Beautiful
DISASTER

Beautiful DISASTER

JAMIE McGUIRE

SIMON & SCHUSTER

London · New York · Sydney · Toronto · New Delhi

A CBS COMPANY

First published in the USA by Atria Books, 2012
A division of Simon and Schuster, Inc.
First published in Great Britain by Simon & Schuster UK Ltd, 2012
A CBS COMPANY

This paperback edition first published, 2012

3 5 7 9 10 8 6 4 2

Simon & Schuster UK Ltd
1st Floor
222 Gray's Inn Road
London WC1X 8HB

www.simonandschuster.co.uk

Simon & Schuster Australia, Sydney
Simon & Schuster India, New Delhi

A CIP catalogue record for this book is available from the British Library

B Format ISBN 978-1-47111-503-5
Ebook ISBN 978-1-47111-504-2

This book is a work of fiction. Names, characters, places and incidents are either
a product of the author's imagination or are used fictitiously. Any resemblance to
actual people, living or dead, events or locales, is entirely coincidental.

Printed and bound by CPI Group (UK) Ltd, Croydon, CR0 4YY

For the fans
whose love for a story
turned a wish
into the book in your hand

Beautiful
DISASTER

Chapter One
Red Flag

Everything in the room screamed that I didn't belong. The stairs were crumbling, the rowdy patrons were shoulder to shoulder, and the air was a medley of sweat, blood, and mold. Voices blurred as they yelled numbers and names back and forth, and arms flailed about, exchanging money and gestures to communicate over the noise. I squeezed through the crowd, following close behind my best friend.

"Keep your cash in your wallet, Abby!" America called to me. Her broad smile gleamed even in the dim light.

"Stay close! It'll get worse once it starts!" Shepley yelled over the noise. America grabbed his hand and then mine as Shepley led us through the sea of people.

The sharp bleating of a bullhorn cut through the smoky air. The noise startled me, and I jumped in reaction, looking for the source of the blast. A man stood on a wooden chair, holding a wad of cash in one hand, the horn in the other. He held the plastic to his lips.

"Welcome to the bloodbath! If you are looking for Economics 101 . . . you are in the wrong fucking place, my friend! If you seek the Circle, this is Mecca! My name is Adam. I make the rules and I call the fight. Betting ends once the opponents are on the floor. No touching the fighters, no assistance, no bet switching, and no encroachment of the ring. If you break these rules, you will get the piss beat out of you and you will be thrown out on your ass without your money! That includes you, ladies! So don't use your hos to scam the system, boys!"

Shepley shook his head. "Jesus, Adam!" he yelled to the emcee over the noise, clearly disapproving of his friend's choice of words.

My heart pounded in my chest. With a pink cashmere cardigan and pearl earrings, I felt like a schoolmarm on the beaches of Normandy. I promised America that I could handle whatever we happened upon, but at ground zero I felt the urge to grip her toothpick of an arm with both hands. She wouldn't put me in any danger, but being in a basement with fifty or so drunken college boys intent on bloodshed and capital, I wasn't exactly confident of our chances to leave unscathed.

After America met Shepley at freshman orientation, she frequently accompanied him to the secret fights held in different basements of Eastern University. Each event was hosted in a different spot, and kept secret until just an hour before the fight.

Because I ran in somewhat tamer circles, I was surprised to learn of an underground world at Eastern; but Shepley knew about it before he had ever enrolled. Travis, Shepley's roommate and cousin, entered his first fight seven months before. As a freshman, he was rumored to be the most lethal competitor Adam had seen in the three years since creating the Circle. Beginning his sophomore year, Travis was unbeatable. Together,

Travis and Shepley easily paid their rent and bills with the winnings.

Adam brought the bullhorn to his mouth once again, and the yelling and movement escalated to a feverish pace.

"Tonight we have a new challenger! Eastern's star varsity wrestler, Marek Young!"

Cheering ensued, and the crowd parted like the Red Sea when Marek entered the room. A circular space cleared, and the mob whistled, booed, and taunted the contender. He bounced up and down and rocked his neck back and forth, his face severe and focused. The crowd quieted to a dull roar, and my hands shot to my ears when music blared through the large speakers on the other side of the room.

"Our next fighter doesn't need an introduction, but because he scares the shit outta me, I'll give him one, anyway! Shake in your boots, boys, and drop your panties, ladies! I give you: Travis 'Mad Dog' Maddox!"

The volume exploded when Travis appeared in a doorway across the room. He made his entrance, shirtless, relaxed, and unaffected. He strolled into the center of the circle as if he were showing up to another day at work. Lean muscles stretched under his tattooed skin as he popped his fists against Marek's knuckles. Travis leaned in and whispered something in Marek's ear, and the wrestler struggled to keep his stern expression. Marek stood toe-to-toe with Travis, and they looked directly into each other's eyes. Marek's expression was murderous; Travis looked mildly amused.

The men took a few steps back, and Adam sounded the horn. Marek took a defensive stance, and Travis attacked.

I stood on my tiptoes when I lost my line of sight, leaning from side to side to get a better view. I inched up, sliding through the screaming crowd. Elbows jabbed into my sides, and shoulders rammed into me, bouncing me back and forth like a pinball. The tops of the fighters' heads became visible, so I continued to push my way forward.

When I finally reached the front, Marek grabbed Travis with his thick arms and tried to throw him to the ground. When Marek leaned down with the motion, Travis rammed his knee into Marek's face. Before Marek could shake off the blow, Travis lit into him, his fists making contact with Marek's bloodied face over and over.

Five fingers sank into my arm and I jerked back.

"What the hell are you doing, Abby?" Shepley said.

"I can't see from back there!" I called to him.

I turned just in time to see Marek land a solid punch. Travis turned, and for a moment I thought he had dodged another blow, but he made a complete circle, crashing his elbow straight into the center of Marek's nose. Blood sprayed my face, and splattered down the front of my cardigan. Marek fell to the concrete floor with a thud, and for a brief moment the room was completely silent.

Adam threw a scarlet square of fabric onto Marek's limp body, and the mob detonated. Cash changed hands once again, and the expressions divided into the smug and the frustrated.

I was pushed around with the movement of those coming and going. America called my name from somewhere in the back, but I was mesmerized by the trail of red from my chest to my waist.

A pair of heavy black boots stepped in front of me, diverting my attention to the floor. My eyes traveled upward; jeans spattered with blood, a set of finely chiseled abs, a bare, tattooed chest drenched in sweat, and finally a pair of warm, brown eyes. I was shoved from behind, and Travis caught me by the arm before I fell forward.

"Hey! Back up off her!" Travis frowned, shoving anyone who came near me. His stern expression melted into a smile at the sight of my shirt, and then he dabbed my face with a towel. "Sorry about that, Pigeon."

Adam patted the back of Travis's head. "C'mon, Mad Dog! You have some dough waitin' on ya!"

Travis's eyes didn't stray from mine. "It's a damn shame about the sweater. It looks good on you." In the next moment he was engulfed by fans, disappearing the way he came.

"What were you thinking, you idiot?" America yelled, yanking my arm.

"I came here to see a fight, didn't I?" I said, smiling.

"You aren't even supposed to be here, Abby," Shepley scolded.

"Neither is America," I said.

"She doesn't try to jump in the circle!" He frowned. "Let's go."

America smiled at me and wiped my face. "You are such a pain in the ass, Abby. God, I love you!" She hooked her arm around my neck, and we made our way up the stairs and into the night.

America followed me into my dorm room and then sneered at my roommate, Kara. I immediately peeled off the bloody cardigan, throwing it into the hamper.

"Gross. Where have you been?" Kara asked from her bed.

I looked to America, who shrugged. "Nosebleed. You haven't seen one of Abby's famous nosebleeds?"

Kara pushed up her glasses and shook her head.

"Oh, you will." She winked at me and then shut the door behind her. Less than a minute later, my cell phone chimed. Per her usual, America texted me seconds after we had said goodbye.

staying w shep c u 2morrow ring queen

I peeked at Kara, who watched me as if my nose would gush at any moment.

"She was kidding," I said.

Kara nodded with indifference and then looked down to the mess of books on her bedspread.

"I guess I'll get a shower," I said, grabbing a towel and my shower bag.

"I'll alert the media," Kara deadpanned, keeping her head down.

THE NEXT DAY, SHEPLEY AND AMERICA JOINED ME FOR lunch. I had intended to sit alone, but as students filtered into the cafeteria, the chairs around me were filled by either Shepley's frat brothers or members of the football team. Some of them had been at the fight, but no one mentioned my ringside experience.

"Shep," a passing voice called.

Shepley nodded, and America and I both turned to see Travis take a seat at the end of the table. He was followed by two voluptuous bottle blondes wearing Sigma Kappa Ts. One of them sat on Travis's lap; the other sat beside him, pawing at his shirt.

"I think I just threw up a little bit in my mouth," America muttered.

The blonde on Travis's lap turned to America. "I heard that, skank."

America grabbed her roll and threw it down the table, narrowly missing the girl's face. Before the girl could say another word, Travis let his knees give way, sending her tumbling to the floor.

"Ouch!" she squealed, looking up at Travis.

"America's a friend of mine. You need to find another lap, Lex."

"Travis!" she whined, scrambling to her feet.

Travis turned his attention to his plate, ignoring her. She looked at her sister and huffed, and they left hand in hand.

Travis winked at America, and, as if nothing had happened, shoveled another bite into his mouth. It was then that I noticed a small cut on his eyebrow. He traded glances with Shepley and then began a conversation with one of the football guys across from him.

Although the crowd at the lunch table had thinned, America, Shepley, and I lingered to discuss our weekend plans. Travis stood up to leave but stopped at our end of the table.

"What?" Shepley asked loudly, holding his hand to his ear.

I tried to ignore him for as long as possible, but when I looked up, Travis was staring at me.

"You know her, Trav. America's best friend? She was with us the other night," Shepley said.

Travis smiled at me in what I assumed was his most charming expression. He oozed sex and rebelliousness with his buzzed brown hair and tattooed forearms, and I rolled my eyes at his attempt to lure me in.

"Since when do you have a best friend, Mare?" Travis asked.

"Since junior year," she answered, pressing her lips together as she smiled in my direction. "Don't you remember, Travis? You ruined her sweater."

Travis smiled. "I ruin a lot of sweaters."

"Gross," I muttered.

Travis spun the empty chair beside me and sat, resting his arms in front of him. "So you're the Pigeon, huh?"

"No," I snapped. "I have a name."

He seemed amused at the way I regarded him, which only served to make me angrier.

"Well? What is it?" he asked.

I took a bite of the last apple spear on my plate, ignoring him.

"Pigeon it is, then," he said, shrugging.

I glanced up at America and then turned to Travis. "I'm trying to eat here."

Travis settled in for the challenge I presented. "My name's Travis. Travis Maddox."

I rolled my eyes. "I know who you are."

"You do, huh?" Travis said, raising his wounded eyebrow.

"Don't flatter yourself. It's hard not to notice when fifty drunks are chanting your name."

Travis sat up a bit taller. "I get that a lot." I rolled my eyes again, and Travis chuckled. "Do you have a twitch?"

"A what?"

"A twitch. Your eyes keep wiggling around." He laughed

again when I glared at him. "Those are some amazing eyes, though," he said, leaning just inches from my face. "What color is that, anyway? Gray?"

I looked down to my plate, letting the long strands of my caramel hair create a curtain between us. I didn't like the way it made me feel when he was so close. I didn't want to be like the scores of other girls at Eastern that blushed in his presence. I didn't want him to affect me in that way at all.

"Don't even think about it, Travis. She's like my sister," America warned.

"Baby," Shepley said, "you just told him no. He's never gonna stop, now."

"You're not her type," she hedged.

Travis feigned offense. "I'm everyone's type!"

I peeked over at him and smiled.

"Ah! A smile. I'm not a rotten bastard after all," he winked. "It was nice to meet you, Pidge." He walked around the table and leaned into America's ear.

Shepley threw a french fry at his cousin. "Get your lips outta my girl's ear, Trav!"

"Networking! I'm networking!" Travis walked backward with his hands up in an innocent gesture.

A few more girls followed behind him, giggling and running their fingers through their hair to get his attention. He opened the door for them, and they nearly squealed in delight.

America laughed. "Oh, no. You're in trouble, Abby."

"What did he say?" I asked, wary.

"He wants you to bring her to the apartment, doesn't he?" Shepley said. America nodded, and he shook his head. "You're a smart girl, Abby. I'm telling you now, if you fall for his shit and then end up getting mad at him, you can't take it out on me and America, all right?"

I smiled. "I won't fall for it, Shep. Do I look like one of the Barbie twins to you?"

"She won't fall for it," America assured him, touching his arm.

"This isn't my first rodeo, Mare. Do you know how many times he's screwed things up for me because he one-nights the best friend? All of a sudden it's a conflict of interest to date me because it's fraternizing with the enemy! I'm tellin' ya, Abby," he looked at me, "don't tell Mare she can't come over or date me because you fall for Trav's line of BS. Consider yourself warned."

"Unnecessary, but appreciated," I said. I tried to reassure Shepley with a smile, but his pessimism was driven by years of being burned by Travis's endeavors.

America waved, leaving with Shepley as I walked to my afternoon class. I squinted in the bright sun, gripping my backpack straps. Eastern was exactly what I hoped it would be, from the smaller classrooms to the unfamiliar faces. It was a new start for me; I could finally walk somewhere without the whispers of those who knew—or thought they knew—anything about my past. I was as indistinguishable as any other wide-eyed, overachieving freshman on her way to class; no staring, no rumors, no pity or judgment. Only the illusion of what I wanted them to see: cashmered, no-nonsense Abby Abernathy.

I sat my backpack on the floor and collapsed into the chair, bending down to fish my laptop from my bag. When I popped up to set it on my desk, Travis slid into the next desk.

"Good. You can take notes for me," he said. He chewed

on the pen in his mouth and smiled, undoubtedly at his most charming.

I shot a disgusted look at him. "You're not even in this class."

"The hell if I'm not. I usually sit up there," he said, nodding to the top row. A small group of girls was staring at me, and I noticed an empty chair in the center.

"I'm not taking notes for you," I said, booting up my computer.

Travis leaned so close that I could feel his breath on my cheek. "I'm sorry . . . did I offend you in some way?"

I sighed and shook my head.

"Then what is your problem?"

I kept my voice low. "I'm not sleeping with you. You should give up, now."

A slow smile crept across his face before he spoke. "I haven't asked you to sleep with me." His eyes drifted to the ceiling in thought. "Have I?"

"I'm not a Barbie twin or one of your little groupies up there," I said, glancing at the girls behind us. "I'm not impressed with your tattoos or your boyish charm or your forced indifference, so you can stop the antics, okay?"

"Okay, Pigeon." He was infuriatingly impervious to my rudeness. "Why don't you come over with America tonight?" I sneered at his request, but he leaned closer. "I'm not trying to bag you. I just wanna hang out."

"Bag me? How do you ever get laid talking like that?"

Travis burst into laughter, shaking his head. "Just come over. I won't even flirt with you, I swear."

"I'll think about it."

Professor Chaney strolled in, and Travis turned his attention to the front of the room. A residual smile lingered on his face, making the dimple in his cheek sink in. The more he smiled, the more I wanted to hate him, and yet it was the very thing that made hating him impossible.

"Who can tell me which president had a cross-eyed wife with a bad case of the uglies?" Chaney asked.

"Make sure you get that down," Travis whispered. "I'm gonna need to know that for job interviews."

"Shhh," I said, typing Chaney's every word.

Travis grinned and relaxed into his chair. As the hour progressed, he alternated between yawning and leaning against my arm to look at my monitor. I made a concentrated effort to ignore him, but his proximity and the muscles bulging from his arm made it difficult. He picked at the black leather band around his wrist until Chaney dismissed us.

I hurried out the door and down the hall. Just when I felt sure I was at a safe distance, Travis Maddox was at my side.

"Have you thought about it?" he asked, slipping on his sunglasses.

A petite brunette stepped in front of us, wide-eyed and hopeful. "Hey, Travis," she lilted, playing with her hair.

I paused, recoiling from her sugary tone, and then walked around her. I'd seen her before, talking normally in the commons area of the girls' dorm, Morgan Hall. Her tone sounded much more mature then, and I wondered what it was about a toddler's voice she thought Travis would find appealing. She babbled in a higher octave for a bit longer until he was next to me once again.

Pulling a lighter from his pocket, he lit a cigarette and blew out a thick cloud of smoke. "Where was I? Oh yeah . . . you were thinking."

I grimaced. "What are you talking about?"

"Have you thought about coming over?"

"If I say yes, will you quit following me?"

He considered my stipulation and then nodded. "Yes."

"Then I'll come over."

"When?"

I sighed. "Tonight. I'll come over tonight."

Travis smiled and stopped in his tracks. "Sweet. See you then, Pidge," he called after me.

I rounded the corner to see America standing with Finch outside our dormitory. The three of us ended up at the same table at freshman orientation, and I knew he would be the welcome third wheel to our well-oiled machine. He wasn't excessively tall, but still he towered over my five feet four inches. His round eyes offset his long, lean features, and his bleached hair was usually fashioned into a spike at the front.

"Travis Maddox? Jesus, Abby, since when did you start fishing in the deep end?" Finch said with disapproving eyes.

America pulled the gum from her mouth in a long string. "You're only making it worse by brushing him off. He's not used to that."

"What do you suggest I do? Sleep with him?"

America shrugged. "It'll save time."

"I told him I'd come over tonight."

Finch and America traded glances.

"What? He promised to quit bugging me if I said yes. You're going over there tonight, right?"

"Well, yeah," America said. "You're really coming?"

I smiled and walked past them into the dorms, wondering if Travis would make good on his promise not to flirt. He wasn't hard to figure out; he either saw me as a challenge, or safely unattractive enough to be a good friend. I wasn't sure which bothered me more.

FOUR HOURS LATER, AMERICA KNOCKED ON MY DOOR TO take me to Shepley and Travis's. She didn't hold back when I walked into the hall.

"Yuck, Abby! You look homeless!"

"Good," I said, smiling at my ensemble. My hair was piled on top of my head in a messy bun. I had scrubbed the makeup from my face and replaced my contacts with rectangular black-rimmed glasses. Sporting a ratty T-shirt and sweatpants, I shuffled along in a pair of flip-flops. The idea had come to me hours before that either way, unattractive was the best plan. Ideally, Travis would be instantly turned off and stop his ridiculous persistence. If he was looking for a buddy, I was aiming for too homely to be seen with.

America rolled down her window and spit out her gum. "You're so obvious. Why didn't you just roll in dog shit to make your outfit complete?"

"I'm not trying to impress anyone," I said.

"Obviously."

We pulled into the parking lot of Shepley's apartment complex, and I followed America to the stairs. Shepley opened the door, laughing as I walked in. "What happened to you?"

"She's trying to be unimpressive," America said.

America followed Shepley into his room. The door closed and I stood alone, feeling out of place. I sat in the recliner closest to the door and kicked off my flip-flops.

Their apartment was more aesthetically pleasing than the typical bachelor pad. The predictable posters of half-naked women and stolen street signs were on the walls, but it was clean, the furniture was new, and the smell of stale beer and dirty clothes was notably absent.

"It's about time you showed up," Travis said, collapsing onto the couch.

I smiled and pushed my glasses up the bridge of my nose, waiting for him to recoil at my appearance. "America had a paper to finish."

"Speaking of papers, have you started the one for History yet?"

He didn't bat an eye at my messy hair, and I frowned at his reaction. "Have you?"

"I finished it this afternoon."

"It's not due until next Wednesday," I said, surprised.

"I just plugged it out. How hard can a two-page essay on Grant be?"

"I'm a procrastinator, I guess," I shrugged. "I probably won't start on it until this weekend."

"Well, if you need help, just let me know."

I waited for him to laugh, or to show some sign that he was joking, but his expression was sincere. I raised an eyebrow. "You're going to help me with my paper?"

"I have an A in that class," he said, a bit miffed at my disbelief.

"He has As in all his classes. He's a freakin' genius. I hate him," Shepley said as he led America into the living room by the hand.

I watched Travis with a dubious expression and his eyebrows shot up. "What? You don't think a guy covered in tats and that trades punches for a living can get the grades? I'm not in school because I have nothing better to do."

"Why do you have to fight at all, then? Why didn't you try for scholarships?" I asked.

"I did. I was awarded half my tuition. But there are books, living expenses, and I gotta come up with the other half sometime. I'm serious, Pidge. If you need help with anything, just ask."

"I don't need your help. I can write a paper." I wanted to leave it at that. I should have left it at that, but this new side of him he'd revealed gnawed at my curiosity. "You can't find something else to do for a living? Less—I don't know—sadistic?"

Travis shrugged. "It's an easy way to make a buck. I can't make that much working at the mall."

"I wouldn't say it's easy if you're getting hit in the face."

"What? You're worried about me?" he winked. I made a face, and he chuckled. "I don't get hit that often. If they swing, I move. It's not that hard."

I laughed once. "You act as if no one else has come to that conclusion."

"When I throw a punch, they take it and try to reciprocate. That's not gonna win a fight."

I rolled my eyes. "What are you, the Karate Kid? Where did you learn to fight?"

Shepley and America glanced at each other, and then their eyes wandered to the floor. It didn't take long to recognize I had said something wrong.

Travis didn't seem affected. "I had a dad with a drinking problem and a bad temper, and four older brothers that carried the asshole gene."

"Oh." My ears smoldered.

"Don't be embarrassed, Pidge. Dad quit drinking, the brothers grew up."

"I'm not embarrassed." I fidgeted with the falling strands of my hair and then decided to pull it down and smooth it into another bun, trying to ignore the awkward silence.

"I like the au naturel thing you have going on. Girls don't come over here like that."

"I was coerced into coming here. It didn't occur to me to impress you," I said, irritated that my plan had failed.

He smiled his boyish, amused grin, and I turned up my anger a notch, hoping it would cover my unease. I didn't know how most girls felt around him, but I'd seen how they behaved. I was experiencing more of a disoriented, nauseated feeling than giggly infatuation, and the harder he worked to make me smile, the more unsettled I felt.

"I'm already impressed. I don't normally have to beg girls to come to my apartment."

"I'm sure," I said, screwing my face into disgust.

He was the worst kind of confident. Not only was he shamelessly aware of his appeal, he was so used to women throwing themselves at him that he regarded my cool demeanor as refreshing instead of an insult. I would have to change my strategy.

America pointed the remote at the television and switched it on. "There's a good movie on tonight. Anyone want to find out where Baby Jane is?"

Travis stood up. "I was just heading out for dinner. You hungry, Pidge?"

"I already ate," I shrugged.

"No you haven't," America said, before realizing her mistake. "Oh . . . er . . . that's right, I forgot you grabbed a . . . pizza? Before we left."

I grimaced at her miserable attempt to fix her blunder, and then waited for Travis's reaction.

He walked across the room and opened the door. "C'mon. You've gotta be hungry."

"Where are you going?"

"Wherever you want. We can hit a pizza place."

I looked down at my clothes. "I'm not really dressed."

He appraised me for a moment and then grinned. "You look fine. Let's go, I'm starvin'."

I stood up and waved to America, passing Travis to walk down the stairs. I stopped in the parking lot, watching in horror as he straddled a matte black motorcycle.

"Uh . . ." I trailed off, scrunching my exposed toes.

He shot an impatient glare in my direction. "Oh, get on. I'll go slow."

"What is that?" I asked, reading the writing on the gas tank too late.

"It's a Harley Night Rod. She's the love of my life, so don't scratch the paint when you get on."

"I'm wearing flip-flops!"

Travis stared at me as if I'd spoken a foreign language. "I'm wearing boots. Get on."

He slipped on his sunglasses, and the engine snarled when

he brought it to life. I climbed on and reached behind me for something to grab on to, but my fingers slipped from leather to the plastic cover of the taillight.

Travis grabbed my wrists and wrapped them around his middle. "There's nothing to hold on to but me, Pidge. Don't let go," he said, pushing the bike backward with his feet. With a flick of his wrist, he pulled onto the street, and we took off like a rocket. The pieces of my hair that hung loose beat against my face, and I ducked behind Travis, knowing I would end up with bug guts on my glasses if I looked over his shoulder.

He gunned the throttle when we pulled into the driveway of the restaurant, and once he slowed to a stop, I wasted no time scrambling to the safety of the concrete.

"You're a lunatic!"

Travis chuckled, leaning his bike onto its kickstand before dismounting. "I went the speed limit."

"Yeah, if we were on the autobahn!" I said, pulling out my bun to separate the rats with my fingers.

Travis watched me pull hair away from my face and then walked to the door, holding it open. "I wouldn't let anything happen to you, Pigeon."

I stormed past him into the restaurant, my head not quite in sync with my feet. Grease and herbs filled the air as I followed him across the red, breadcrumb-speckled carpet. He chose a booth in the corner, away from the patches of students and families, and then ordered two beers. I scanned the room, watching the parents coaxing their boisterous children to eat, and looking away from the inquisitive glances of Eastern students.

"Sure, Travis," the waitress said, writing down our drink

orders. She looked a bit high from his presence as she returned to the kitchen.

I tucked the windblown hair behind my ears, suddenly embarrassed by my appearance. "Come here often?" I asked acerbically.

Travis leaned on the table with his elbows, his brown eyes fixated on mine. "So what's your story, Pidge? Are you a man-hater in general, or do you just hate me?"

"I think it's just you," I grumbled.

He laughed once, amused at my mood. "I can't figure you out. You're the first girl that's ever been disgusted with me before sex. You don't get all flustered when you talk to me, and you don't try to get my attention."

"It's not a ploy. I just don't like you."

"You wouldn't be here if you didn't like me."

My frown involuntarily smoothed and I sighed. "I didn't say you're a bad person. I just don't like being a foregone conclusion for the sole reason of having a vagina." I focused on the grains of salt on the table until I heard a choking noise from Travis's direction.

His eyes widened and he quivered with howling laughter. "Oh my God! You're killing me! That's it. We have to be friends. I won't take no for an answer."

"I don't mind being friends, but that doesn't mean you have to try to get in my panties every five seconds."

"You're not sleeping with me. I get it."

I tried not to smile, but failed.

His eyes brightened. "You have my word. I won't even think about your panties . . . unless you want me to."

I rested my elbows on the table and leaned into them. "And that won't happen, so we can be friends."

An impish grin sharpened his features as he leaned in a bit closer. "Never say never."

"So what's your story?" I asked. "Have you always been Travis 'Mad Dog' Maddox, or is that just since you came here?" I used two fingers on each hand as quotation marks when I said his nickname, and for the first time his confidence waned. He looked a bit embarrassed.

"No. Adam started that after my first fight."

His short answers were beginning to bug me. "That's it? You're not going to tell me anything about yourself?"

"What do you wanna know?"

"The normal stuff. Where you're from, what you want to be when you grow up . . . things like that."

"I'm from here, born and raised, and I'm a Criminal Justice major."

With a sigh, he unrolled his silverware and straightened them beside his plate. He looked over his shoulder, his jaw tense. Two tables seating the Eastern soccer team erupted in laughter, and Travis seemed to be annoyed at what they were laughing about.

"You're joking," I said in disbelief.

"No, I'm a local," he said, distracted.

"I meant about your major. You don't look like the criminal justice type."

His eyebrows pulled together, suddenly focused on our conversation. "Why?"

I scanned the tattoos covering his arm. "I'll just say that you seem more criminal and less justice."

"I don't get in any trouble . . . for the most part. Dad was pretty strict."

"Where was your mom?"

"She died when I was a kid," he said, matter-of-fact.

"I'm ... I'm sorry," I said, shaking my head. His answer caught me off guard.

He dismissed my sympathy. "I don't remember her. My brothers do, but I was just three when she died."

"Four brothers, huh? How did you keep them straight?" I teased.

"I kept them straight by who hit the hardest, which also happened to be oldest to youngest. Thomas; the twins, Taylor and Tyler; and then Trenton. You never, ever got caught alone in a room with Taylor and Ty. I learned half of what I do in the Circle from them. Trenton was the smallest, but he's fast. He's the only one that can land a punch on me now."

I shook my head, dumbfounded at the thought of five Travises running around in one household. "Do they all have tattoos?"

"Pretty much. Except Thomas. He's an ad exec in California."

"And your dad? Where's he?"

"Around," he said. His jaws were working again, increasingly irritated with the soccer team.

"What are they laughing about?" I asked, gesturing to the rowdy table. He shook his head, clearly not wanting to share. I crossed my arms and squirmed in my seat, nervous about what they were saying that caused him so much aggravation. "Tell me."

"They're laughing about me having to take you to dinner, first. It's not usually ... my thing."

"First?" When the realization settled on my face, Travis

winced at my expression. I spoke before I thought. "And I was afraid they were laughing about you being seen with me dressed like this, and they think I'm going to sleep with you," I grumbled.

"Why wouldn't I be seen with you?"

"What were we talking about?" I asked, warding off the heat rising in my cheeks.

"You. What's your major?" he asked.

"Oh, er . . . General Ed, for now. I'm still undecided, but I'm leaning toward Accounting."

"You're not a local, though. You must be a transplant."

"Wichita. Same as America."

"How did you end up here from Kansas?"

I picked at the label of my beer bottle. "We just had to get away."

"From what?"

"My parents."

"Oh. What about America? She has parent issues, too?"

"No, Mark and Pam are great. They practically raised me. She sort of tagged along; she didn't want me to come alone."

Travis nodded. "So, why Eastern?"

"What's with the third degree?" I said. The questions were drifting from small talk to personal, and I was beginning to get uncomfortable.

Several chairs knocked together as the soccer team left their seats. They traded one last joke before they meandered toward the door. Their pace quickened when Travis stood up. Those in the back of the group pushed those in front to escape before Travis made his way across the room. He sat down, forcing the frustration and anger away.

I raised an eyebrow.

"You were going to say why you chose Eastern," he prompted.

"It's hard to explain," I said, shrugging. "I guess it just felt right."

He smiled as he opened his menu. "I know what you mean."

Chapter Two
Pig

FAMILIAR FACES FILLED THE SEATS OF OUR FAVORITE lunch table. America sat on one side of me, Finch on the other, and the rest of the spaces were picked off by Shepley and his Sigma Tau brothers. It was hard to hear with the low roar inside the cafeteria, and the air conditioner seemed to be on the fritz again. The air was thick with the smells of fried foods and sweaty skin, but somehow everyone seemed to be more energetic than usual.

"Hey, Brazil," Shepley said, greeting the man sitting in front of me. His olive skin and chocolate eyes offset the white Eastern Football hat pulled low on his forehead.

"Missed you after the game Saturday, Shep. I drank a beer or six for ya," he said with a broad white grin.

"I appreciate it. I took Mare out to dinner," he said, leaning over to kiss the top of America's long blond hair.

"You're sittin' in my chair, Brazil."

Brazil turned to see Travis standing behind him, and then looked to me, surprised. "Oh, is she one of your girls, Trav?"

"Absolutely not," I said, shaking my head.

Brazil looked to Travis, who stared at him expectantly. Brazil shrugged and then took his tray to the end of the table.

Travis smiled at me as he settled into the seat. "What's up, Pidge?"

"What is that?" I asked, unable to look away from his tray. The mystery food on his plate looked like a wax display.

Travis laughed and took a drink from his water glass. "The cafeteria ladies scare me. I'm not about to critique their cooking skills."

I didn't miss the appraising eyes of those sitting at the table. Travis's behavior piqued their curiosity, and I subdued a smile at being the only girl they had seen him insist on sitting with.

"Ugh . . . that Bio test is after lunch," America groaned.

"Did you study?" I asked.

"God, no. I spent the night reassuring my boyfriend that you weren't going to sleep with Travis."

The football players seated at the end of our table stopped their obnoxious laughter to listen more closely, making the other students take notice. I glared at America, but she was unconcerned with any blame, nudging Shepley with her shoulder.

"Jesus, Shep. You've got it that bad, huh?" Travis asked, throwing a packet of ketchup at his cousin. Shepley didn't answer, but I smiled appreciatively at Travis for the diversion.

America rubbed his back. "He's going to be okay. It's just going to take him a while to believe Abby is resistant to your charms."

"I haven't tried to charm her," Travis sniffed, seeming offended. "She's my friend."

I looked to Shepley. "I told you. You have nothing to worry about."

Shepley finally met my eyes, and upon seeing my sincere expression, his eyes brightened a bit.

"Did you study?" Travis asked me.

I frowned. "No amount of studying is going to help me with Biology. It's just not something I can wrap my head around."

Travis stood up. "C'mon."

"What?"

"Let's go get your notes. I'm going to help you study."

"Travis . . ."

"Get your ass up, Pidge. You're gonna ace that test."

I tugged on one of America's long yellow braids as I passed. "See you in class, Mare."

She smiled. "I'll save you a seat. I'll need all the help I can get."

Travis followed me to my room, and I pulled out my study guide while he popped open my book. He quizzed me relentlessly, and then clarified a few things I didn't understand. In the way that he explained it, the concepts went from being confusing to obvious.

". . . and somatic cells use mitosis to reproduce. That's when you have the phases. They sound sort of like a woman's name: Prometa Anatela."

I laughed. "Prometa Anatela?"

"Prophase, metaphase, anaphase, and telophase."

"Prometa Anatela," I repeated, nodding.

He smacked the top of my head with the papers. "You got this. You know this study guide backward and forward."

I sighed. "Well . . . we'll see."

"I'm going to walk you to class. I'll quiz you on the way."

I locked the door behind us. "You're not going to be mad if I flunk this test, are you?"

"You're not going to flunk, Pidge. We need to start earlier for the next one, though," he said, keeping in step with me to the science building.

"How are you going to tutor me, do your homework, study, and train for your fights?"

Travis chuckled. "I don't train for my fights. Adam calls me, tells me where the fight is, and I go."

I shook my head in disbelief as he held the paper in front of him to ask the first question. We had nearly finished a second round of the study guide when we reached my class.

"Kick ass," he smiled, handing me the notes and leaning against the doorjamb.

"Hey, Trav."

I turned to see a tall, somewhat lanky man smile at Travis on his way into the classroom.

"Parker," Travis nodded.

Parker's eyes brightened a bit when he looked to me, and he smiled. "Hi, Abby."

"Hi," I said, surprised that he knew my name. I had seen him in class, but we'd never met.

Parker continued to his seat, joking with those sitting beside him. "Who's that?" I asked.

Travis shrugged, but the skin around his eyes seemed tenser than before. "Parker Hayes. He's one of my Sig Tau brothers."

"You're in a frat?" I asked, doubtful.

"Sigma Tau, same as Shep. I thought you knew that," he said, looking beyond me to Parker.

"Well . . . you don't seem the . . . fraternity type," I said, eyeing the tattoos on his forearms.

Travis turned his attention to me and grinned. "My dad is an alumnus, and my brothers are all Sig Tau. It's a family thing."

"And they expected you to pledge?" I asked, skeptical.

"Not really. They're just good guys," he said, flicking my papers. "Better get to class."

"Thanks for helping me," I said, nudging him with my elbow. America passed, and I followed her to our seats.

"How did it go?" she asked.

I shrugged. "He's a good tutor."

"Just a tutor?"

"He's a good friend, too."

She seemed disappointed, and I giggled at the fallen expression on her face.

It had always been a dream of America's for us to date friends, and roommates-slash-cousins, for her, was hitting the jackpot. She wanted us to room together when she decided to come with me to Eastern, but I vetoed her idea, hoping to spread my wings a bit. Once she finished pouting, she focused on finding a friend of Shepley's to introduce me to.

Travis's healthy interest in me had surpassed her ideas.

I breezed through the test and sat on the steps outside the building, waiting for America. When she slumped down beside me in defeat, I waited for her to speak.

"That was awful!" she cried.

"You should study with us. Travis explains it really well."

America groaned and leaned her head on my shoulder. "You were no help at all! Couldn't you have given me a courtesy nod or something?" I hooked my arm around her neck and walked her to our dorm.

◆ ◆ ◆

OVER THE NEXT WEEK, TRAVIS HELPED WITH MY HIS-
tory paper and tutored me in Biology. We stood together scanning the grade board outside Professor Campbell's office. My
student number was three spots from the top.

"Third-highest test grade in the class! Nice, Pidge!" he
said, squeezing me. His eyes were bright with excitement and
pride, and an awkward feeling made me take a step back.

"Thanks, Trav. Couldn't have done it without you," I said,
pulling on his T-shirt.

He tossed me over his shoulder, making his way through the
crowd behind us. "Make way! Move it, people! Let's make room
for this poor woman's hideously disfigured, ginormous brain!
She's a fucking genius!"

I giggled at the amused and curious expressions of my classmates.

AS THE DAYS WENT BY, WE FIELDED THE PERSISTENT RU-
mors about a relationship. Travis's reputation helped to quiet
the gossip. He had never been known to stay with one girl longer than a night, so the more times we were seen together, the
more people understood our platonic relationship for what it
was. Even with the constant questions about our involvement, the
stream of attention Travis received from his coeds didn't recede.

He continued to sit next to me in History and eat with me at
lunch. It didn't take long to realize I had been wrong about him,
even finding myself defensive toward those who didn't know
Travis the way that I did.

In the cafeteria, Travis set a can of orange juice in front
of me.

"You didn't have to do that. I was going to grab one," I said, peeling off my jacket.

"Well, now you don't have to," he said, flashing the dimple on his left cheek.

Brazil snorted. "Did she turn you into a cabana boy, Travis? What's next, fanning her with a palm tree leaf, wearing a Speedo?"

Travis shot him a murderous glare, and I jumped to his defense. "You couldn't fill a Speedo, Brazil. Shut the hell up."

"Easy, Abby! I was kidding!" Brazil said, holding up his hands.

"Just . . . don't talk about him like that," I said, frowning.

Travis's expression was a mixture of surprise and gratitude. "Now I've seen it all. I was just defended by a girl," he said, standing up. Before he left with his tray, he offered one more warning glare to Brazil, and then walked outside to stand with a small group of fellow smokers outside the building.

I tried not to watch him while he laughed and talked. Every girl in the group subtly competed for the space next to him, and America shoved her elbow into my ribs when she noticed my attention was elsewhere.

"Whatcha lookin' at, Abby?"

"Nothing. I'm not looking at anything."

She rested her chin on her hand and shook her head. "They're so obvious. Look at the redhead. She's run her fingers through her hair as many times as she's blinked. I wonder if Travis gets tired of that."

Shepley nodded. "He does. Everyone thinks he's this asshole, but if they only knew how much patience he has dealing with every girl that thinks she can tame him . . . He can't go anywhere without them bugging him. Trust me; he's much more polite than I would be."

"Oh, like you wouldn't love it," America said, kissing his cheek.

Travis was finishing his cigarette outside the cafeteria when I passed. "Wait up, Pidge. I'll walk you."

"You don't have to walk me to every class, Travis. I know how to get there on my own."

Travis was easily sidetracked by a girl with long black hair and a short skirt. She walked by, smiling at him. He followed her with his eyes and nodded in the girl's direction, throwing down his cigarette.

"I'll catch up with you later, Pidge."

"Yeah," I said, rolling my eyes as he jogged to the girl's side.

Travis's seat remained empty during class, and I found myself a bit irritated with him for missing over a girl he didn't know. Professor Chaney dismissed early, and I hurried across the lawn, aware that I was to meet Finch at three to give him Sherri Cassidy's Music Appreciation notes. I looked at my watch and quickened my pace.

"Abby?"

Parker jogged across the grass to walk beside me. "I don't think we've officially met," he said, holding out his hand. "Parker Hayes."

I took his hand and smiled. "Abby Abernathy."

"I was behind you when you got your Bio test grade. Congratulations," he smiled, shoving his hands in his pockets.

"Thanks. Travis helped, or I would've been at the bottom of that list, trust me."

"Oh, are you guys . . . ?"

"Friends."

Parker nodded and smiled. "Did he tell you there's a party at the House this weekend?"

"We mostly just talk about Biology and food."

Parker laughed. "That sounds like Travis."

At the door of Morgan Hall, Parker scanned my face with his big green eyes. "You should come. It'll be fun."

"I'll talk to America. I don't think we have any plans."

"Are you a package deal?"

"We made a pact this summer. No parties solo."

"Smart." He nodded in approval.

"She met Shep at orientation, so I haven't really had to tag along with her much. This will be the first time I've needed to ask her, so I'm sure she'll be happy to come." I inwardly cringed. Not only was I babbling, I'd made it obvious that I didn't get asked to parties.

"Great. I'll see you there," he said. He flashed his perfect Banana Republic–model smile with his square jaw and naturally tan skin, turning to walk across campus.

I watched him walk away; he was tall, clean-shaven, with a pressed pin-striped dress shirt and jeans. His wavy dark-blond hair bounced when he walked.

I bit my lip, flattered by his invitation.

"Now, he's more your speed," Finch said in my ear.

"He's cute, huh?" I asked, unable to stop smiling.

"Hell, yes. In that preppy, missionary-position kind of way."

"Finch!" I cried, smacking him on the shoulder.

"Did you get Sherri's notes?"

"I did," I said, pulling them from my bag. He lit a cigarette, held it between his lips, and squinted at the papers.

"Fucking brilliant," he said, scanning the pages. He folded them away in his pocket, and then took another drag. "Good thing Morgan's boilers are out. You'll need a cold shower after getting ogled by that tall drink of water."

"The dorm doesn't have hot water?" I wailed.

"That's the word," Finch said, sliding his backpack over his shoulder. "I'm off to Algebra. Tell Mare I said not to forget me this weekend."

"I'll tell her," I grumbled, glaring up at the antique brick walls of our dormitory. I stomped up to my room, pushed through the door, and let my backpack fall to the floor.

"No hot water," Kara mumbled from her side of the desk.

"I heard."

My cell phone buzzed and I clicked it open, reading a text message from America cursing the boilers. A few moments later there was a knock on the door.

America walked in and plopped onto my bed, arms crossed. "Can you believe this shit? How much are we paying and we can't even take a hot shower?"

Kara sighed. "Stop whining. Why don't you just stay with your boyfriend? Haven't you been staying with him, anyway?"

America's eyes darted in Kara's direction. "Good idea, Kara. The fact that you're a total bitch comes in handy sometimes."

Kara kept her eyes on her computer monitor, unfazed by America's jab.

America pulled out her cell phone and clicked out a text message with amazing precision and speed. Her phone chirped, and she smiled at me. "We're staying with Shep and Travis until they fix the boilers."

"What? I'm not!" I cried.

"Oh, yes you are. There's no reason for you to be stuck here freezing in the shower when Travis and Shep have two bathrooms at their place."

"I wasn't invited."

"I'm inviting you. Shep already said it was fine. You can sleep on the couch . . . if Travis isn't using it."

"And if he's using it?"

America shrugged. "Then you can sleep in Travis's bed."

"No way!"

She rolled her eyes. "Don't be such a baby, Abby. You guys are friends, right? If he hasn't tried anything by now, I don't think he will."

Her words made my open mouth snap shut. Travis had been around me in one way or another every night for weeks. I had been so occupied with making sure everyone knew we were just friends, it hadn't occurred to me that he really was interested only in friendship. I wasn't sure why, but I felt insulted.

Kara looked at us with disbelief. "Travis Maddox hasn't tried to sleep with you?"

"We're friends!" I said in a defensive tone.

"I know, but he hasn't even tried? He's slept with everyone."

"Except us," America said, looking her over. "And you."

Kara shrugged. "Well, I've never met him. I've just heard."

"Exactly," I snapped. "You don't even know him."

Kara returned to her monitor, oblivious to our presence.

I sighed. "All right, Mare. I need to pack."

"Make sure you pack for a few days; who knows how long it will take them to fix the boilers?" she said, entirely too excited.

Dread settled over me as if I were about to sneak into enemy territory. "Ugh . . . all right."

America bounced when she hugged me. "This is going to be so fun!"

Half an hour later we loaded down her Honda and headed for the apartment. America hardly took a breath between ramblings as she drove. She honked her horn as she slowed to a stop in her usual parking space. Shepley jogged down the steps and pulled both of our suitcases from the trunk, following us up the stairs.

"It's open," he puffed.

America pushed the door and held it open. Shepley grunted when he dropped our luggage to the floor. "Christ, baby! Your suitcase is twenty more pounds than Abby's!"

America and I froze when a woman emerged from the bathroom, buttoning her blouse.

"Hi," she said, surprised. Her mascara-smeared eyes examined us before settling on our luggage. I recognized her as the leggy brunette Travis had followed from the cafeteria.

America glared at Shepley.

He held up his hands. "She's with Travis!"

Travis rounded the corner in a pair of boxer shorts and yawned. He looked at his guest and then patted her backside. "My company's here. You'd better go."

She smiled and wrapped her arms around him, kissing his neck. "I'll leave my number on the counter."

"Eh . . . don't worry about it," Travis said in a casual tone.

"What?" she asked, leaning back to look in his eyes.

"Every time!" America said. She looked at the woman. "How are you surprised by this? He's Travis Fucking Maddox! He is famous for this very thing, and every time they're surprised!" she said, turning to Shepley. He put his arm around her, gesturing for her to calm down.

The girl narrowed her eyes at Travis and then grabbed her purse and stormed out, slamming the door behind her.

Travis walked into the kitchen and opened the fridge as if nothing had happened.

America shook her head and walked down the hall. Shepley followed her, angling his body to compensate for the weight of her suitcase as he trailed behind.

I collapsed against the recliner and sighed, wondering if I was crazy for agreeing to come. I didn't realize Shepley's apartment was a revolving door for clueless bimbos.

Travis stood behind the breakfast bar, crossed his arms over his chest, and smiled. "What's wrong, Pidge? Hard day?"

"No, I'm thoroughly disgusted."

"With me?" He was smiling. I should have known that he expected the conversation. It only made me less inclined to hold back.

"Yes, you. How can you just use someone like that and treat them that way?"

"How did I treat her? She offered her number, I declined."

My mouth fell open at his lack of remorse. "You'll have sex with her, but you won't take her number?"

Travis leaned on the counter with his elbows. "Why would I want her number if I'm not going to call her?"

"Why would you sleep with her if you're not going to call her?"

"I don't promise anyone anything, Pidge. She didn't stipulate a relationship before she spread-eagled on my couch."

I stared at the couch with revulsion. "She's someone's daughter, Travis. What if, down the line, someone treats your daughter like that?"

"My daughter better not drop her panties for some jackass she just met, let's put it that way."

I crossed my arms, angry that he made sense. "So, besides admitting that you're a jackass, you're saying that because she slept with you, she deserved to be tossed out like a stray cat?"

"I'm saying that I was honest with her. She's an adult, it was consensual . . . she was a little too eager about it, if you want to know the truth. You act like I committed a crime."

"She didn't seem as clear about your intentions, Travis."

"Women usually justify their actions with whatever they make up in their heads. She didn't tell me up front that she expected a relationship any more than I told her I expected sex with no strings. How is it any different?"

"You're a pig."

Travis shrugged. "I've been called worse."

I stared at the couch, the cushions still askew and bunched up from its recent use. I recoiled at the thought of how many women had given themselves away against the fabric. Itchy fabric at that.

"I guess I'm sleeping on the recliner," I grumbled.

"Why?"

I glared at him, furious over his confused expression. "I'm not sleeping on that thing! God knows what I'd be lying in!"

He lifted my luggage off the floor. "You're not sleeping on the couch or the recliner. You're sleeping in my bed."

"Which is more unsanitary than the couch, I'm sure."

"There's never been anyone in my bed but me."

I rolled my eyes. "Give me a break!"

"I'm absolutely serious. I bag 'em on the couch. I don't let them in my room."

"Then why am I allowed in your bed?"

One corner of his mouth pulled up into an impish grin. "Are you planning on having sex with me tonight?"

"No!"

"That's why. Now get your cranky ass up, take your hot shower, and then we can study some Bio."

I glared at him for a moment and then grudgingly did as he commanded. I stood under the shower entirely too long, letting the water wash away my aggravation. Massaging the shampoo through my hair, I sighed at how wonderful it was to shower in a noncommunal bathroom again—no flip-flops, no toiletry bag, just the relaxing blend of water and steam.

The door opened, and I jumped. "Mare?"

"No, it's me," Travis said.

I automatically wrapped my arms over the parts I didn't want him to see. "What are you doing in here? Get out!"

"You forgot a towel, and I brought your clothes, and your toothbrush, and some weird face cream I found in your bag."

"You went through my stuff?" I shrieked. He didn't answer. Instead, I heard the faucet turn on and the sound of his toothbrush against his teeth.

I peeked out of the plastic curtain, holding it against my chest. "Get out, Travis."

He looked up at me, his lips covered in suds from his toothpaste. "I can't go to bed without brushing my teeth."

"If you come within two feet of this curtain, I will poke out your eyes while you sleep."

"I won't peek, Pidge," he chuckled.

I waited under the water with my arms wrapped tightly across my chest. He spit, gurgled, and spit again, and then the door closed. I rinsed the soap from my skin, dried as quickly as possible, and then pulled my T-shirt and shorts on, slipping on my glasses and raking a comb through my hair. The night moisturizer Travis had brought caught my eye, and I couldn't help but smile. He was thoughtful and almost nice when he wanted to be.

Travis opened the door again. "C'mon, Pidge! I'm gettin' old, here!"

I threw my comb at him and he ducked, shutting the door and laughing to himself all the way to his room. I brushed my teeth and then shuffled down the hall, passing Shepley's bedroom on the way.

"Night, Abby," America called from the darkness.

"Night, Mare."

I hesitated before landing two soft knocks on Travis's door.

"Come in, Pidge. You don't have to knock."

He pulled the door open and I walked in, seeing his black iron-rod bed parallel to the line of windows on the far side of the room. The walls were bare except for a lone sombrero above his headboard. I half expected his room to be covered in posters of barely clothed women, but I didn't even see an advertisement for a beer brand. His bed was black, his carpet gray; everything else in the room was white. It looked as if he'd just moved in.

"Nice PJs," Travis said, noting my yellow-and-navy plaid shorts and gray Eastern T. He sat on his bed and patted the pillow beside him. "Well, come on. I'm not going to bite you."

"I'm not afraid of you," I said, walking over to the bed and dropping my Biology book beside him. "Do you have a pen?"

He nodded to his night table. "Top drawer."

I reached across the bed and pulled open the drawer, finding three pens, a pencil, a tube of K-Y Jelly, and a clear glass bowl overflowing with packages of different brands of condoms. Revolted, I grabbed a pen and shoved the drawer shut.

"What?" he asked, turning a page of my book.

"Did you rob the health clinic?"

"No. Why?"

I pulled the cap off the pen, unable to keep the sickened expression from my face. "Your lifetime supply of condoms."

"Better safe than sorry, right?"

I rolled my eyes. Travis returned to the pages, a wry smile breaking across his lips. He read the notes to me, highlighting the main points while he asked me questions and patiently explained what I didn't comprehend.

After an hour, I pulled off my glasses and rubbed my eyes. "I'm beat. I can't memorize one more macromolecule."

Travis smiled, closing my book. "All right."

I paused, unsure of our sleeping arrangements. Travis left the room and walked down the hall, mumbling something into Shepley's room before turning on the shower. I turned back the covers and then pulled them up to my neck, listening to the high-pitched whine of the water running through the pipes.

Ten minutes later, the water shut off, and the floor creaked under Travis's steps. He strolled across the room with a towel wrapped around his hips. He had tattoos on opposite sides of his chest, and black tribal art covering each of his bulging shoulders.

On his right arm, the black lines and symbols spanned from his shoulder to his wrist; on the left, the tattoos stopped at his elbow, with one single line of script on the underside of his forearm. I intentionally kept my back to him while he stood in front of his dresser and dropped his towel to slip on a pair of boxers.

After flipping off the light, he crawled into the bed beside me.

"You're sleeping here, too?" I asked, turning to look at him. The full moon outside the windows cast shadows across his face. "Well, yeah. This is my bed."

"I know, but I . . ." I paused. My only other options were the couch or the recliner.

Travis grinned and shook his head. "Don't you trust me by now? I'll be on my best behavior, I swear," he said, holding up fingers that I was sure the Boy Scouts of America had never considered using.

I didn't argue, I simply turned away and rested my head on the pillow, tucking the covers behind me to create a clear barrier between his body and mine.

"Goodnight, Pigeon," he whispered into my ear. I could feel his minty breath on my cheek, giving rise to goose bumps on every inch of my flesh. Thank God it was dark enough that he couldn't see my embarrassing reaction or the flush of my cheeks that followed.

IT SEEMED LIKE I HAD JUST CLOSED MY EYES WHEN I heard the alarm. I reached over to turn it off, but wrenched back my hand in horror when I felt warm skin beneath my fingers. I tried to recall where I was. When the answer hit, it mortified me that Travis might think I'd done it on purpose.

"Travis? Your alarm," I whispered. He still didn't move. "Travis!" I said, nudging him. When he still didn't stir, I reached across him, fumbling in the dim light until I felt the top of the clock. Unsure of how to turn it off, I smacked the top of it until I hit the snooze button, and then fell against my pillow with a huff.

Travis chuckled.

"You were awake?"

"I promised I'd behave. I didn't say anything about letting you lay on me."

"I didn't lie on you," I protested. "I couldn't reach the clock. That has to be the most annoying alarm I've ever heard. It sounds like a dying animal."

He reached over and flipped a button. "You want breakfast?"

I glared at him, and then shook my head. "I'm not hungry."

"Well, I am. Why don't you ride with me down the street to the café?"

"I don't think I can handle your lack of driving skills this early in the morning," I said. I swung my feet over the side of the bed and shoved them into my slippers, shuffling to the door.

"Where are you going?" he asked.

"To get dressed and go to class. Do you need an itinerary while I'm here?"

Travis stretched, and then walked over to me, still in his boxers. "Are you always so temperamental, or will that taper off once you believe I'm not just creating some elaborate scheme to get into your pants?" His hands cupped my shoulders, and I felt his thumbs caress my skin in unison.

"I'm not temperamental."

He leaned in close and whispered in my ear. "I don't want to sleep with you, Pidge. I like you too much."

He walked past me to the bathroom, and I stood, stunned. Kara's words replayed in my mind. Travis Maddox slept with everyone; I couldn't help but feel deficient in some way, knowing he had no desire to even try to sleep with me.

The door opened again, and America walked through. "Wakey, wakey, eggs 'n' bakey!" she smiled, yawning.

"You're turning into your mother, Mare," I grumbled, rifling through my suitcase.

"Oooh . . . did someone miss some sleep last night?"

"He barely breathed in my direction," I said acerbically.

A knowing smile brightened America's face. "Oh."

"Oh, what?"

"Nothing," she said, returning to Shepley's room.

Travis was in the kitchen, humming a random tune while scrambling eggs. "You sure you don't want some?" he asked.

"I'm sure. Thanks, though."

Shepley and America walked in, and Shepley pulled two plates from the cabinet, holding them out as Travis shoveled a pile of steaming eggs onto each one. Shepley set the plates on the bar, and he and America sat together, satisfying the appetite they more than likely worked up the night before.

"Don't look at me like that, Shep. I'm sorry, I just don't want to go," America said.

"Baby, the House has a date party twice a year," Shepley spoke as he chewed. "It's a month away. You'll have plenty of time to find a dress and do all that girl stuff."

"I would, Shep . . . that's really sweet . . . but I'm not gonna know anyone there."

"A lot of the girls that come don't know a lot of people there," he said, surprised at the rejection.

She slumped in her chair. "The sorority bitches get invited to those things. They'll all know each other . . . it'll be weird."

"C'mon, Mare. Don't make me go alone."

"Well . . . maybe you could find someone to take Abby?" she said, looking at me, and then at Travis.

Travis raised an eyebrow, and Shepley shook his head. "Trav doesn't go to the date parties. It's something you take your girlfriend to . . . and Travis doesn't . . . you know."

America shrugged. "We could set her up with someone."

I narrowed my eyes at her. "I can hear you, you know."

America used the face she knew I couldn't say no to. "Please, Abby? We'll find you a nice guy that's funny and witty, and you know I'll make sure he's hot. I promise you'll have a good time! And who knows? Maybe you'll hit it off."

Travis threw the pan in the sink. "I didn't say I wouldn't take her."

I rolled my eyes. "Don't do me any favors, Travis."

"That's not what I meant, Pidge. Date parties are for the guys with girlfriends, and it's common knowledge that I don't do the girlfriend thing. But I won't have to worry about you expecting an engagement ring afterward."

America jutted her lip out. "Pretty please, Abby?"

"Don't look at me like that!" I complained. "Travis doesn't want to go, I don't want to go . . . we won't be much fun."

Travis crossed his arms and leaned against the sink. "I didn't say I didn't want to go. I think it'd be fun if the four of us went," he shrugged.

Everyone's eyes focused on me, and I recoiled. "Why don't we hang out here?"

America pouted and Shepley leaned forward. "Because I

have to go, Abby. I'm a freshman. I have to make sure everything's moving smoothly, everyone has a beer in their hand, things like that."

Travis walked across the kitchen and wrapped his arm around my shoulders, pulling me to his side. "C'mon, Pidge. Will you go with me?"

I looked at America, then at Shepley, and finally to Travis. "Yes," I sighed.

America squealed and hugged me, and then I felt Shepley's hand on my back. "Thanks, Abby," Shepley said.

Chapter Three
Cheap Shot

Finch took another drag. The smoke flowed from his nose in two thick streams. I angled my face toward the sun as he regaled me with his recent weekend of dancing, booze, and a very persistent new friend.

"If he's stalking you, then why do you let him buy you drinks?" I laughed.

"It's simple, Abby. I'm broke."

I laughed again, and Finch jabbed his elbow into my side when he caught sight of Travis walking toward us.

"Hey, Travis," Finch lilted, winking at me.

"Finch," Travis said with a nod. He dangled his keys. "I'm headed home, Pidge. You need a ride?"

"I was just going in," I said, grinning up at him through my sunglasses.

"You're not staying with me tonight?" he asked. His face was a combination of surprise and disappointment.

"No, I am. I just had to grab a few things that I forgot."

"Like what?"

"Well, my razor for one. What do you care?"

"It's about time you shaved your legs. They've been tearing the hell outta mine," he said with an impish grin.

Finch's eyes bulged as he gave me a quick once-over, and I made a face at Travis. "That's how rumors get started!" I looked at Finch and shook my head. "I'm sleeping in his bed . . . just sleeping."

"Right," Finch said with a smug smile.

I smacked Finch's arm before yanking the door open and climbing the stairs. By the time I reached the second floor, Travis was beside me.

"Oh, don't be mad. I was just kidding."

"Everyone already assumes we're having sex. You're making it worse."

"Who cares what they think?"

"I do, Travis! I do!" I pushed open my door, shoved random items into a small tote, and then stormed out, with Travis trailing behind. He chuckled as he took the bag from my hand, and I glared at him. "It's not funny. Do you want the whole school to think I'm one of your sluts?"

Travis frowned. "No one thinks that. And if they do, they better hope I don't hear about it."

He held the door open for me, and after walking through, I stopped abruptly in front of him.

"Whoa!" he said, slamming into me.

I flipped around. "Oh my God! People probably think we're together and you're shamelessly continuing your . . . lifestyle. I must look pathetic!" I said, coming to the realization as I spoke. "I don't think I should stay with you anymore. We should just stay away from each other in general for a while."

I took my bag from him, and he snatched it back.

"No one thinks we're together, Pidge. You don't have to quit talking to me to prove a point."

We engaged in a tug-of-war with the tote, and when he refused to let go, I growled loudly in frustration. "Have you ever had a girl—that's a friend—stay with you? Have you ever given girls rides to and from school? Have you eaten lunch with them every day? No one knows what to think about us, even when we tell them!"

He walked to the parking lot, holding my effects hostage. "I'll fix this, okay? I don't want anyone thinking less of you because of me," he said with a troubled expression. His eyes brightened and he smiled. "Let me make it up to you. Why don't we go to the Dutch tonight?"

"That's a biker bar," I sneered, watching him fasten my tote to his bike.

"Okay, then let's go to the club. I'll take you to dinner and then we can go to the Red Door. My treat."

"How will going out to dinner and then to a club fix the problem? When people see us out together it will make it worse."

He straddled his bike. "Think about it. Me, drunk, in a room full of scantily clad women? It won't take long for people to figure out we're not a couple."

"So what am I supposed to do? Take a guy home from the bar to drive the point home?"

"I didn't say that. No need to get carried away," he said with a frown.

I rolled my eyes and climbed onto the seat, wrapping my arms around his middle. "Some random girl is going to follow us home from the bar? That's how you're going to make it up to me?"

"You're not jealous, are you, Pigeon?"

"Jealous of what? The STD-infested imbecile you're going to piss off in the morning?"

Travis laughed, and then started his Harley. He flew toward his apartment at twice the speed limit, and I closed my eyes to block out the trees and cars we left behind.

After climbing off his bike, I smacked his shoulder. "Did you forget I was with you? Are you trying to get me killed?"

"It's hard to forget you're behind me when your thighs are squeezing the life out of me." A smirk came with his next thought. "I couldn't think of a better way to die, actually."

"There is something very wrong with you."

We had barely made it inside when America shuffled out of Shepley's bedroom. "We were thinking about going out tonight. You guys in?"

I looked at Travis and grinned. "We're going to swing by the sushi place before we go to Red."

America's smile spanned from one side of her face to the other. "Shep!" she cried, scampering into the bathroom. "We're going out tonight!"

I was the last one in the shower, so Shepley, America, and Travis were impatiently standing by the door when I stepped out of the bathroom in a black dress and hot pink heels.

America whistled. "Hot damn, Mama!"

I smiled in appreciation, and Travis held out his hand. "Nice legs."

"Did I mention that it's a magic razor?"

"I don't think it's the razor," he smiled, pulling me out the door.

We were far too loud and obnoxious in the sushi bar, and had already had a night's worth to drink before we stepped foot in the Red Door. Shepley pulled into the parking lot, taking time to find a space.

"Sometime tonight, Shep," America muttered.

"Hey, I have to find a wide space. I don't want some drunken idiot dinging the paint."

Once we parked, Travis leaned the seat forward and helped me out. "I meant to ask you about your IDs. They're flawless. You didn't get them around here."

"Yeah, we've had them for a while. It was necessary . . . in Wichita," I said.

"'Necessary?'" Travis asked.

"It's a good thing you have connections," America said. She hiccupped and covered her mouth, giggling.

"Dear God, woman," Shepley said, holding America's arm as she awkwardly stepped along the gravel. "I think you're already done for the night."

Travis made a face. "What are you talking about, Mare? What connections?"

"Abby has some old friends that—"

"They're fake IDs, Trav," I interrupted. "You have to know the right people if you want them done right, right?"

America purposefully looked away from Travis, and I waited.

"Right," he said, extending his hand for mine.

I grabbed three of his fingers and smiled, knowing by his expression that he wasn't satisfied with my answer.

"I need another drink!" I said as a second attempt to change the subject.

"Shots!" America yelled.

Shepley rolled his eyes. "Oh, yeah. That's what you need, another shot."

Once inside, America immediately pulled me onto the dance floor. Her blond hair was everywhere, and I laughed at the duck face she made when she moved to the music. When the song was over, we joined the boys at the bar. An excessively voluptuous platinum blonde was already at Travis's side, and America's face screwed into revulsion.

"It's going to be like this all night, Mare. Just ignore them," Shepley said, nodding to a small group of girls standing a few feet away. They eyed the blonde, waiting for their turn.

"It looks like Vegas threw up on a flock of vultures," America sneered.

Travis lit a cigarette as he ordered two more beers, and the blonde bit her puffy, glossed lip and smiled. The bartender popped the tops open and slid the bottles to Travis. The blonde picked up one of the beers, but Travis pulled it from her hand.

"Uh . . . not yours," he said to her, handing it to me.

My initial thought was to toss the bottle in the trash, but the woman looked so offended, I smiled and took a drink. She walked off in a huff, and I chuckled that Travis didn't seem to notice.

"Like I would buy a beer for some chick at a bar," he said, shaking his head. I held up my beer, and he pulled up one side of his mouth into a half smile. "You're different."

I clinked my bottle against his. "To being the only girl a guy with no standards doesn't want to sleep with," I said, taking a swig.

"Are you serious?" he asked, pulling the bottle from my mouth. When I didn't recant, he leaned toward me. "First of all . . . I have standards. I've never been with an ugly woman. Ever. Second of all, I wanted to sleep with you. I thought about throwing you over my couch fifty different ways, but I haven't because I don't see you that way anymore. It's not that I'm not attracted to you, I just think you're better than that."

I couldn't hold back the smug smile that crept across my face. "You think I'm too good for you."

He sneered at my second insult. "I can't think of a single guy I know that's good enough for you."

The smugness melted away, replaced with a touched, appreciative smile. "Thanks, Trav," I said, setting my empty bottle on the bar.

Travis pulled on my hand. "C'mon," he said, tugging me through the crowd to the dance floor.

"I've had a lot to drink! I'm going to fall!"

Travis smiled and pulled me to him, grabbing my hips. "Shut up and dance."

America and Shepley appeared beside us. Shepley moved like he'd been watching too many Usher videos. Travis had me near panic with the way he pressed against me. If he used any of those moves on the couch, I could see why so many girls chanced humiliation in the morning.

He cinched his hands around my hips, and I noticed that his expression was different, almost serious. I ran my hands over his flawless chest and six-pack as they stretched and tensed under his tight shirt to the music. I turned my back to him, smiling when he wrapped his arms around my waist. Coupled with the alcohol in my system, when he pulled my body against his, things came to mind that were anything but friendly.

The next song bled into the one we were dancing to, and Travis showed no signs of wanting to return to the bar. The sweat beaded on the back of my neck, and the multicolored strobe lights made me feel a bit dizzy. I closed my eyes and leaned my head against his shoulder. He grabbed my hands and pulled them up and around his neck. His hands ran down my arms and down my ribs, finally returning to my hips. When I felt his lips and then his tongue against my neck, I pulled away from him.

He chuckled, looking a bit surprised. "What, Pidge?"

My temper flared, making the sharp words I wanted to say stick in my throat. I retreated to the bar and ordered another Corona. Travis took the stool beside me, holding up his finger to order one for himself. As soon as the bartender set the bottle in front of me, I tipped it up and drank half the contents before slamming it to the bar.

"You think that is going to change anyone's mind about us?" I said, pulling my hair to the side, covering the spot he kissed.

He laughed once. "I don't give a damn what they think about us."

I shot him a dirty look and then turned to face forward.

"Pigeon," he said, touching my arm.

I pulled away from him. "Don't. I could never get drunk enough to let you get me on that couch."

His face twisted in anger, but before he could say anything, a dark-haired stunner with pouty lips, enormous blue eyes, and far too much cleavage approached him.

"Well, if it isn't Travis Maddox," she said, bouncing in all the right places.

He took a drink, and then his eyes locked on mine. "Hey, Megan."

"Introduce me to your girlfriend," she smiled. I rolled my eyes.

Travis tipped his head back to finish his beer, and then slid his empty bottle down the bar. Everyone waiting to order watched it until it fell into the trash can at the end. "She's not my girlfriend."

He grabbed Megan's hand, and she happily traipsed behind him to the dance floor. He all but mauled her for one song, and then another, and another. They were causing a scene with the way she let him grope her, and when he bent her over I turned my back to them.

"You look pissed," a man said as he sat next to me. "Is that your boyfriend out there?"

"No, he's just a friend," I grumbled.

"Well, that's good. That could have been pretty awkward for you if he was." He faced the dance floor, shaking his head at the spectacle.

"Tell me about it," I said, drinking the last of my beer. I barely tasted the last two I had put away, and my teeth were numb.

"Would you like another one?" he asked. I looked over at him and he smiled. "I'm Ethan."

"Abby," I said, taking his outstretched hand.

He held up two fingers to the bartender, and I smiled. "Thanks."

"So, you live here?" he asked.

"In Morgan Hall at Eastern."

"I have an apartment in Hinley."

"You go to State?" I asked. "What is that . . . like, an hour away? What are you doing over here?"

"I graduated last May. My little sister goes to Eastern. I'm staying with her this week while I apply for jobs."

"Uh-oh . . . living in the real world, huh?"

Ethan laughed. "And it's everything they say it is."

I pulled the gloss out of my pocket and smeared it across my lips, using the mirror lining the wall behind the bar.

"That's a nice shade," he said, watching me press my lips together.

I smiled, feeling the anger at Travis and the heaviness of the alcohol. "Maybe you can try it on later."

Ethan's eyes brightened as I leaned in closer, and I smiled when he touched my knee. He pulled back his hand when Travis stepped between us.

"You ready, Pidge?"

"I'm talking, Travis," I said, moving him back. His shirt was damp from the circus on the dance floor, and I made a show of wiping my hand on my skirt.

Travis made a face. "Do you even know this guy?"

"This is Ethan," I said, sending my new friend the best flirty smile I could manage.

He winked at me, and then looked at Travis, extending his hand. "Nice to meet you."

Travis watched me expectantly until I finally gave in, waving my hand in his general direction. "Ethan, this is Travis," I muttered.

"Travis Maddox," he said, staring at Ethan's hand as if he wanted to rip it off.

Ethan's eyes grew wide, and he awkwardly pulled back his hand. "Travis Maddox? Eastern's Travis Maddox?"

I rested my cheek on my fist, dreading the inevitable testosterone-fueled story swapping that would soon ensue.

Travis stretched his arm behind me to grip the bar. "Yeah, what of it?"

"I saw you fight Shawn Smith last year, man. I thought I was about to witness someone's death!"

Travis glowered down at him. "You wanna see it again?"

Ethan laughed once, his eyes darting back and forth between us. When he realized Travis was serious, he smiled at me apologetically and left.

"Are you ready, now?" he snapped.

"You are a complete asshole, you know that?"

"I've been called worse," he said, helping me off the stool.

We followed America and Shepley to the car, and when Travis tried to grab my hand to lead me across the parking lot, I yanked it away. He wheeled around and I jerked to a stop, leaning back when he came within a few inches of my face.

"I should just kiss you and get it over with!" he yelled. "You're being ridiculous! I kissed your neck, so what?"

I could smell the beer and cigarettes on his breath and pushed him away. "I'm not your fuck buddy, Travis."

He shook his head in disbelief. "I never said you were! You're around me 24-7, you sleep in my bed, but half the time you act like you don't wanna be seen with me!"

"I came here with you!"

"I have never treated you with anything but respect, Pidge."

I stood my ground. "No, you just treat me like your property. You had no right to run Ethan off like that!"

"Do you know who Ethan is?" he asked. When I shook my head, he leaned in closer. "I do. He was arrested last year for sexual battery, but the charges were dropped."

I crossed my arms. "Oh, so you have something in common?"

Travis's eyes narrowed, and the muscles in his jaws twitched under his skin. "Are you calling me a rapist?" he said in a cold, low tone.

I pressed my lips together, even angrier that he was right. I had taken it too far. "No, I'm just pissed at you!"

"I've been drinking, all right? Your skin was three inches from my face, and you're beautiful, and you smell fucking awesome when you sweat. I kissed you! I'm sorry! Get over yourself!"

His excuse made the corners of my mouth turn up. "You think I'm beautiful?"

He frowned with disgust. "You're gorgeous and you know it. What are you smiling about?"

I tried to quell my amusement, to no avail. "Nothing. Let's go."

Travis laughed once and shook his head. "Wha . . . ? You . . . ? You're a pain in my ass!" he yelled, glaring at me. I couldn't stop smiling, and after a few seconds, Travis's mouth turned up. He shook his head again, and then hooked his arm around my neck. "You're making me crazy. You know that, right?"

At the apartment, we all stumbled through the door. I made a beeline for the bathroom to wash the smoke out of my hair.

When I stepped out of the shower, I saw that Travis had brought me one of his T-shirts and a pair of his boxers to change into.

The shirt swallowed me, and the boxers disappeared under the shirt. I crashed into the bed and sighed, still smiling at what he'd said in the parking lot.

Travis stared at me for a moment, and I felt a twinge in my chest. I had an almost ravenous urge to grab his face and plant my mouth on his, but I fought against the alcohol and hormones raging through my bloodstream.

"Night, Pidge," he whispered, turning over.

I fidgeted, not yet ready to sleep. "Trav?" I said, leaning up to rest my chin on his shoulder.

"Yeah?"

"I know I'm drunk, and we just got into a ginormous fight over this, but . . ."

"I'm not having sex with you, so quit asking," he said, his back still turned to me.

"What? No!" I cried.

Travis laughed and turned, looking at me with a soft expression. "What, Pigeon?"

I sighed. "This," I said, laying my head on his chest and stretching my arm across his middle, snuggling as close to him as I could.

He stiffened and held his hands up, as if he didn't know how to react. "You are drunk."

"I know," I said, too intoxicated to be embarrassed.

He relaxed one hand against my back, and the other on my wet hair, and then pressed his lips to my forehead. "You are the most confusing woman I've ever met."

"It's the least you can do after scaring off the only guy that approached me tonight."

"You mean Ethan the rapist? Yeah, I owe you for that one."

"Never mind," I said, feeling the beginning of a rejection coming on.

He grabbed my arm and held it on his stomach to keep me from pulling away. "No, I'm serious. You need to be more careful. If I wasn't there . . . I don't even want to think about it. And now you expect me to apologize for running him off?"

"I don't want you to apologize. It's not even about that."

"Then what's it about?" he asked, searching my eyes for something. His face was just a few inches from mine, and I could feel his breath on my lips.

I frowned. "I'm drunk, Travis. It's the only excuse I have."

"You just want me to hold you until you fall asleep?"

I didn't answer.

He shifted to look straight into my eyes. "I should say no to prove a point," he said, his eyebrows pulling together. "But I would hate myself later if I said no and you never asked me again."

I nestled my cheek against his chest, and he tightened his arms, sighing. "You don't need an excuse, Pigeon. All you have to do is ask."

I CRINGED AT THE SUNLIGHT POURING THROUGH THE window and the alarm blaring into my ear. Travis was still asleep, surrounding me with both his arms and his legs. I maneuvered an arm free to reach over and pound the snooze button. Wiping my face, I looked over at him, sleeping soundly two inches from me.

"Oh my God," I whispered, wondering how we'd managed to become so tangled. I took a deep breath and held it as I worked to free myself from his grip.

"Stop it, Pidge, I'm sleepin'," he mumbled, squeezing me against him.

After several attempts, I finally slid from his grip and sat on the edge of the bed, looking back at his half-naked body draped in covers. I watched him for a moment and sighed. The lines were becoming blurred, and it was my fault.

His hand slid across the sheets and touched my fingers. "What's wrong, Pigeon?" he said, his eyes barely open.

"I'm going to get a glass of water, you want anything?" Travis shook his head and closed his eyes, his cheek flat against the mattress.

"Morning, Abby," Shepley said from the recliner when I rounded the corner.

"Where's Mare?"

"Still sleeping. What are you doing up so early?" he asked, looking at the clock.

"The alarm went off, but I always wake up early after I drink. It's a curse."

"Me, too," he nodded.

"You better get Mare up. We have class in an hour," I said, turning on the tap, and leaning over to take a sip.

Shepley nodded. "I was just going to let her sleep."

"Don't do that. She'll be mad if she misses."

"Oh," he said, standing up. "Better wake her, then." He wheeled around. "Hey, Abby?"

"Yeah?"

"I don't know what's going on with you and Travis, but

I know that he's going to do something stupid to piss you off. It's a tic he has. He doesn't get close with anyone very often, and for whatever reason he's let you in. But you have to overlook his demons. It's the only way he'll know."

"Know what?" I asked, raising an eyebrow at his melodramatic speech.

"If you'll climb over the wall," he answered simply.

I shook my head and chuckled. "Whatever you say, Shep."

Shepley shrugged, and then disappeared into his bedroom. I heard soft murmurs, a protesting groan, and then America's sweet giggling.

I swirled the oatmeal around in my bowl, and squeezed the chocolate syrup in as I stirred.

"That's sick, Pidge," Travis said, wearing only a pair of green plaid boxers. He rubbed his eyes and pulled a box of cereal from the cabinet.

"Good morning to you, too," I said, snapping the cap on the bottle.

"I hear your birthday is coming up. Last stand of your teenage years," he grinned, his eyes puffy and red.

"Yeah . . . I'm not a big birthday person. I think Mare is going to take me to dinner or something." I smiled. "You can come if you want."

"All right," he shrugged. "It's a week from Sunday?"

"Yes. When's your birthday?"

He poured the milk, dunking the flakes with his spoon, "Not 'til April. April first."

"Shut up."

"No, I'm serious," he said, chewing.

"Your birthday is on April Fools'?" I asked again, raising an eyebrow.

He laughed. "Yes! You're gonna be late. I better get dressed."

"I'm riding with Mare."

I could tell he was being intentionally cool when he shrugged. "Whatever," he said, turning his back to me to finish his cereal.

Chapter Four
The Bet

"HE'S DEFINITELY STARING AT YOU," AMERICA WHISpered, leaning back to peek across the room.

"Stop looking, dummy, he's going to see you."

America smiled and waved. "He's already seen me. He's still staring."

I hesitated for a moment and then finally worked up enough courage to look in his direction. Parker was looking right at me, grinning.

I returned his smile and then pretended to type something on my laptop.

"Is he still staring?" I murmured.

"Yep," she giggled.

After class, Parker stopped me in the hall.

"Don't forget about the party this weekend."

"I won't," I said, trying not to bat my eyes or do anything else ridiculous.

America and I made our way across the lawn to the cafeteria to meet Travis and Shepley for lunch. She was still laughing about Parker's behavior when they approached.

"Hey, baby," America said, kissing her boyfriend square on the mouth.

"What's so funny?" Shepley asked.

"Oh, a guy in class was staring at Abby all hour. It was adorable."

"As long as he was staring at Abby," Shepley winked.

"Who was it?" Travis grimaced.

I adjusted my backpack, prompting Travis to slide it off my arms and hold it. I shook my head. "Mare's imagining things."

"Abby! You big fat liar! It was Parker Hayes, and he was being so obvious. The guy was practically drooling."

Travis's expression twisted into disgust. "Parker Hayes?"

Shepley pulled on America's hand. "We're headed to lunch. Will you be enjoying the fine cafeteria cuisine this afternoon?"

America kissed him again in answer, and Travis and I followed behind. I sat my tray between America and Finch, but Travis didn't sit in his normal seat across from me. Instead, he sat a few seats down. It was then that I realized he hadn't said much during our walk to the cafeteria.

"Are you okay, Trav?" I asked.

"Me? Fine, why?" he said, smoothing the features of his face.

"You've just been quiet."

Several members of the football team approached the table and sat down, laughing loudly. Travis looked a bit annoyed as he rolled his food around on his plate.

Chris Jenks tossed a french fry onto Travis's tray. "What's up, Trav? I heard you bagged Tina Martin. She's been raking your name through the mud today."

"Shut up, Jenks," Travis said, keeping his eyes on his food.

I leaned forward so the brawny giant sitting in front of Travis could experience the full force of my glare. "Knock it off, Chris."

Travis's eyes bored into mine. "I can take care of myself, Abby."

"I'm sorry, I . . ."

"I don't want you to be sorry. I don't want you to be anything," he snapped, shoving away from the table and storming out the door.

Finch looked over at me with raised eyebrows. "Whoa. What was that about?"

I stabbed a Tater Tot with my fork and puffed. "I don't know."

Shepley patted my back. "It's nothing you did, Abby."

"He just has stuff going on," America added.

"What kind of stuff?" I asked.

Shepley shrugged and turned his attention to his plate. "You should know by now that it takes patience and a forgiving attitude to be friends with Travis. He's his own universe."

I shook my head. "That's the Travis everyone else sees . . . not the Travis I know."

Shepley leaned forward. "There's no difference. You just have to ride the wave."

After class, I rode with America to the apartment to find Travis's motorcycle gone. I went into his room and curled into a ball on his bed, resting my head on my arm. Travis had been fine that morning. As much time as we had spent together, I couldn't believe I didn't see that something had been bothering him. Not only that, it disturbed me that America seemed to know what was going on and I didn't.

My breathing evened out and my eyes grew heavy; it wasn't long before I fell asleep. When my eyes opened again, the night sky had darkened the window. Muffled voices filtered down the hall from the living room, including Travis's deep tone. I crept down the hall, and then froze when I heard my name.

"Abby gets it, Trav. Don't beat yourself up," Shepley said.

"You're already going to the date party. What's the harm in asking her out?" America asked.

I stiffened, waiting for his response. "I don't want to date her; I just want to be around her. She's . . . different."

"Different how?" America asked, sounding irritated.

"She doesn't put up with my bullshit, it's refreshing. You said it yourself, Mare: I'm not her type. It's just not . . . like that with us."

"You're closer to her type than you know," America said.

I backed up as quietly as I could, and when the wooden boards creaked beneath my bare feet, I reached over to pull Travis's bedroom door shut and then walked down the hall.

"Hey, Abby," America said with a grin. "How was your nap?"

"I was out for five hours. That's closer to a coma than a nap."

Travis stared at me for a moment, and when I smiled at him, he walked straight toward me, grabbed my hand, and pulled me down the hall to his bedroom. He shut the door, and I felt my heart pounding in my chest, bracing for him to say something else to crush my ego.

His eyebrows pulled in. "I'm so sorry, Pidge. I was an asshole to you earlier."

I relaxed a bit, seeing the remorse in his eyes. "I didn't know you were mad at me."

"I wasn't mad at you. I just have a bad habit of lashing out at those I care about. It's a piss-poor excuse, I know, but I am sorry," he said, enveloping me in his arms.

I nestled my cheek against his chest, settling in. "What were you mad about?"

"It's not important. The only thing I'm worried about is you."

I leaned back to look up at him. "I can handle your temper tantrums."

His eyes scanned my face for several moments before a small smile spread across his lips. "I don't know why you put up with me, and I don't know what I'd do if you didn't."

I could smell the mixture of cigarettes and mint on his breath, and I looked at his lips, my body reacting to how close we were. Travis's expression changed and his breathing staggered—he had noticed, too.

He leaned in infinitesimally, and then we both jumped when his cell phone rang. He sighed, pulling it from his pocket.

"Yeah. Hoffman? Jesus . . . all right. That'll be an easy grand. Jefferson?" He looked at me and winked. "We'll be there." He hung up and took my hand. "Come with me." He pulled me down the hall. "That was Adam," he said to Shepley. "Brady Hoffman will be at Jefferson in ninety minutes."

Shepley nodded and stood up, digging his cell phone from his pocket. He quickly tapped in the information, sending exclusive text invitations to those who knew about the Circle. Those ten or so members would text ten members on their list, and so on, until every member knew exactly where the floating fight ring would be held.

"Here we go," America said, smiling. "We'd better freshen up!"

The air in the apartment was tense and buoyant at the same time. Travis seemed the least affected, slipping on his boots and a white tank top as if he were leaving to run an errand.

America led me down the hall to Travis's bedroom and frowned. "You have to change, Abby. You can't wear that to the fight."

"I wore a freaking cardigan last time and you didn't say anything!" I protested.

"I didn't think you'd go last time. Here," she threw clothes at me, "put this on."

"I am not wearing this!"

"Let's go!" Shepley called from the living room.

"Hurry up!" America snapped, running into Shepley's room.

I pulled on the deep-cut yellow halter top and tight low-rise jeans America had thrown at me, and then slipped on a pair of heels, raking a brush through my hair as I shuffled down the hall. America came out of her room with a short green baby-doll dress and matching heels, and when we rounded the corner, Travis and Shepley were standing at the door.

Travis's mouth fell open. "Oh, hell no. Are you trying to get me killed? You've gotta change, Pidge."

"What?" I asked, looking down.

America grabbed her hips. "She looks cute, Trav, leave her alone!"

Travis took my hand and led me down the hall. "Get a T-shirt on . . . and some sneakers. Something comfortable."

"What? Why?"

"Because I'll be more worried about who's looking at your tits in that shirt instead of Hoffman," he said, stopping at his door.

"I thought you said you didn't give a damn what anyone else thought?"

"That's a different scenario, Pigeon." Travis looked down at my chest and then up at me. "You can't wear this to the fight, so please . . . just . . . please just change," he stuttered, shoving me into the room and shutting me in.

"Travis!" I yelled. I kicked off my heels, and shoved my feet into my Converses. Then I wiggled out of my halter top, throwing it across the room. The first cotton shirt that touched my hands I yanked over my head, and then ran down the hall, standing in the doorway.

"Better?" I huffed, pulling my hair into a ponytail.

"Yes!" Travis said, relieved. "Let's go!"

We raced to the parking lot. I jumped on the back of Travis's motorcycle as he ripped the engine and peeled out, flying down the road to the college. I squeezed his middle in anticipation; the rushing to get out the door sent adrenaline surging through my veins.

Travis drove over the curb, parking his motorcycle in the shadows behind the Jefferson Liberal Arts building. He pushed his sunglasses to the top of his head and then grabbed my hand, smiling as we snuck to the back of the building. He stopped at an open window near the ground.

My eyes widened with realization. "You're joking."

Travis smiled. "This is the VIP entrance. You should see how everyone else gets in."

I shook my head as he worked his legs through, and then disappeared. I leaned down and called into oblivion, "Travis!"

"Down here, Pidge. Just come in feet first, I'll catch you."

"You're out of your damn mind if you think I'm jumping into the dark!"

"I'll catch you! I promise! Now get your ass in here!"

I sighed, touching my forehead with my hand. "This is insane!"

I sat down, and then scooted forward until half of my body was dangling in the dark. I turned onto my stomach and pointed my toes, feeling for the floor. I waited for my feet to touch Travis's hand, but I lost my grip, squealing when I fell backward. A pair of hands grabbed me, and I heard Travis's voice in the darkness.

"You fall like a girl," he chuckled.

He lowered my feet to the ground and then pulled me deeper into the blackness. After a dozen steps, I could hear the familiar yelling of numbers and names, and then the room was illuminated. A lantern sat in the corner, lighting the room just enough that I could make out Travis's face.

"What are we doing?"

"Waiting. Adam has to run through his spiel before I go in."

I fidgeted. "Should I wait here, or should I go in? Where do I go when the fight starts? Where's Shep and Mare?"

"They went in the other way. Just follow me out; I'm not sending you into that shark pit without me. Stay by Adam; he'll keep you from getting crushed. I can't look out for you and throw punches at the same time."

"Crushed?"

"There's going to be more people here tonight. Brady Hoffman is from State. They have their own Circle there. It will be our crowd and their crowd, so the room's gonna get crazy."

"Are you nervous?" I asked.

He smiled, looking down at me. "No. You look a little nervous, though."

"Maybe," I admitted.

"If it'll make you feel better, I won't let him touch me. I won't even let him get one in for his fans."

"How are you going to manage that?"

He shrugged. "I usually let them get one in—to make it look fair."

"You . . . ? You let people hit you?"

"How much fun would it be if I just massacred someone and they never got a punch in? It's not good for business, no one would bet against me."

"What a load of crap," I said, crossing my arms.

Travis raised an eyebrow. "You think I'm yankin' your chain?"

"I find it hard to believe that you only get hit when you let them hit you."

"Would you like to make a wager on that, Abby Abernathy?" he smiled, his eyes animated.

I smiled. "I'll take that bet. I think he'll get one in on you."

"And if he doesn't? What do I win?" he asked. I shrugged as the yelling on the other side of the wall grew to a roar. Adam greeted the crowd, and then went over the rules.

Travis's mouth stretched into a wide grin. "If you win, I'll go without sex for a month." I raised an eyebrow, and he smiled again. "But if I win, you have to stay with me for a month."

"What? I'm staying with you anyway! What kind of bet is that?" I shrieked over the noise.

"They fixed the boilers at Morgan today," Travis said with a smile and a wink.

A smirk softened my expression as Adam called Travis's name. "Anything is worth watching you try abstinence for a change."

Travis kissed my cheek, and then walked out, standing tall. I followed behind, and when we crossed into the next room, I was startled by the number of people packed together in the small space. It was standing room only, but the shoving and shouting only amplified once we entered the room. Travis nodded in my direction, and then Adam's hand was on my shoulder, pulling me to his side.

I leaned into Adam's ear. "I've got two on Travis," I said.

Adam's eyebrows shot up as he watched me pull two Benjamins from my pocket. He held out his palm, and I slapped the bills into his hand.

"You're not the Goody Two-shoes I thought you were," he said, giving me a once-over.

Brady was at least a head taller than Travis, and I gulped when I saw them stand toe-to-toe. Brady was massive, twice Travis's size and solid muscle. I couldn't see Travis's expression, but it was obvious that Brady was out for blood.

Adam pressed his lips against my ear. "You might want to plug your ears, kiddo."

I cupped my hands on each side of my head, and Adam sounded the horn. Instead of attacking, Travis took a few steps back. Brady swung, and Travis dodged to the right. Brady swung again, and Travis ducked and sidestepped to the other side.

"What the hell? This ain't a boxing match, Travis!" Adam yelled.

Travis landed a punch to Brady's nose. The volume in the basement was deafening then. Travis sank a left hook into Brady's jaw, and my hands flew over my mouth when Brady attempted a few more punches, each one catching air. Brady fell against his entourage when Travis elbowed him in the face. Just when I thought it was almost over, Brady came out swinging again. Throw after throw, Brady couldn't seem to keep up. Both men were covered in sweat, and I gasped when Brady missed another punch, slamming his hand into a cement pillar. When he folded over, cradling his fist beneath him, Travis went in for the kill.

He was relentless, first bringing his knee to Brady's face and then pummeling him over and over until Brady stumbled and hit the ground. The noise level boomed as Adam left my side to throw the red square on Brady's bloodied face.

Travis disappeared behind his fans, and I pressed my back against the wall, feeling my way to the doorway we came in. Reaching the lantern was a huge relief. I worried about being knocked down and trampled.

My eyes focused on the doorway, waiting for the crowd to spill into the small room. After several minutes and no sign of Travis, I prepared to retrace my steps to the window. With the number of people trying to leave at once, it wasn't safe enough to chance wandering around.

Just as I stepped into the darkness, footsteps crunched against the loose concrete on the floor. Travis was looking for me in a panic.

"Pigeon!"

"I'm here!" I called out, running into his arms.

Travis looked down and frowned. "You scared the shit out of me! I almost had to start another fight just to get to you . . . I finally get here and you're gone!"

"I'm glad you're back. I wasn't looking forward to trying to find my way in the dark."

All worry left his face, and he smiled widely. "I believe you lost the bet."

Adam stomped in, looked at me, and then glowered at Travis. "We need to talk."

Travis winked at me. "Stay put. I'll be right back."

They disappeared into the darkness. Adam raised his voice a few times, but I couldn't make out what he was saying. Travis returned, shoving a wad of cash into his pocket, and then he offered a half smile. "You're going to need more clothes."

"You're really going to make me stay with you for a month?"

"Would you have made me go without sex for a month?"

I laughed, knowing I would. "We better stop at Morgan."

Travis beamed. "This should be interesting."

As Adam passed, he slammed my winnings into my palm, and then merged into the dissipating mob.

Travis raised an eyebrow. "You put in?"

I smiled and shrugged. "I thought I should get the full experience."

He led me to the window and then crawled out, turning to help me up and out into the fresh night air. The crickets were chirping in the shadows, stopping just long enough to let us pass. The monkey grass that lined the sidewalk waved in the gentle breeze, reminding me of the sound the ocean makes when I wasn't quite close enough to hear the waves breaking. It wasn't too hot or too cold; it was the perfect night.

"Why on earth would you want me to stay with you, anyway?" I asked.

Travis shrugged, shoving his hands in his pockets. "I don't know. Everything's better when you're around."

The warm and fuzzies I felt from his words quickly faded with the sight of the red blotchy mess on his shirt. "Ew. You have blood all over you."

Travis looked down with indifference and then opened the door, gesturing for me to walk in. I breezed by Kara, who studied on her bed, held captive by the textbooks that surrounded her.

"The boilers were fixed this morning," she said.

"I heard," I said, rifling through my closet.

"Hi," Travis said to Kara.

Kara's face twisted as she scanned Travis's sweaty, bloody form.

"Travis, this is my roommate, Kara Lin. Kara, Travis Maddox."

"Nice to meet you," Kara said, pushing her glasses up the bridge of her nose. She glanced at my bulging bags. "Are you moving out?"

"Nope. Lost a bet."

Travis burst into laughter, grabbing my bags. "Ready?"

"Yeah. How am I going to get all of this to your apartment? We're on your bike."

Travis smiled and pulled out his cell phone. He carried my luggage to the street, and minutes later, Shepley's black vintage Charger pulled up.

The passenger-side window rolled down, and America poked her head out. "Hey, chickie!"

"Hey yourself. The boilers are working again at Morgan. Are you still staying with Shep?"

She winked. "Yeah, I thought I'd stay tonight. I heard you lost a bet."

Before I could speak, Travis shut the trunk and Shep sped off, with America squealing as she fell back into the car.

We walked to his Harley, and he waited for me to settle into my seat. When I wrapped my arms around him, he rested his hand on mine.

"I'm glad you were there tonight, Pidge. I've never had so much fun at a fight in my life."

I perched my chin on his shoulder and smiled. "That was because you were trying to win our bet."

He angled his neck to face me. "Damn right I was." There was no amusement in his eyes; he was serious, and he wanted me to see it.

My eyebrows shot up. "Is that why you were in such a bad mood today? Because you knew they'd fixed the boilers, and I would be leaving tonight?"

Travis didn't answer; he only smiled as he started his motorcycle. The drive to the apartment was uncharacteristically slow. At every stoplight, Travis would either cover my hands with his, or he would rest his hand on my knee. The lines were blurring again, and I wondered how we would spend a month together and not ruin everything. The loose ends of our friendship were tangling in a way I never imagined.

When we arrived in the apartment parking lot, Shepley's Charger sat in its usual spot.

I stood in front of the steps. "I always hate it when they've been home for a while. I feel like we're going to interrupt them."

"Get used to it. This is your place for the next four weeks," Travis smiled and turned his back to me. "Get on."

"What?" I smiled.

"C'mon, I'll carry you up."

I giggled and hopped onto his back, interlacing my fingers on his chest as he ran up the stairs. America opened the door before we made it to the top and smiled.

"Look at you two. If I didn't know better . . ."

"Knock it off, Mare," Shepley said from the couch.

America smiled as if she'd said too much, and then opened the door wide so we could both fit through. Travis collapsed against the recliner. I squealed when he leaned against me.

"You're awfully cheerful this evening, Trav. What gives?" America prompted.

I leaned over to see his face. I'd never seen him so pleased.

"I just won a shitload of money, Mare. Twice as much as I thought I would. What's not to be happy about?"

America grinned. "No, it's something else," she said, watching Travis's hand as he patted my thigh. She was right; he was different. There was an air of peace around him, almost as if some kind of new contentment had settled into his soul.

"Mare," Shepley warned.

"Fine, I'll talk about something else. Didn't Parker invite you to the Sig Tau party this weekend, Abby?"

Travis's smile vanished and he turned to me, waiting for an answer.

"Er . . . yeah? Aren't we all going?"

"I'll be there," Shepley said, distracted by the television.

"And that means I'm going," America said, looking expectantly at Travis.

Travis watched me for a moment, and then nudged my leg. "Is he picking you up or something?"

"No, he just told me about the party."

America's mouth spread into a mischievous grin, almost bobbing in anticipation. "He said he'd see you there, though. He's really cute."

Travis shot an irritated glance in America's direction and then looked to me. "Are you going?"

"I told him I would," I shrugged. "Are you going?"

"Yeah," he said without hesitation.

Shepley's attention turned to Travis then. "You said last week you weren't."

"I changed my mind, Shep. What's the problem?"

"Nothing," he grumbled, retreating to his bedroom.

America frowned at Travis. "You know what the problem is," she said. "Why don't you quit driving him crazy and just get it over with." She joined Shepley in his room, and their voices were reduced to murmuring behind the closed door.

"Well, I'm glad everyone else knows," I said.

Travis stood up. "I'm going to take a quick shower."

"Is there something going on with them?" I asked.

"No, he's just paranoid."

"It's because of us," I guessed. Travis's eyes lit up and he nodded.

"What?" I asked, eyeing him suspiciously.

"You're right. It's because of us. Don't fall asleep, okay? I wanna talk to you about something."

He walked backward a few steps, and then disappeared

behind the bathroom door. I twisted my hair around my finger, mulling over the way he emphasized the word "us," and the look on his face when he'd said it. I wondered if there had ever been lines at all, and if I was the only one who considered Travis and I just friends anymore.

Shepley burst out of his room, and America ran after him. "Shep, don't!" she pleaded.

He looked back to the bathroom door, and then to me. His voice was low, but angry. "You promised, Abby. When I told you to spare judgment, I didn't mean for you two to get involved! I thought you were just friends!"

"We are," I said, shaken by his surprise attack.

"No, you're not!" he fumed.

America touched his shoulder. "Baby, I told you it will be fine."

He pulled away from her grip. "Why are you pushing this, Mare? I told you what's going to happen!"

She grabbed his face with both hands. "And I told you it won't! Don't you trust me?"

Shepley sighed, looked at her, at me, and then stomped into his room.

America fell into the recliner beside me, and puffed. "I just can't get it into his head that whether you and Travis work out or not, it won't affect us. But he's been burned too many times. He doesn't believe me."

"What are you talking about, Mare? Travis and I aren't together. We are just friends. You heard him earlier . . . he's not interested in me that way."

"You heard that?"

"Well, yeah."

"And you believe it?"

I shrugged. "It doesn't matter. It'll never happen. He told me he doesn't see me like that, anyway. Besides, he's a total commitmentphobe, I'd be hard pressed to find a girlfriend outside of you that he hasn't slept with, and I can't keep up with his mood swings. I can't believe Shep thinks otherwise."

"Because not only does he know Travis . . . he's talked to Travis, Abby."

"What do you mean?"

"Mare?" Shepley called from the bedroom.

America sighed. "You're my best friend. I think I know you better than you know yourself sometimes. I see you two together, and the only difference between me and Shep and you and Travis is that we're having sex. Other than that? No difference."

"There is a huge, huge difference. Is Shep bringing home different girls every night? Are you going to the party tomorrow to hang out with a guy with definite dating potential? You know I can't get involved with Travis, Mare. I don't even know why we're discussing it."

America's expression turned to disappointment. "I'm not seeing things, Abby. You have spent almost every moment with him for the last month. Admit it, you have feelings for him."

"Let it go, Mare," Travis said, tightening his towel around his waist.

America and I jumped at the sound of Travis's voice, and when my eyes met his, I could see the happiness was gone. He walked down the hall without another word, and America looked at me with a sad expression.

"I think you're making a mistake," she whispered. "You don't need to go that party to meet a guy, you've got one that's crazy about you right here," she said, leaving me alone.

I rocked in the recliner, letting everything that had happened in the last week replay in my mind. Shepley was angry with me, America was disappointed in me, and Travis . . . he went from being happier than I'd ever seen him to so offended that he was speechless. Too nervous to crawl into bed with him, I watched the clock change from minute to minute.

An hour had passed when Travis came out of his room and down the hall. When he rounded the corner, I expected him to ask me to come to bed, but he was dressed and had his bike keys in his hand. His sunglasses were hiding his eyes, and he popped a cigarette in his mouth before grabbing the knob of the door.

"You're leaving?" I asked, sitting up. "Where are you going?"

"Out," he said, yanking the door open, and then slamming it closed behind him.

I fell back in the recliner and huffed. I had somehow become the villain and had no idea how I'd managed to get there.

When the clock above the television read two a.m., I finally resigned myself to going to bed. The mattress was lonely without him, and the idea of calling his cell kept creeping into my mind. I had nearly fallen asleep when Travis's motorcycle pulled into the parking lot. Two car doors shut shortly after, and then several pairs of footsteps climbed the stairs. Travis fumbled with the lock, and then the door opened. He laughed and mumbled, and then I heard not one, but two female voices. Their giggling was interrupted by the distinct sounds of kissing and moaning. My heart sank, and I was instantly angry that I felt that way. My eyes clenched shut when one of the girls squealed, and then

I was sure the next sound was the three of them collapsing onto the couch.

I considered asking America for her keys, but Shepley's door was directly in view of the couch, and I couldn't stomach witnessing the picture that went along with the noises in the living room. I buried my head under the pillow, and then shut my eyes when the door popped open. Travis walked across the room, opened the top night-table drawer, picked through his bowl of condoms, and then shut the drawer, jogging down the hall. The girls giggled for what seemed like half an hour, and then it was quiet.

Seconds later, moans, humming, and shouting filled the apartment. It sounded as if a pornographic movie were being filmed in the living room. I covered my face with my hands, and shook my head. Whatever lines had blurred or disappeared in the last week, an impenetrable stone wall had gone up in their place. I shook off my ridiculous emotions, forcing myself to relax. Travis was Travis, and we were, without a doubt, friends, and only friends.

The shouting and other nauseating noises quieted down after an hour, followed by whining, and then grumbling by the women after being dismissed. Travis showered and then collapsed onto his side of the bed, turning his back to me. Even after his shower, he smelled like he'd drunk enough whiskey to sedate a horse, and I was livid that he'd driven his motorcycle home in such a state.

After the awkwardness faded and the anger weakened, I still couldn't sleep. When Travis's breaths were deep and even, I sat up to look at the clock. The sun was going to rise in less than an hour. I ripped the covers off of me, walked down the hall, and took a blanket from the hall cabinet. The only evidence of Travis's threesome was two empty condom packages on the floor. I stepped over them and fell into the recliner.

I closed my eyes. When I opened them again, America and Shepley were sitting quietly on the couch, watching a muted television. The sun lit the apartment, and I cringed when my back complained at any attempted movement.

America's attention darted to me. "Abby?" she said, rushing to my side. She watched me with wary eyes. She was waiting for anger, or tears, or another emotionally charged outburst.

Shepley looked miserable. "I'm sorry about last night, Abby. This is my fault."

I smiled. "It's okay, Shep. You don't have to apologize."

America and Shepley traded glances, and then she grabbed my hand. "Travis went to the store. He is . . . ugh, it doesn't matter what he is. I packed your stuff, and I'll take you to the dorms before he gets home so you don't have to deal with him."

It wasn't until that moment that I felt like crying; I had been kicked out. I worked to keep my voice smooth before I spoke. "Do I have time to take a shower?"

America shook her head. "Let's just go, Abby, I don't want you to have to see him. He doesn't deserve to—"

The door flew open, and Travis walked in, his arms laden with grocery sacks. He walked straight into the kitchen, furiously working to get the cans and boxes into the cabinets.

"When Pidge wakes up, let me know, okay?" he said in a soft voice. "I got spaghetti, and pancakes, and strawberries, and that oatmeal shit with the chocolate packets, and she likes Fruity Pebbles cereal, right, Mare?" he asked, turning.

When he saw me, he froze. After an awkward pause, his expression melted, and his voice was smooth and sweet. "Hey, Pigeon."

I couldn't have been more confused if I had woken up in a foreign country. Nothing made sense. At first I thought I had been evicted, and then Travis comes home with bags full of my favorite foods.

He took a few steps into the living room, nervously shoving his hands in his pockets. "You hungry, Pidge? I'll make you some pancakes. Or there's, uh... there's some oatmeal. And I got you some of that pink foamy shit that girls shave with, and a hair dryer, and a ... a ... just a sec, it's in here," he said, rushing to the bedroom.

The door opened and shut, and then he rounded the corner, the color gone from his face. He took a deep breath, and his eyebrows pulled in. "Your stuff's packed."

"I know," I said.

"You're leaving," he said, defeated.

I looked to America, who glowered at Travis as if she could kill him. "You actually expected her to stay?"

"Baby," Shepley whispered.

"Don't fucking start with me, Shep. Don't you dare defend him to me," America seethed.

Travis looked desperate. "I am so sorry, Pidge. I don't even know what to say."

"Come on, Abby," America said. She stood and pulled on my arm.

Travis took a step, but America pointed her finger at him. "So help me God, Travis! If you try to stop her, I will douse you with gasoline and light you on fire while you sleep!"

"America," Shepley said, sounding a bit desperate himself. I could see that he was torn between his cousin and the woman he loved, and I felt terrible for him. The situation was exactly what he had tried to avoid all along.

"I'm fine," I said, exasperated by the tension in the room.

"What do you mean, you're fine?" Shepley asked, almost hopeful.

I rolled my eyes. "Travis brought women home from the bar last night, so what?"

America looked worried. "Huh-uh, Abby. Are you saying you're okay with what happened?"

I looked to all of them. "Travis can bring home whoever he wants. It's his apartment."

America stared at me as if I'd lost my mind, Shepley was on the verge of a smile, and Travis looked worse than before.

"You didn't pack your things?" Travis asked.

I shook my head and looked at the clock; it was after two in the afternoon. "No, and now I'm going to have to unpack it all. I still have to eat, and shower, and get dressed . . ." I said, walking into the bathroom. Once the door closed behind me, I leaned against it and slid down to the floor. I was sure I had pissed off America beyond repair, but I'd made Shepley a promise, and I intended to keep my word.

A soft knock tapped on the door above me. "Pidge?" Travis said.

"Yeah?" I said, trying to sound normal.

"You're staying?"

"I can go if you want me to, but a bet's a bet."

The door vibrated with the soft bump of Travis's forehead

against it. "I don't want you leave, but I wouldn't blame you if you did."

"Are you saying I'm released from the bet?"

There was a long pause. "If I say yes, will you leave?"

"Well, yeah. I don't live here, silly," I said, forcing a small laugh.

"Then no, the bet's still in effect."

I looked up and shook my head, feeling tears burn my eyes. I had no idea why I was crying, but I couldn't stop. "Can I take a shower, now?"

"Yeah . . ." he sighed.

I heard America's shoes enter the hall and stomp by Travis. "You're a selfish bastard," she growled, slamming Shepley's door behind her.

I pushed myself up from the floor, turned on the shower, and then undressed, pulling the curtain closed behind me.

After another knock on the door, Travis cleared his throat. "Pigeon? I brought some of your stuff."

"Just set it on the sink. I'll get it."

Travis walked in and shut the door behind him. "I was mad. I heard you spitting out everything that's wrong with me to America and it pissed me off. I just meant to go out and have a few drinks and try to figure some things out, but before I knew it, I was piss drunk, and those girls . . ." He paused. "I woke up this morning and you weren't in bed, and when I found you on the recliner and saw the wrappers on the floor, I felt sick."

"You could have just asked me instead of spending all that money at the grocery store just to bribe me to stay."

"I don't care about the money, Pidge. I was afraid you'd leave and never speak to me again."

I cringed at his explanation. I hadn't stopped to think how it would make him feel to hear me talk about how wrong for me he was, and now the situation was too messed up to salvage.

"I didn't mean to hurt your feelings," I said, standing under the water.

"I know you didn't. And I know it doesn't matter what I say now, because I fucked things up . . . just like I always do."

"Trav?"

"Yeah?"

"Don't drive drunk on your bike anymore, okay?"

I waited for a full minute until he finally took a deep breath and spoke. "Yeah, okay," he said, shutting the door behind him.

Chapter Five
Parker Hayes

"COME IN," I CALLED, HEARING A KNOCK ON THE DOOR. Travis froze in the doorway. "Wow."

I smiled and looked down at my dress. A bustier that elongated into a short skirt, it was admittedly more daring than what I had worn in the past. The material was thin, black, and see-through over a nude shell. Parker would be at that party, and I had every intention of being noticed.

"You look amazing," he said as I slid on my heels.

I gave his white dress shirt and jeans an approving nod. "You look nice, too."

His sleeves were bunched above his elbows, revealing the intricate tattoos on his forearms. I noticed that his favorite black leather cuff was around his wrist when he shoved his hands in his pockets.

America and Shepley waited for us in the living room.

"Parker is going to piss himself when he sees you," America giggled as Shepley led the way to the car.

Travis opened the door, and I slid into the backseat of Shepley's Charger. Although we had occupied that seat countless times before, it was suddenly awkward to sit next to him.

Cars lined the street; some even parked on the front lawn. The house was bursting at the seams, and people were still walking down the street from the dorms. Shepley pulled into the grass lot in the back, and America and I followed the boys inside.

Travis brought me a red plastic cup full of beer and then leaned in to whisper in my ear. "Don't take these from anyone but me or Shep. I don't want anyone slipping anything into your drink."

I rolled my eyes. "No one is going to put anything in my drink, Travis."

"Just don't drink anything that doesn't come from me, okay? You're not in Kansas anymore, Pigeon."

"I haven't heard that one before," I said sarcastically, taking a drink.

An hour had passed, and Parker was still a no-show. America and Shepley were dancing to a slow song in the living room when Travis tugged on my hand. "Wanna dance?"

"No, thanks," I said.

His face fell.

I touched his shoulder. "I'm just tired, Trav."

He put his hand on mine and began to speak, but when I looked beyond him I saw Parker. Travis noticed my expression and turned.

"Hey, Abby! You made it!" Parker smiled.

"Yeah, we've been here for an hour or so," I said, pulling my hand from under Travis's.

"You look incredible!" he yelled over the music.

"Thanks!" I grinned, glancing over to Travis. His lips were pressed together, and a line had formed between his eyebrows.

Parker nodded toward the living room and smiled. "You wanna dance?"

I wrinkled my nose and shook my head. "Nah, I'm kinda tired."

Parker looked at Travis then. "I thought you weren't coming."

"I changed my mind," Travis said, irritated that he had to explain.

"I see that," Parker said, looking to me. "You wanna get some air?"

I nodded and then followed Parker up the stairs. He paused, reaching to take my hand as we climbed to the second floor. When we reached the top, he pushed open a pair of French doors to the balcony.

"Are you cold?" he asked.

"A little chilly," I said, smiling when he pulled off his jacket and covered my shoulders. "Thanks."

"You're here with Travis?"

"We rode together."

Parker's mouth stretched across his face in a broad grin, and then he looked out onto the lawn. A group of girls were in a huddle, arms hooked together to fight the cold. Crepe paper and beer cans littered the grass along with empty bottles of liquor. Amid the clutter, Sig Tau brothers were standing around their masterpiece: a pyramid of kegs decorated with white lights.

Parker shook his head. "This place is going to be destroyed in the morning. The cleanup crew is going to be busy."

"You have a cleanup crew?"

"Yeah," he smiled, "we call them freshmen."

"Poor Shep."

"He's not on it. He gets a pass because he's Travis's cousin, and he doesn't live in the House."

"Do you live in the House?"

Parker nodded. "The last two years. I need to get an apartment, though. I need a quieter place to study."

"Let me guess . . . Business major?"

"Biology, with a minor in Anatomy. I've got one more year left, take the MCAT, and then hopefully I'm off to Harvard Med."

"You already know you're in?"

"My dad went to Harvard. I mean, I don't know for sure, but he's a generous alumnus, if you know what I mean. I carry a 4.0, got a 2200 on my SATs, thirty-six on my ACTs. I'm in a good position for a spot."

"Your dad's a doctor?"

Parker confirmed it with a good-natured smile. "Orthopedic surgeon."

"Impressive."

"How about you?" he asked.

"Undecided."

"Typical freshman answer."

I sighed in dramatic fashion. "I guess I just blew my chances at being exceptional."

"Oh, you don't have to worry about that. I noticed you the first day of class. What are you doing in Calculus Three as a freshman?"

I smiled and twisted my hair around my finger. "Math is sort of easy for me. I packed on the classes in high school and took two summer courses at Wichita State."

"Now that's impressive," he said.

We stood on the balcony for over an hour, talking about everything from local eateries to how I became such good friends with Travis.

"I wouldn't mention it, but the two of you seem to be the topic of conversation."

"Great," I murmured.

"It's just unusual for Travis. He doesn't befriend women. He tends to make enemies of them more often than not."

"Oh, I don't know. I've seen more than a few who either have short-term memory loss or are all too forgiving when it comes to him."

Parker laughed. His white teeth gleamed against his golden tan. "People just don't understand your relationship. You have to admit, it's a bit ambiguous."

"Are you asking if I'm sleeping with him?"

He smiled. "You wouldn't be here with him if you were. I've known him since I was fourteen, and I'm well aware of how he operates. I'm curious about your friendship, though."

"It is what it is," I shrugged. "We hang out, eat, watch TV, study, and argue. That's about it."

Parker laughed out loud, shaking his head at my honesty. "I've heard you're the only person who's allowed to put Travis in his place. That's an honorable title."

"Whatever that means. He's not as bad as everyone makes him out to be."

The sky turned purple and then pink as the sun broke above the horizon. Parker looked at his watch, glancing over the railing to the thinning crowd on the lawn. "Looks like the party's over."

"I better track down Shep and Mare."

"Would you mind if I drove you home?" he asked.

I tried to subdue my excitement. "Not at all. I'll let America know." I walked through the door, and then cringed before turning around. "Do you know where Travis lives?"

Parker's thick brown eyebrows pulled in. "Yes, why?"

"That's where I'm staying," I said, bracing for his reaction.

"You're staying with Travis?"

"I sort of lost a bet, so I'm there for a month."

"A month?"

"It's a long story," I said, shrugging sheepishly.

"But you two are just friends?"

"Yes."

"Then I'll take you to Travis's," he smiled.

I trotted down the stairs to find America and passed a sullen Travis, who seemed annoyed with the drunken girl speaking to him. He followed me into the hall as I tugged on America's dress.

"You guys can go ahead. Parker offered me a ride home."

"What?" America said with excitement in her eyes.

"What?" Travis asked, angry.

"Is there a problem?" America asked him.

He glared at America, and then pulled me around the corner, his jaw flitting under his skin. "You don't even know the guy."

I pulled my arm from his grip. "This is none of your business, Travis."

"The hell if it's not. I'm not letting you ride home with a complete stranger. What if he tries something on you?"

"Good! He's cute!"

Travis's expression contorted from surprise to anger, and

I braced myself for what he might say next. "Parker Hayes, Pidge? Really? Parker Hayes," he repeated with disdain. "What kind of name is that, anyway?"

I crossed my arms. "Stop it, Trav. You're being a jerk."

He leaned in, seeming flustered. "I'll kill him if he touches you."

"I like him," I said, emphasizing every word.

He seemed stunned at my confession, and then his features turned severe. "Fine. If he ends up holding you down in the backseat of his car, don't come crying to me."

My mouth popped open; I was offended and instantly furious. "Don't worry, I won't," I said, shouldering past him.

Travis grabbed my arm and sighed, peering at me over his shoulder. "I didn't mean it, Pidge. If he hurts you—if he even makes you feel uncomfortable—you let me know."

The anger subsided, and my shoulders fell. "I know you didn't. But you have got to curb this overprotective big-brother thing you've got going on."

Travis laughed once. "I'm not playing the big brother, Pigeon. Not even close."

Parker rounded the corner and pushed his hands inside his pockets, offering his elbow to me. "All set?"

Travis clenched his jaw, and I stepped to the other side of Parker to distract him from Travis's expression. "Yeah, let's go." I took Parker's arm and walked with him a few steps before turning to say goodbye to Travis, but he was glowering at the back of Parker's head. His eyes darted to me, and then his features smoothed.

"Stop it," I said through my teeth, following Parker through the remnants of the crowd to his car.

"I'm the silver one." The headlights of his car blinked twice when he hit the keyless entry.

He opened the passenger side door, and I laughed. "You drive a Porsche?"

"She's not just a Porsche. She's a Porsche 911 GT3. There's a difference."

"Let me guess, it's the love of your life?" I said, quoting Travis's statement about his motorcycle.

"No, it's a car. The love of my life will be a woman with my last name."

I allowed a small smile, trying not to be overly affected by his sentiment. He held my hand to help me into the car, and when he slid behind the wheel, he leaned his head against his seat and smiled at me.

"What are you doing tonight?"

"Tonight?" I asked.

"It's morning. I want to ask you to dinner before someone else beats me to it."

A grin extended across my face. "I don't have any plans."

"I'll pick you up at six?"

"Okay," I said, watching him slink his fingers between mine.

Parker took me straight to Travis's, keeping to the speed limit, my hand in his. He pulled behind the Harley, and like before, opened my door. Once we reached the landing, he leaned down to kiss my cheek.

"Get some rest. I'll see you tonight," he whispered in my ear.

"'Bye," I said, turning the knob. When I pushed, the door gave way and I surged forward.

Travis grabbed my arm before I fell. "Easy there, Grace."

I turned to see Parker staring at us with an uncomfortable

expression. He leaned over to peer into the apartment. "Any humiliated, stranded girls in there I need to give a ride?"

Travis glared at Parker. "Don't start with me."

Parker smiled and winked. "I'm always giving him a hard time. I don't get to quite as often since he realized it's easier if he can get them to drive their own cars."

"I guess that does simplify things," I said, teasing Travis.

"Not funny, Pidge."

"Pidge?" Parker asked.

"It's, uh . . . short for Pigeon. It's just a nickname, I don't even know where he came up with it," I said. It was the first time I'd felt awkward about the name Travis had bestowed on me the night we met.

"You're going to have to fill me in when you find out. Sounds like a good story," Parker smiled. "Night, Abby."

"Don't you mean good morning?" I said, watching him trot down the stairs.

"That, too," he called back with a sweet smile.

Travis slammed the door, and I had to jerk my head back before it caught me in the face. "What?" I snapped.

Travis shook his head and walked to his bedroom. I followed him and then hopped on one foot to pull off my heel. "He's nice, Trav."

He sighed and walked over to me. "You're gonna hurt yourself," he said, hooking his arm around my waist with one hand and pulling off my heels with the other. He tossed them into the closet and then pulled off his shirt, making his way to the bed.

I unzipped my dress and shimmied it over my hips, kicking it into the corner. I yanked a T-shirt over my head and then unsnapped my bra, pulling it through the sleeve of my shirt. When

I wrapped my hair into a bun on top of my head, I noticed him staring.

"I'm sure there's nothing I have that you haven't seen before," I said, rolling my eyes. I slid under the covers and settled against my pillow, curling into a ball. He unbuckled his belt and pulled his jeans down, stepping out of them.

I waited while he stood quietly for a moment. I had my back to him, so I wondered what he was doing, standing beside the bed in silence. The bed concaved when he finally crawled onto the mattress beside me, and I stiffened when his hand rested on my hip.

"I missed a fight tonight," he said. "Adam called. I didn't go."

"Why?" I said, turning to face him.

"I wanted to make sure you got home."

I wrinkled my nose. "You didn't have to babysit me."

He traced the length of my arm with his finger, sending shivers up my spine. "I know. I guess I still feel bad about the other night."

"I told you I didn't care."

He sat up on his elbow, a dubious frown on his face. "Is that why you slept on the recliner? Because you didn't care?"

"I couldn't fall asleep after your . . . friends left."

"You slept just fine in the recliner. Why couldn't you sleep with me?"

"You mean next to a guy who still smelled like the pair of barflies he had just sent home? I don't know! How selfish of me!"

Travis winced. "I said I was sorry."

"And I said I didn't care. Good night," I said, turning over.

Several moments of silence passed. He slid his hand across

the top of my pillow, resting his hand on mine. He caressed the delicate pieces of skin between my fingers, and then he pressed his lips against my hair. "As worried as I was that you'd never speak to me again . . . I think it's worse that you're indifferent."

My eyes closed. "What do you want from me, Travis? You don't want me to be upset about what you did, but you want me to care. You tell America that you don't want to date me, but you get so pissed off when I say the same thing that you storm out and get ridiculously drunk. You don't make any sense."

"Is that why you said those things to America? Because I said I wouldn't date you?"

My teeth clenched. He had just insinuated that I was playing games with him. I formed the most direct answer I could think of. "No, I meant what I said. I just didn't mean it as an insult."

"I just said that because," he scratched his short hair nervously, "I don't want to ruin anything. I wouldn't even know how to go about being who you deserve. I was just trying to get it worked out in my head."

"Whatever that means. I have to get some sleep. I have a date tonight."

"With Parker?" he asked, anger seeping through his tone.

"Yes. Can I please go to sleep?"

"Sure," he said, shoving himself off the bed and then slamming the door behind him. The recliner squeaked under his weight, and then muffled voices from the television drifted down the hall. I forced my eyes shut and tried to calm down enough to doze off, even if it was just for a few hours.

The clock read three p.m. when I peeled my eyes open. I grabbed a towel and my robe, and then trudged into the bathroom. As soon as I closed the shower curtain, the door opened and shut. I waited for someone to speak, but the only sound was the toilet lid smacking against porcelain.

"Travis?"

"Nope, it's me," America said.

"Do you have to pee in here? You have your own bathroom."

"Shep has been in there for half an hour with the beer shits. Not going in there."

"Nice."

"I hear you have a date tonight. Travis is pissed!" she lilted.

"At six! He is so sweet, America. He's just . . ." I trailed off, sighing. I was gushing, and it wasn't like me to gush. I kept thinking about how perfect he had been since the moment we'd met. He was exactly what I needed: the polar opposite of Travis.

"Rendered you speechless?" she giggled.

I poked my head from the curtain. "I didn't want to come home! I could have talked to him forever!"

"Sounds promising. Isn't it kind of weird that you're here, though?"

I ducked under the water, rinsing away the suds. "I explained it to him."

The toilet flushed, and the faucet turned on, making the water flash cold for a moment. I cried out and the door flew open.

"Pidge?" Travis said.

America laughed. "I just flushed the toilet, Trav, calm down."

"Oh. You all right, Pigeon?"

"I'm great. Get out." The door shut again and I sighed. "Is it too much to ask for locks on the doors?" America didn't answer. "Mare?"

"It's really too bad you two couldn't get on the same page. You're the only girl who could have . . ." She sighed. "Never mind. It doesn't matter, now."

I turned off the water and wrapped myself in a towel. "You're as bad as he is. It's a sickness . . . no one here makes sense. You're pissed at him, remember?"

"I know," she nodded.

I turned on my new hair dryer and began the process of primping for my date with Parker. I curled my hair and painted my nails and lips a deep shade of red. It was a bit much for a first date. I frowned at myself in the mirror. It wasn't Parker I was trying to impress. I wasn't in a position to be insulted when Travis accused me of playing games, after all.

As I took one last glance at myself in the mirror, guilt washed over me. Travis was trying so hard, and I was being a stubborn brat. I walked out into the living room and Travis smiled, not the reaction I had expected at all.

"You . . . are beautiful."

"Thank you," I said, rattled by the absence of irritation or jealousy in his voice.

Shepley whistled. "Nice choice, Abby. Guys dig red."

"And the curls are gorgeous," America added.

The doorbell chimed and America smiled, waving with exaggerated excitement. "Have fun!"

I opened the door. Parker held a small bouquet of flowers, wearing slacks and a tie. His eyes did a quick once-over from my dress to my shoes and then back up.

"You are the most beautiful creature I've ever seen," he said, enamored.

I looked behind me to wave to America, whose smile was so wide I could see every one of her teeth. Shepley wore the expression of a proud father, and Travis kept his eyes on the television.

Parker held out his hand, leading me to his shiny Porsche. Once we were inside, he let out a puff of air.

"What?" I asked.

"I have to say, I was a bit nervous about picking up the woman Travis Maddox is in love with . . . from his apartment. You don't know how many people have accused me of insanity today."

"Travis is not in love with me. He can barely stand to be near me sometimes."

"Then it's a love-hate relationship? Because when I broke it to my brothers that I was taking you out tonight, they all said the same thing. He's been behaving so erratically—even more than usual—that they've all come to the same conclusion."

"They're wrong," I insisted.

Parker shook his head as if I were utterly clueless. He rested his hand on mine. "We'd better go. I have a table waiting."

"Where?"

"Biasetti's. I took a chance . . . I hope you like Italian."

I raised one eyebrow. "Wasn't it short notice for reservations? That place is always packed."

"Well . . . it's our restaurant. Half, anyway."

"I like Italian."

Parker drove to the restaurant at exactly the speed limit, using his turn signal appropriately and slowing at a reasonable rate for each yellow light. When he spoke, he barely took his eyes from the road. When we arrived at the restaurant, I giggled.

"What?" he asked.

"You're just . . . a very cautious driver. It's a good thing."

"Different from the back of Travis's motorcycle?" he smiled.

I should have laughed, but the difference didn't feel like a good thing. "Let's not talk about Travis tonight. Okay?"

"Fair enough," he said, leaving his seat to open my door.

We were seated right away at a table by a large bay window. Although I was in a dress, I looked impoverished compared to the other women in the restaurant. They were dripping with diamonds and wearing cocktail dresses. I'd never eaten anywhere so swanky.

We ordered, and Parker closed his menu, smiling at the waiter. "And bring us a bottle of the Allegrini Amarone, please."

"Yes, sir," the waiter said, taking our menus.

"This place is unbelievable," I whispered, leaning against the table.

His green eyes softened. "Thank you, I'll let my father know you think so."

A woman approached our table. Her blond hair was pulled into a tight French bun, a gray streak interrupting the smooth wave of her bangs. I tried not to stare at the sparkling jewels resting around her neck, or those swaying back and forth on her ears, but they were made to be noticed. Her squinty blue eyes targeted me.

She quickly turned away to look at my date. "Who's your friend, Parker?"

"Mother, this is Abby Abernathy. Abby, this is my mother, Vivienne Hayes."

I extended my hand and she shook it once. In a well-practiced move, interest lit the sharp features of her face, and she looked to Parker. "Abernathy?"

I gulped, worried that she had recognized the name.

Parker's expression turned impatient. "She's from Wichita, Mom. You don't know her family. She goes to Eastern."

"Oh?" Vivienne eyed me again. "Parker is leaving next year for Harvard."

"That's what he said. I think that's great. You must be very proud."

The tension around her eyes smoothed a bit, and the corners of her mouth turned up in a smug grin. "We are. Thank you."

I was amazed at how her words were so polite, and yet they dripped with insult. It wasn't a talent she had developed overnight. Mrs. Hayes must have spent years impressing her superiority upon others.

"It's good to see you, Mom. Good night." She kissed his cheek, rubbed the lipstick off with her thumb, and then returned to her table. "Sorry about that, I didn't know she would be here."

"It's fine. She seems . . . nice."

Parker laughed. "Yes, for a piranha." I stifled a giggle, and he offered an apologetic smile. "She'll warm up. It just takes her a while."

"Hopefully by the time you leave for Harvard."

We talked endlessly about the food, Eastern, calculus, and even the Circle. Parker was charming and funny and said all the right things. Various people approached Parker to greet him, and he always introduced me with a proud smile. He was regarded as a celebrity within the walls of the restaurant, and when we left, I felt the appraising eyes of everyone in the room.

"Now what?" I asked.

"I'm afraid I have a midterm in Comparative Vertebrate

Anatomy first thing Monday morning. I have some studying to do," he said, covering my hand with his.

"Better you than me," I said, trying not to seem too disappointed.

He drove to the apartment, and then led me up the stairs by the hand.

"Thank you, Parker." I was aware of the ridiculous grin on my face. "I had a fantastic time."

"Is it too early to ask for a second date?"

"Not at all," I beamed.

"I'll call you tomorrow?"

"Sounds perfect."

Then came the moment of awkward silence. The element of dates I dread. To kiss or not to kiss, I hated that question.

Before I had a chance to wonder whether he would kiss me or not, he touched each side of my face and pulled me to him, pressing his lips against mine. They were soft and warm and wonderful. He pulled back once and then kissed me again.

"Talk to you tomorrow, Abs."

I waved, watching him walk down the steps to his car. "'Bye."

Once again, when I turned the knob, the door yanked away and I fell forward. Travis caught me, and I regained my footing.

"Would you stop that?" I said, closing the door behind me.

"'Abs'? What are you, a workout video?" he sneered.

"'Pigeon'?" I said with the same amount of disdain. "An annoying bird that craps all over the sidewalk?"

"You like Pigeon," he said defensively. "It's a dove, an attractive girl, a winning card in poker, take your pick. You're my Pigeon."

I grabbed his arm to remove my heels and then walked to

his room. As I changed into my pajamas, I tried my best to stay mad at him.

Travis sat on the bed and crossed his arms. "Did you have a good time?"

"I had," sigh, "a fantastic time. A perfect time. He's . . ." I couldn't think of an adequate word to describe him, so I just shook my head.

"He kissed you?"

I pressed my lips together and nodded. "He's got really soft lips."

Travis recoiled. "I don't care what kind of lips he has."

"Trust me, it's important. I get so nervous with first kisses, too, but this one wasn't so bad."

"You get nervous about a kiss?" he asked, amused.

"Just first kisses. I loathe them."

"I'd loathe them, too, if I had to kiss Parker Hayes."

I giggled and left for the bathroom to scrub the makeup from my face. Travis followed, leaning against the doorjamb. "So you're going out again?"

"Yep. He's calling me tomorrow." I dried my face and scampered down the hall, hopping into the bed.

Travis stripped down to his boxers, and sat down with his back to me. A bit slumped over, he looked exhausted. The lean muscles of his back stretched as he did, and he glanced back at me for a moment. "If you had such a good time, why are you home so early?"

"He has a big test on Monday."

Travis wrinkled his nose. "Who cares?"

"He's trying to get into Harvard. He has to study."

He huffed, crawling onto his stomach. I watched him shove

his hands under his pillow, seeming irritated. "Yeah, that's what he keeps telling everyone."

"Don't be an ass. He has priorities . . . I think it's responsible."

"Shouldn't his girl top his priorities?"

"I'm not his girl. We've been on one date, Trav," I scolded.

"So what did you guys do?" I shot him a dirty look and he laughed. "What? I'm curious!"

Seeing that he was sincere, I described everything, from the restaurant to the food to the sweet and funny things Parker said. I knew my mouth was frozen in a ridiculous grin, but I couldn't stop smiling while describing my perfect evening.

Travis watched me with an amused smile while I blathered on, even asking questions. Although he seemed frustrated with the situation regarding Parker, I had the distinct feeling that he enjoyed seeing me so happy.

Travis settled in on his side of the bed, and I yawned. We stared at each other for a moment before he sighed. "I'm glad you had a good time, Pidge. You deserve it."

"Thanks," I grinned. The ringtone of my cell phone reverberated from the night table, and I jerked up to look at the display.

"Hello?"

"It's tomorrow," Parker said.

I looked at the clock and laughed. It was 12:01. "It is."

"So what about Monday night?" he asked.

I covered my mouth for a moment and then took a deep breath. "Uh, yeah. Monday night is great."

"Good. I'll see you Monday," he said. I could hear the smile in his voice.

I hung up and glanced at Travis, who watched with mild annoyance. I turned away from him and curled into a ball, tensing with excitement.

"You're such a girl," Travis said, turning his back to me.

I rolled my eyes.

He turned over, pulling me to face him. "You really like Parker?"

"Don't ruin this for me, Travis!"

He stared at me for a moment, and then shook his head, turning away once again. "Parker Hayes."

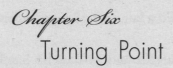

Chapter Six
Turning Point

Monday night's date met my every expectation. We ate Chinese food while I giggled at Parker's skills with chopsticks. When he brought me home, Travis opened the door before he could kiss me. When we went out the following Wednesday night, Parker made sure to kiss me in the car.

Thursday at lunch, Parker met me in the cafeteria and surprised everyone when he sat in Travis's spot. When Travis finished his cigarette and came inside, he walked past Parker with indifference, sitting at the end of the table. Megan approached him but was instantly disappointed when he waved her off. Everyone at the table was quiet after that, and I found it difficult to focus on anything Parker talked about.

"I'm assuming I just wasn't invited," Parker said, catching my attention.

"What?"

"I heard your birthday party is on Sunday. I wasn't invited?"

America peeked at Travis, who glared at Parker as if he were seconds away from mowing him down.

"It was a surprise party, Parker," America said softly.

"Oh," Parker said, cringing.

"You're throwing me a surprise party?" I asked America.

She shrugged. "It was Trav's idea. It's at Brazil's on Sunday. Six o'clock."

Parker's cheeks flushed a faint red. "I suppose I'm really not invited, now."

"No! Of course you are!" I said, holding his hand on top of the table. Twelve pairs of eyes zeroed in on our hands. I could see that Parker was just as uncomfortable with the attention as I was, so I let go and pulled my hands onto my lap.

Parker stood up. "I have a few things I need to do before class. I'll call you later."

"Okay," I said, offering an apologetic smile.

Parker leaned over the table and kissed my lips. The silence was cafeteria-wide, and America elbowed me after Parker walked out.

"Isn't it creepy how everyone watches you?" she whispered. She glanced around the room with a frown. "What?" America yelled. "Mind your business, perverts!" One by one, heads turned away, and murmuring ensued.

I covered my eyes with my hands. "You know, before I was pathetic because I was thought to be Travis's poor clueless girlfriend. Now I'm evil because everyone thinks I'm bouncing back and forth between Travis and Parker like a Ping-Pong ball." When America didn't comment, I looked up. "What? Don't tell me you're buying into that crap, too!"

"I didn't say anything!" she said.

I stared at her in disbelief. "But that's what you think?"

America shook her head, but she didn't speak. The icy stares from the other students were suddenly apparent, and I stood up, walking to the end of the table.

"We need to talk," I said, tapping Travis's shoulder. I tried to sound polite, but the anger bubbling inside me put an edge to my words. The entire student populace, including my best friend, thought I was juggling two men. There was only one solution.

"So talk," Travis said, popping something breaded and fried into his mouth.

I fidgeted, noticing the curious eyes of everyone within earshot. When Travis still didn't move, I grabbed his arm and gave it a good tug. He stood up and followed me outside with a grin on his face.

"What, Pidge?" he said, looking at my hand on his arm and then at me.

"You've got to let me out of the bet," I begged.

His face fell. "You want to leave? Why? What'd I do?"

"You didn't do anything, Trav. Haven't you noticed everyone staring? I am quickly becoming the pariah of Eastern U."

Travis shook his head and lit a cigarette. "Not my problem."

"Yes, it is. Parker said everyone thinks he has a death wish because you're in love with me."

Travis's eyebrows shot up and he choked on the puff of smoke he'd just inhaled. "People are saying that?" he said between coughs.

I nodded. He looked away with wide eyes, taking another drag.

"Travis! You have to release me from the bet! I can't date Parker and live with you at the same time. It looks terrible!"

"So quit dating Parker."

I glared at him. "That's not the problem and you know it."

"Is that the only reason you want to leave? Because of what people are saying?"

"At least before I was clueless and you were the bad guy," I grumbled.

"Answer the question, Pidge."

"Yes!"

Travis looked beyond me to the students entering and leaving the cafeteria. He was deliberating, and I grew impatient while he took his time making his decision.

Finally, he stood tall, resolved. "No."

I shook my head, sure that I had misunderstood. "Excuse me?"

"No. You said so yourself: A bet's a bet. After the month's up, you'll be off with Parker, he'll become a doctor, you'll get married and have your 2.5 children, and I'll never see you again." He grimaced at his own words. "I still have three weeks. I'm not giving that up for lunchroom gossip."

I looked through the glass window to see the entire cafeteria watching us. The unwelcome attention made my eyes burn. I shouldered past him to walk to my next class.

"Pigeon," Travis called after me.

I didn't turn around.

That night, America sat on the tile floor of the bathroom, babbling about the boys while I stood in front of the mirror and pulled my hair into a ponytail. I was only half listening, thinking about how patient Travis had been—for Travis—knowing he didn't like the idea of Parker picking me up from his apartment every other night.

The expression on Travis's face when I asked him to let me out of the bet, and again when I told him people were saying he was in love with me, flashed in my mind. I couldn't stop wondering why he didn't deny it.

"Well, Shep thinks you're being too hard on him. He's never had anyone he's cared enough to—"

Travis poked his head in and smiled as he watched me fuss with my hair. "Wanna grab dinner?" he asked.

America stood up to look at herself in the mirror, combing her fingers through her golden hair. "Shep wants to check out that new Mexican place downtown if you guys wanna go."

Travis shook his head. "I thought me and Pidge could go alone tonight."

"I'm going out with Parker."

"Again?" he said, annoyed.

"Again," I said in a singsong voice.

The doorbell rang, and I hurried past Travis to open the door. Parker stood in front of me, his naturally wavy blond hair framing his clean-shaven face.

"Do you ever look less than gorgeous?" Parker asked.

"Based on the first time she came over here, I'm going to say yes," Travis said from behind me.

I rolled my eyes and smiled, holding up a finger to Parker to signal him to wait. I turned and threw my arms around Travis. He stiffened with surprise and then relaxed, pulling me tight against him.

I looked into his eyes and smiled. "Thanks for organizing my birthday party. Can I take a rain check on dinner?"

A dozen emotions scrolled across Travis's face, and then the corners of his mouth turned up. "Tomorrow?"

I squeezed him and grinned. "Absolutely." I waved to him as Parker grabbed my hand.

"What was that about?" Parker asked.

"We haven't been getting along lately. That was my version of an olive branch."

"Should I be worried?" he asked, opening my door.

"No." I kissed his cheek.

At dinner, Parker talked about Harvard, and the House, and his plans to search for an apartment. His eyebrows pulled in. "Will Travis be escorting you to your birthday party?"

"I'm not really sure. He hasn't said anything about it."

"If he doesn't mind, I'd like to take you." He took my hand in his and kissed my fingers.

"I'll ask him. The party was his idea, so . . ."

"I understand. If not, I'll just see you there," he smiled.

Parker took me to the apartment, slowing to a stop in the parking lot. When he kissed me goodbye, his lips lingered on mine. He yanked up the parking brake as his lips traveled along the ridge of my jaw to my ear and then halfway down my neck. It took me off guard, and I let out a quiet sigh in response.

"You are so beautiful," he whispered. "I've been distracted all night, with your hair pulled away from your neck." He peppered my neck with kisses and I exhaled, a hum escaping with my breath.

"What took you so long?" I smiled, lifting my chin to give him better access.

Parker focused on my lips. He grabbed each side of my face, kissing me a bit firmer than usual. We didn't have much room in the car, but we made the space available work to our advantage. He leaned against me, and I bent my knee as I fell against the window. His tongue slipped inside my mouth, and his hand grabbed my ankle and then slid up my leg to my thigh. The windows fogged within minutes with our labored breath sticking to the cool windows. His lips grazed my collarbone, and then his head jerked up when the glass vibrated with several loud thumps.

Parker sat up, and I righted myself, adjusting my dress. I jumped when the door flew open. Travis and America stood beside the car. America wore a sympathetic frown, and Travis seemed just short of flying into a blind rage.

"What the hell, Travis?" Parker yelled.

The situation suddenly felt dangerous. I'd never heard Parker raise his voice, Travis's knuckles were white as he balled them into fists at his sides—and I was in the way. America's hand seemed tiny when she placed it on Travis's bulky arm, shaking her head at Parker in silent warning.

"C'mon, Abby. I need to talk to you," she said.

"About what?"

"Just come on!" she snapped.

I looked to Parker, seeing the irritation in his eyes. "I'm sorry, I have to go."

"No, it's fine. Go ahead."

Travis helped me from the Porsche and then kicked the door shut. I flipped around and stood between him and the car, shoving his shoulder. "What is wrong with you? Knock it off!"

America seemed nervous. It didn't take long to figure out why. Travis reeked of whiskey; she had insisted on accompanying him, or he'd asked her to come. Either way she was a deterrent to violence.

The wheels of Parker's shiny Porsche squealed out of the

parking lot, and Travis lit a cigarette. "You can go in, now, Mare."

She tugged on my skirt. "C'mon, Abby."

"Why don't you stay, Abs," he seethed.

I nodded for America to go ahead and she reluctantly complied. I crossed my arms, ready for a fight, preparing myself to lash out at him after the inevitable lecture. Travis took several drags from his cigarette, and when it was obvious that he wasn't going to explain, my patience ran out.

"Why did you do that?" I asked.

"Why? Because he was mauling you in front of my apartment!" he yelled. His eyes were unfocused, and I could see that he was incapable of rational conversation.

I kept my voice calm. "I may be staying with you, but what I do and who I do it with is my business."

He flicked his cigarette to the ground. "You're so much better than that, Pidge. Don't let him fuck you in a car like a cheap prom date."

"I wasn't going to have sex with him!"

He gestured to the empty space where Parker's car sat. "What were you doing, then?"

"Haven't you ever made out with someone, Travis? Haven't you just messed around without letting it get that far?"

He frowned and shook his head as if I were speaking gibberish. "What's the point in that?"

"The concept exists for a lot of people . . . especially those that date."

"The windows were all fogged up, the car was bouncing . . . how was I supposed to know?" he said, waving his arms in the direction of the empty parking slot.

"Maybe you shouldn't spy on me!"

He rubbed his face and shook his head. "I can't stand this, Pigeon. I feel like I'm going crazy."

I threw out my hands and let them hit my thighs. "You can't stand what?"

"If you sleep with him, I don't wanna know about it. I'll go to prison for a long time if I find out he . . . just don't tell me."

"Travis," I seethed. "I can't believe you just said that! That's a big step for me!"

"That's what all girls say!"

"I don't mean the sluts you deal with! I mean me!" I said, holding my hand to my chest. "I haven't . . . ugh! Never mind." I walked away from him, but he grabbed my arm, twirling me around to face him.

"You haven't what?" he asked, weaving a bit. I didn't answer—I didn't have to. I could see the recognition light up his face and he laughed once. "You're a virgin?"

"So what?" I said, the blood under my cheeks igniting.

His eyes drifted from mine, in and out of focus as he tried to think through the whiskey. "That's why America was so sure it wouldn't get too far."

"I had the same boyfriend all four years of high school. He was an aspiring Baptist youth minister! It never came up!"

Travis's anger vanished, and relief was apparent in his eyes. "A youth minister? What happened after all that hard-earned abstinence?"

"He wanted to get married and stay in . . . Kansas. I didn't." I was desperate to change the subject. The amusement in Travis's eyes was humiliating enough. I didn't want him digging further into my past.

He took a step toward me and held each side of my face. "A virgin," he said, shaking his head. "I would have never guessed with the way you danced at the Red."

"Very funny," I said, stomping up the stairs.

Travis attempted to follow me but tripped and fell, rolling onto his back and laughing hysterically.

"What are you doing? Get up!" I said, helping him to his feet.

He hooked his arm around my neck, and I helped him up the stairs. Shepley and America were already in bed, so with no help in sight, I kicked off my heels to avoid breaking my ankles while walking Travis to the bedroom. He fell on his back to the bed, pulling me with him.

When we landed, my face was just inches from his. His expression was suddenly serious. He leaned up, nearly kissing me, but I pushed him away. Travis's eyebrows pulled in.

"Knock it off, Trav," I said.

He held me tight against him until I quit struggling, and then he flicked the strap of my dress, causing it to hang off my shoulder. "Since the word virgin came out of those beautiful lips of yours . . . I have a sudden urge to help you out of that dress."

"Well, that's too bad. You were ready to kill Parker for the same thing twenty minutes ago, so don't be a hypocrite."

"Fuck Parker. He doesn't know you like I do."

"Trav, c'mon. Let's get your clothes off and get you in bed."

"That's what I'm talkin' about," he chuckled.

"How much did you drink?" I asked, finally getting my footing between his legs.

"Enough," he smiled, pulling at the hem of my dress.

"You probably surpassed enough a gallon ago," I said, slapping his hand away. I planted my knee on the mattress beside him and pulled his shirt over his head. He reached for me again and I grabbed his wrist, sniffing at the pungent stench in the air. "God, Trav, you reek of Jack Daniel's."

"Jim Beam," he corrected with a drunken nod.

"It smells like burned wood and chemicals."

"It tastes like it, too," he laughed. I pulled open his belt buckle and yanked it from the loops. He laughed with the jerking motion and then lifted his head to look at me. "Better guard your virginity, Pidge. You know I like it rough."

"Shut up," I said, unbuttoning his jeans, slipping them down over his hips and then off his legs. I threw the denim to the floor and stood with my hands on my hips, breathing hard. His legs were hanging off the end of the bed, his eyes closed, his breathing deep and heavy. He had passed out.

I walked to the closet, shaking my head as I rifled through our clothes. I unzipped my dress and shoved it down over my hips, letting it fall to my ankles. Kicking it into the corner, I pulled off my ponytail holder and shook out my hair.

The closet was bursting with his clothes and mine, and I puffed, blowing my hair from my face as I searched through the mess for a T-shirt. As I pulled one off the hanger, Travis slammed into my back, wrapping his arms around my waist.

"You scared the shit outta me!" I complained.

He ran his hands over my skin. They felt different, slow and deliberate. I closed my eyes when he pulled me against him and buried his face in my hair, nuzzling my neck. As I felt his bare skin against mine, it took me a moment to protest.

"Travis . . ."

He pulled my hair to one side and grazed his lips along my

back from one shoulder to the other, unsnapping the clasp of my bra. He kissed the bare skin at the base of my neck and I closed my eyes; the warm softness of his mouth felt too good to make him stop. A quiet moan escaped from his throat when he pressed his pelvis against mine, and I could feel how much he wanted me through his boxers. I held my breath, knowing the only thing keeping us from that big step I was so opposed to a few moments before was two thin pieces of fabric.

Travis turned me to face him, and then pressed against me, leaning my back against the wall. Our eyes met, and I could see the ache in his expression as he scanned the bare pieces of my skin. I had seen him peruse women before, but this was different. He didn't want to conquer me; he wanted me to say yes.

He leaned in to kiss me, stopping just an inch away. I could feel the heat from his skin radiating against my lips, and I had to stop myself from drawing him in the rest of the way. His fingers were digging into my skin as he deliberated, and then his hands slid from my back to the hem of my panties. His index fingers slid down my hips in between my skin and the lacy fabric, and in the same moment that he was about to slip the delicate threads down my legs, he hesitated. Just when I opened my mouth to say yes, he clenched his eyes shut.

"Not like this," he whispered, brushing his lips across mine. "I want you, but not like this."

He stumbled, falling backward against the bed, and I stood for a moment with my arms crossed across my stomach. When his breathing evened out, I shoved my arms through the shirt I still had in my hand and yanked it over my head. Travis didn't move, and I blew out a slow breath of air, knowing I couldn't restrain either of us if I crawled in bed and he woke up with a less honorable perspective.

I hurried to the recliner and collapsed into it, covering my face with my hands. I felt the layers of frustration dancing and crashing into each other inside of me. Parker had left feeling slighted, Travis waited until I was seeing someone—someone I truly liked—to show an interest in me, and I seemed to be the only girl he couldn't bring himself to sleep with, even when he was wasted.

The next morning, I poured orange juice into a tall glass and took a sip as I bobbed my head to the music playing from my iPod. I had awakened before the sun and then squirmed in the recliner until eight. After that, I decided to clean up the kitchen to pass the time until my less ambitious roommates awoke. I loaded the dishwasher and swept and mopped, and then wiped the counters down. When the kitchen was sparkling, I grabbed the basket of clean clothes and sat on the couch, folding until there were a dozen or more piles surrounding me.

Murmuring came from Shepley's room. America giggled and then it was quiet for a few minutes more, followed by noises that made me feel a bit uncomfortable sitting alone in the living room.

I stacked the piles of folded clothes in the basket and carried it to Travis's room, smiling when I saw that he hadn't moved from where he had fallen the night before. I set the basket down and pulled the blanket over him, stifling a laugh when he turned over.

"View, Pigeon," he said, mumbling something inaudible before his breathing returned to slow and deep.

I couldn't help but watch him sleep; knowing he was dreaming about me sent a thrill through my veins that I couldn't explain. Travis seemed to settle back into a quiet sleep, so I decided to take a shower, hoping the sound of someone up and around would quiet Shepley and America's moans and the creaking and banging of the bed against the wall. When I turned off the water, I realized they weren't worried about who could hear.

I combed my hair, rolling my eyes at America's high-pitched yelps, more closely resembling a poodle than a porn star. The doorbell rang, and I grabbed my blue terry-cloth robe and tightened the belt, jogging across the living room floor. The noises from Shepley's bedroom immediately cut off, and I opened the door to Parker's smiling face.

"Good morning," he said.

I raked my wet hair back with my fingers. "What are you doing here?"

"I didn't like the way we said goodbye last night. I went out this morning to get your birthday present, and I couldn't wait to give it to you. So," he said, pulling a shiny box from his jacket pocket, "Happy Birthday, Abs."

He set the silver package in my hand, and I leaned in to kiss his cheek. "Thank you."

"Go ahead. I want to see your face when you open it."

I slipped my finger under the tape on the underside of the box, and then pulled the paper off, handing it to him. A rope of shimmering diamonds sat snugly in a white gold bracelet.

"Parker," I whispered.

He beamed. "You like it?"

"I do," I said, holding it in front of my face in awe, "but it's too much. I couldn't accept this if we'd been dating a year, much less a week."

Parker grimaced. "I thought you might say that. I searched high and low all morning for the perfect birthday present, and when I saw this, I knew there was only one place it could ever belong," he said, taking it from my fingers and clasping it around my wrist. "And I was right. It looks incredible on you."

I held up my wrist and shook my head, hypnotized by the brilliance of colors reacting to the sunlight. "It's the most beautiful thing I've ever seen. No one's ever given me anything so . . ." *expensive* came to mind, but I didn't want to say that, "elaborate. I don't know what to say."

Parker laughed, and then kissed my cheek. "Say that you'll wear it tomorrow."

I grinned from ear to ear. "I'll wear it tomorrow," I said, looking to my wrist.

"I'm glad you like it. The look on your face was worth the seven stores I went to."

I sighed. "You went to seven stores?" He nodded, and I took his face in my hands. "Thank you. It's perfect," I said, kissing him quickly.

He hugged me tight. "I have to get back. I'm having lunch with my parents, but I'll call you later, okay?"

"Okay. Thank you!" I called after him, watching him trot down the stairs.

I hurried into the apartment, unable to take my eyes off of my wrist.

"Holy shit, Abby!" America said, grabbing my hand. "Where did you get this?"

"Parker brought it. It's my birthday present," I said.

America gawked at me, and then down at the bracelet. "He bought you a diamond tennis bracelet? After a week? If I didn't know better, I'd say you have a magic crotch!"

I laughed out loud, beginning a ridiculous giggle-fest in the living room.

Shepley emerged from his bedroom, looking tired and satisfied. "What are you fruitcakes shrieking about in here?"

America held up my wrist. "Look! Her birthday present from Parker!"

Shepley squinted, and then his eyes popped open. "Whoa."

"I know, right?" America said, nodding.

Travis stumbled around the corner, looking a bit beat up. "You guys are loud as fuck," he groaned, buttoning his jeans.

"Sorry," I said, pulling my hand from America's grip. Our almost moment crept into my mind, and I couldn't seem to look him in the eyes.

He downed the rest of my orange juice, and then wiped his mouth. "Who in the hell let me drink that much last night?"

America sneered, "You did. You went out and bought a fifth after Abby left with Parker and killed the whole thing by the time she got back."

"Damn," he said, shaking his head. "Did you have fun?" he asked, looking to me.

"Are you serious?" I asked, showing my anger before thinking. "What?"

America laughed. "You pulled her out of Parker's car, seeing red when you caught them making out like high schoolers. They fogged up the windows and everything!"

Travis's eyes unfocused, scanning his memories of the night before. I worked to stifle my temper. If he didn't remember pulling me from the car, he wouldn't remember how close I came to handing my virginity to him on a silver platter.

"How pissed are you?" he asked, wincing.

"Pretty pissed." I was angrier that my feelings had nothing to do with Parker. I tightened my robe and stomped down the hall. Travis's footsteps were right behind me.

"Pidge," he said, catching the door when I shut it in his face. He slowly pushed it open and stood before me, waiting to suffer my wrath.

"Do you remember anything you said to me last night?" I asked.

"No. Why? Was I mean to you?" His bloodshot eyes were heavy with worry, which only served to amplify my anger.

"No, you weren't mean to me! You . . . we . . ." I covered my eyes with my hands and then froze when I felt Travis's hand on my wrist.

"Where'd this come from?" he said, glaring at the bracelet.

"It's mine," I said, pulling away from him.

He didn't take his eyes from my wrist. "I've never seen it before. It looks new."

"It is."

"Where'd you get it?"

"Parker gave it to me about fifteen minutes ago," I said, watching his face morph from confusion to rage.

"What the fuck was that douchebag doing here? Did he stay the night?" he asked, his voice rising with each question.

I crossed my arms. "He went shopping for my birthday present this morning and brought it by."

"It's not your birthday yet." His face turned a deep shade of red as he worked to keep his temper under control.

"He couldn't wait," I said, lifting my chin with stubborn pride.

"No wonder I had to drag your ass out of his car, sounds like you were . . ." he trailed off, pressing his lips together.

I narrowed my eyes. "What? Sounds like I was what?"

His jaws tensed and he took a deep breath, blowing it out from his nose. "Nothing. I'm just pissed off, and I was going to say something shitty that I didn't mean."

"It's never stopped you before."

"I know. I'm working on it," he said, walking to the door. "I'll let you get dressed."

When he reached for the knob, he paused, rubbing his arm. As soon as his fingers touched the tender splatter of purple pooling under his skin, he pulled up his elbow and noticed the bruise. He stared at it for a moment and then turned to me.

"I fell on the stairs last night. And you helped me to bed . . ." he said, sifting through the blurry images in his mind.

My heart was pounding, and I swallowed hard as I watched realization strike. His eyes narrowed. "We," he began, taking a step toward me, looking at the closet and then to the bed.

"No, we didn't. Nothing happened," I said, shaking my head.

He cringed, the memory obviously replaying in his mind. "You fog up Parker's windows, I pull you out of the car, and then I try to . . ." he said, shaking his head. He turned for the door and grabbed the knob, his knuckles white. "You're turning me into a fucking psycho, Pigeon," he growled over his shoulder. "I don't think straight when I'm around you."

"So it's my fault?"

He turned. His eyes fell from my face to my robe, to my

legs, and then my feet, returning to my eyes. "I don't know. My memory is a little hazy . . . but I don't recall you saying no."

I took a step forward, ready to argue that irrelevant little fact, but I couldn't. He was right. "What do you want me to say, Travis?"

He looked at the bracelet and then back at me with accusing eyes. "You were hoping I wouldn't remember?"

"No! I was pissed that you forgot!"

His brown eyes bored into mine. "Why?"

"Because if I would have . . . if we would have . . . and you didn't . . . I don't know why! I just was!"

He stormed across the room, stopping inches from me. His hands touched my cheeks, his breathing quick as he scanned my face. "What are we doin', Pidge?"

My eyes began at his belt and then rose over the muscles and tattoos of his stomach and chest, finally settling on the warm brown of his irises. "You tell me."

Chapter Seven
Nineteen

"ABBY?" SHEPLEY SAID, KNOCKING ON THE DOOR. "Mare was going to run some errands; she wanted me to let you know in case you needed to go."

Travis hadn't taken his eyes from mine. "Pidge?"

"Yeah," I called to Shepley. "I have some stuff I need to take care of."

"All right, she's ready to go when you are," Shepley said, his footsteps disappearing down the hall.

"Pidge?"

I pulled a few things from the closet and slid past him. "Can we talk about this later? I have a lot to do today."

"Sure," he said with a contrived smile.

It was a relief to escape to the bathroom. I quickly closed the door behind me. Two weeks left in the apartment and no way to put off the conversation—at least, not for that long. The logical part of my brain insisted that Parker was my type: attractive, smart, and interested in me. Why I bothered with Travis was something I would never understand.

Whatever the reason, it was making us both insane. I had

been divided into two separate people: the docile, polite person I was with Parker, and the angry, confused, frustrated person I turned into around Travis. The entire school had witnessed Travis going from unpredictable before to damn near volatile now.

I dressed quickly, leaving Travis and Shepley to go downtown with America. She giggled about her morning sexcapade with Shepley, and I listened with dutiful nods in all the right places. It was hard to focus on the topic at hand with the diamonds of my bracelet creating tiny dots of light on the ceiling of the car, reminding me of the choice I was suddenly faced with. Travis wanted an answer, and I didn't have one.

"Okay, Abby. What's going on? You've been quiet."

"This thing with Travis . . . it's just a mess."

"Why?" she said, her sunglasses pushing up when she wrinkled her nose.

"He asked me what we were doing."

"What are you doing? Are you with Parker or what?"

"I like him, but it's been a week. We're not serious or anything."

"You have feelings for Travis, don't you?"

I shook my head. "I don't know how I feel about him. I just don't see it happening, Mare. He's too much of a bad thing."

"Neither one of you will just come out and say it, that's the problem. You're both so scared of what might happen that you're fighting it tooth and nail. I know for a fact that if you looked Travis in the eye and told him you wanted him, he would never look at another woman again."

"You know that for a fact?"

"Yes. I have the inside track, remember?"

I paused in thought for a moment. Travis had been talking to Shepley about me, but Shepley wouldn't encourage a relationship by telling America. He knew she would tell me. This led me to the only conclusion: America had overheard them. I wanted to ask her what was said, but thought better of it.

"That situation is a broken heart just waiting to happen," I said, shaking my head. "I don't think he's capable of being faithful."

"He wasn't capable of carrying on a friendship with a female, either, but you two sure shocked the whole of Eastern."

I fingered my bracelet and sighed. "I don't know. I don't mind how things are. We can just be friends."

America shook her head. "Except that you're not just friends," she sighed. "You know what? I'm over this conversation. Let's go get our hair and makeup done. I'll buy you a new outfit for your birthday."

"I think that's exactly what I need," I said.

After hours of manicures, pedicures, being brushed, waxed, and powdered, I stepped into my shiny yellow high heels and tugged on my new gray dress.

"Now that's the Abby I know and love!" America laughed, shaking her head at my ensemble. "You have to wear that to your party tomorrow."

"Wasn't that the plan all along?" I said, smirking. My cell phone buzzed in my purse, and I held it to my ear. "Hello?"

"It's dinner time! Where the hell did you two run off to?" Travis said.

"We indulged in a little pampering. You and Shep knew how to eat before we came along. I'm sure you can manage."

"Well, no shit. We worry about you, ya know."

I looked at America and smiled. "We're fine."

"Tell him I'll have you back in no time. I have to stop by Brazil's to pick up some notes for Shep, and then we'll be home."

"Did you get that?" I asked.

"Yeah. See you then, Pidge."

We drove to Brazil's in silence. America turned off the ignition, staring at the apartment building ahead. Shepley asking America to drive over surprised me; we were just a block from Shepley and Travis's apartment.

"What's wrong, Mare?"

"Brazil just gives me the creeps. The last time I was here with Shep, he was being all flirty."

"Well, I'll go in with you. If he so much as winks at you, I'll stab him in the eye with my new heels, okay?"

America smiled and hugged me. "Thanks, Abby!"

We walked to the back of the building, and America took a deep breath before knocking on the door. We waited, but no one came.

"I guess he's not here?" I asked.

"He's here," she said, irritated. She banged on the wood with the side of her fist and then the door swung open.

"HAPPY BIRTHDAY!" the crowd inside yelled.

The ceiling was pink-and-black bubbles, every inch covered by helium balloons with long silver strings hanging down in the faces of the guests. The crowd separated, and Travis approached me with a broad smile, touching each side of my face and kissing my forehead.

"Happy birthday, Pigeon."

"It's not 'til tomorrow," I said. Still in shock, I tried smiling at everyone around us.

Travis shrugged. "Well, since you were tipped off, we had to make some last minute changes to surprise you. Surprised?"

"Very!" I said as Finch hugged me.

"Happy birthday, baby!" Finch said, kissing my lips.

America nudged me with her elbow. "Good thing I got you to run errands with me today or you would have shown up looking like ass!"

"You look great," Travis said, scanning my dress.

Brazil hugged me, pressing his cheek to mine. "And I hope you know America's Brazil-is-creepy story was just a line to get you in here."

I looked at America and she laughed. "It worked, didn't it?"

Once everyone took turns hugging me and wishing me a happy birthday, I leaned into America's ear. "Where's Parker?"

"He'll be here later," she whispered. "Shepley couldn't get him on the phone to let him know until this afternoon."

Brazil cranked up the volume on the stereo, and everyone screamed. "Come here, Abby!" he said, walking to the kitchen. He lined up shot glasses along the counter and pulled a bottle of tequila from the bar. "Happy birthday from the football team, baby girl," he smiled, pouring each shot glass full of Patrón. "This is the way we do birthdays: You turn nineteen, you have nineteen shots. You can drink 'em or give 'em away, but the more you drink, the more of these you get," he said, fanning out a handful of twenties.

"Oh my God!" I squealed.

"Drink 'em up, Pidge!" Travis said.

I looked to Brazil, suspicious. "I get a twenty for every shot I drink?"

"That's right, lightweight. Gauging by the size of you, I'm

going to say we'll get away with losing sixty bucks by the end of the night."

"Think again, Brazil," I said, grabbing the first shot glass, rolling it across my lip, tipping my head back to empty the glass and then rolling it the rest of the way, dropping it into my other hand.

"Holy shit!" Travis exclaimed.

"This is really a waste, Brazil," I said, wiping the corners of my mouth. "You shoot Cuervo, not Patrón."

The smug smile on Brazil's face faded, and he shook his head and shrugged. "Get after it, then. I've got the wallets of twelve football players that say you can't finish ten."

I narrowed my eyes. "Double or nothing says I can drink fifteen."

"Whoa!" Shepley cried. "You're not allowed to hospitalize yourself on your birthday, Abby!"

"She can do it," America said, staring at Brazil.

"Forty bucks a shot?" Brazil said, looking unsure.

"Are you scared?" I asked.

"Hell no! I'll give you twenty a shot, and when you make it to fifteen, I'll double your total."

"That's how Kansans do birthdays," I said, popping back another shot.

An hour and three shots later, I was in the living room dancing with Travis. The song was a rock ballad, and Travis mouthed the words to me as we danced. He dipped me at the end of the first chorus, and I let my arms fall behind me. He popped me back up, and I sighed.

"You can't do that when I start getting into the double-digit shots," I giggled.

"Did I tell you how incredible you look tonight?"

I shook my head and hugged him, laying my head on his shoulder. He tightened his grip, and buried his face in my neck, making me forget about decisions or bracelets or my separate personalities; I was exactly where I wanted to be.

When the music changed to a faster beat, the door opened.

"Parker!" I said, running over to hug him. "You made it!"

"Sorry I'm late, Abs," he said, pressing his lips against mine. "Happy birthday."

"Thanks," I said, seeing Travis stare at us from the corner of my eye.

Parker lifted my wrist. "You wore it."

"I said I would. Wanna dance?"

He shook his head. "Uh . . . I don't dance."

"Oh. Well, you wanna witness my sixth shot of Patrón?" I smiled, holding up my five twenties. "I make double if I get to fifteen."

"That's a bit dangerous, isn't it?"

I leaned into his ear. "I am totally hustling them. I've played this game with my dad since I was sixteen."

"Oh," he said, frowning with disapproval. "You drank tequila with your dad?"

I shrugged. "It was his way of bonding."

Parker seemed unimpressed as his eyes left mine, scanning the crowd. "I can't stay long. I'm leaving early for a hunting trip with my father."

"It's a good thing my party was tonight, or you wouldn't have made it tomorrow," I said, surprised to hear of his plans.

He smiled and took my hand. "I would have made it back in time."

I pulled him to the kitchen, picked up another shot glass, and killed it, slamming it on the counter upside down like I had the previous five. Brazil handed me another twenty, and I danced into the living room. Travis grabbed me, and we danced with America and Shepley.

Shepley slapped me on the butt. "One!"

America added a second swat on my backside, and then the entire party joined in, sans Parker.

At number nineteen, Travis rubbed his hands together. "My turn!"

I rubbed my sore posterior. "Be easy! My ass hurts!"

With an evil smirk, he reared his hand far above his shoulder. I closed my eyes tight. After a few moments, I peeked back. Just before his hand made contact, he stopped and gave me a gentle pat.

"Nineteen!" he exclaimed.

The guests cheered, and America started a drunken rendition of "Happy Birthday." I laughed when the part came to say my name and the entire room sang "Pigeon."

Another slow song came over the stereo, and Parker pulled me to the makeshift dance floor. It didn't take me long to figure out why he didn't dance.

"Sorry," he said after stepping on my toes for the third time.

I leaned my head on his shoulder. "You're doing just fine," I lied.

He pressed his lips against my temple. "What are you doing Monday night?"

"Going to dinner with you?"

"Yes. In my new apartment."

"You found one!"

He laughed and nodded. "We'll order in, though. My cooking isn't exactly edible."

"I'd eat it, anyway," I said, smiling up at him.

Parker glanced around the room and then led me to a hallway. He gently pressed me against the wall, kissing me with his soft lips. His hands were everywhere. At first I played along, but after his tongue infiltrated my lips, I got the distinct feeling that I was doing something wrong.

"Okay, Parker," I said, maneuvering away.

"Everything all right?"

"I just think it's rude of me to make out with you in a dark corner when I have guests out there."

He smiled and kissed me again. "You're right, I'm sorry. I just wanted to give you a memorable birthday kiss before I left."

"You're leaving?"

He touched my cheek. "I have to wake up in four hours, Abs."

I pressed my lips together. "Okay. I'll see you Monday?"

"You'll see me tomorrow. I'll stop by when I get back."

He led me to the door and then kissed my cheek before he left. I noticed that Shepley, America, and Travis were all staring at me.

"Daddy's gone!" Travis yelled when the door closed. "Time to get the party started!"

Everyone cheered, and Travis pulled me to the center of the floor.

"Hang on . . . I'm on a schedule," I said, leading him by the hand to the counter. I knocked back another shot, and laughed when Travis took one from the end, sucking it down. I grabbed another and swallowed, and he did the same.

"Seven more, Abby," Brazil said, handing me two more twenty-dollar bills.

I wiped my mouth as Travis pulled me to the living room again. I danced with America and then Shepley, but when Chris Jenks from the football team tried to dance with me, Travis pulled him back by the shirt and shook his head. Chris shrugged and turned, dancing with the first girl he saw.

The tenth shot hit hard, and I felt a little dizzy standing on Brazil's couch with America, dancing like clumsy grade-schoolers. We giggled over nothing, waving our arms around to the beat.

I stumbled, nearly falling off the couch backward, but Travis's hands were instantly on my hips to steady me.

"You've made your point," he said. "You've drunk more than any girl we've ever seen. I'm cutting you off."

"The hell you are," I slurred. "I have six hundred bucks waiting on me at the bottom of that shot glass, and you of all people aren't going to tell me I can't do something extreme for cash."

"If you're that hard up for money, Pidge . . ."

"I'm not borrowing money from you," I sneered.

"I was gonna suggest pawning that bracelet," he smiled.

I smacked him on the arm just as America started the count-down to midnight. When the hands of the clock superimposed on the twelve, we all celebrated.

I was nineteen.

America and Shepley kissed each of my cheeks, and then Travis lifted me off the ground, twirling me around.

"Happy birthday, Pigeon," he said with a soft expression.

I stared into his warm brown eyes for a moment, feeling lost inside of them. The room was frozen in time as we stared at each other, so close I could feel his breath on my skin.

"Shots!" I said, stumbling to the counter.

"You look torn up, Abby. I think it's time to call it a night," Brazil said.

"I'm not a quitter," I said. "I wanna see my money."

Brazil placed a twenty under the last two glasses, and then he yelled at his teammates, "She's gonna drink 'em! I need fifteen!"

They all groaned and rolled their eyes, pulling out their wallets to form a stack of twenties behind the last shot glass. Travis had emptied the other four shots on the other side of my fifteen.

"I would have never believed that I could lose fifty bucks on a fifteen-shot bet with a girl," Chris complained.

"Believe it, Jenks," I said, picking up a glass in each hand.

I knocked back each of the glasses and waited for the vomit rising in my throat to settle.

"Pigeon?" Travis asked, taking a step in my direction.

I raised a finger and Brazil smiled. "She's going to lose it," he said.

"No, she won't," America shook her head. "Deep breath, Abby."

I closed my eyes and inhaled, picking up the last shot.

"Holy God, Abby! You're going to die of alcohol poisoning!" Shepley cried.

"She's got this," America assured him.

I tipped my head and let the tequila flow down my throat. My teeth and lips had been numb since shot number eight, and the kick of the eighty proof had long since lost its edge. The entire party erupted into whistles and yells as Brazil handed me the stack of money.

"Thank you," I said with pride, tucking the money away in my bra.

"You are incredibly sexy right now," Travis said in my ear as we walked to the living room.

We danced into the morning, and the tequila running through my veins eased me into oblivion.

Chapter Eight
Rumors

WHEN MY EYES FINALLY PEELED OPEN, I SAW THAT MY pillow consisted of denim and legs. Travis sat with his back against the tub; his head leaned against the wall, passed out cold. He looked as rough as I felt. I pulled the blanket off of me and stood up, gasping at my horrifying reflection in the mirror above the sink.

I looked like death.

Mascara smeared, black tearstains down my cheek, lipstick smudged across my mouth, and my hair had balls of rats on each side.

Sheets, towels, and blankets surrounded Travis. He had fashioned a soft pallet to sleep on while I expelled the fifteen shots of tequila I'd consumed the night before. Travis had held my hair out of the toilet, and sat with me all night.

I turned on the faucet, holding my hand under the water until it was the temperature I wanted. Scrubbing the mess from my face, I heard a moan from the floor. Travis stirred, rubbed his eyes, and stretched, and then looked beside him, jerking in a panic.

"I'm right here," I said. "Why don't you go to bed? Get some sleep?"

"You okay?" he said, wiping his eyes once more.

"Yeah, I'm good. Well, good as I can be. I'll feel better once I get a shower."

He stood up. "You took my crazy title last night, just so you know. I don't know where that came from, but I don't want you to do it again."

"It's pretty much what I grew up around, Trav. Not a big deal."

He took my chin in his hands and wiped the remaining smeared mascara from under my eyes with his thumbs. "It was a big deal to me."

"Fine, I won't do it again. Happy?"

"Yes. But I have something to tell you, if you promise not to freak out."

"Oh, God, what did I do?"

"Nothing, but you need to call America."

"Where is she?"

"At Morgan. She got into it with Shep last night."

I rushed through my shower and yanked on the clothes Travis had set on the sink. When I emerged from the bathroom, Shepley and Travis were sitting in the living room.

"What did you do to her?" I demanded.

Shepley's face fell. "She's really pissed at me."

"What happened?"

"I was mad that she encouraged you to drink so much. I thought we were going to end up taking you to the hospital. One thing led to another, and the next thing I know, we're screaming at each other. We were both drunk, Abby. I said some things I can't take back," he shook his head, looking to the floor.

"Like what?" I said, angry.

"I called her a few names I'm not proud of and then told her to leave."

"You let her leave here drunk? Are you some kind of idiot?" I said, grabbing at my purse.

"Easy, Pidge. He feels bad enough," Travis said.

I fished my cell phone out of my purse, dialing America's number.

"Hello?" she answered. She sounded awful.

"I just heard," I sighed. "Are you okay?" I walked down the hall for privacy, glancing back once to shoot a dirty look at Shepley.

"I'm fine. He's an asshole." Her words were abrupt, but I could hear the hurt in her voice. America had mastered the art of hiding her emotions, and she could have hidden it from anyone but me.

"I'm sorry I didn't go with you."

"You were out of it, Abby," she said dismissively.

"Why don't you come get me? We can talk about it."

She breathed into the phone. "I don't know. I don't really feel like seeing him."

"I'll tell him to stay inside, then."

After a long pause, I heard keys clink in the background. "All right. I'll be there in a minute."

I walked into the living room, pulling my purse over my shoulder. They watched me open the door to wait for America, and Shepley scooted forward on the couch.

"She's coming here?"

"She doesn't want to see you, Shep. I told her you'd stay inside."

He sighed and fell against the cushion. "She hates me."

"I'll talk to her. You better get one amazing apology together, though."

Ten minutes later, a car horn beeped twice outside, and I closed the door behind me. When I reached the bottom of the stairs, Shepley rushed past me to America's red Honda, and hunched over to see her through the window. I stopped in my tracks, watching America snub him as she looked straight ahead. She rolled down her window, and Shepley seemed to be explaining, and then they began to argue. I went inside to give them their privacy.

"Pigeon?" Travis said, trotting down the stairs.

"It doesn't look good."

"Let them figure it out. Come inside," he said, intertwining his fingers in mine to lead me up the stairs.

"Was it that bad?" I asked.

He nodded. "It was pretty bad. They're just getting out of the honeymoon stage, though. They'll work it out."

"For someone that's never had a girlfriend, you seem to know about relationships."

"I have four brothers and a lot of friends," he said, grinning to himself.

Shepley stomped into the apartment and slammed the door behind him. "She's fucking impossible!"

I kissed Travis on the cheek. "That's my cue."

"Good luck," Travis said.

I slid in beside America, and she huffed. "He's fucking impossible!"

I giggled, but she shot a glare in my direction. "Sorry," I said, forcing my smile to fade.

We set out for a drive and America yelled and cried and yelled some more. At times she broke into rants that seemed to be directed at Shepley, as if he were sitting in my place. I sat quietly, letting her work it out in a way only America can.

"He called me irresponsible! Me! As if I don't know you! As if I haven't seen you rob your dad of hundreds of dollars drinking twice as much. He doesn't know what the hell he's talking about! He doesn't know what your life was like! He doesn't know what I know, and he acts like I'm his child instead of his girlfriend!" I rested my hand on hers, but she pulled it away. "He thought you would be the reason we wouldn't work out, and then he ended up doing the job on his own. And speaking of you, what the hell was that last night with Parker?"

The sudden change of topic took me by surprise. "What do you mean?"

"Travis threw you that party, Abby, and you go off and make out with Parker. And you wonder why everyone is talking about you!"

"Hold on a minute! I told Parker we shouldn't be back there. What does it matter if Travis threw me that party or not? I'm not with him!"

America looked straight ahead, blowing a puff of air from her nose.

"All right, Mare. What is it? You're mad at me now?"

"I'm not mad at you. I just don't associate with complete idiots."

I shook my head and then looked out the window before I said something I couldn't take back. America had always been able to make me feel like shit on command.

"Do you even see what's going on?" she asked. "Travis quit

fighting. He doesn't go out without you. He hasn't brought any girls home since the bimbo twins, has yet to murder Parker, and you're worried that people are saying you're playing them both. You know why that is, Abby? Because it's the truth!"

I turned, slowly craning my neck in her direction, trying to give her the dirtiest look I knew how. "What the hell is wrong with you?

"You're dating Parker now, and you're so happy," she said in a mocking tone. "Then why aren't you at Morgan?"

"Because I lost the bet, you know that!"

"Give me a break, Abby! You talk about how perfect Parker is, you go on these amazing dates with him, talk to him for hours on the phone, and then you lie next to Travis every night. Do you see what's wrong with this situation? If you really liked Parker, your stuff would be at Morgan right now."

I clenched my teeth. "You know I've never welshed on a bet, Mare."

"That's what I thought," she said, twisting her hands around the steering wheel. "Travis is what you want, and Parker is what you think you need."

"I know it looks that way, but—"

"It looks that way to everyone. So if you don't like the way people are talking about you—change. It's not Travis's fault. He's done a 180 for you. You're reaping the rewards, and Parker's getting the benefits."

"A week ago you wanted to pack me up and never let Travis come near me again! Now you're defending him?"

"Abigail! I'm not defending him, stupid! I'm looking out for you! You're both crazy about each other! Do something about it!"

"How could you possibly think I should be with him?" I wailed. "You are supposed to be keeping me away from people like him!"

She pressed her lips together, clearly losing her patience. "You have worked so hard to separate yourself from your father. That's the only reason you're even considering Parker! He's the complete opposite of Mick, and you think Travis is going to land you right back where you were. He's not like your dad, Abby."

"I didn't say he was, but it's putting me in a prime position to follow in his footsteps."

"Travis wouldn't do that to you. I think you underestimate just how much you mean to him. If you'd just tell him—"

"No. We didn't leave everything behind to have everyone here look at me the way they did in Wichita. Let's focus on the problem at hand. Shep is waiting for you."

"I don't want to talk about Shep," she said, slowing to a stop at the light.

"He's miserable, Mare. He loves you."

Her eyes filled with tears and her bottom lip quivered. "I don't care."

"Yes, you do."

"I know," she whimpered, leaning against my shoulder.

She cried until the light changed, and then I kissed her head. "Green light."

She sat up, wiping her nose. "I was pretty mean to him earlier. I don't think he'll talk to me now."

"He'll talk to you. He knew you were mad."

America wiped her face and then made a slow U-turn. I was worried it would take a lot of coaxing on my part to get her to come in with me, but Shepley ran down the stairs before she turned off the ignition.

He yanked open her car door, pulling her to her feet. "I'm so sorry, baby. I should have minded my own business, I . . . please don't leave. I don't know what I'd do without you."

America took his face in her hands and smiled. "You're an arrogant ass, but I still love you."

Shepley kissed her over and over like he hadn't seen her in months, and I smiled at a job well done. Travis stood in the doorway, grinning as I made my way into the apartment.

"And they lived happily ever after," Travis said, shutting the door behind me.

I collapsed on the couch, and he sat next to me, pulling my legs onto his lap.

"What do you wanna do today, Pidge?"

"Sleep. Or rest . . . or sleep."

"Can I give you your present first?"

I pushed his shoulder. "Shut up. You got me a present?"

His mouth curved into a nervous smile. "It's not a diamond bracelet, but I thought you'd like it."

"I'll love it, sight unseen."

He lifted my legs off of his lap and then disappeared into Shepley's bedroom. I raised an eyebrow when I heard him murmuring, and then he emerged with a box. He sat it on the floor at my feet, crouching behind it.

"Hurry, I want you to be surprised," he smiled.

"Hurry?" I asked, lifting the lid.

My mouth fell open when a pair of big, dark eyes looked up at me.

"A puppy?" I shrieked, reaching into the box. I lifted the

dark, wiry-haired baby to my face, and it covered my mouth in warm, wet kisses.

Travis beamed, triumphant. "You like him?"

"Him? I love him! You got me a puppy!"

"It's a cairn terrier. I had to drive three hours to pick him up Thursday after class."

"So when you said you were going with Shepley to take his car to the shop . . ."

"We went to get your present," he nodded.

"He's wiggly!" I laughed.

"Every girl from Kansas needs a Toto," Travis said, helping me hang on to the tiny fuzz ball in my lap.

"He does look like Toto! That's what I'm going to call him," I said, wrinkling my nose at the squirmy pup.

"You can keep him here. I'll take care of him for you when you're back at Morgan," his mouth pulled up into a half smile, "and it's my security that you'll visit when your month is up."

I pressed my lips together. "I would have come back anyway, Trav."

"I'd do anything for that smile that's on your face right now."

"I think you need a nap, Toto. Yes, you do," I cooed to the puppy.

Travis nodded, pulled me onto his lap, and then stood up. "Come on, then."

He carried me into his bedroom, pulled back the covers, and then lowered me to the mattress. Crawling over me, he reached over to pull the curtains closed and then fell onto his pillow.

"Thanks for staying with me last night," I said, stroking Toto's soft fur. "You didn't have to sleep on the bathroom floor."

"Last night was one of the best nights of my life."

I turned to see his expression. When I saw that he was serious, I shot him a dubious look. "Sleeping in between the toilet and the tub on a cold, hard tile floor with a vomiting idiot was one of your best nights? That's sad, Trav."

"No, sitting up with you when you're sick and you falling asleep in my lap was one of my best nights. It wasn't comfortable, I didn't sleep worth a shit, but I brought in your nineteenth birthday with you, and you're actually pretty sweet when you're drunk."

"I'm sure between the heaving and purging I was very charming."

He pulled me close, patting Toto, who was snuggled up to my neck. "You're the only woman I know that still looks incredible with your head in the toilet. That's saying something."

"Thanks, Trav. I won't make you babysit me again."

He leaned against his pillow. "Whatever. No one can hold your hair back like I can."

I giggled and closed my eyes, letting myself sink into the darkness.

"GET UP, ABBY!" AMERICA YELLED, SHAKING ME.

Toto licked my cheek. "I'm up! I'm up!"

"We have class in half an hour!"

I jumped from the bed. "I've been asleep for . . . fourteen hours? What the hell?"

"Just get in the shower! If you're not ready in ten minutes, I'm leaving your ass here!"

"I don't have time to take a shower!" I said, changing out of the clothes I fell asleep in.

Travis propped his head on his hand and chuckled. "You

girls are ridiculous. It's not the end of the world if you're late for one class."

"It is if you're America. She doesn't miss and she hates being late," I said, pulling a shirt over my head and stepping into my jeans.

"Let Mare go ahead. I'll take you."

I hopped on one foot and then the other, pulling my boots on. "My bag is in her car, Trav."

"Whatever," he shrugged, "just don't hurt yourself getting to class." He lifted Toto, cradling him with one arm like a tiny football, taking him down the hall.

America rushed me out the door and into the car. "I can't believe he got you that puppy," she said, looking behind her as she backed out from the parking spot.

Travis stood in the morning sun in his boxers and bare feet, clutching his arms around him from the cold. He watched Toto sniff a small patch of grass, coaxing him like a proud father.

"I've never had a dog before," I said. "This should be interesting."

America glanced at Travis before shoving the Honda into gear. "Look at him," she said, shaking her head. "Travis Maddox: Mr. Mom."

"Toto is adorable. Even you will be putty in his paws."

"You can't take it back to the dorm with you, you know. I don't think Travis thought this out."

"Travis said he'd keep him at the apartment."

She raised one eyebrow. "Of course he will. Travis thinks ahead, I'll give him that," she said, shaking her head as she slammed on the gas.

I puffed, sliding into my seat with one minute to spare. Once the adrenaline absorbed into my system, the heaviness from my postbirthday coma settled over my body. America elbowed me when class was dismissed, and I followed her to the cafeteria.

Shepley met us at the door, and I noticed right away that something was wrong.

"Mare," Shepley said, grabbing her arm.

Travis jogged to where we stood and grabbed his hips, puffing until he caught his breath.

"Is there a mob of angry women chasing you?" I teased.

He shook his head. "I was trying to catch you . . . before you . . . went in," he breathed.

"What's going on?" America asked Shepley.

"There's a rumor," Shepley began. "Everyone's saying that Travis took Abby home and . . . the details are different, but it's pretty bad."

"What? Are you serious?" I cried.

America rolled her eyes. "Who cares, Abby? People have been speculating about you and Trav for weeks. It's not the first time someone has accused you two of sleeping together."

Travis and Shepley traded glances.

"What?" I said. "There's something else, isn't there?"

Shepley winced. "They're saying you slept with Parker at Brazil's, and then you let Travis . . . take you home, if you know what I mean."

My mouth fell open. "Great! So I'm the school slut now?"

Travis's eyes darkened and his jaws tensed. "This is my fault. If it was anyone else, they wouldn't be saying that about you." He walked into the cafeteria, his hands in fists at his sides.

America and Shepley followed behind him. "Let's just hope no one is stupid enough to say anything to him," America said.

"Or her," Shepley added.

Travis sat a few seats across and down from me, brooding over his Reuben. I waited for him to look at me, wanting to offer a comforting smile. Travis had a reputation, but I let Parker take me into the hall.

Shepley elbowed me while I stared at his cousin. "He just feels bad. He's probably trying to deflect the rumor."

"You don't have to sit down there, Trav. Come on, come sit," I said, patting the empty surface in front of me.

"I heard you had quite a birthday, Abby," Chris Jenks said, throwing a piece of lettuce on Travis's plate.

"Don't start with her, Jenks," Travis warned, glowering.

Chris smiled, pushing up his round, pink cheeks. "I heard Parker is furious. He said he came by your apartment yesterday, and you and Travis were still in bed."

"They were taking a nap, Chris," America sneered.

My eyes darted to Travis. "Parker came by?"

He shifted uncomfortably in his chair. "I was gonna tell you."

"When?" I snapped.

America leaned into my ear. "Parker heard the rumor, and came by to confront you. I tried to stop him, but he walked down the hall and . . . totally got the wrong idea."

I planted my elbows on the table, covering my face with my hands. "This just keeps getting better."

"So you guys really didn't do the deed?" Chris asked. "Damn, that sucks. Here I thought Abby was right for you after all, Trav."

"You better stop now, Chris," Shepley warned.

"If you didn't sleep with her, mind if I take a shot?" Chris said, chuckling to his teammates.

My face burned with the initial embarrassment, but then America screamed in my ear, reacting to Travis jumping from his seat. He reached over the table and grabbed Chris by the throat with one hand and a fistful of T-shirt in the other. The linebacker slid across the table, and dozens of chairs grated across the floor as people stood to watch. Travis punched him repeatedly in the face, his elbow spiking high in the air before he landed each blow. The only thing Chris could do was to cover his face with his hands.

No one touched Travis. He was out of control, and his reputation left everyone afraid to get in his way. The football players ducked and winced as they watched their teammate being assaulted without mercy on the tile floor.

"Travis!" I screamed, running around the table.

In midpunch, Travis withheld his fist and then released Chris's shirt, letting him fall to the floor. He was panting when he turned to look at me; I'd never seen him look so frightening. I swallowed and took a step back as he shouldered past me.

I took a step to follow him, but America grabbed my arm. Shepley kissed her quickly and then followed his cousin out the door.

"Jesus," America whispered.

We turned to watch Chris's teammates pick him off the floor, and I cringed at his red and puffy face. Blood trickled from his nose, and Brazil handed him a napkin from the table.

"That crazy son of a bitch!" Chris groaned, sitting on the chair and holding his hand to his face. He looked at me. "I'm sorry, Abby. I was just kidding."

I had no words to reply. I couldn't explain what had just happened any more than he could.

"She didn't sleep with either of them," America said.

"You never know when to shut up, Jenks," Brazil said, disgusted.

America pulled on my arm. "C'mon. Let's go."

She didn't waste time tugging me to her car. When she put the gear in drive, I grabbed her wrist. "Wait! Where are we going?"

"We're going to Shep's. I don't want him to be alone with Travis. Did you see him? Dude's gone off the deep end!"

"Well, I don't want to be around him, either!"

America stared at me in disbelief. "There's obviously something going on with him. Don't you want to know what it is?"

"My sense of self-preservation is outweighing my curiosity at this point, Mare."

"The only thing that stopped him was your voice, Abby. He'll listen to you. You need to talk to him."

I sighed and released her wrist, falling against the back of my seat. "All right. Let's go."

We pulled into the parking lot, and America slowed to a stop between Shepley's Charger and Travis's Harley. She walked to the stairs, putting her hands on her hips with a touch of her own dramatic flair.

"C'mon, Abby!" America called, motioning for me to follow.

Hesitant, I finally followed, stopping when I saw Shepley hurry down the stairs to speak quietly in America's ear. He looked at me, shook his head, and then whispered to her once again.

"What?" I asked.

"Shep doesn't . . ." she fidgeted. "Shep doesn't think it's a good idea that we go in. Travis is still pretty mad."

"You mean he doesn't think I should go in," I said. America shrugged sheepishly and then looked to Shepley.

Shepley touched my shoulder. "You didn't do anything wrong, Abby. He just doesn't . . . he doesn't want to see you right now."

"If I didn't do anything wrong, then why doesn't he want to see me?"

"I'm not sure; he won't talk to me about it. I think he's embarrassed that he lost his temper in front of you."

"He lost his temper in front of the entire cafeteria! What do I have to do with it?"

"More than you think," Shepley said, dodging my eyes.

I watched them for a moment, and then pushed past them, running up the stairs. I burst through the doors to find an empty living room. The door to Travis's room was closed, so I knocked.

"Travis? It's me, open up."

"Walk away, Pidge," he called from the other side of the door.

I peeked in to see him sitting on the edge of his bed, facing the window. Toto pawed at his back, unhappy about being ignored.

"What is going on with you, Trav?" I asked. He didn't answer, so I stood beside him, crossing my arms. His jaw tensed, but he no longer wore the frightening expression he had in the cafeteria. He seemed sad. The deep, hopeless kind.

"You're not going to talk to me about this?"

I waited, but he remained quiet. I turned for the door, and he finally sighed. "You know the other day when Brazil mouthed off to me and you rushed to my defense? Well . . . that's what happened. I just got a little carried away."

"You were angry before Chris said anything," I said, returning to sit beside him on the bed.

He continued to stare out the window. "I meant what I said before. You need to walk away, Pidge. God knows I can't walk away from you."

I touched his arm. "You don't want me to leave."

Travis's jaws tensed again, and then he took me under his arm. He paused for a moment and then kissed my forehead, pressing his cheek against my temple. "It doesn't matter how hard I try. You're going to hate me when it's all said and done."

I wrapped my arms around him. "We have to be friends. I won't take no for an answer," I quoted.

His eyebrows pulled in, and then he cradled me to him with both arms, still staring out the window. "I watch you sleeping a lot. You always look so peaceful. I don't have that kind of quiet. I have all this anger and rage boiling inside of me—except when I watch you sleep.

"That's what I was doing when Parker walked in," he continued. "I was awake, and he walked in and just stood there with this shocked look on his face. I knew what he thought, but I didn't set him straight. I didn't explain because I wanted him to think something happened. Now the whole school thinks you were with us both in the same night."

Toto nuzzled his way onto my lap, and I rubbed his ears. Travis reached over to pet him once and then rested his hand on mine. "I'm sorry."

I shrugged. "If he believes the gossip, it's his own fault."

"It's hard to think anything else when he sees us in bed together."

"He knows I'm staying with you. I was fully clothed, for Christ's sake."

Travis sighed. "He was probably too pissed to notice. I know you like him, Pidge. I should have explained. I owe you that much."

"It doesn't matter."

"You're not mad?" he asked, surprised.

"Is that what you're so upset about? You thought I'd be mad at you when you told me the truth?"

"You should be. If someone single-handedly sunk my reputation, I'd be a little pissed."

"You don't care about reputations. What happened to the Travis that doesn't give a shit what anyone thinks?" I teased, nudging him.

"That was before I saw the look on your face when you heard what everyone's saying. I don't want you to get hurt because of me."

"You would never do anything to hurt me."

"I'd rather cut off my arm," he sighed.

He relaxed his cheek against my hair. I didn't have a reply, and Travis seemed to have said everything he needed to, so we sat in silence. Once in a while, Travis would squeeze me tighter to his side. I gripped his shirt, not knowing how else to make him feel better other than to just let him hold me.

When the sun began to set, I heard a faint knock at the door. "Abby?" America's voice sounded small on the other side of the wood.

"Come in, Mare," Travis answered.

America walked in with Shepley, and she smiled at the sight

of us tangled in each other's arms. "We were going to grab a bite to eat. You two feel like making a Pei Wei run?"

"Ugh . . . Asian again, Mare? Really?" Travis asked.

I smiled. He sounded like himself again.

America noticed as well. "Yes, really. You guys coming or not?"

"I'm starving," I said.

"Of course you are, you didn't get to eat lunch," he said, frowning. He stood up, bringing me with him. "Come on. Let's get you some food."

He kept his arm around me and didn't let go until we were in the booth at Pei Wei.

As soon as Travis left for the bathroom, America leaned in. "So? What did he say?"

"Nothing," I shrugged.

She raised an eyebrow. "You were in his room for two hours. He didn't say anything?"

"He usually doesn't when he's that mad," Shepley said.

"He had to have said something," America prodded.

"He said he got a little carried away taking up for me, and that he didn't tell Parker the truth when he walked in. That's it," I said, straightening the salt and pepper.

Shepley shook his head, closing his eyes.

"What, baby?" America asked, sitting taller.

"Travis is," he sighed, rolling his eyes. "Forget it."

America wore a stubborn expression. "Oh, hell no, you can't just—"

She cut off when Travis sat down and swung his arm behind me. "Damn it! The food's not here yet?"

We laughed and joked until the restaurant closed, and then

filed into the car for the ride home. Shepley carried America up the stairs on his back, but Travis stayed behind, tugging on my arm to keep me from following. He looked up at our friends until they disappeared behind the door and then offered a regretful smile. "I owe you an apology for today, so I'm sorry."

"You've already apologized. It's fine."

"No, I apologized for Parker. I don't want you thinking I'm some psycho that goes around attacking people over the tiniest thing," he said, "but I owe you an apology because I didn't defend you for the right reason."

"And that would be . . ." I prompted.

"I lunged at him because he said he wanted to be next in line, not because he was teasing you."

"Insinuating there is a line is plenty reason for you to defend me, Trav."

"That's my point. I was pissed because I took that as him wanting to sleep with you."

After processing what Travis meant, I grabbed the sides of his shirt and pressed my forehead against his chest. "You know what? I don't care," I said, looking up at him. "I don't care what people are saying or that you lost your temper or why you messed up Chris's face. The last thing I want is a bad reputation, but I'm tired of explaining our friendship to everyone. To hell with 'em."

Travis's eyes turned soft, and the corners of his mouth turned up. "Our friendship? Sometimes I wonder if you listen to me at all."

"What do you mean?"

"Let's go in. I'm tired."

I nodded, and he held me against his side until we were

inside the apartment. America and Shepley had already shut themselves in their bedroom, and I slipped in and out of the shower. Travis sat with Toto outside while I dressed in my pajamas, and within half an hour, we were both in bed.

I rested my head on my arm, breathing out a long, relaxing puff of air. "Just two weeks left. What are you going to do for drama when I move back to Morgan?"

"I don't know," he said. I could see his tormented frown, even in the darkness.

"Hey," I touched his arm. "I was kidding."

I watched him for a long time, breathing, blinking, and trying to relax. He fidgeted a bit and then looked over at me. "Do you trust me, Pidge?"

"Yeah, why?"

"C'mere," he said, pulling me against him. I stiffened for a second or two before resting my head on his chest. Whatever was going on with him, he needed me near him, and I couldn't have objected even if I'd wanted to. It felt right lying next to him.

Chapter Nine
Promise

Finch shook his head. "okay, so you're with Parker, or with Travis? I'm confused."

"Parker's not talking to me, so that's sort of up in the air right now," I said, bouncing to readjust my backpack.

He blew out a puff of smoke and then picked a piece of tobacco from his tongue. "So are you with Travis?"

"We're friends, Finch."

"You realize everyone thinks you two are having some sort of freaky friends-with-benefits thing going on that you're not admitting to, right?"

"I don't care. They can think what they want."

"Since when? What happened to the nervous, mysterious, guarded Abby I know and love?"

"She died from the stress of all the rumors and assumptions."

"That's too bad. I'm going to miss pointing and laughing at her."

I smacked Finch's arm, and he laughed. "Good. It's about time you quit pretending," he said.

"What do you mean?"

"Honey, you're talking to someone who's lived most of his life pretending. I spotted you a mile away."

"What are you trying to say, Finch? That I'm a closet lesbian?"

"No, that you're hiding something. The cardigans, the demure sophisticate that goes to fancy restaurants with Parker Hayes . . . that's not you. Either you were a small-town stripper or you've been to rehab. The latter's my guess."

I laughed out loud. "You are a terrible guesser!"

"So what's your secret?"

"If I told you, it wouldn't be a secret, now would it?"

His features sharpened with an impish grin. "I've shown you mine, now show me yours."

"I hate to be the bearer of bad news, but your sexual orientation isn't exactly a secret, Finch."

"Fuck! And I thought I had the mysterious sex-kitten thing going for me," he said, taking another drag.

I cringed before I spoke. "Did you have a good home life, Finch?"

"My mom's great . . . my dad and I had a lot of issues to work out, but we're good, now."

"I had Mick Abernathy for a father."

"Who's that?"

I giggled. "See? It's not a big deal if you don't know who he is."

"Who is he?"

"A mess. The gambling, the drinking, the bad temper . . . it's hereditary in my family. America and I came here so I could start fresh, without the stigma of being the daughter of a drunken has-been."

"A gambling has-been from Wichita?"

"I was born in Nevada. Everything Mick touched turned to gold back then. When I turned thirteen, his luck changed."

"And he blamed you."

"America gave up a lot to come here with me so I could get away, but I get here and walk face-first into Travis."

"And when you look at Travis . . ."

"It's all too familiar."

Finch nodded, flicking his cigarette to the ground. "Shit, Abby. That sucks."

I narrowed my eyes. "If you tell anyone what I just told you, I'll call the Mob. I know some of them, you know."

"Bullshit."

I shrugged. "Believe what you want."

Finch eyed me suspiciously, and then smiled. "You are officially the coolest person I know."

"That's sad, Finch. You should get out more," I said, stopping at the cafeteria entrance.

He pulled my chin up. "It'll all work out. I'm a firm believer in the whole things-happening-for-a-reason adage. You came here, America met Shep, you found your way to the Circle, something about you turned Travis Maddox's world upside down. Think about it," he said, planting a quick kiss on my lips.

"Hey now!" Travis said. He grabbed me by the waist, lifted me off my feet, returning me to the ground behind him. "You're the last person I'd have to worry about that shit from, Finch! Throw me a bone, here!" he teased.

Finch leaned to the side of Travis and winked. "Later, Cookie."

When Travis turned to face me, his smile faded. "What's the frown for?"

I shook my head, trying to let the adrenaline run its course. "I just don't like that nickname. It has some bad memories attached to it."

"Term of endearment from the youth minister?"

"No," I grumbled.

Travis punched his palm. "Do you want me to go beat the piss out of Finch? Teach him a lesson? I'll take him out."

I couldn't help but smile. "If I wanted to take Finch out, I'd just tell him Prada went out of business, and he'd finish the job for me."

Travis laughed, nudging toward the door. "Let's go! I'm wasting away, here!"

We sat at the lunch table together picking on each other with pinches and elbows to the ribs. Travis's mood was as optimistic as on the night I lost the bet. Everyone at the table noticed, and when he instigated a mini–food fight with me, it garnered the attention of those sitting at the tables around us.

I rolled my eyes. "I feel like a zoo animal."

Travis watched me for a moment, noted those staring, and then stood up. "I CAN'T!" he yelled. I stared in awe as the entire room jerked their heads in his direction. Travis bobbed his head a couple of times to a beat in his head.

Shepley closed his eyes. "Oh, no."

Travis smiled. "Get no . . . sa . . . tis . . . faction," he sang. He kept belting out the lyrics as he climbed onto the table as everyone stared.

He pointed to the football players at the end of the table and they smiled and yelled the lyrics back in unison. The whole room clapped to the beat.

Travis sang into his fist and danced past me.

The whole room chanted in harmony.

Travis jerked his hips, and a few whistles and squeals from the girls in the room fired off. He walked by me again, singing the chorus to the other side of the room, the football players his backup singers.

He pointed to his clapping audience. Some people stood and danced with him, but most just watched with amused amazement.

He jumped to the adjacent table and America squealed and clapped, elbowing me. I shook my head; I had died and woken up in *High School Musical*.

The football players were humming the base line, "Na, na, nanana! Na, na, na! Na na, nanana!"

Travis held his fist-microphone high, then jumped down, leaned across the table, and sang into my face.

The room clapped to the beat, and as he hit the final note, he stood smiling and breathless.

The entire room exploded into applause, even a few whistles. I shook my head after he kissed my forehead, and then stood up to take a bow. When he returned to his seat in front of me, he chuckled.

"They're not looking at you, now, are they?" he panted.

"Thanks. You really shouldn't have," I said.

"Abs?"

I looked up to see Parker standing at the end of the table. All eyes were on me once again.

"We need to talk," Parker said, seeming nervous. I looked at America, Travis, and then to Parker. "Please?" he asked, shoving his hands in his pockets.

I nodded, following him outside. He walked past the windows to the privacy of the side of the building. "I didn't mean to draw attention to you again. I know how you hate that."

"Then you might have just called if you wanted to talk," I said.

He nodded, looking to the ground. "It wasn't my intention to find you in the cafeteria. I saw the commotion, and then you, and I just went in. I'm sorry."

I waited, and he spoke again, "I don't know what happened with you and Travis. It's none of my business . . . you and I have only been on a handful of dates. I was upset at first, but then I realized that it wouldn't have bothered me if I didn't have feelings for you."

"I didn't sleep with him, Parker. He held my hair while I hurled a pint of Patrón in his toilet. That's as romantic as it got."

He laughed once. "I don't think we've really gotten a fair shot . . . not with you living with Travis. The truth is, Abby, I like you. I don't know what it is, but I can't seem to stop thinking about you." I smiled and he took my hand, running his finger over my bracelet. "I probably scared you off with this ridiculous present, but I've never been in this situation before. I feel like I'm constantly competing with Travis for your attention."

"You didn't scare me off with the bracelet."

He pressed his lips together. "I'd like to take you out again in a couple of weeks, after your month is up with Travis. Then we can concentrate on getting to know each other without the distraction."

"Fair enough."

He leaned down and closed his eyes, pressing his lips against mine. "I'll call you soon."

I waved goodbye, and then returned to the cafeteria, passing Travis.

He grabbed me, pulling me onto his lap. "Breakin' up is hard to do?"

"He wants to try again when I'm back at Morgan."

"Shit, I'm going to have to think of another bet," he said, pulling my plate in front of me.

The next two weeks flew by. Other than class, I spent every waking moment with Travis, and most of that time we spent alone. He took me to dinner, for drinks and dancing at the Red, bowling; and he was called out to two fights. When we weren't laughing ourselves silly, we were play-wrestling, or snuggling on the couch with Toto, watching a movie. He made a point to ignore every girl that batted an eyelash at him, and everyone talked about the new Travis.

My last night in the apartment, America and Shepley were inexplicably absent, and Travis labored over a special Last Night dinner. He bought wine, set out napkins, and even brought home new silverware for the occasion. He sat our plates on the breakfast bar and pulled his stool to the other side to sit across from me. For the first time, I got the distinct feeling we were on a date.

"This is really good, Trav. You've been holding out on me," I said as I chewed the Cajun chicken pasta he had prepared.

He forced a smile, and I could see he was working hard to keep the conversation light. "If I told you before, you would have expected it every night." His smile faded, and his eyes fell to the table.

I rolled my food around on my plate. "I'm going to miss you, too, Trav."

"You're still gonna come over, right?"

"You know I will. And you'll be at Morgan's, helping me study just like you did before."

"But it won't be the same," he sighed. "You'll be dating Parker, we're going to get busy . . . go in different directions."

"It's not going to change that much."

He managed a single laugh. "Who would have thought from the first time we met that we'd be sitting here? You couldn't have told me three months ago that I'd be this miserable over saying goodbye to a girl."

My stomach sank. "I don't want you to be miserable."

"Then don't go," he said. His expression was so desperate that the guilt formed a lump in my throat.

"I can't move in here, Travis. That's crazy."

"Says who? I just had the best two weeks of my life."

"Me, too."

"Then why do I feel like I'm never gonna see you again?"

I didn't have a reply. His jaws tensed, but he wasn't angry. The urge to go to him grew insistent, so I stood up and walked around the bar, sitting on his lap. He didn't look at me, so I hugged his neck, pressing my cheek against his.

"You're going to realize what a pain in the ass I was, and then you'll forget all about missing me," I said into his ear.

He puffed a breath of air as he rubbed my back. "Promise?"

I leaned back and looked into his eyes, touching each side of his face with my hands. I caressed his jaw with my thumb; his expression was heartbreaking. I closed my eyes and leaned down to kiss the corner of his mouth, but he turned so that I caught more of his lips than I'd intended.

Even though the kiss surprised me, I didn't pull back right away.

Travis kept his lips on mine, but he didn't take it any further.

I finally pulled away, playing it off with a smile. "I have a big day tomorrow. I'm going to clean up the kitchen, and then I'm going to head to bed."

"I'll help you," he said.

We did the dishes together in silence, with Toto asleep at our feet. He dried the last dish and set it in the rack and then led me down the hall, holding my hand a bit too tight. The distance from the mouth of the hallway to his bedroom door seemed to take twice as long. We both knew that goodbye was just a few hours away.

He didn't even try to pretend not to watch this time as I changed into one of his T-shirts for bed. He stripped down to his boxers and climbed under the blanket, waiting for me to join him.

Once I did, Travis flipped off the lamp, and then pulled me against him without permission or apology. He tensed his arms and sighed, and I nestled my face into his neck. I shut my eyes tight, trying to savor the moment. I knew I would wish for that moment back every day of my life, so I lived it with everything I had.

He looked out the window. The trees cast a shadow across his face. Travis clenched his eyes shut, and a sinking feeling settled over me. It was agonizing to see him suffer, knowing that not only was I the cause of it . . . I was the only one that could take it away.

"Trav? Are you okay?" I asked.

There was a long pause before he finally spoke. "I've never been less okay in my life."

I pressed my forehead against his neck, and he squeezed me tighter. "This is silly," I said. "We're going to see each other every day."

"You know that's not true."

The weight of the grief we both felt was crushing, and an irrepressible need came over me to save us both. I lifted my chin, but hesitated; what I was about to do would change everything. I reasoned that Travis didn't see intimacy as anything but a way to pass the time, and I shut my eyes again and swallowed back my fears. I had to do something, knowing we would both lie awake, dreading every passing minute until morning.

My heart pounded as I touched his neck with my lips and then tasted his flesh in a slow, tender kiss. He looked down with surprise, and then his eyes softened with the realization of what I wanted.

He leaned down, pressing his lips against mine with a delicate sweetness. The warmth from his lips traveled all the way to my toes, and I pulled him closer to me. Now that we had taken the first step, I had no intention of stopping there.

I parted my lips, letting Travis's tongue find its way to mine. "I want you," I said.

Suddenly, the kiss slowed, and he tried to pull away. Determined to finish what I had started, my mouth worked against his more anxiously. In reaction, Travis backed away until he was on his knees. I rose with him, keeping our mouths melded together.

He gripped each of my shoulders to hold me at bay. "Wait a

sec," he whispered with an amused smile, breathing hard. "You don't have to do this, Pidge. This isn't what tonight is about."

He was holding back, but I could see it in his eyes that his self-control wouldn't last long.

I leaned in again, and this time his arms gave way just enough for me to brush my lips against his. I looked up at him from under my brows, resolute. It took me a moment to say the words, but I would say them. "Don't make me beg," I whispered against his mouth.

With those four words, his reservations vanished. He kissed me, hard and eager. My fingers ran down the length of his back and settled on the elastic of his boxers, nervously running along the gather of the fabric. His lips grew impatient then, and I fell against the mattress when he crashed into me. His tongue found its way to mine once again, and when I gained the courage to slide my hand between his skin and the boxers, he groaned.

Travis yanked the T-shirt over my head, and then his hand impatiently traveled down my side, gripping my panties and slipping them down my legs with one hand. His mouth returned to mine once more as his hand slid up the inside of my thigh, and I let out a long, faltering breath when his fingers wandered where no man had touched me before. My knees arched and twitched with each movement of his hand, and when I dug my fingers into his flesh, he positioned himself above me.

"Pigeon," he said, panting, "it doesn't have to be tonight. I'll wait until you're ready."

I reached for the top drawer of his nightstand, pulling it open. Feeling the plastic between my fingers, I touched the corner to my mouth, tearing the package open with my teeth.

His free hand left my back, and then he pulled his boxers down, kicking them off as if he couldn't stand them between us.

The package crackled in his fingertips, and after a few moments, I felt him between my thighs. I closed my eyes.

"Look at me, Pigeon."

I peered up at him, and his eyes were intent and soft at the same time. He tilted his head, leaning down to kiss me tenderly, and then his body tensed, pushing himself inside of me in a small, slow movement. When he pulled back, I bit my lip with the discomfort; when he rocked into me again, I clenched my eyes shut with the pain. My thighs tightened around his hips, and he kissed me again.

"Look at me," he whispered.

When I opened my eyes, he pressed inside me again, and I cried out with the wonderful burning it caused. Once I relaxed, the motion of his body against mine was more rhythmic. The nervousness I had felt in the beginning had disappeared, and Travis grabbed at my flesh as if he couldn't get enough. I pulled him into me, and he moaned when the way it felt became too much.

"I've wanted you for so long, Abby. You're all I want," he breathed against my mouth.

He grabbed my thigh with one hand and propped himself up with his elbow, just inches above me. A thin sheet of sweat began to bead on our skin, and I arched my back as his lips traced my jaw and then followed a single line down my neck.

"Travis," I sighed.

When I said his name, he pressed his cheek against mine, and his movements became more rigid. The noises from his throat grew louder, and he finally pressed inside me one last time, groaning and quivering above me.

After a few moments, he relaxed and let his breathing slow.

"That was some first kiss," I said with a tired, content expression.

He scanned my face and smiled. "Your last first kiss."

I was too shocked to reply.

He collapsed beside me on his stomach, stretching one arm across my middle, and resting his forehead against my cheek. I ran my fingers along the bare skin of his back until I heard his breathing even out.

I lay awake for hours, listening to Travis's deep breaths and the wind weaving through the trees outside. America and Shepley came in the front door quietly, and I heard them tiptoe down the hall, murmuring to each other.

We had packed my things earlier in the day, and I flinched at how uncomfortable the morning would be. I had thought once Travis slept with me his curiosity would be satiated, but instead he was talking about forever. My eyes snapped shut with the thought of his expression when he learned that what had happened between us wasn't a beginning, it was closure. I couldn't go down that road, and he would hate me when I told him.

I maneuvered out from under his arm and got dressed, carrying my shoes with me down the hall to Shepley's room. America sat on the bed, and Shepley was pulling off his shirt in front of the closet.

"Everything okay, Abby?" Shepley asked.

"Mare?" I said, signaling for her to join me in the hall.

She nodded, watching me with cautious eyes. "What's going on?"

"I need you to take me to Morgan now. I can't wait 'til tomorrow."

One side of her mouth turned up with a knowing smile. "You never could handle goodbyes."

Shepley and America helped me with my bags, and I stared out the window of America's car on my journey back to Morgan Hall. When we set down the last of the bags in my room, America grabbed me.

"It's going to be so different in the apartment, now."

"Thanks for bringing me home. The sun will be up in a few hours. You better go," I said, squeezing once before letting go.

America didn't look back when she left my room, and I chewed my lip nervously, knowing how angry she would be when she realized what I'd done.

My shirt crackled as I pulled it over my head; the static in the air had intensified with the coming winter. Feeling a bit lost, I curled into a ball underneath my thick comforter and inhaled through my nose; Travis's scent still lingered on my skin.

The bed felt cold and foreign, a sharp contrast to the warmth of Travis's mattress. I had spent thirty days in a cramped apartment with Eastern's most infamous tramp, and after all the bickering and late-night houseguests, it was the only place I wanted to be.

THE PHONE CALLS BEGAN AT EIGHT IN THE MORNING, and then every five minutes for an hour.

"Abby!" Kara groaned. "Answer your stupid phone!"

I reached over and turned it off. It wasn't until I heard the banging on the door that I realized I wouldn't be allowed to spend the day holed up in my room as planned.

Kara yanked on the knob. "What?"

America pushed past her, and stood beside my bed. "What in the hell is going on?" she yelled. Her eyes were red and puffy, and she was still in her pajamas.

I sat up. "What, Mare?"

"Travis is a fucking wreck! He won't talk to us, he's trashed the apartment, threw the stereo across the room . . . Shep can't talk any sense into him!"

I rubbed my eyes with the heels of my hand and blinked. "I don't know."

"Bullshit! You're going to tell me what in the hell is going on, and you're going to tell me now!"

Kara grabbed her shower bag and fled. She slammed the door behind her, and I frowned, afraid she would tell the resident adviser, or worse, the dean of students.

"Keep it down, America, Jesus," I whispered.

She clenched her teeth. "What did you do?"

I assumed he would be upset with me; I didn't know he'd fly into a rage. "I . . . don't know," I swallowed.

"He took a swing at Shep when he found out we helped you leave. Abby! Please tell me!" she pleaded, her eyes glossing over. "It's scaring me!"

The fear in her eyes forced only the partial truth. "I just couldn't say goodbye. You know it's hard for me."

"It's something else, Abby. He's gone fucking nuts! I heard him call your name, and then he stomped all over the apartment looking for you. He barged into Shep's room, demanding to know where you were. Then he tried to call you. Over and over and over," she sighed. "His face was . . . Jesus, Abby. I've never seen him like that.

"He ripped his sheets off the bed, and threw them away, threw his pillows away, shattered his mirror with his fist, kicked his door . . . broke it from the hinges! It was the scariest thing I've ever seen in my life!"

I closed my eyes, forcing the tears that had pooled in my eyes down my cheeks.

America thrust her cell phone at me. "You have to call him. You have to at least tell him you're okay."

"Okay, I'll call him."

She shoved her phone at me again. "No, you're calling him now."

I took her phone in my hand and fingered the buttons, trying to imagine what I could possibly say to him. She snatched it out of my hand, dialed, and then handed it to me. I held the phone to my ear and took a deep breath.

"Mare?" Travis answered, his voice thick with worry.

"It's me."

The line was quiet for several moments before he finally spoke. "What the fuck happened to you last night? I wake up this morning, and you're gone and you . . . you just leave and don't say goodbye? Why?"

"I'm sorry. I—"

"You're sorry? I've been going crazy! You don't answer your phone, you sneak out and—wh-why? I thought we finally had everything figured out!"

"I just needed some time to think."

"About what?" He paused. "Did I . . . did I hurt you?"

"No! It's nothing like that! I'm really, really sorry. I'm sure America told you. I don't do goodbyes."

"I need to see you," he said, his voice desperate.

I sighed. "I have a lot to do today, Trav. I have to unpack and I have piles of laundry."

"You regret it," he said, his voice breaking.

"It's not . . . that's not what it is. We're friends. That's not going to change."

"Friends? Then what the fuck was last night?" he said, anger bleeding through his voice.

I closed my eyes tight. "I know what you want. I just can't . . . do that right now."

"So you just need some time?" he asked in a calmer voice. "You could have told me that. You didn't have to run out on me."

"It just seemed like the easiest way."

"Easier for who?"

"I couldn't sleep. I kept thinking about what it would be like in the morning, loading Mare's car and . . . I couldn't do it, Trav," I said.

"It's bad enough that you aren't going to be here anymore. You can't just drop out of my life."

I forced a smile. "I'll see you tomorrow. I don't want anything to be weird, okay? I just need to sort some stuff out. That's all."

"Okay," he said. "I can do that."

I hung up the phone, and America glared at me. "You slept with him? You bitch! You weren't even going to tell me?"

I rolled my eyes and fell against the pillow. "This isn't about you, Mare. This has just become one convoluted clusterfuck."

"What's so difficult about it? You two should be deliriously happy, not breaking doors and hiding in your room!"

"I can't be with him," I whispered, keeping my eyes on the ceiling.

Her hand covered mine, and she spoke softly. "Travis needs

work. Trust me, I understand any and all reservations you have about him, but look how much he's already changed for you. Think about the last two weeks, Abby. He's not Mick."

"I'm Mick! I get involved with Travis and everything we've worked for . . . poof!" I snapped my fingers. "Just like that!"

"Travis wouldn't let that happen."

"It's not up to him, now is it?"

"You're going to break his heart, Abby. You're going to break his heart! The one girl he trusts enough to fall for, and you're going to nail him to the wall!"

I turned away from her, unable to see the expression that went with the pleading tone in her voice. "I need the happy ending. That's why we came here."

"You don't have to do this. It could work."

"Until my luck runs out."

America threw up her hands, letting them fall into her lap. "Jesus, Abby, not this shit again. We talked about this."

My phone rang, and I looked at the display. "It's Parker."

She shook her head. "We're still talking."

"Hello?" I answered, avoiding America's glare.

"Abs! Day one of freedom! How does it feel?" he said.

"It feels . . . free," I said, unable to muster up any enthusiasm.

"Dinner tomorrow night? I've missed you."

"Yeah," I wiped my nose with my sleeve. "Tomorrow's great."

After I hung up the phone, America frowned. "He's going to ask me when I get back," she said. "He's going to want to know what we talked about. What am I supposed to tell him?"

"Tell him that I'll keep my promise. By this time tomorrow, he won't miss me."

Chapter Ten
Poker Face

Two tables over, one table back. America and Shepley were barely visible from my seat, and I hunched over, watching Travis stare at the empty chair I usually occupied, before sitting at the end of the lunch table. I felt ridiculous for hiding, but I wasn't prepared to sit across from him for an entire hour. When I finished my meal, I took a deep breath and walked outside to where Travis was finishing his cigarette.

I had spent most of the night trying to form a plan to get us to where we were before. If I treated our encounter the way he regarded sex in general, I would have a better chance. The plan risked losing him altogether, but I hoped his enormous male ego would force him to play it off the same way.

"Hey," I said.

He grimaced. "Hey. I thought you'd be at lunch."

"I had to run in and out; I have to study," I shrugged, doing my best impression of casual.

"Need some help?"

"It's Calculus. I think I've got it handled."

"I can just hang out for moral support." He smiled, digging

his hand into his pocket. The solid muscles in his arm tensed with the movement, and the thought of them flexing as he thrust himself inside me replayed with vivid detail in my head.

"Er . . . what?" I asked, disoriented from the sudden erotic thought that had flashed in my mind.

"Are we supposed to pretend the other night never happened?"

"No, why?" I feigned confusion and he sighed, frustrated with my behavior.

"I don't know . . . because I took your virginity?" He leaned toward me, saying the words in a hushed voice.

I rolled my eyes. "I'm sure it's not the first time you've deflowered a virgin, Trav."

Just as I had feared, my casual demeanor made him angry. "As a matter of fact, it was."

"C'mon . . . I said I didn't want any weirdness between us."

Travis took one last drag of his cigarette and flicked it to the ground. "Well, if I've learned anything in the last few days, it's that you don't always get what you want."

"Hey, Abs," Parker said, kissing my cheek.

Travis gave Parker a murderous expression.

"I'll pick you up around six?" Parker said.

I nodded. "Six."

"See you in a bit," he said, continuing to class. I watched him walk away, afraid to endure the consequences of the last ten seconds.

"You're going out with him tonight?" Travis seethed. His jaw was clenched, and I could see it working under his skin.

"I told you he was going to ask me out after I got back to Morgan. He called me yesterday."

"Things have changed a little bit since that conversation, don't you think?"

"Why?"

He walked away from me, and I swallowed, trying to keep the tears at bay. Travis stopped and came back, leaning into my face. "That's why you said I wouldn't miss you after today! You knew I'd find out about you and Parker, and you thought I'd just . . . what? Get over you? Do you not trust me, or am I just not good enough? Tell me, damn it! Tell me what the fuck I did to you to make you do this!"

I stood my ground, staring straight into his eyes. "You didn't do anything to me. Since when is sex so life or death to you?"

"Since it was with you!"

I glanced around, seeing that we were making a scene. People were walking by slowly, staring and whispering to each other. I felt my ears burn, and it spread across my face, making my eyes water.

He closed his eyes, trying to compose himself before he spoke again. "Is that it? You don't think it meant anything to me?"

"You are Travis Maddox."

He shook his head, disgusted. "If I didn't know any better, I'd think you were shoving my past in my face."

"I don't think four weeks ago constitutes the past." His face contorted and I laughed. "I'm kidding! Travis, it's fine. I'm fine, you're fine. There's no need to make a big deal of it."

All emotion disappeared from his face and he took a deep breath through his nose. "I know what you're trying to do." His eyes unfocused for a moment, lost in thought. "I'll just have to prove it to you, then." His eyes narrowed as he looked into mine, as determined as he was before one of his fights. "If you think I'm just going to go back to fucking around, you're wrong. I don't want anyone else. You wanna be friends? Fine, we're friends. But you and I both know that what happened wasn't just sex."

He stormed past me and I closed my eyes, exhaling the breath I didn't know I'd been holding. Travis glanced back at me and then continued to his next class. An escaping tear fell down my cheek and I quickly wiped it away. The curious stares of my classmates targeted my back as I plodded to class.

Parker was on the second row, and I slid into the desk next to him.

A grin stretched across his face. "I'm looking forward to tonight."

I took a breath and smiled, trying to change gears from my conversation with Travis. "What's the plan?"

"Well, I'm all settled in my apartment. I thought we'd have dinner there."

"I'm looking forward to tonight, too," I said, trying to convince myself.

With America's refusal to help, Kara was a reluctant assistant to aid me in choosing a dress for my date with Parker. As soon as I pulled it on over my head, I yanked it off and slipped on a pair of jeans instead. After brooding about my failed plan all afternoon, I couldn't talk myself into dressing up. Keeping the cool weather in mind, I pulled on a thin ivory cashmere sweater over a brown tank top, and waited by the door. When Parker's shiny Porsche pulled in front of Morgan, I pushed my way out the door before he had time to make it up the walk.

"I was going to come get you," he said, disappointed as he held open the door.

"Then I saved you a trip," I said, buckling my seat belt.

He slid in beside me and leaned over, touching each side of my face, kissing me with his plush, soft lips. "Wow," he breathed, "I've missed your mouth."

His breath was minty, his cologne smelled incredible, his hands were warm and soft, and he looked fantastic in his jeans and green dress shirt, but I couldn't shake the feeling that something was missing. That excitement I had in the beginning was noticeably absent, and I silently cursed Travis for taking that away.

I forced a smile. "I'm going to take that as a compliment."

His apartment was exactly as I had imagined: immaculate, with expensive electronics in every corner, and most likely decorated by his mother.

"So? What do you think?" he said, grinning like a child showing off a new toy.

"It's great," I nodded.

His expression changed from playful to intimate, and he pulled me into his arms, kissing my neck. Every muscle in my body tensed. I wanted to be anywhere but in that apartment.

My cell phone rang, and I offered him an apologetic smile before answering.

"How's the date goin', Pidge?"

I turned my back to Parker and whispered into the phone. "What do you need, Travis?" I tried to make my tone sharp, but it was softened by my relief to hear his voice.

"I wanna go bowling tomorrow. I need my partner."

"Bowling? You couldn't have called me later?" I felt like a hypocrite for saying the words, knowing I had hoped for an excuse to keep Parker's lips off of me.

"How am I supposed to know when you're gonna get done? Oh. That didn't come out right . . ." he trailed off, sounding amused with himself.

"I'll call you tomorrow and we can talk about it then, okay?"

"No, it's not okay. You said you wanna be friends, but we can't hang out?" I rolled my eyes, and Travis huffed. "Don't roll your eyes at me. Are you coming or not?"

"How did you know I rolled my eyes? Are you stalking me?" I asked, noting the drawn curtains.

"You always roll your eyes. Yes? No? You're wasting precious date time."

He knew me so well. I fought the urge to ask him to pick me up right then. I couldn't help but smile at the thought.

"Yes!" I said in a hushed voice, trying not to laugh. "I'll go."

"I'll pick you up at seven."

I turned to Parker, grinning like the Cheshire Cat.

"Travis?" he asked with a knowing expression.

"Yes," I frowned, caught.

"You're still just friends?"

"Still just friends," I nodded once.

We sat at the table, eating Chinese takeout. I warmed up to him after a while, and he reminded me of how charming he was. I felt lighter, almost giggly, a marked change from earlier. As hard as I tried to push the thought from my head, I couldn't deny that it was my plans with Travis that had brightened my mood.

After dinner, we sat on the couch to watch a movie, but before the beginning credits were over, Parker had me on my back. I was glad I had chosen to wear jeans; I wouldn't have been able to fend him off as easily in a dress. His lips traveled down to my collarbone, and his hand stopped at my belt. He clumsily worked to pull it open, and once it popped, I slid out from under him to stand up.

"Okay! I think a single is all you'll be hitting tonight," I said, buckling my belt.

"What?"

"First base . . . second base? Never mind. It's late, I better go."

He sat up and gripped my legs. "Don't go, Abs. I don't want you to think that's why I brought you here."

"Isn't it?"

"Of course not," he said, pulling me onto his lap. "You're all I've thought about for two weeks. I apologize for being impatient."

He kissed my cheek, and I leaned into him, smiling when his breath tickled my neck. I turned to him and pressed my lips against his, trying my hardest to feel something—but I didn't. I pulled away from him and sighed.

Parker furrowed his brow. "I said I was sorry."

"I said it was late."

We drove to Morgan, and Parker squeezed my hand after he kissed me goodnight. "Let's try again. Biasetti's tomorrow?"

I pressed my lips together. "I'm bowling with Travis tomorrow."

"Wednesday, then?"

"Wednesday's great," I said, offering a contrived smile.

Parker shifted in his seat. He was working up to something. "Abby? There's a date party in a couple weekends at the House . . ."

I inwardly cringed, dreading the discussion we would inevitably have.

"What?" he asked, chuckling nervously.

"I can't go with you," I said, letting myself out of the car.

He followed, meeting me at the Morgan entrance. "You have plans?"

I winced. "Travis already asked me."

"Travis asked you what?"

"To the date party," I explained, a bit frustrated.

Parker's face flushed, and he shifted his weight. "You're going to the date party with Travis? He doesn't go to those things. And you're just friends. It doesn't make sense for you to go with him."

"America wouldn't go with Shep unless I went."

He relaxed. "Then you can go with me," he smiled, intertwining his fingers in mine.

I grimaced at his solution. "I can't cancel with Travis and then go with you."

"I don't see the problem," he shrugged. "You can be there for America, and Travis will get out of having to go. He is a staunch advocate for doing away with date parties. He thinks it's a platform for our girlfriends to force us to declare a relationship."

"It was me that didn't want to go. He talked me into it."

"Now you have an excuse," he shrugged. He was maddeningly confident that I was going to change my mind.

"I didn't want to go at all."

Parker's patience had run out. "I just want to be clear; you don't want to go to the date party. Travis wants to go, he asked you, and you won't cancel with him to go with me, even though you didn't want to go in the first place?"

I had a hard time meeting his glare. "I can't do that to him, Parker, I'm sorry."

"Do you understand what a date party is? It's something you go to with your boyfriend."

His patronizing tone made any empathy I'd felt for him disappear. "Well, I don't have a boyfriend, so technically I shouldn't go at all."

"I thought we were going to try again. I thought we had something."

"I am trying."

"What do you expect me to do? Sit at home alone while you're at my fraternity's date party with someone else? Should I ask another girl?"

"You can do what you want," I said, irritated with his threat.

He looked up and shook his head. "I don't want to ask another girl."

"I don't expect you not to go to your own party. I'll see you there."

"You want me to ask someone else? And you're going with Travis. Do you not see how completely absurd that is?"

I crossed my arms, ready for a fight. "I told him I would go before you and I ever went out, Parker. I can't cancel on him."

"You can't, or you don't want to?"

"Same difference. I'm sorry that you don't understand." I pulled the door open to Morgan, and Parker put his hand on mine.

"All right," he sighed in resignation. "This is obviously an issue I'm going to have to work through. Travis is one of your best friends; I do understand that. I don't want it to affect our relationship. Okay?"

"Okay," I said, nodding.

He opened the door and gestured to me to walk through,

kissing my cheek before I walked inside. "See you Wednesday at six?"

"Six," I said, waving as I walked up the stairs.

America was walking out of the shower room when I turned the corner, and her eyes brightened when she recognized me. "Hey, chickie! How'd it go?"

"It went," I said, deflated.

"Uh-oh."

"Don't tell Travis, okay?"

She huffed. "I won't. What happened?"

"Parker asked me to the date party."

America tightened her towel. "You're not bailing on Trav, are you?"

"No, and Parker's not happy about it."

"Understandable," she said, nodding. "It's also too damn bad."

America pulled the strands of her long, wet hair over one shoulder, and drops of water trickled down her bare skin. She was a walking contradiction. She applied to Eastern so we could move together. She was my self-proclaimed conscience, intent on stepping in when I gave in to my imbedded tendencies to fly off track. It went against everything we talked about for me to get involved with Travis, and she had become his overly enthusiastic cheerleader.

I leaned against the wall. "Would you be mad if I didn't go at all?"

"No, I would be unbelievably and irrevocably pissed off. That's grounds for a full-blown cat fight, Abby."

"Then I guess I'm going," I said, shoving my key in the lock. My cell phone rang, and a picture of Travis making a funny face appeared on the display. "Hello?"

"You home yet?"

"Yeah, he dropped me off about five minutes ago."

"I'll be there in five more."

"Wait! Travis?" I said after he'd hung up.

America laughed. "You just had a disappointing date with Parker, and you smiled when Travis called. Are you really that dense?"

"I didn't smile," I protested. "He's coming here. Will you meet him outside and tell him I went to bed?"

"You did, too, and no . . . go tell him yourself."

"Yes, Mare, me going out there to tell him I'm in bed is so gonna work." She turned her back to me, walking to her room. I threw up my hands, letting them fall to my thighs. "Mare! Please?"

"Have fun, Abby," she smiled, disappearing into her room.

I walked down the stairs to see Travis on his motorcycle, parked at the front steps. He wore a white T-shirt with black artwork, setting off the tattoos on his arms.

"Aren't you cold?" I asked, tugging my jacket tighter.

"You look nice. Did you have a good time?"

"Uh . . . yeah, thanks," I said, distracted. "What are you doing here?"

He pulled back the throttle, and the engine snarled. "I was going to take a ride to clear my head. I want you to come with me."

"It's cold, Trav."

"You want me to go get Shep's car?"

"We're going bowling tomorrow. Can't you wait until then?"

"I went from being with you every second of the day to seeing you for ten minutes if I'm lucky."

I smiled and shook my head. "It's only been two days, Trav."

"I miss you. Get your ass on the seat and let's go."

I couldn't argue. I missed him, too. More than I would ever admit to him. I zipped up my jacket and climbed on behind him, slipping my fingers through the belt loops of his jeans. He pulled my wrists to his chest and then folded them across one another. Once he was satisfied that I was holding him tightly enough, he took off, racing down the road.

I rested my cheek against his back and closed my eyes, breathing in his scent. It reminded me of his apartment and his sheets and the way he smelled when he walked around with a towel around his waist. The city blurred past us, and I didn't care how fast he was driving or how cold the wind was as it whipped across my skin; I wasn't even paying attention to where we were. The only thing I could think about was his body against mine. We had no destination or time frame, and we drove the streets long after they had been abandoned by everyone but us.

Travis pulled into a gas station and parked. "You want anything?" he asked.

I shook my head, climbing off the bike to stretch my legs. He watched me rake my fingers through the tangles in my hair and smiled.

"Quit it. You're fucking beautiful."

"Just point me to the nearest eighties rock video," I said.

He laughed and then yawned, swatting at the moths that buzzed around him. The nozzle clicked, sounding louder than it should in the quiet night. We seemed to be the only two people on earth.

I pulled out my cell phone to check the time. "Oh my God, Trav. It's three in the morning."

"You wanna go back?" he asked, his face shadowed with disappointment.

I pressed my lips together. "We better."

"We're still going bowling tonight?"

"I told you I would."

"And you're still going to Sig Tau with me in a couple weeks, right?"

"Are you insinuating that I don't follow through? I find that a little insulting."

He pulled the nozzle from his tank and hooked it on its base. "I just never know what you're going to do anymore."

He sat on his bike and helped me to climb on behind him. I hooked my fingers in his belt loops and then thought better of it, wrapping my arms around him.

He sighed and leaned the bike upright, reluctant to start the engine. His knuckles turned white as he gripped the handlebars. He took a breath, beginning to speak, and then shook his head.

"You're important to me, you know," I said, squeezing him.

"I don't understand you, Pigeon. I thought I knew women, but you're so fucking confusing I don't know which way is up."

"I don't understand you, either. You're supposed to be Eastern's ladies' man. I'm not getting the full freshmen experience they promised in the brochure," I teased.

"Well, that's a first. I've never had a girl sleep with me to get me to leave her alone," he said, keeping his back to me.

"That's not what it was, Travis," I lied, ashamed that he had guessed my intentions without realizing how right he was.

He shook his head and started the engine, pulling out onto the street. He drove uncharacteristically slow, stopping at all the yellow lights, taking the long way to campus.

When we pulled in front of the entrance to Morgan Hall, the same sadness I felt the night I left the apartment consumed me. It was ridiculous to be so emotional, but each time I did something to push him away, I was terrified it would work.

He walked me to the door, and I pulled out my keys, avoiding his eyes. As I fumbled with the metal in my hand, his hand was suddenly at my chin, his thumb softly touching my lips.

"Did he kiss you?" he asked.

I pulled away, surprised that his fingers caused a burning feeling that seared every nerve from my mouth to my toes. "You really know how to screw up a perfect night, don't you?"

"You thought it was perfect, huh? Does that mean you had a good time?"

"I always do when I'm with you."

He looked to the ground and his eyebrows pulled together. "Did he kiss you?"

"Yes," I sighed, irritated.

His eyes closed tight. "Is that all?"

"That is none of your business!" I said, yanking open the door.

Travis pushed it closed and stood in my way, his expression apologetic. "I need to know."

"No you don't! Move, Travis!"

"Pigeon . . ."

"You think because I'm no longer a virgin, I'll screw anyone that'll have me? Thanks!" I said, shoving him.

"I didn't say that, damn it! Is it too much to ask for a little peace of mind?"

"Why would it give you peace of mind to know if I'm sleeping with Parker?"

"How can you not know? It's obvious to everyone else but you!" he said, exasperated.

"I guess I'm just an idiot, then. You're on a roll tonight, Trav," I said, reaching for the door handle.

He gripped my shoulders. "The way I feel about you . . . it's crazy."

"You got the crazy part right," I snapped, pulling away from him.

"I practiced this in my head the whole time we were on the bike, so just hear me out," he said.

"Travis—"

"I know we're fucked up, all right? I'm impulsive and hot-tempered, and you get under my skin like no one else. You act like you hate me one minute, and then you need me the next. I never get anything right, and I don't deserve you . . . but I fucking love you, Abby. I love you more than I've loved anyone or anything, ever. When you're around, I don't need booze or money or the fighting or the one-night stands . . . all I need is you. You're all I think about. You're all I dream about. You're all I want."

My plan to feign ignorance was an epic fail. I couldn't pretend to be impervious when he had laid all of his cards on the table. When we met, something inside both of us had changed, and whatever that was, it made us need each other. For reasons unknown to me, I was his exception, and as much as I had tried to fight my feelings, he was mine.

He shook his head, cupped each side of my face, and looked into my eyes. "Did you sleep with him?"

Hot tears filled my eyes as I shook my head no. He slammed his lips against mine, and his tongue entered my mouth without hesitation. Unable to control myself, I gripped his shirt in my fists, and pulled him to me. He hummed in his amazing deep voice and gripped me so tight that it was difficult to breathe.

He pulled back, breathless. "Call Parker. Tell him you don't wanna see him anymore. Tell him you're with me."

I closed my eyes. "I can't be with you, Travis."

"Why the hell not?" he said, letting go.

I shook my head, afraid of his reaction to the truth.

He laughed once. "Unbelievable. The one girl I want, and she doesn't want me."

I swallowed, knowing I would have to get closer to the truth than I had in months. "When America and I moved out here, it was with the understanding that my life was going to turn out a certain way. Or that it wouldn't turn out a certain way. The fighting, the gambling, the drinking . . . it's what I left behind. When I'm around you . . . it's all right there for me in an irresistible, tattooed package. I didn't move hundreds of miles away to live it all over again."

He pulled my chin up so that I would face him. "I know you deserve better than me. You think I don't know that? But if there was any woman made for me . . . it's you. I'll do whatever I have to do, Pidge. Do you hear me? I'll do anything."

I turned away from his grip, ashamed that I couldn't tell him the truth. I was the one that wasn't good enough. I would be the one to ruin everything, to ruin him. He would hate me one day, and I couldn't see the look in his eye when he came to that conclusion.

He held the door shut with his hand. "I'll stop fighting the second I graduate. I won't drink a single drop again. I'll give you the happy ever after, Pigeon. If you just believe in me, I can do it."

"I don't want you to change."

"Then tell me what to do. Tell me and I'll do it," he pleaded.

Any thoughts of being with Parker were long gone, and I knew it was because of my feelings for Travis. I thought about the different paths my life would take from that moment— trusting Travis with a leap of faith and risking the unknown, or pushing him away and knowing exactly where I would end up, which included a life without him—either decision terrified me.

"Can I borrow your phone?" I asked.

Travis pulled his brows together, confused. "Sure," he said, pulling his phone from his pocket, handing it to me.

I dialed, and then closed my eyes as it rang in my ear.

"Travis? What the hell? Do you know what time it is?" Parker answered. His voice was deep and raspy, and I instantly felt my heart vibrating in my chest. It hadn't occurred to me that he would know I had called from Travis's phone.

My next words somehow found their way to my trembling lips. "I'm sorry for calling you so early, but this couldn't wait. I . . . can't go to dinner with you on Wednesday."

"It's almost four in the morning, Abby. What's going on?"

"I can't see you at all, actually."

"Abs . . ."

"I'm . . . pretty sure I'm in love with Travis," I said, bracing for his reaction.

After a few moments of shocked silence, he hung up in my ear.

My eyes still focused on the pavement, I handed Travis his

phone and then reluctantly peered up at his expression. A combination of confusion, shock, and adoration scrolled across his face.

"He hung up," I grimaced.

He scanned my face with careful hope in his eyes. "You love me?"

"It's the tattoos," I shrugged.

A wide smile stretched across his face, making his dimple sink into his cheek. "Come home with me," he said, enveloping me in his arms.

My eyebrows shot up. "You said all that to get me in bed? I must have made quite an impression."

"The only thing I'm thinking about right now is holding you in my arms all night."

"Let's go," I said.

Despite the excessive speed and the shortcuts, the ride to the apartment seemed endless. When we finally arrived, Travis carried me up the stairs. I giggled against his lips as he fumbled to unlock the door. When he set me on my feet and closed the door behind us, he let out a long, relieved sigh.

"It hasn't seemed like home since you left," he said, kissing my lips.

Toto scampered down the hall and wagged his tiny tail, pawing at my legs. I cooed at him as I lifted him off the floor.

Shepley's bed squeaked, and then his feet stomped across the floor. His door flew open as he squinted from the light. "Fuck no, Trav, you're not pulling this shit! You're in love with Ab . . ."—his eyes focused and he recognized his mistake— ". . . by. Hey, Abby."

"Hey, Shep," I said, setting Toto on the floor.

Travis pulled me past his still-shocked cousin and kicked the door shut behind us, pulling me into his arms and kissing me without a second thought, as if we had done it a million times before. I pulled his shirt over his head, and he slipped my jacket off my shoulders. I stopped kissing him long enough to remove my sweater and tank top and then crashed into him again. We undressed each other, and within seconds he lowered me to his mattress. I reached above my head to pull open the drawer and plunged my hand inside, searching for anything that crackled.

"Shit," he said, panting and frustrated. "I got rid of them."

"What? All of them?" I breathed.

"I thought you didn't . . . if I wasn't with you, I wasn't going to need them."

"You're kidding me!" I said, letting my head fall against the headboard.

His forehead fell against my chest. "Consider yourself the opposite of a foregone conclusion."

I smiled and kissed him. "You've never been with anyone without one?"

He shook his head. "Never." I looked around for a moment, lost in thought. He laughed once at my expression. "What are you doing?

"Ssh, I'm counting." Travis watched me for a moment and then leaned down to kiss my neck. "I can't concentrate while you're doing tha . . ."—I sighed—"the twenty-fifth and two days . . ." I breathed.

Travis chuckled. "What the hell are you talkin' about?"

"We're good," I said, sliding down so I was directly beneath him.

He pressed his chest against mine, and kissed me tenderly. "Are you sure?"

I let my hands glide from his shoulders to his backside and pulled him against me. He closed his eyes and let out a long, deep groan.

"Oh my God, Abby," he breathed. He rocked into me again, another hum emanating from his throat. "Holy shit, you feel amazing."

"Is it different?"

He looked into my eyes. "It's different with you, anyway, but"—he took in a deep breath and tensed again, closing his eyes for a moment—"I'm never going to be the same after this."

His lips searched every inch of my neck, and when he found his way to my mouth, I sunk my fingertips into the muscles of his shoulders, losing myself in the intensity of the kiss.

Travis brought my hands above my head and intertwined his fingers with mine, squeezing my hands with each thrust. His movements became a bit rougher, and I dug my nails into his hands, my insides tensing with incredible force.

I cried out, biting my lip and clenching my eyes shut.

"Abby," he whispered, sounding conflicted, "I need a . . . I need to . . ."

"Don't stop," I begged.

He rocked into me again, groaning so loudly that I covered his mouth. After a few labored breaths, he looked into my eyes and then kissed me over and over. His hands cupped each side of my face and then he kissed me again, slower, more tender. He touched his lips to mine, and then my cheeks, my forehead, my nose, and then finally returned to my lips.

I smiled and sighed, exhaustion setting in. Travis pulled me next to him, situating the covers over us. I rested my cheek against his chest, and he kissed my forehead once more, locking his fingers together behind me.

"Don't leave this time, okay? I wanna wake up just like this in the morning."

I kissed his chest, feeling guilty that he had to ask. "I'm not going anywhere."

Chapter Eleven
Jealousy

I AWOKE ON MY STOMACH, NAKED AND TANGLED IN TRA-vis Maddox's sheets. I kept my eyes closed, feeling his fingers caressing my arm and back.

He exhaled with a deep, contented sigh, speaking in a hushed voice. "I love you, Abby. I'm going to make you happy, I swear it."

The bed concaved as he shifted, and then his lips were on my back in slow, small kisses. I remained still, and just as he had made his way up to the skin just below my ear, he left me to walk across the room. His footsteps leisurely plodded down the hall, and the pipes whined with the water pressure of the shower.

I opened my eyes and sat up, stretching. Every muscle in my body ached, muscles that I never knew I had. I held the sheet to my chest, looking out the window, watching the yellow and red leaves spiral from their branches to the ground.

His cell phone vibrated somewhere on the floor, and after clumsily searching the crumpled clothes next to the bed, I found it in his jeans pocket. The display was lit with only a number, no name.

"Hello?"

"Is uh . . . is Travis there?" a woman asked.

"He's in the shower, can I take a message?"

"Of course he is. Tell him that Megan called, would ya?"

Travis walked in, tightening his towel around his water-splotched waist, and smiled as I held out his phone.

"It's for you," I said.

He kissed me before looking at the display, and then shook his head. "Yeah? It was my girlfriend. What do you need, Megan?" He listened for a moment and then smiled, "Well, Pigeon's special, what can I say?" After a long pause, he rolled his eyes. I could only imagine what she was saying. "Don't be a bitch, Megan. Listen, you can't call my phone anymore . . . Well, love'll do that to ya," he said, looking at me with a soft expression. "Yes, with Abby. I mean it, Meg, no more phone calls . . . Later."

He tossed his phone on the bed, and then sat beside me. "She was a little pissy. Did she say anything to you?"

"No, she just asked for you."

"I erased the few numbers I had on my phone, but I guess that doesn't stop them from calling me. If they don't figure it out on their own, I'll set them straight."

He watched me expectantly, and I couldn't help but smile. I had never seen this side of him. "I trust you, you know."

He pressed his lips to mine. "I wouldn't blame you if you expected me to earn it."

"I've got to get in the shower. I've already missed one class."

"See? I'm a good influence already."

I stood up, and he tugged on the sheet. "Megan said there's a Halloween party this weekend at the Red Door. I went with her last year, it was pretty fun."

"I'm sure it was," I said, raising an eyebrow.

"I just mean a lot of people come out. They have a pool tournament and cheap drinks . . . wanna go?"

"I'm not really . . . I don't do the dress-up thing. I never have."

"I don't, either. I just go," he shrugged.

"Are we still going bowling tonight?" I asked, wondering if the invitation was just to get some alone time with me that he no longer needed.

"Well, hell yeah! I'm gonna kick your ass, too!"

I narrowed my eyes at him. "Not this time you're not. I have a new superpower."

He laughed. "And what's that? Harsh language?"

I leaned over to kiss his neck once, and then ran my tongue up to his ear, kissing his earlobe. He froze in place.

"Distraction," I breathed into his ear.

He grabbed my arms and flipped me onto my back. "You're going to miss another class."

AFTER FINALLY TALKING HIM INTO LEAVING THE APART-ment long enough to attend history class, we raced to campus and slid into our seats just before Professor Chaney began. Travis turned his red baseball cap backward to plant a kiss on my lips in full view of everyone in the classroom.

On our way to the cafeteria, he took my hand in his, intertwining our fingers as we walked. He seemed so proud to be holding my hand, announcing to the world that we were finally together. Finch noticed, looking at our hands and then to me with a ridiculous grin. He wasn't the only one; our simple display of affection generated stares and murmuring from everyone we passed.

At the door of the cafeteria, Travis blew out his last puff of smoke, looking to me when I hesitated. America and Shepley were already inside, and Finch had lit another cigarette, leaving me to go in with Travis alone. I was certain the gossip had soared to a new level since Travis had kissed me in full view of everyone in our history class, and I dreaded walking out onto the stage the cafeteria presented.

"What, Pigeon?" he said, tugging on my hand.

"Everyone is watching us."

He pulled my hand to his mouth and kissed my fingers. "They'll get over it. It's just the initial shock. Remember when we first started hanging out? Their curiosity died down after a while and they got used to seeing us together. C'mon," he said, pulling me through the door.

One of the reasons I had chosen Eastern U was its modest population, but the exaggerated interest in scandal that came with it was at times exhausting. It was a running joke; everyone was aware of how ridiculous the rumor mill was, and yet they all shamelessly participated in it.

We sat down in our usual spots with our food. America smiled at me with a knowing expression. She chatted as if everything was normal, but the football players at the other end of the table were staring at me like I was on fire.

Travis tapped my apple with his fork. "You gonna eat that, Pidge?"

"No, you can have it, baby."

Heat consumed my ears when America's head jerked to look at me.

"It just came out," I said, shaking my head. I peeked up at Travis, whose expression was a mixture of amusement and adoration.

We had exchanged the term a few times that morning, and it hadn't occurred to me that it was new to everyone else until it tumbled from my mouth.

"You two have just reached the level of annoyingly cute," America grinned.

Shepley tapped my shoulder. "You staying over tonight?" he asked, his words garbled amid the bread in his mouth. "I promise I won't come out of my room cussing at you."

"You were defending my honor, Shep. You're forgiven," I said.

Travis took a bite of the apple and chewed, looking as happy as I'd ever seen him. The peace in his eyes had returned, and even as the dozens of people watched our every move, everything felt . . . right.

I thought of all the times I had insisted being with Travis was the wrong decision and how much time I had wasted fighting my feelings for him. Looking across the table at his soft brown eyes and the dimple dancing in his cheek as he chewed, I couldn't remember what I was so worried about.

"He looks awful happy. Did you finally give it up, Abby?" Chris said, elbowing his teammates.

"You're not very smart, are ya, Jenks?" Shepley said, frowning.

The blood instantly rose to my cheeks, and I looked to Travis who had murder in his eyes. My embarrassment took a backseat to Travis's anger, and I shook my head dismissively. "Just ignore him."

After another tense moment, his shoulders relaxed a bit, and he nodded once, taking a deep breath. After a few seconds, he winked at me.

I reached my hand across the table, sliding my fingers into his. "You meant what you said last night, didn't you?"

He began to speak, but Chris's laughter filled the cafeteria. "Holy God! Travis Maddox is whipped?"

"Did you mean it when you said you didn't want me to change?" he asked, squeezing my hand.

I looked down at Chris laughing to his teammates and then turned to Travis. "Absolutely. Teach that asshole some manners."

A mischievous grin spread across his face, and he walked down to the end of the table where Chris sat. Silence spread across the room, and Chris swallowed back his laughter.

"Hey, I was just givin' you a hard time, Travis," he said, looking up at him.

"Apologize to Pidge," Travis said, glowering down at him.

Chris looked down at me with a nervous grin. "I . . . I was just kidding, Abby. I'm sorry."

I glared at him as he looked up to Travis for approval. When Travis walked away, Chris snickered and then whispered something to Brazil. My heart began to pound when I saw Travis stop in his tracks and ball his hands into fists at his side.

Brazil shook his head and huffed in an exasperated sigh. "Just remember when you wake up, Chris . . . that you bring it on yourself."

Travis lifted Finch's tray off the table and swung it into Chris's face, knocking him off his chair. Chris tried to scramble under the table, but Travis pulled him out by his legs and then began to whale on him.

Chris curled into a ball, and then Travis kicked him in the back. Chris arched and turned, holding his hands out, allowing Travis to land several punches to his face. The blood began to flow, and Travis stood up, winded.

"If you even look at her, you piece of shit, I'll break your fuckin' jaw!" Travis yelled. I winced when he kicked Chris in the leg one last time.

The women working in the cafeteria scampered out, shocked at the bloody mess on the floor.

"Sorry," Travis said, wiping Chris's blood from his cheek.

Some of the students stood up to get a better look; others remained seated, watching with mild amusement. The football team simply stared at Chris's limp body on the floor, shaking their heads.

Travis turned, and Shepley stood, grabbing both my arm and America's hand, and pulled us out the door behind his cousin. We walked the short distance to Morgan Hall, and America and I sat on the front steps, watching Travis pace back and forth.

"You okay, Trav?" Shepley asked.

"Just . . . give me a minute," he said, putting his hands low on his hips as he walked.

Shepley shoved his hands into his pockets. "I'm surprised you stopped."

"Pidge said to teach him some manners, Shep, not kill him. It took everything I had to quit when I did."

America slipped on her large, square sunglasses to look up at Travis. "What did Chris say that set you off, anyway?"

"Something he'll never say again," Travis seethed.

America looked to Shepley, who shrugged. "I didn't hear it."

Travis's hands balled into fists again. "I'm goin' back in there."

Shepley touched Travis's shoulder. "Your girl's out here. You don't need to go back in there."

Travis looked at me, forcing himself to stay calm. "He said . . . everyone thinks Pidge has . . . Jesus, I can't even say it."

"Just say it already," America muttered, picking at her nails.

Finch walked up behind Travis, clearly thrilled by all the excitement. "Every straight guy at Eastern wants to try her out because she landed the unattainable Travis Maddox," he shrugged. "That's what they're saying in there now, at least."

Travis shouldered past Finch, heading for the cafeteria. Shepley bolted after him, grabbing his arm. My hands flew to my mouth when Travis swung, and Shepley ducked. My eyes darted to America who was unaffected, accustomed to their routine.

I could think of only one thing to do to stop him. I scrambled off the steps, wheeling around, directly in his path. I jumped on him, wrapping my legs around his waist, and he gripped my thighs as I grabbed each side of his face, planting a long, deep kiss on his mouth. I could feel his anger melt away as he kissed me, and when I pulled away, I knew I had won.

"We don't care what they think, remember? You can't start now," I said, smiling with confidence. I had more of an effect on him than I ever thought possible.

"I can't let them talk about you like that, Pigeon," he said with a frustrated frown, lowering me to my feet.

I slid my arms under his, interlocking my fingers behind his back. "Like what? They think I have something special because you've never settled down before. Do you disagree?"

"Hell no, I just can't stand the thought of every guy in this school wanting to bag you because of it." He pressed his forehead against mine. "This is going to make me crazy. I can already tell."

"Don't let them get to you, Travis," Shepley said. "You can't fight everybody."

Travis sighed. "Everybody. How would you feel if everybody thought about America like that?"

"Who says they don't?" America said, offended. We all laughed, and America made a face. "I wasn't kidding."

Shepley pulled her to her feet by her hands and kissed her cheek. "We know, baby. I gave up being jealous a long time ago. I'd never have time to do anything else."

America smiled in appreciation, and then hugged him. Shepley had an uncanny ability to make everyone around him feel at ease, no doubt the result from growing up around Travis and his brothers. It was probably more of a defense mechanism than anything.

Travis nuzzled my ear, and I giggled until I saw Parker approach. The same sense of urgency I'd felt when Travis wanted to return to the cafeteria overcame me, and I instantly let go of Travis to quickly walk the ten or so feet to intercept Parker.

"I need to talk to you," he said.

I glanced behind me, and then shook my head as a warning.

"Now is not a good time, Parker. It's a really, really bad time, actually. Travis and Chris got into it at lunch, and he's still a little raw. You need to go."

Parker eyed Travis, and then returned his attention to me, determined. "I just heard what happened in the cafeteria. I don't think you realize what you're getting yourself into. Travis is bad news, Abby. Everyone knows it. No one is talking about how great it is that you've turned him around . . . they're all waiting for him to do what he does best. I don't know what he's told you, but you have no clue what kind of person he is."

I felt Travis's hands on my shoulders. "Why don't you tell her, then?"

Parker shifted nervously. "Do you know how many humiliated girls I've taken home from parties after they've spent a few hours alone in a room with him? He's going to hurt you."

Travis's fingers tightened in reaction, and I rested my hand on his until he relaxed. "You should go, Parker."

"You should listen to what I'm saying, Abs."

"Don't fucking call her that," Travis growled.

Parker didn't take his eyes from mine. "I'm worried about you."

"I appreciate it, but it's unnecessary."

Parker shook his head. "He saw you as a long-term challenge, Abby. He has you thinking you're different from the other girls so he could get you in the sack. He's going to get tired of you. He has the attention span of a toddler."

Travis stepped around me, standing so close to Parker that their noses nearly touched. "I let you have your say. My patience has run out." Parker tried to look at me, but Travis leaned in his way. "Don't you fucking look at her. Look at me, you spoiled shit stain." Parker focused on Travis's eyes and waited. "If you so much as breathe in her direction, I'll make sure you'll be limping through med school."

Parker took a few steps back until I was in his line of sight. "I thought you were smarter than that," he said, shaking his head before turning away.

Travis watched him leave, and then turned around, his eyes searching mine. "You know that's a bunch of bullshit, right? It's not true."

"I'm sure that's what everyone is thinking," I grumbled, noting the interest of those walking by.

"Then I'll prove them wrong."

AS THE WEEK WORE ON, TRAVIS TOOK HIS PROMISE VERY seriously. He no longer humored the girls that stopped him on his way to and from class, and at times he was rude about it. By the time we walked into the Red for the Halloween party, I was a little nervous about how he planned to keep the intoxicated coeds away.

America, Finch, and I sat at a nearby table while watching Shepley and Travis play pool against two of their Sig Tau brothers.

"Go, baby!" America called, standing up on the rungs of her stool.

Shepley winked at her and then took his shot, sinking it into the far right pocket.

"Wooo!" she squealed.

A trio of women dressed as Charlie's Angels approached Travis while he waited his turn, and I smiled as he tried his best to ignore them. When one of them traced the line of one of his tattoos, Travis pulled his arm away. He waved her off so he could make a shot, and she pouted to her friends.

"Can you believe how ridiculous they are? The girls here are shameless," America said.

Finch shook his head in awe. "It's Travis. I think it's the bad-boy thing. They either want to save him or think they're immune to his wicked ways. I'm not sure which."

"It's probably both," I laughed, giggling at the girls waiting for Travis to pay them attention. "Can you imagine hoping you're the one he'll pick? Knowing you'll be used for sex?"

"Daddy issues," America said, taking a sip of her drink.

Finch put out his cigarette and tugged on our dresses. "Come on, girls! The Finch wants to dance!"

"Only if you promise not to call yourself that ever again," America said.

Finch jutted out his bottom lip, and America smiled. "Come on, Abby. You don't wanna make Finch cry, do you?"

We joined the policemen and vampires on the dance floor, and Finch broke out his Timberlake moves. I glanced at Travis over my shoulder and caught him watching me from the corner of his eye, pretending to watch Shepley sink the eight ball for the game. Shepley collected their winnings, and Travis walked to the long, shallow table that bordered the dance floor, taking a drink. Finch flailed about on the dance floor, finally sandwiching himself between America and me. Travis rolled his eyes, chuckling as he returned to our table with Shepley.

"I'm going to get another drink. Want anything?" America shouted over the music.

"I'll go with you," I said, looking to Finch and pointing at the bar.

Finch shook his head and continued to dance. America and I shouldered through the crowd to the bar. The bartenders were overwhelmed, so we settled in for a long wait.

"The boys are making a killing tonight," America said.

I leaned into her ear. "Why anyone bets against Shep I'll never understand."

"For the same reason they bet against Travis. They're idiots," she smiled.

A man in a toga leaned against the bar beside America and smiled. "What are you ladies drinking this evening?"

"We buy our own beverages, thanks," America said, facing forward.

"I'm Mike," he said, and then pointed to his friend, "This is Logan."

I smiled politely, looking to America, who made her best go-away expression. The bartender took our order and then nodded to the men behind us, turning to make America's drink. She brought over a square glass full of pink, frothy liquid and three beers. Mike handed her some money, and she nodded.

"This is something else," Mike said, scanning the crowd.

"Yeah," America said, annoyed.

"I saw you dancing out there," Logan said to me, nodding to the dance floor. "You looked good."

"Uh . . . thanks," I said, trying to remain polite, wary that Travis was just a few yards away.

"You wanna dance?" he asked.

I shook my head. "No, thanks. I'm here with my—"

"Boyfriend," Travis said, appearing out of nowhere. He

glared at the men standing in front of us, and they backed away a bit, clearly intimidated.

America couldn't contain her smug smile as Shepley wrapped his arm around her. Travis nodded across the room. "Run along, now."

The men glanced at America and me and then took a few cautious steps backward before retreating behind the safety of the crowd.

Shepley kissed America. "I can't take you anywhere!" She giggled, and I smiled at Travis, who was glowering down at me.

"What?"

"Why did you let him buy your drink?"

America let go of Shepley, noticing Travis's mood. "We didn't, Travis. I told them not to."

Travis took the bottle from my hand. "Then what's this?"

"Are you serious?" I asked.

"Yes, I'm fucking serious," he said, tossing the beer in the trash can by the bar. "I've told you a hundred times . . . you can't be taking drinks from random guys. What if he put something in it?"

America held up her glass. "The drinks were never out of our sight, Trav. You're overreacting."

"I'm not talking to you," Travis said, his eyes boring into mine.

"Hey!" I said, instantly angry. "Don't talk to her like that."

"Travis," Shepley warned, "let it go."

"I don't like you letting other guys buy you drinks," Travis said.

I raised an eyebrow. "Are you trying to pick a fight?"

"Would it bother you to walk up to the bar and see me sharing a drink with some chick?"

I nodded once. "Okay. You're oblivious to all women, now. I get it. I should be making the same effort."

"It would be nice." He was clearly trying to subdue his temper, and it was a bit unnerving to be on the wrong side of his wrath. His eyes were still bright with anger, and an innate urge to go on the offensive bubbled to the surface.

"You're going to have to tone down the jealous-boyfriend thing, Travis. I didn't do anything wrong."

Travis shot me an incredulous look. "I walk up here, and some guy is buying you a drink!"

"Don't yell at her!" America said.

Shepley put his hand on Travis's shoulder. "We've all had a lot to drink. Let's just get out of here." Shepley's usually calming effect was lost on Travis, and I was instantly annoyed that his tantrum had ended our night.

"I have to tell Finch we're leaving," I grumbled, shouldering past Travis to the dance floor.

A warm hand encapsulated my wrist. I wheeled around, seeing Travis's fingers locked without regret. "I'll go with you."

I twisted my arm from his grip. "I am fully capable of walking a few feet by myself, Travis. What is wrong with you?"

I spied Finch in the middle and pushed my way out to him. "We're leaving!"

"What?" Finch yelled over the music.

"Travis is in a pissy mood! We're leaving!"

Finch rolled his eyes and shook his head, waving as I left the dance floor. Just as I spotted America and Shepley, I was tugged backward by a man in a pirate costume.

"Where do you think you're going?" he smiled, bumping up against me.

I laughed and shook my head at the silly face he was making. Just as I turned to walk away, he grabbed my arm. It didn't take long for me to realize he wasn't grabbing at me, he was grabbing for me—for protection.

"Whoa!" he cried, looking beyond me with wide eyes.

Travis barreled his way onto the dance floor, and plunged his fist straight into the pirate's face, the force sending both of us to the ground. With my palms flat on the wooden floor, I blinked my eyes in stunned disbelief. Feeling something warm and wet on my hand, I turned it over and recoiled. It was covered in blood from the man's nose. His hand was cupped over his face, but the bright red liquid poured down his forearm as he writhed on the floor.

Travis scrambled to pick me up, seeming as shocked as I was. "Oh shit! Are you all right, Pidge?"

When I got to my feet, I yanked my arm from his grip. "Are you insane?"

America grabbed my wrist and pulled me through the crowd to the parking lot. Shepley unlocked his doors and after I slid into my seat, Travis turned to me.

"I'm sorry, Pigeon, I didn't know he had a hold of you."

"Your fist was two inches from my face!" I said, catching the oil-stained towel Shepley had thrown at me. I wiped the blood from my hand, revolted.

The seriousness of the situation darkened his face and he

winced. "I wouldn't have swung if I thought I could have hit you. You know that, right?"

"Shut up, Travis. Just shut up," I said, staring at the back of Shepley's head.

"Pidge . . ." Travis began.

Shepley hit his steering wheel with the heel of his hand. "Shut up, Travis! You said you're sorry, now shut the fuck up!"

The trip home was made in complete silence. Shepley pulled his seat forward to let me out of the car, and I looked to America, who nodded with understanding.

She kissed her boyfriend good night. "I'll see you tomorrow, baby."

Shep nodded in resignation and kissed her. "Love you."

I walked past Travis to America's Honda, and he jogged to my side. "C'mon. Don't leave mad."

"Oh, I'm not leaving mad. I'm furious."

"She needs some time to cool off, Travis," America warned, unlocking her door.

When the passenger side lock popped, Travis held his hand against the door. "Don't leave, Pigeon. I was out of line. I'm sorry."

I held up my hand, showing him the remnants of dried blood on my palm. "Call me when you grow up."

He leaned against the door with his hip. "You can't leave."

I raised an eyebrow, and Shepley jogged around the car beside us. "Travis, you're drunk. You're about to make a huge mistake. Just let her go home, cool off . . . you can both talk tomorrow when you're sober."

Travis's expression turned desperate. "She can't leave," he said, staring into my eyes.

"It's not going to work, Travis," I said, tugging on the door. "Move!"

"What do you mean it's not gonna work?" Travis asked, grabbing my arm.

"I mean the sad face. I'm not falling for it," I said, pulling away.

Shepley watched Travis for a moment, and then turned to me. "Abby . . . this is the moment I was talking about. Maybe you should . . ."

"Stay out of it, Shep," America snapped, starting the car.

"I'm gonna fuck up. I'm gonna fuck up a lot, Pidge, but you have to forgive me."

"I'm going to have a huge bruise on my ass in the morning! You hit that guy because you were pissed at me! What should that tell me? Because red flags are going up all over the place right now!"

"I've never hit a girl in my life," he said, surprised at my words.

"And I'm not about to be the first one!" I said, tugging on the door. "Move, damn it!"

Travis nodded, and then took a step back. I sat beside America, slamming the door. She put the car in reverse, and Travis leaned down to look at me through the window.

"You're going to call me tomorrow, right?" he said, touching the windshield.

"Just go, Mare," I said, refusing to meet his eyes.

The night was long. I kept looking at the clock and cringed when I saw that another hour had passed. I couldn't stop thinking about Travis and whether or not I would call him, wondering if he was awake as well. I finally resorted to sticking the earbuds of my iPod in my ear and listening to every loud, obnoxious song on my playlist.

The last time I looked at the clock, it was after four. The birds were already chirping outside my window, and I smiled when my eyes began to feel heavy. It seemed like just a few moments later when I heard a knock at the door, and America burst through it. She pulled the earbuds from my ears and then fell into my desk chair.

"Mornin', sunshine. You look like hell," she said, blowing a pink bubble from her mouth and then letting it smack loudly as it popped.

"Shut UP, America!" Kara said from under her covers.

"You realize people like you and Trav are going to fight, right?" America said, filing her nails as she chewed the huge wad of gum in her mouth.

I turned over on the bed. "You are officially fired. You are a terrible conscience."

She laughed. "I just know you. If I handed you my keys right now, you'd drive straight over there."

"I would not!"

"Whatever," she lilted.

"It's eight o'clock in the morning, Mare. They're probably still passed out cold."

Just then, I heard a faint knock on the door. Kara's arm shot out from under her comforter and turned the knob. The door slowly opened, revealing Travis in the doorway.

"Can I come in?" he asked in a low, raspy voice. The purple circles under his eyes announced his lack of sleep, if he'd had any at all.

I sat up in bed, startled by his exhausted appearance. "Are you okay?"

He walked in and fell to his knees in front of me. "I'm so sorry, Abby. I'm sorry," he said, wrapping his arms around my waist and burying his head in my lap.

I cradled his head in my arms and peered up at America.

"I'm uh . . . I'm gonna go," she said, awkwardly fumbling for the door handle.

Kara rubbed her eyes and sighed and then grabbed her shower bag. "I'm always very clean when you're around, Abby," she grumbled, slamming the door behind her.

Travis looked up at me. "I know I get crazy when it comes to you, but God knows I'm tryin', Pidge. I don't wanna screw this up."

"Then don't."

"This is hard for me, ya know. I feel like any second you're going to figure out what a piece of shit I am and leave me. When you were dancing last night, I saw a dozen different guys watching you. You go to the bar, and I see you thank that guy for your drink. Then that douchebag on the dance floor grabs you."

"You don't see me throwing punches every time a girl talks to you. I can't stay locked up in the apartment all the time. You're going to have to get a handle on your temper."

"I will. I've never wanted a girlfriend before, Pigeon. I'm not used to feeling this way about someone . . . about anyone. If you'll be patient with me, I swear I'll get it figured out."

"Let's get something straight; you're not a piece of shit, you're amazing. It doesn't matter who buys me drinks or who asks me to dance or who flirts with me. I'm going home with you. You've asked me to trust you, and you don't seem to trust me."

He frowned. "That's not true."

"If you think I'm going to leave you for the next guy that comes along, then you don't have much faith in me."

He tightened his grip. "I'm not good enough for you, Pidge. That doesn't mean I don't trust you, I'm just bracing for the inevitable."

"Don't say that. When we're alone, you're perfect. We're perfect. But then you let everyone else ruin it. I don't expect a 180, but you have to pick your battles. You can't come out swinging every time someone looks at me."

He nodded. "I'll do anything you want. Just . . . tell me you love me."

"You know I do."

"I need to hear you say it," he said, his brows pulling together.

"I love you," I said, touching my lips to his. "Now quit being such a baby."

He laughed, crawling into the bed with me. We spent the next hour in the same spot under the covers, giggling and kissing, barely noticing when Kara returned from the shower.

"Could you get out? I have to get dressed," Kara said to Travis, tightening her robe.

Travis kissed my cheek, and then stepped into the hall. "See ya in a sec."

I fell against my pillow as Kara rummaged through her closet. "What are you so happy about?" she grumbled.

"Nothing," I sighed.

"Do you know what codependency is, Abby? Your boyfriend is a prime example, which is creepy considering he went from having no respect for women at all to thinking he needs you to breathe."

"Maybe he does," I said, refusing to let her spoil my mood.

"Don't you wonder why that is? I mean . . . he's been through half the girls at this school. Why you?"

"He says I'm different."

"Sure he does. But why?"

"Why do you care?" I snapped.

"It's dangerous to need someone that much. You're trying to save him, and he's hoping you can. You two are a disaster."

I smiled at the ceiling. "It doesn't matter what or why it is. When it's good, Kara . . . it's beautiful."

She rolled her eyes. "You're hopeless."

Travis knocked on the door, and Kara let him in.

"I'm going to the commons to study. Good luck," she said in the most insincere voice she could muster.

"What was that about?" Travis asked.

"She said we're a disaster."

"Tell me something I don't know," he smiled. His eyes were suddenly focused, and he kissed the tender skin behind my ear. "Why don't you come home with me?"

I rested my hand on the back of his neck and sighed at the feeling of his soft lips against my skin. "I think I'm going to stay here. I'm constantly at your apartment."

His head popped up. "So? You don't like it there?"

I touched his cheek and sighed. He was so quick to worry. "Of course I do, but I don't live there."

He ran the tip of his nose up my neck. "I want you there. I want you there every night."

"I'm not moving in with you," I said, shaking my head.

"I didn't ask you to move in with me. I said I want you there."

"Same thing!" I laughed.

Travis frowned. "You're really not staying with me tonight?"

I shook my head, and his eyes traveled up my wall to the ceiling. I could almost see the wheels spinning inside his head. "What are you up to?" I asked, narrowing my eyes.

"I'm trying to think of another bet."

Chapter Twelve
Two of a Kind

I FLIPPED A TINY WHITE PILL IN MY MOUTH AND SWAL-
lowed, chasing it with a large glass of water. I was standing in
the middle of Travis's bedroom in a bra and panties, getting
ready to slip into my pajamas.

"What's that?" Travis asked from the bed.

"Uh . . . my pill?"

He frowned. "What pill?"

"The pill, Travis. You have yet to replenish your top drawer
and the last thing I need is to worry about whether or not I'm
going to get my period."

"Oh."

"One of us has to be responsible," I said, raising an eyebrow.

"My God, you're sexy," Travis said, propping his head up
with his hand. "The most beautiful woman at Eastern is my
girlfriend. That's insanity."

I rolled my eyes and slipped the purple silk over my head,
crawling in bed beside him. I straddled his lap and kissed his
neck, giggling when he let his head fall against the headboard.
"Again? You're gonna kill me, Pidge."

"You can't die," I said, covering his face with kisses. "You're too damn mean."

"No, I can't die because there are too many jackasses falling over themselves to take my place! I may live forever just to spite them!"

I giggled against his mouth and he flipped me onto my back. His finger slid under the delicate purple ribbon tied at the crest of my shoulder and slid it down my arm, kissing the skin it left behind.

"Why me, Trav?"

He leaned back, searching my eyes. "What do you mean?"

"You've been with all these women, refused to settle down, refuse to even take a phone number . . . so why me?"

"Where is this coming from?" he said, his thumb caressing my cheek.

I shrugged. "I'm just curious."

"Why me? You have half the men at Eastern just waiting for me to screw up."

I wrinkled my nose. "That's not true. Don't change the subject."

"It is true. If I hadn't been chasing you from the beginning of school, you'd have more than Parker Hayes following you around. He's just too self-absorbed to be scared of me."

"You're avoiding my question! And poorly, I might add."

"Okay! Why you?" A smile spread across his face and he leaned down to touch his lips to mine. "I had a thing for you since the night of that first fight."

"What?" I said with a dubious expression.

"It's true. You in that cardigan with blood all over you? You looked absolutely ridiculous," he chuckled.

"Thanks."

His smiled faded. "It was when you looked up at me. That was the moment. You had this wide-eyed, innocent look . . . no pretenses. You didn't look at me like I was Travis Maddox," he said, rolling his eyes at his own words, "you looked at me like I was . . . I don't know, a person, I guess."

"News flash, Trav. You are a person."

He brushed my bangs from my face. "No, before you came, Shepley was the only one that treated me like anyone else. You didn't get all awkward or flirt or run your fingers through your hair. You saw me."

"I was a complete bitch to you."

He kissed my neck. "That's what sealed the deal."

I slipped my hands down his back and into his boxers. "I hope this gets old soon. I don't see myself ever getting tired of you."

"Promise?" he asked, smiling.

His phone buzzed on the night table and he smiled again, holding it to his ear. "Yeah? . . . Oh, hell no, I got Pidge here with me. We're just gettin' ready to go to bed . . . Shut the fuck up, Trent, that's not funny . . . Seriously? What's he doin' in town?" He looked at me and sighed. "All right. We'll be there in half an hour . . . You heard me, douchebag. Because I don't go anywhere without her, that's why. Do you want me to pound your face when I get there?" Travis hung up and shook his head.

I raised an eyebrow. "That is the weirdest conversation I've ever heard."

"That was Trent. Thomas is in town and it's poker night at my dad's."

"Poker night?" I swallowed.

"Yeah, they usually take all of my money. Cheatin' bastards."

"I'm going to meet your family in thirty minutes?"

He looked at his watch. "Twenty-seven minutes to be exact."

"Oh my God, Travis!" I wailed, jumping out of bed.

"What are you doing?" he sighed.

I rummaged through the closet and yanked on a pair of jeans, hopping up and down to pull them up, and then pulled the nightgown over my head, throwing it into Travis's face. "I can't believe you gave me twenty minutes' notice to meet your family! I could kill you right now!"

He pulled my nightgown from his eyes and laughed at my desperate attempt to look presentable. I grabbed a black V-neck shirt and tugged it to its proper position and then ran to the bathroom, brushing my teeth and ripping a brush through my hair. Travis walked up behind me, fully dressed and ready, and wrapped his arms around my waist.

"I'm a mess!" I said, frowning in the mirror.

"Do you even realize how beautiful you are?" he asked, kissing my neck.

I huffed, scampering into his room to slip on a pair of heels, and then took Travis's hand as he led me to the door. I stopped, zipping up my black leather jacket and pulling my hair up into a tight bun in preparation for the blustery ride to his father's house.

"Calm down, Pigeon. It's just a bunch of guys sitting around a table."

"This is the first time I'm meeting your dad and your

brothers . . . all at the same time . . . and you want me to calm down?" I said, climbing onto his bike behind him.

He angled his neck, touching my cheek as he kissed me. "They're going to love you, just like I do."

When we arrived, I let my hair fall down my back and ran my fingers through it a few times before Travis led me through the door.

"Holy Christ! It's the asshat!" one of the boys called.

Travis nodded once. He tried to look annoyed, but I could see that he was excited to see his brothers. The house was dated, with yellow-and-brown faded wallpaper and shag carpet in different shades of brown. We walked down a hall to a room straight ahead with the door wide open. Smoke wafted into the hallway, and his brothers and father were seated at a round wooden table with mismatched chairs.

"Hey, hey . . . watch the language around the young lady," his dad said, the cigar in his mouth bobbing while he talked.

"Pidge, this is my dad, Jim Maddox. Dad, this is Pigeon."

"Pigeon?" Jim asked, an amused expression on his face.

"Abby," I said, shaking his hand.

Travis pointed to his brothers. "Trenton, Taylor, Tyler, and Thomas."

They all nodded, and all but Thomas looked like older versions of Travis: buzz cuts, brown eyes, their T-shirts stretched over their bulging muscles, and covered in tattoos. Thomas wore a dress shirt and loosened tie, his eyes were hazel green, and his dark blond hair was longer by about an inch.

"Does Abby have a last name?" Jim asked.

"Abernathy," I nodded.

"It's nice to meet you, Abby," Thomas said, smiling.

"Really nice," Trenton said, giving me an impish once-over. Jim slapped the back of his head and he yelped. "What'd I say?" he said, rubbing the back of his head.

"Have a seat, Abby. Watch us take Trav's money," one of the twins said. I couldn't tell which was which; they were carbon copies of each other, even their tattoos matched.

The room was peppered with vintage pictures of poker games, pictures of poker legends posing with Jim and someone I assumed to be Travis's grandfather, and antique playing cards along the shelves.

"You knew Stu Ungar?" I asked, pointing to a dusty photo.

Jim's squinty eyes brightened. "You know who Stu Ungar is?"

I nodded. "My dad's a fan, too."

He stood up, pointing to the picture beside it. "And that's Doyle Brunson, there."

I smiled. "My dad saw him play, once. He's unbelievable."

"Trav's granddaddy was a professional . . . we take poker very seriously around here," Jim smiled.

I sat between Travis and one of the twins while Trenton shuffled the deck with moderate skill. The boys put in their cash and Jim divvied out the chips.

Trenton raised an eyebrow. "You wanna play, Abby?"

I smiled politely and shook my head. "I don't think I should."

"You don't know how?" Jim asked.

I couldn't hold back a smile. Jim looked so serious, almost paternal. I knew what answer he expected, and I hated to disappoint him.

Travis kissed my forehead. "Play . . . I'll teach you."

"You should just kiss your money goodbye, now, Abby," Thomas laughed.

I pressed my lips together and dug into my purse, pulling out two fifties. I held them out to Jim and waited patiently as he traded them for chips. Trenton's mouth tightened into a smug smile, but I ignored him.

"I have faith in Travis's teaching skills," I said.

One of the twins clapped his hands together. "Hells yeah! I'm going to get rich tonight!"

"Let's start small this time," Jim said, throwing in a five-dollar chip.

Trenton dealt, and Travis fanned out my hand for me. "Have you ever played cards?"

"It's been a while," I nodded.

"Go Fish doesn't count, Pollyanna," Trenton said, looking at his cards.

"Shut your hole, Trent," Travis said, glancing up at his brother before looking back down to my hand. "You're shooting for higher cards, consecutive numbers, and if you're really lucky, in the same suit."

The first hand, Travis looked at my cards and I looked at his. I mainly nodded and smiled, playing when I was told. Both Travis and I lost, and my chips had dwindled by the end of the first round.

After Thomas dealt to begin the second round, I wouldn't let Travis see my cards. "I think I've got this," I said.

"You sure?" he asked.

"I'm sure, baby," I said.

Three hands later, I had won back my chips and annihilated

the stacked chips of the others with a pair of aces, a straight, and the high card.

"Bullshit!" Trenton whined. "Beginner's luck sucks!"

"You've got a fast learner, Trav," Jim said, moving his mouth around his cigar.

Travis swigged his beer. "You're makin' me proud, Pigeon!" His eyes were bright with excitement, and his smile was different than I'd ever seen before.

"Thanks."

"Those that cannot do, teach," Thomas said, smirking.

"Very funny, asshole," Travis murmured.

Four hands later, I tipped back the last of my beer and narrowed my eyes at the only man at the table who hadn't folded. "The action's on you, Taylor. You gonna be a baby or you going to put in like a man?"

"Fuck it," he said, throwing the last of his chips in.

Travis looked at me, his eyes animated. It reminded me of the expressions of those watching his fights.

"Whatdya got, Pigeon?"

"Taylor?" I prompted.

A wide grin spread across his face. "Flush!" he smiled, spreading his cards faceup on the table.

Five pairs of eyes turned to me. I scanned the table and then slammed my cards down. "Read 'em and weep, boys! Aces and eights!" I said, giggling.

"A full house? What the fuck?" Trenton cried.

"Sorry. I've always wanted to say that," I said, pulling in my chips.

Thomas's eyes narrowed. "This isn't just beginner's luck. She plays."

Travis eyed Thomas for a moment and then looked to me. "Have you played before, Pidge?"

I pressed my lips together and shrugged, displaying my best innocent smile. Travis's head fell back, bursting into a barrage of laughter. He tried to speak but couldn't and then hit the table with his fist.

"Your girlfriend just fucking hustled us!" Taylor said, pointing in my direction.

"NO FUCKING WAY!" Trenton wailed, standing up.

"Good plan, Travis. Bring a card shark to poker night," Jim said, winking at me.

"I didn't know!" he said, shaking his head.

"Bullshit," Thomas said, eyeing me.

"I didn't!" he said through his laughter.

"I hate to say it, bro. But I think I just fell in love with your girl," Tyler said.

"Hey, now," Travis said, his smile quickly fading into a grimace.

"That's it. I was going easy on you, Abby, but I'm winning my money back, now," Trenton warned.

Travis sat out for the last few rounds, watching his brothers try their hardest to regain their money. Hand after hand, I pulled in their chips, and hand after hand, Thomas watched me more closely. Every time I laid my cards down, Travis and Jim laughed, Taylor cursed, Tyler proclaimed his undying love for me, and Trenton threw a full-blown tantrum.

I cashed in my chips and gave them each one hundred dollars once we settled into the living room. Jim refused, but the brothers accepted with gratitude. Travis grabbed my hand and we walked to the door.

I could see he was unhappy, so I squeezed his fingers in mine. "What's wrong?"

"You just gave away four hundred bucks, Pidge!" Travis frowned.

"If this was poker night at Sig Tau, I would have kept it. I can't rob your brothers the first time I meet them."

"They would have kept your money!" he said.

"And I wouldn't have lost a second of sleep over it, either," Taylor said.

Thomas stared at me in silence from the corner of the room.

"Why do you keep starin' at my girl, Tommy?"

"What did you say your last name was?" Thomas asked.

I shifted my weight nervously. My mind raced for something witty or sarcastic to say to deflect the question. I picked at my nails instead, silently cursing myself. I should have known better than to win all those hands. Thomas knew. I could see it in his eyes.

Travis, noticing my unease, turned to his brother and put his arm around my waist. I wasn't sure if he was doing it in protective reaction, or if he was bracing himself for what his brother might say.

Travis shifted, visibly uncomfortable with his brother's questioning. "It's Abernathy. What of it?"

"I can see why you didn't put it together before tonight, Trav, but now you don't have an excuse," Thomas said, smug.

"What the fuck are you talking about?" Travis asked.

"Are you related to Mick Abernathy by any chance?" Thomas asked.

All heads turned in my direction, and I nervously raked my hair back with my fingers. "How do you know Mick?"

Travis angled his head to look into my eyes. "He's only one of the best poker players that ever lived. Do you know him?"

I winced, knowing I had finally been cornered into telling the truth. "He's my father."

The entire room exploded.

"NO FUCKING WAY!"

"I KNEW IT!"

"WE JUST PLAYED MICK ABERNATHY'S DAUGH-TER!"

"MICK ABERNATHY? HOLY SHIT!"

Thomas, Jim, and Travis were the only ones not shouting. "I told you guys I shouldn't play," I said.

"If you would have mentioned you were Mick Abernathy's daughter, I think we would have taken you more seriously," Thomas said.

I peered over at Travis, who stared at me in awe. "You're Lucky Thirteen?" he asked, his eyes a bit hazy.

Trenton stood and pointed at me, his mouth opened wide. "Lucky Thirteen is in our house! No way! I don't fucking believe it!"

"That was the nickname the papers gave me. And the story wasn't exactly accurate," I said, fidgeting.

"I need to get Abby home, guys," Travis said, still staring at me.

Jim peered at me over his glasses. "Why wasn't it accurate?"

"I didn't take my dad's luck. I mean, how ridiculous," I chuckled, twisting my hair nervously around my finger.

Thomas shook his head. "No, Mick gave that interview. He said at midnight on your thirteenth birthday his luck ran dry."

"And yours picked up," Travis added.

"You were raised by mobsters!" Trenton said, smiling with excitement.

"Uh . . . no." I laughed once. "They didn't raise me. They were just . . . around a lot."

"That was a damn shame, Mick running your name through the mud like that in all the papers. You were just a kid," Jim said, shaking his head.

"If anything it was beginner's luck," I said, desperately trying to hide my humiliation.

"You were taught by Mick Abernathy," Jim said, shaking his head in awe. "You were playing pros, and winning, at thirteen years old, for Christ's sakes." He looked at Travis and smiled. "Don't bet against her, son. She doesn't lose."

Travis looked at me, then, his expression still shocked and disoriented. "Uh . . . we gotta go, Dad. Bye, guys."

The deep, excited chatter of Travis's family faded as he pulled me out the door and to his bike. I twisted my hair into a bun and zipped up my coat, waiting for him to speak. He climbed onto his bike without a word, and I straddled the seat behind him.

I was sure he felt that I hadn't been honest with him, and he was probably embarrassed that he found out about such an important part of my life the same time his family had. I expected a huge argument when we returned to his apartment, and I went over a dozen different apologies in my head before we reached the front door.

He led me down the hall by my hand, and then helped me with my coat.

I pulled at the caramel knot on the crown of my head, and

my hair fell past my shoulders in thick waves. "I know you're mad," I said, unable to look him in the eye. "I'm sorry I didn't tell you, but it's not something I talk about."

"Mad at you?" he said. "I am so turned on I can't see straight. You just robbed my asshole brothers of their money without batting an eyelash, you have achieved legend status with my father, and I know for a fact that you purposely lost that bet we made before my fight."

"I wouldn't say that . . ."

He lifted his chin. "Did you think you were going to win?"

"Well . . . no, not exactly," I said, pulling off my heels.

Travis smiled. "So you wanted to be here with me. I think I just fell in love with you all over again."

"How are you not mad right now?" I asked, tossing my shoes to the closet.

He sighed and nodded. "That's pretty big, Pidge. You should have told me. But I understand why you didn't. You came here to get away from all of that. It's like the sky opened up . . . everything makes sense, now."

"Well, that's a relief."

"Lucky Thirteen," he said, shaking his head and pulling my shirt over my head.

"Don't call me that, Travis. It's not a good thing."

"You're fucking famous, Pigeon!" he said, surprised at my words. He unbuttoned my jeans and pulled them down around my ankles, helping me to step out of them.

"My father hated me after that. He still blames me for all his problems."

Travis yanked off his shirt and hugged me to him. "I still

can't believe the daughter of Mick Abernathy is standing in front of me, and I've been with you this whole time and had no idea."

I pushed away from him. "I'm not Mick Abernathy's daughter, Travis! That's what I left behind. I'm Abby. Just Abby!" I said, walking over to the closet. I yanked a T-shirt off its hanger and pulled it over my head.

He sighed. "I'm sorry. I'm a little starstruck."

"It's just me!" I held the palm of my hand to my chest, desperate for him to understand.

"Yeah, but . . ."

"But nothing. The way you're looking at me right now? This is exactly why I didn't tell you." I closed my eyes. "I won't live like that anymore, Trav. Not even with you."

"Whoa! Calm down, Pigeon. Let's not get carried away." His eyes focused and he walked over to wrap me in his arms. "I don't care what you were or what you're not anymore. I just want you."

"I guess we have that in common, then."

He led me to the bed, smiling down at me. "It's just you and me against the world, Pidge."

I curled up beside him, settling into the mattress. I had never planned on anyone besides myself and America knowing about Mick, and I never expected that my boyfriend would belong to a family of poker buffs. I heaved a heavy sigh, pressing my cheek against his chest.

"What's wrong?" he asked.

"I don't want anyone to know, Trav. I didn't want you to know."

"I love you, Abby. I won't mention it again, okay? Your secret's safe with me," he said, kissing my forehead.

✦ ✦ ✦

"MR. MADDOX, THINK YOU COULD TONE IT DOWN UNTIL after class?" Professor Chaney said, reacting to my giggling as Travis nuzzled my neck.

I cleared my throat, feeling my cheeks radiate with embarrassment.

"I don't think so, Dr. Chaney. Have you gotten a good look at my girl?" Travis said, gesturing to me.

Laughter echoed throughout the room, and my face caught fire. Professor Chaney glanced at me with a half-amused, half-awkward expression and then shook his head at Travis.

"Just do your best," Chaney said.

The class laughed again, and I sunk into my seat. Travis rested his arm on the back of my chair, and the lecture continued. After class had been dismissed, Travis walked me to my next class.

"Sorry if I embarrassed you. I can't help myself."

"Try."

Parker walked by, and when I returned his nod with a polite smile, his eyes brightened. "Hey, Abby. See you inside." He walked into the classroom, and Travis glowered at him for a few tense moments.

"Hey," I tugged on his hand until he looked at me. "Forget about him."

"He's been telling the guys at the House that you're still calling him."

"That's not true," I said, unaffected.

"I know that, but they don't. He said he's just biding his time. He told Brad that you're just waiting for the right time to dump me, and how you call him to say how unhappy you are. He's starting to piss me off."

"He has quite an imagination." I glanced at Parker, and when he met my eyes and smiled, I glared at him.

"Would you get mad if I embarrassed you one more time?"

I shrugged and Travis wasted no time leading me into the classroom. He stopped at my desk, setting my bag on the floor. He looked over at Parker and then pulled me to him, one hand on the nape of my neck, one hand on my backside, and then kissed me, deep and determined. He worked his lips against mine in the way he usually reserved for his bedroom, and I couldn't help but grab his shirt with both fists.

The murmuring and giggles grew louder after it became clear that Travis wasn't going to let go anytime soon.

"I think he just got her pregnant!" someone from the back of the room said, laughing.

I pulled away with my eyes closed, trying to regain my composure. When I looked at Travis, he was staring at me with the same forced restraint.

"I was just trying to make a point," he whispered.

"Good point," I nodded.

Travis smiled, kissed my cheek, and then looked to Parker, who was fuming in his seat.

"I'll see you at lunch," he winked.

I fell against my seat and sighed, trying to shake off the tingling between my thighs.

I labored through Calculus, and when class was over I noticed Parker standing against the wall by the door.

"Parker," I nodded, determined not to give him the reaction he was hoping for.

"I know you're with him. He doesn't have to violate you in front of an entire class on my account."

I stopped in my tracks and poised to attack. "Then maybe you should stop telling your frat brothers that I'm calling you. You're going to push him too far, and I'm not going to feel sorry for you when he puts his boot in your ass."

He wrinkled his nose. "Listen to you. You've been around Travis too much."

"No, this is me. It's just a side of me you know nothing about."

"You didn't exactly give me a chance, did you?"

I sighed. "I don't want to fight with you, Parker. It just didn't work out, okay?"

"No, it's not okay. You think I enjoy being the laughingstock of Eastern? Travis Maddox is the one we all appreciate because he makes us look good. He uses girls, tosses them aside, and even the biggest jerks at Eastern look like Prince Charming after Travis."

"When are you going to open your eyes and realize that he's different now?"

"He doesn't love you, Abby. You're a shiny new toy. Although, after the scene he made in class, I'm assuming you're not all that shiny anymore."

I slapped his face with a loud smack before I realized what I'd done.

"If you would have waited two seconds, I could have saved you the effort, Pidge," Travis said, pulling me behind him.

I grabbed his arm. "Travis, don't."

Parker looked a bit nervous as a perfect red outline of my hand appeared on his cheek.

"I warned you," Travis said, shoving Parker violently against the wall.

Parker's jaws tensed and he glared at me. "Consider this closure, Travis. I can see now that you two are made for each other."

"Thanks," Travis said, hooking his arm around my shoulders.

Parker pushed himself from the wall and quickly rounded the corner to descend the stairs with a quick glance to make sure Travis didn't follow.

"Are you okay?" Travis asked.

"My hand stings."

He smiled. "That was badass, Pidge. I'm impressed."

"He'll probably sue me and I'll end up paying his way into Harvard. What are you doing here? I thought we were meeting in the cafeteria?"

One side of his mouth pulled up in an impish grin. "I couldn't concentrate in class. I'm still feelin' that kiss."

I looked down the hall and then to him. "Come with me."

His eyebrows pulled together over his smile. "What?"

I walked backward, pulling him along until I felt the knob of the Physics lab. The door swung open, and I glanced behind me, seeing that it was empty and dark. I tugged on his hand, giggling at his confused expression, and then locked the door, pushing him against it.

I kissed him and he chuckled. "What are you doin'?"

"I don't want you to be unable to concentrate in class," I said, kissing him again. He lifted me up and I wrapped my legs around him.

"I'm not sure what I ever did without you," he said, holding me up with one hand and unbuckling his belt with the other, "but I don't ever want to find out. You're everything I've ever wanted, Pigeon."

"Just remember that when I take all of your money in the next poker game," I said, pulling off my shirt.

Chapter ~~Thirteen~~ Fourteen
Full House

I TWIRLED AROUND, SCRUTINIZING MY REFLECTION with a skeptical eye. The dress was white, backless, and dangerously short, the bodice held up by a short string of rhinestones that formed a halter around my neck.

"Wow! Travis is going to piss himself when he sees you in that!" America said.

I rolled my eyes. "How romantic."

"You're getting that one. Don't try any more on, that's the one," she said, clapping with excitement.

"You don't think it's too short? Mariah Carey shows less skin."

America shook her head. "I insist."

I took a turn on the bench while America tried on one dress after another, more indecisive when it came to choosing one for herself. She settled on an extremely short, tight, flesh-colored number that left one of her shoulders bare.

We rode in her Honda to the apartment to find the Charger gone and Toto alone. America pulled out her phone and dialed, smiling when Shepley answered.

"Where'd you go, baby?" She nodded and then looked at me. "Why would I be mad? What kind of surprise?" she said. She looked at me again and then walked into Shepley's bedroom, closing the door.

I rubbed Toto's black pointy ears while America murmured in the bedroom. When she emerged, she tried to subdue the smile on her face.

"What are they up to now?" I asked.

"They're on their way home. I'll let Travis tell you," she said, grinning from ear to ear.

"Oh, God . . . what?" I asked.

"I just said I can't tell you. It's a surprise."

I fidgeted with my hair and picked at my nails, unable to sit still while I waited for Travis to unveil his latest surprise. A birthday party, a puppy—I couldn't imagine what could be next.

The loud engine of Shepley's Charger announced their arrival. The boys laughed as they walked up the stairs.

"They're in a good mood," I said. "That's a good sign."

Shepley walked in first. "I just didn't want you to think there was a reason that he got one and I didn't."

America stood up to greet her boyfriend and threw her arms around him. "You're so silly, Shep. If I wanted an insane boyfriend, I'd date Travis."

"It doesn't have anything to do with how I feel about you," Shepley added.

Travis walked through the door with a square gauze bandage on his wrist. He smiled at me and then collapsed on the couch, resting his head on my lap.

I couldn't look away from the bandage. "Okay . . . what did you do?"

Travis smiled and pulled me down to kiss him. I could feel the nervousness radiating from him. Outwardly he was smiling, but I had the distinct feeling he wasn't sure how I would react to what he had done.

"I got a few things today."

"Like what?" I asked, suspicious.

Travis laughed. "Calm down, Pidge. It's nothing bad."

"What happened to your wrist?" I said, pulling his hand up by his fingers.

A thunderous diesel motor pulled up outside and Travis hopped up from the couch, opening the door. "It's about fucking time! I've been home for at least five minutes!" he said with a smile.

One man walked in backward, carrying a plastic-covered gray sofa, followed by another man bringing in the rear. Shepley and Travis moved the couch—with me and Toto still on it—forward, and then the men sat the new one in its place. Travis pulled off the plastic and then lifted me in his arms, setting me on the soft cushions.

"You got a new one?" I asked, grinning from ear to ear.

"Yep, and a couple of other things, too. Thanks, guys," he said as the movers lifted the old couch and left the way they came.

"There goes a lot of memories," I smirked.

"None that I want to hold on to." He sat beside me and sighed, watching me for a moment before he pulled off the tape that held the gauze on his arm. "Don't freak out."

My mind raced with what could be under that bandage. I imagined a burn or stitches or something equally gruesome.

He pulled the bandage back and I gasped at the black script

tattooed across the underside of his wrist, the skin around it red and shiny from the antibiotic he had smeared on. I shook my head in disbelief as I read the word.

Pigeon

"Do you like it?" he asked.

"You had my name tattooed on your wrist?" I said the words, but it didn't sound like my voice. My mind stretched in every direction, and yet I managed to speak in a calm, even tone.

"Yeah." He kissed my cheek as I stared in disbelief at the permanent ink in his skin.

"I tried to talk him out of it, Abby. He hasn't done anything crazy in a while. I think he was having withdrawal," Shepley said, shaking his head.

"What do you think?" Travis prompted.

"I don't know what to think," I said.

"You should have asked her first, Trav," America said, shaking her head and covering her mouth with her fingers.

"Asked her what? If I could get a tattoo?" he frowned, turning to me. "I love you. I want everyone to know I'm yours."

I shifted nervously. "That's permanent, Travis."

"So are we," he said, touching my cheek.

"Show her the rest," Shepley said.

"The rest?" I said, looking down to his other wrist.

Travis stood, pulling up his shirt. His impressive six-pack stretched and tightened with the movement. Travis turned, and on his side was another fresh tattoo spanning the length of his ribs.

"What is that?" I asked, squinting at the vertical symbols.

"It's Hebrew," Travis said with a nervous grin.

"What does it mean?"

"It says, 'I belong to my beloved, and my beloved is mine.'"

My eyes darted to his. "You weren't happy with just one tattoo, you had to get two?"

"It's something I always said I would do when I met The One. I met you . . . I went and got the tats." His smile faded when he saw my expression. "You're pissed, aren't you?" he said, pulling his shirt down.

"I'm not mad. I'm just . . . it's a little overwhelming."

Shepley squeezed America to his side with one arm. "Get used to it now, Abby. Travis is impulsive and goes balls to the wall on everything. This'll tide him over until he can get a ring on your finger."

America's eyebrows shot up, first to me, and then to Shepley. "What? They just started dating!"

"I . . . think I need a drink," I said, walking into the kitchen.

Travis chuckled, watching me rifle the cabinets. "He was kidding, Pidge."

"I was?" Shepley asked.

"He wasn't talking about anytime soon," Travis hedged. He turned to Shepley and grumbled, "Thanks a lot, asshole."

"Maybe you'll quit talking about it, now," Shepley grinned.

I poured a shot of whiskey into a glass and jerked my head back, swallowing it all at once. My face compressed as the liquid burned down my throat.

Travis gently wrapped his arms around my middle from behind. "I'm not proposing, Pidge. They're tattoos."

"I know," I said, nodding my head as I poured another drink. Travis pulled the bottle from my hand and twisted the cap on, shoving it back into the cabinet. When I didn't turn around, he pivoted my hips so that I would face him.

"Okay. I should have talked to you about it first, but I decided to buy the couch, and then one thing led to another. I got excited."

"This is very fast for me, Travis. You've mentioned moving in together, you just branded yourself with my name, you're telling me you love me . . . this is all very . . . fast."

Travis frowned. "You're freakin' out. I told you not to freak out."

"It's hard not to! You found out about my dad and everything you felt before has suddenly been amplified!"

"Who's your dad?" Shepley asked, clearly unhappy about being out of the loop. When I didn't acknowledge his question, he sighed. "Who's her dad?" he asked America. America shook her head dismissively.

Travis's expression twisted with disgust. "My feelings for you have nothing to do with your dad."

"We're going to this date party tomorrow. It's supposed to be this big deal where we're announcing our relationship or something, and now you have my name on your arm and this proverb talking about how we belong to each other! It's freaky, okay? I'm freaked out!"

Travis grabbed my face and planted his mouth on mine, and then he lifted me off the floor, setting me on the counter. His tongue begged entrance into my mouth, and when I let him in, he moaned.

His fingers dug into my hips, pulling me closer. "You are so fucking hot when you're mad," he said against my lips.

"Okay," I breathed, "I'm calm."

He smiled, pleased that his plan of distraction had worked. "Everything's still the same, Pidge. It's still just you and me."

"You two are nuts," Shepley said, shaking his head.

America playfully smacked Shepley's shoulder. "Abby bought something for Travis today, too."

"America!" I scolded.

"You found a dress?" he asked, smiling.

"Yeah." I wrapped my legs and arms around him. "Tomorrow it's going to be your turn to be freaked out."

"I'm looking forward to it," he said, pulling me off the counter. I waved to America as Travis carried me down the hall.

FRIDAY AFTER CLASS, AMERICA AND I SPENT THE AFTER-noon downtown, primping and indulging. We had our nails and toes done, errant hairs waxed, skin bronzed, and hair highlighted. When we returned to the apartment, every surface had been covered with bouquets of roses. Reds, pinks, yellows, and whites—it looked like a floral shop.

"Oh my God!" America squealed when she walked through the door.

Shepley looked around him, standing proud. "We went to buy you two flowers, but neither of us thought just one bouquet would do it."

I hugged Travis. "You guys are . . . you're amazing. Thank you."

He smacked my backside. "Thirty minutes until the party, Pidge."

The boys dressed in Travis's room while we slipped on our dresses in Shepley's. Just as I fastened my silver heels, there was a knock on the door.

"Time to go, ladies," Shepley said.

America walked out, and Shepley whistled.

"Where is she?" Travis asked.

"Abby's having some trouble with her shoe. She'll be out in just a sec," America explained.

"The suspense is killin' me, Pigeon!" Travis called.

I walked out, fidgeting with my dress while Travis stood in front of me, blank-faced.

America elbowed him and he blinked. "Holy shit."

"Are you ready to be freaked out?" America asked.

"I'm not freaked out—she looks amazing," Travis said.

I smiled and then slowly turned around to show him the steep dip of the fabric in the back of the dress.

"Okay, now I'm freakin' out," he said, walking over to me and turning me around.

"You don't like it?" I asked.

"You need a jacket." He jogged to the rack and then hastily draped my coat over my shoulders.

"She can't wear that all night, Trav," America chuckled.

"You look beautiful, Abby," Shepley said as an apology for Travis's behavior.

Travis's expression was pained as he spoke. "You do. You look incredible . . . but you can't wear that. Your skirt is . . . wow, your legs are . . . your skirt is too short and it's only half a dress! It doesn't even have a back on it!"

I couldn't help but smile. "That's the way it's made, Travis."

"Do you two live to torture each other?" Shepley frowned.

"Do you have a longer dress?" Travis asked.

I looked down. "It's actually pretty modest in the front. It's just the back that shows off a lot of skin."

"Pigeon," he winced with his next words, "I don't want you to be mad, but I can't take you to my frat house looking like that. I'll get in a fight the first five minutes."

I leaned up on the balls of my feet and kissed his lips. "I have faith in you."

"This night is gonna suck," he groaned.

"This night is going to be fantastic," America said, offended.

"Just think of how easy it will be to get it off later," I said, kissing his neck.

"That's the problem. Every other guy there will be thinking the same thing."

"But you're the only one that gets to find out," I lilted. He didn't respond, and I leaned back to assess his expression. "Do you really want me to change?"

Travis scanned my face, my dress, my legs, and then exhaled. "No matter what you wear, you're gorgeous. I should just get used to it, now, right?" I shrugged and he shook his head. "All right, we're already late. Let's go."

I huddled next to Travis for warmth as we walked from the car to the Sigma Tau house. The air was smoky but warm. Music boomed from the basement, and Travis bobbed his head to the beat. Everyone seemed to turn at once. I wasn't sure if they were staring because Travis was at a date party or because he was wearing slacks or because of my dress, but they were all staring.

America leaned over to whisper in my ear. "I'm so glad you're here, Abby. I feel like I just walked into a Molly Ringwald movie."

"Glad I could help," I grumbled.

Travis and Shepley took our coats and then led us across the room to the kitchen. Shepley took four beers out of the fridge and handed one to America and then one to me. We stood in the kitchen, listening to Travis's frat brothers discuss his last fight. The sorority sisters accompanying them happened to be the same busty blondes who followed Travis into the cafeteria the first time we spoke.

Lexie was easy to recognize. I couldn't forget the look on her face when Travis pushed her from his lap for insulting America. She watched me with curiosity, seeming to study my every word. I knew she was curious why Travis Maddox apparently found me irresistible, and I found myself making an effort to show her. I kept my hands on Travis, inserting clever quips at precise moments of conversation, and joked with him about his new tattoos.

"Dude, you got your girl's name on your wrist? What in the hell possessed you to do that?" Brad said.

Travis proudly turned over his hand to reveal my name. "I'm crazy about her," he said, looking down at me with soft eyes.

"You barely know her," Lexie scoffed.

He didn't take his eyes from mine. "I know her." He furrowed his brow. "I thought the tat freaked you out. Now you're bragging about it?"

I leaned up to kiss his cheek and shrugged. "It's growing on me."

Shepley and America made their way downstairs, and we followed hand in hand. Furniture had been pushed along the walls for a makeshift dance floor. Just as we descended the stairs, a slow song began to play.

Travis didn't hesitate to pull me into the middle, holding me close and pulling my hand to his chest. "I'm glad I've never gone to one of these things before. It's right that I've only brought you."

I smiled and pressed my cheek against his chest. He held his hand against my lower back, warm and soft against my bare skin.

"Everyone's staring at you in this dress," he said. I looked up, expecting to see a tense expression, but he was smiling. "I guess it's kinda cool . . . being with the girl everyone wants."

I rolled my eyes. "They don't want me. They're curious why you want me. And anyway, I feel sorry for anyone that thinks they have a chance. I am hopelessly and completely in love with you."

A pained look shadowed his face. "You know why I want you? I didn't know I was lost until you found me. I didn't know what alone was until the first night I spent without you in my bed. You're the one thing I've got right. You're what I've been waiting for, Pigeon."

I reached up to take his face between my hands and he wrapped his arms around me, lifting me off the floor. I pressed my lips against his, and he kissed me with the emotion of everything he'd just said. It was in that moment that I realized why he'd gotten the tattoo, why he had chosen me, and why I was different. It wasn't just me, and it wasn't just him, it was what we were together that was the exception.

A faster beat vibrated the speakers, and Travis lowered me to my feet. "Still wanna dance?"

America and Shepley appeared beside us and I raised an eyebrow. "If you think you can keep up with me."

Travis smirked. "Try me."

I moved my hips against his and ran my hand up his shirt,

unfastening his top two buttons, Travis chuckled and shook his head, and I turned around, moving against him to the beat. He grabbed my hips and I reached around, grabbing his backside. I leaned forward and his fingers dug into my skin. When I stood up, he touched his lips to my ear.

"Keep that up and we'll be leaving early."

I turned around and smiled, throwing my arms around his neck. He pressed himself against me and I untucked his shirt, slipping my hands up his back, pressing my fingers into his lean muscles, and then smiling at the noise he made when I tasted his neck.

"Jesus, Pigeon, you're killin' me," he said, gripping the hem of my skirt, pulling it up just enough to graze my thighs with his fingertips.

"I guess we know what the appeal is," Lexie sneered from behind us.

America spun, stomping toward Lexie on the warpath. Shepley grabbed her just in time.

"Say it again!" America said. "I dare you, bitch!"

Lexie cowered behind her boyfriend, shocked at America's threat.

"Better get a muzzle on your date, Brad," Travis warned.

Two songs later, the hair on the back of my neck was heavy and damp. Travis kissed the skin just below my ear. "C'mon, Pidge. I need a smoke."

He led me up the stairs, and then grabbed my coat before leading me up to the second floor. We walked out onto the balcony to find Parker and his date. She was taller than I, her short, dark hair pinned back with a single bobby pin. I noticed her pointy stilettos immediately, with her leg hooked around

Parker's hip. She stood with her back against the brick, and when Parker noticed us walk out, he pulled his hand from underneath her skirt.

"Abby," he said, surprised and breathless.

"Hey, Parker," I said, stifling a laugh.

"How, uh . . . how have you been?"

I smiled politely. "I've been great. You?"

"Uh," he looked at his date, "Abby, this is Amber. Amber . . . Abby."

"Abby Abby?" she asked.

Parker gave one quick, uncomfortable nod. Amber shook my hand with a disgusted look on her face, and then eyed Travis as if she had just encountered the enemy. "Nice to meet you . . . I guess."

"Amber," Parker warned.

Travis laughed once and then opened the doors for them to walk through. Parker grabbed Amber's hand and retreated into the house.

"That was . . . awkward," I said, shaking my head as I folded my arms, leaning against the railing. It was cold, and there were only a handful of couples outside.

Travis was all smiles. Not even Parker could dampen his mood. "At least he's moved on from trying his damnedest to get you back."

"I don't think he was trying to get me back so much as trying to keep me away from you."

Travis wrinkled his nose. "He took one girl home for me once. Now he acts like he's made a habit of swooping in and saving every freshman I bagged."

I gave him a wry look from the corner of my eye. "Did I ever tell you how much I loathe that word?"

"Sorry," he said, pulling me to his side. He lit his cigarette and took a deep breath. The smoke he blew out was thicker than usual, mixing with the winter air. He turned his hand over and took a long look at his wrist. "How weird is it that this tat isn't just my new favorite, but it makes me feel at ease to know it's there?"

"Pretty weird." Travis raised an eyebrow and I laughed. "I'm kidding. I can't say I understand it, but it's sweet . . . in a Travis Maddox sort of way."

"If it feels this good to have this on my arm, I can't imagine how it's going to feel to get a ring on your finger."

"Travis . . ."

"In four or maybe five years," he added.

I took a breath. "We need to slow down. Way, way down."

"Don't start this, Pidge."

"If we keep going at this pace, I'm going to be barefoot and pregnant before I graduate. I'm not ready to move in with you, I'm not ready for a ring, and I'm certainly not ready to settle down."

Travis gripped my shoulders and turned me to face him. "This isn't the 'I wanna see other people' speech, is it? Because I'm not sharing you. No fucking way."

"I don't want anyone else," I said, exasperated. He relaxed and released my shoulders, gripping the railing.

"What are you saying, then?" he asked, staring across the horizon.

"I'm saying we need to slow down. That's all I'm saying." He nodded, clearly unhappy. I touched his arm. "Don't be mad."

"It seems like we take one step forward and two steps back, Pidge. Every time I think we're on the same page, you put up a wall. I don't get it . . . most girls are hounding their boyfriends to get serious, to talk about their feelings, to take the next step . . ."

"I thought we established that I'm not most girls?"

He let his head drop, frustrated. "I'm tired of guessing. Where do you see this going, Abby?"

I pressed my lips against his shirt. "When I think about my future, I see you."

Travis relaxed, pulling me close. We both watched the night clouds move across the sky. The lights of the school dotted the darkened block, and partygoers folded their arms against thick coats, scurrying to the warmth of the fraternity house.

I saw the same peace in Travis's eyes that I had witnessed only a handful of times. And it hit me that just like on the other nights, his content expression was a direct result of reassurance from me.

I had experienced insecurity: those living one stroke of bad luck to another, men who were afraid of their own shadow. It was easy to be afraid of the dark side of Vegas, the side the neon and glitter never seemed to touch. But Travis Maddox wasn't afraid to fight or to defend someone he cared about or to look into the humiliated and angry eyes of a scorned woman. He could walk into a room and stare down someone twice his size, believing that no one could touch him—that he was invincible to anything that tried make him fall.

He was afraid of nothing. Until he'd met me.

I was the one part of his life that was unknown, the wild card, the variable he couldn't control. Regardless of the moments of peace I had given him, in every other moment of every other day, the turmoil he felt without me was made ten times worse in my presence. The anger that took hold of him before was only harder for him to manage. Being the exception was no longer a mysterious, special thing. I had become his weakness.

Just as I was to my father.

"Abby! There you are! I've been looking all over for you!" America said, bursting through the door. She held up her cell phone. "I just got off the phone with my dad. Mick called them last night."

"Mick?" My face screwed into disgust. "Why would he call them?"

America raised her eyebrows as if I should know the answer. "Your mother kept hanging up on him."

"What did he want?" I said, feeling sick.

She pressed her lips together. "To know where you were."

"They didn't tell him, did they?"

America's face fell. "He's your father, Abby. Dad felt he had a right to know."

"He's going to come here," I said, feeling my eyes burn. "He's going to come here, Mare!"

"I know! I'm sorry!" she said, trying to hug me. I pulled away from her and covered my face with my hands.

A familiar pair of strong, protective hands rested on my shoulders. "He won't hurt you, Pigeon," Travis said. "I won't let him."

"He'll find a way," America said, watching me with heavy eyes. "He always does."

"I have to get out of here." I pulled my coat around me and pulled at the handles of the French doors. I was too upset to slow down long enough to coordinate pushing down the handles while pulling at the doors at the same time. Just as frustrated tears fell down my frozen cheeks, Travis's hand covered mine. He pressed down, helping me to push the handles, and then with his other hand he pulled open the doors. I looked at him, conscious of the ridiculous scene I was making, expecting to see a confused or disapproving look on his face, but he looked down at me only with understanding.

Travis took me under his arm and together we went through the house, down the stairs and through the crowd to the front door. The three of them struggled to keep up with me as I made a beeline for the Charger.

America's hand shot out and grabbed my coat, stopping me in my tracks. "Abby!" she whispered, pointing to a small group of people.

They were crowded around an older, disheveled man who pointed frantically to the house, holding up a picture. The couples were nodding, discussing the photo among one another.

I stormed over to the man and pulled the photo from his hands. "What in the hell are you doing here?"

The crowd dispersed, walking into the house, and Shepley and America stood on each side of me. Travis cupped my shoulders from behind.

Mick looked at my dress and clicked his tongue in disapproval. "Well, well, Cookie. You can take the girl out of Vegas . . ."

"Shut up. Shut up, Mick. Just turn around," I pointed behind him, "and go back to wherever you came from. I don't want you here."

"I can't, Cookie. I need your help."

"What else is new?" America sneered.

Mick narrowed his eyes at America and then looked to me. "You look awful pretty. You've grown up. I wouldn't've recognized you on the street."

I sighed, impatient with the small talk. "What do you want?"

He held up his hands and shrugged. "I seemed to have gotten myself in a pickle, kiddo. Old Dad needs some money."

I closed my eyes. "How much?"

"I was doing good, I really was. I just had to borrow a bit to get ahead and . . . you know."

"I know," I snapped. "How much do you need?"

"Twenty-five."

"Well, shit, Mick, twenty-five hundred? If you'll get the hell outta here . . . I'll give that to you now," Travis said, pulling out his wallet.

"He means twenty-five thousand," I said, glaring at my father.

Mick's eyes scanned over Travis. "Who's this clown?"

Travis's eyebrows shot up from his wallet and I felt his weight lean into my back. "I can see, now, why a smart guy like yourself has been reduced to asking your teenage daughter for an allowance."

Before Mick could speak, I pulled out my cell phone. "Who do you owe this time, Mick?"

Mick scratched his greasy, graying hair. "Well, it's a funny story, Cookie—"

"Who?" I shouted.

"Benny."

My mouth fell open and I took a step back, into Travis. "Benny? You owe Benny? What in the hell were you . . ." I took a breath; there was no point. "I don't have that kind of money, Mick."

He smiled. "Something tells me you do."

"Well, I don't! You've really done it, this time, haven't you? I knew you wouldn't stop until you got yourself killed!"

He shifted; the smug grin on his face had vanished. "How much ya got?"

I clenched my jaw. "Eleven thousand. I was saving for a car."

America's eyes darted in my direction. "Where did you get eleven thousand dollars, Abby?"

"Travis's fights," I said, my eyes boring into Mick's.

Travis pulled on my shoulders to look into my eyes. "You made eleven thousand off my fights? When were you betting?"

"Adam and I had an understanding," I said, unconcerned with Travis's surprise.

Mick's eyes were suddenly animated. "You can double that in a weekend, Cookie. You could get me the twenty-five by Sunday, and Benny won't send his thugs for me."

My throat felt dry and tight. "It'll clean me out, Mick. I have to pay for school."

"Oh, you can make it back in no time," he said, waving his hand dismissively.

"When is your deadline?" I asked.

"Monday mornin'. Midnight," he said, unapologetic.

"You don't have to give him a fucking dime, Pigeon," Travis said, tugging on my arm.

Mick grabbed my wrist. "It's the least you could do! I wouldn't be in this mess if it weren't for you!"

America slapped his hand away and then shoved him. "Don't

you dare start that shit again, Mick! She didn't make you borrow money from Benny!"

Mick looked at me with loathing in his eyes. "If it weren't for her, I woulda had my own money. You took everything from me, Abby. I have nothin'!"

I thought time away from Mick would lessen the pain that came with being his daughter, but the tears flowing from my eyes said otherwise. "I'll get your money to Benny by Sunday. But when I do, I want you to leave me the hell alone. I won't do this again, Mick. From now on, you're on your own, do you hear me? Stay. Away."

He pressed his lips together and then nodded. "Have it your way, Cookie."

I turned around and headed for the car, hearing America behind me. "Pack your bags, boys. We're going to Vegas."

Chapter Fifteen
City of Sin

TRAVIS SET DOWN OUR BAGS AND LOOKED AROUND THE room. "This is nice, right?"

I glared at him and he raised his brow. "What?"

The zipper of my suitcase whined as I pulled it around its borders, and I shook my head. Different strategies and the lack of time crowded my head. "This isn't a vacation. You shouldn't be here, Travis."

In the next moment he was behind me, crossing his arms around my middle. "I go where you go."

I leaned my head against his chest and sighed. "I have to get on the floor. You can stay here or check out the Strip. I'll see you later, okay?"

"I'm going with you."

"I don't want you there, Trav." A hurt expression weighted his face, and I touched his arm. "If I'm going to win fourteen thousand dollars in one weekend, I have to concentrate. I don't like who I'm going to be while I'm at those tables, and I don't want you see it, okay?"

He brushed my hair from my eyes and kissed my cheek. "Okay, Pidge."

Travis waved to America as he left the room, and she approached me in the same dress she had worn to the date party. I changed into a short gold number and slipped on a pair of heels, grimacing at the mirror. America pulled back my hair and then handed me a black tube.

"You need about five more coats of mascara, and they're going to toss your ID on sight if you don't slather on some more blush. Have you forgotten how this game is played?"

I snatched the mascara from her hand and spent another ten minutes on my makeup. Once I finished, my eyes began to gloss over. "Dammit, Abby, don't cry," I said, looking up and dabbing under my eyes with a tissue.

"You don't have to do this. You don't owe him anything." America cupped my shoulders as I stood in front of the mirror one last time.

"He owes Benny money, Mare. If I don't, they'll kill him."

Her expression was one of pity. I had seen her look at me that way many times before, but this time she was desperate. She'd seen him ruin my life more times than either of us could count. "What about the next time? And the next time? You can't keep doing this."

"He agreed to stay away. Mick Abernathy is a lot of things, but he's no welsher."

We walked down the hall and stepped into an empty elevator. "You have everything you need?" I asked, keeping the cameras in mind.

America clicked her fake driver's license with her nails and smiled. "The name's Candy. Candy Crawford," she said in her flawless southern accent.

I held out my hand. "Jessica James. Nice to meet you, Candy."

We both slipped on our sunglasses and stood stone-faced as the elevator opened, revealing the neon lights and bustle of the casino floor. People moved in all directions from all walks of life. Vegas was heavenly hell, the one place you could find dancers in ostentatious feathers and stage makeup, prostitutes with insufficient yet acceptable attire, businessmen in luxurious suits, and wholesome families in the same building. We strutted down an aisle lined with red ropes and handed a man in a red jacket our IDs. He eyed me for a moment and I pulled down my glasses.

"Anytime today would be great," I said, bored.

He returned our IDs and stood aside, letting us pass. We passed aisle after aisle of slot machines and the blackjack tables and then stopped at the roulette wheel. I scanned the room, watching the various poker tables, settling on the one with older gentlemen in the seats.

"That one," I said, nodding across the way.

"Start off aggressive, Abby. They won't know what hit 'em."

"No. They're old Vegas. I have to play it smart this time."

I walked over to the table, using my most charming smile. Locals could smell a hustler from a mile away, but I had two things in my favor that covered the scent of any con: youth . . . and tits.

"Good evening, gentlemen. Mind if I join you?"

They didn't look up. "Sure, sweet cheeks. Grab a seat and look pretty. Just don't talk."

"I want in," I said, handing America my sunglasses. "There's not enough action at the blackjack tables."

One of the men chewed on his cigar. "This is a poker table, Princess. Five-card draw. Try your luck on the slot machines."

I sat in the only empty seat, making a show of crossing my legs. "I've always wanted to play poker in Vegas. And I have all these chips," I said, setting my rack of chips on the table, "and I'm really good online."

All five men looked at my chips and then at me. "There's a minimum ante, Sugar," the dealer said.

"How much?"

"Five hundred, Peach. Listen . . . I don't want to make you cry. Do yourself a favor and pick out a shiny slot machine."

I pushed forward my chips, shrugging my shoulders in the way a reckless and overly confident girl might before realizing she'd just lost her college fund. The men looked at each other. The dealer shrugged and tossed in his own.

"Jimmy," one of the players said, offering his hand. When I took it, he pointed at the other men. "Mel, Pauli, Joe, and that's Winks." I looked over to the skinny man chewing on a toothpick, and as predicted, he winked at me.

I nodded and waited with fake anticipation as the first hand was dealt. I purposely lost the first two, but by the fourth hand, I was up. It didn't take as long for the Vegas veterans to figure me out as it did Thomas.

"You said you played online?" Pauli asked.

"And with my dad."

"You from here?" Jimmy asked.

"Wichita," I said.

"She's no online player, I'll tell you that," Mel grumbled.

An hour later, I had taken twenty-seven hundred dollars from my opponents, and they were beginning to sweat.

"Fold," Jimmy said, throwing down his cards with a frown.

"If I didn't see it with my own eyes, I would have never believed," I heard behind me.

America and I turned at the same time, and my lips stretched across my face in a wide smile. "Jesse." I shook my head. "What are you doing here?"

"This is my place you're scamming, Cookie. What are you doing here?"

I rolled my eyes and turned to my suspicious new friends. "You know I hate that, Jess."

"Excuse us," Jesse said, pulling me by the arm to my feet. America eyed me warily as I was ushered a few feet away.

Jesse's father ran the casino, and it was more than just a surprise that he had joined the family business. We used to chase each other down the halls of the hotel upstairs, and I always beat him when we raced elevators. He had grown up since I'd seen him last. I remembered him as a gangly prepubescent teenager; the man before me was a sharply dressed pit boss, not at all gangly and certainly all man. He still had the silky brown skin and green eyes I remembered, but the rest of him was a pleasant surprise.

His emerald irises sparkled in the bright lights. "This is surreal. I thought it was you when I walked by, but I couldn't convince myself that you would come back here. When I saw this Tinker Bell cleaning up at the vets' table, I knew it was you."

"It's me," I said.

"You look . . . different."

"So do you. How's your dad?"

"Retired," he smiled. "How long are you here?"

"Just until Sunday. I have to get back to school."

"Hey, Jess," America said, taking my arm.

"America," he chuckled. "I should have known. You are each other's shadows."

"If her parents ever knew that I brought her here, all that would have come to an end a long time ago."

"It's good to see you, Abby. Why don't you let me buy you dinner?" he asked, scanning my dress.

"I'd love to catch up, but I'm not here for fun, Jess."

He held out his hand and smiled. "Neither am I. Hand over your ID."

My face fell, knowing I had a fight on my hands. Jesse wouldn't give in to my charms so easily. I knew I would have to tell him the truth. "I'm here for Mick. He's in trouble."

Jesse shifted. "What kind of trouble?"

"The usual."

"I wish I could help. We go way back, and you know I respect your dad, but you know I can't let you stay."

I grabbed his arm and squeezed. "He owes Benny money."

Jesse closed his eyes and shook his head. "Jesus."

"I have until tomorrow. I'm calling in a solid IOU, Jesse. Just give me until then."

He touched his palm to my cheek. "I'll tell you what . . . if you have dinner with me tomorrow, I'll give you until midnight."

I looked at America and then to Jesse. "I'm here with someone."

He shrugged. "Take it or leave it, Abby. You know how things are done here. You can't have something for nothing."

I sighed, defeated. "Fine. I'll meet you tomorrow night at Ferraro's if you give me until midnight."

He leaned down and kissed my cheek. "It was good to see

you again. See you tomorrow . . . five o'clock, all right? I'm on the floor at eight."

I smiled as he walked away, but it quickly faded when I saw Travis staring at me from the roulette table.

"Oh shit," America said, tugging on my arm.

Travis glared at Jesse as he passed, and then made his way to me. He shoved his hands in his pockets and glanced at Jesse, who was watching us from the corner of his eye.

"Who was that?"

I nodded in Jesse's direction. "That is Jesse Viveros. I've known him a long time."

"How long?"

I looked back at the vet table. "Travis, I don't have time for this."

"I guess he chucked the youth minister idea," America said, sending a flirtatious grin in Jesse's direction.

"That's your ex-boyfriend?" Travis asked, instantly angry. "I thought you said he was from Kansas?"

I shot America an impatient glare and then took Travis's chin in my hand, insisting on his full attention. "He knows I'm not old enough to be in here, Trav. He gave me until midnight. I will explain everything later, but for now I have to get back to the game, all right?"

Travis's jaws fluttered under his skin, and then he closed his eyes, taking a deep breath. "All right. I'll see you at midnight." He bent down to kiss me, but his lips were cold and distant. "Good luck."

I smiled as he melted into the crowd, and then I turned my attention to the men. "Gentlemen?"

"Have a seat, Shirley Temple," Jimmy said. "We'll be making our money back now. We don't appreciate being hustled."

"Do your worst." I smiled.

"You have ten minutes," America whispered.

"I know," I said.

I tried to block out the time and America's knee bobbing nervously under the table. The pot was at sixteen thousand dollars—the night's all-time high, and it was all or nothing.

"I've never seen anything like you, kid. You've had almost a perfect game. And she's got no tell, Winks. You notice?" Pauli said.

Winks nodded; his cheerful demeanor had evaporated a bit more with every hand. "I noticed. Not a rub or a smile, even her eyes stay the same. It's not natural. Everybody's got a tell."

"Not everybody," America said, smug.

I felt a familiar pair of hands touch my shoulders. I knew it was Travis, but I didn't dare turn around, not with three thousand dollars sitting in the middle of the table.

"Call," Jimmy said.

Those who had crowded around us applauded when I laid down my hand. Jimmy was the only one close enough to touch me with three of a kind. Nothing my straight couldn't handle.

"Unbelievable!" Pauli said, throwing his two deuces to the table.

"I'm out," Joe grumbled, standing up and stomping away from the table.

Jimmy was a bit more gracious. "I can die tonight and feel I've played a truly worthy opponent, kiddo. It's been a pleasure, Abby."

I froze. "You knew?"

Jimmy smiled. The years of cigar smoke and coffee stained his large teeth. "I've played you before. Six years ago. I've wanted a rematch for a long time."

Jimmy extended his hand. "Take care, kid. Tell your dad Jimmy Pescelli says hello."

America helped gather my winnings, and I turned to Travis, looking at my watch. "I need more time."

"Wanna try the blackjack tables?"

"I can't lose money, Trav."

He smiled. "You can't lose, Pidge."

America shook her head. "Blackjack's not her game."

Travis nodded. "I won a little. I'm up six hundred. You can have it."

Shepley handed me his chips. "I only made three. It's yours."

I sighed. "Thanks, guys, but I'm still short five grand."

I looked at my watch again and then looked up to see Jesse approaching. "How did you do?" he asked, smiling.

"I'm five K short, Jess. I need more time."

"I've done all I can, Abby."

I nodded, knowing I had already asked too much. "Thanks for letting me stay."

"Maybe I can get my dad to talk to Benny for you?"

"It's Mick's mess. I'm going to ask him for an extension."

Jesse shook his head. "You know that's not going to happen, Cookie, no matter how much you come up with. If it's less than what he owes, Benny's going to send someone. You stay as far away from him as you can."

I felt my eyes burn. "I have to try."

Jesse took a step forward, leaning in to keep his voice low. "Get on a plane, Abby. You hear me?"

"I hear you," I snapped.

Jesse sighed, and his eyes grew heavy with sympathy. He wrapped his arms around me and kissed my hair. "I'm sorry. If it wasn't my job at stake, you know I'd try to figure something out."

I nodded, pulling away from him. "I know. You did what you could."

He lifted my chin with his finger. "I'll see you tomorrow at five." He bent down to kiss the corner of my mouth and then walked past me without another word.

I glanced to America, who watched Travis. I didn't dare meet his eyes; I couldn't imagine what angry expression was on his face.

"What's at five?" Travis said, his voice dripping with subdued anger.

"She agreed to dinner if Jesse would let her stay. She didn't have a choice, Trav," America said. I could tell by the cautious tone of her voice that Travis was beyond angry.

I peered up at him, and he glowered at me with the same betrayed expression Mick had on his face the night he realized I'd taken his luck.

"You had a choice."

"Have you ever dealt with the Mob, Travis? I'm sorry if your feelings are hurt, but a free meal with an old friend isn't a high price to pay to keep Mick alive."

I could see that Travis wanted to lash out at me, but there was nothing he could say.

"C'mon, you guys, we have to find Benny," America said, pulling me by the arm.

Travis and Shepley followed behind in silence as we walked down the Strip to Benny's building. The traffic—both cars and people on the thoroughfare—were just beginning to concentrate. With each step, I felt a sick, hollow feeling in my stomach, my mind racing to think of a compelling argument to make Benny see reason. By the time we knocked on the large green door I had seen so many times before, I had come up as short as my bankroll.

It wasn't a surprise to see the enormous doorman—black, frightening, and as wide as he was tall—but I was stunned to see Benny standing beside him.

"Benny," I breathed.

"My, my . . . you're not Lucky Thirteen anymore, now, are ya? Mick didn't tell me what a looker you've grown into. I've been waiting for you, Cookie. I hear you have a payment for me."

I nodded and Benny gestured to my friends. I lifted my chin to feign confidence. "They're with me."

"I'm afraid your companions will have to wait outside," the doorman said in an abnormally deep bass tone.

Travis immediately took me by the arm. "She's not going in there alone. I'm coming with her."

Benny eyed Travis and I swallowed. When Benny looked up to his doorman and the corners of his mouth turned up, I relaxed a bit.

"Fair enough," Benny said. "Mick will be glad to know you have such a good friend with you."

I followed him inside, turning to see the worried look on America's face. Travis kept a firm grip on my arm, purposefully standing between me and the doorman. We followed Benny into an elevator and traveled up four floors in silence, and then the doors opened.

A large mahogany desk sat in the middle of a vast room. Benny hobbled to his plush chair and sat down, gesturing for us to take the two empty seats facing his desk. When I sat down, the leather felt cold beneath me, and I wondered how many people had sat in that same chair, moments from their death. I reached over to grab Travis's hand, and he gave me a reassuring squeeze.

"Mick owes me twenty-five thousand. I trust you have the full amount," Benny said, scribbling something on a notepad.

"Actually," I paused, clearing my throat, "I'm five K short, Benny. But I have all day tomorrow to get that. And five thousand is no problem, right? You know I'm good for it."

"Abigail," Benny said, frowning, "You disappoint me. You know my rules better than that."

"P-please, Benny. I'm asking you to take the 19,900 and I'll have the rest for you tomorrow."

Benny's beady eyes darted from me to Travis and then back again. It was then that I noticed two men taking a step forward from the shadowed corners of the room. Travis's grip on my hand grew tighter, and I held my breath.

"You know I don't take anything but the full amount. The fact that you're trying to hand me less tells me something. You know what it tells me? That you're not sure if you can get the full amount."

The men from the corners took another step forward.

"I can get your money, Benny," I giggled nervously. "I won eighty-nine hundred in six hours."

"So are you saying you'll bring me eighty-nine hundred in six more hours?" Benny smiled his devilish grin.

"The deadline isn't until midnight tomorrow," Travis said, glancing behind us and then watching the approaching shadow men.

"W-what are you doing, Benny?" I asked, my posture rigid.

"Mick called me tonight. He said you're taking care of his debt."

"I'm doing him a favor. I don't owe you any money," I said sternly, my survival instincts kicking in.

Benny leaned both of his fat, stubby elbows onto his desk. "I'm considering teaching Mick a lesson, and I'm curious just how lucky you are, kiddo."

Travis shot out of his chair, pulling me with him. He jerked me behind him, backing up toward the door.

"Josiah is outside the door, young man. Where exactly do you think you're going to escape to?"

I was wrong. When I was thinking about persuading Benny to see reason, I should have anticipated Mick's will to survive and Benny's penchant for retribution.

"Travis," I warned, watching Benny's henchmen approach us.

Travis pushed me behind him a few feet and stood tall. "I hope you know, Benny, that when I take out your men, I mean no disrespect. But I'm in love with this girl, and I can't let you hurt her."

Benny burst into a loud cackle. "I gotta hand it to you, son. You've got the biggest balls of anyone that's come through those doors. I'll prepare you for what you're about to get. The rather large fella to your right is David, and if he can't take you out with his fists, he's going to use that knife in his holster. The man to your left is Dane, and he's my best fighter. He's got a fight tomorrow, as a matter of fact, and he's never lost. Mind you don't hurt your hands, Dane. I've got a lot of money riding on you."

Dane smiled at Travis with wild, amused eyes. "Yes, sir."

"Benny, stop! I can get you the money!" I cried.

"Oh no . . . this is going to get interesting very fast," Benny chuckled, settling back into his seat.

David rushed Travis and my hands flew up to my mouth. The man was strong but clumsy and slow. Before David could swing or reach for his knife, Travis incapacitated him, shoving David's face straight down into his knee. When Travis threw a punch, he wasted no time, throwing every bit of strength he had into the man's face. Two punches and an elbow later, David was lying on the floor in a bloody heap.

Benny's head fell back, laughing hysterically and pounding his desk with the delight of a child watching Saturday morning cartoons. "Well, go on, Dane. He didn't scare you, did he?"

Dane approached Travis more carefully, with the focus and precision of a professional fighter. His fist flew at Travis's face with incredible speed, but Travis dodged, ramming his shoulder into Dane at full force. They fell against Benny's desk, and then Dane grabbed Travis with both arms, hurling him to the ground. They scuffled on the floor for a moment, and then Dane gained ground, positioning himself to get in a few punches on Travis while he was trapped beneath him on the floor. I covered my face, unable to watch.

I heard a cry of pain, and then I looked up to see Travis hovering over Dane, holding him by his shaggy hair, jabbing punch after punch into the side of his head. Dane's face rammed into the front of Benny's desk with each blow, and then he scrambled to his feet, disoriented and bleeding.

Travis watched him for a moment, and then attacked again, grunting with every strike, once again using the full force of his strength. Dane dodged once and landed his knuckles on Travis's jaw.

Travis smiled and held up his finger. "That's your one."

I couldn't believe my ears. Travis had let Benny's thug hit him. He was enjoying himself. I had never seen Travis fight without constraint; it was a bit frightening to see him unleash everything he had on these trained killers and have the upper hand. Until that moment, I hadn't realized just what Travis was capable of.

With Benny's disturbing laughter in the background, Travis finished Dane off, landing his elbow in the center of Dane's face, knocking him out before he hit the ground. I followed his body as it bounced once on Benny's imported rug.

"Amazing, young man! Simply amazing!" Benny said, clapping with delight.

Travis pulled me behind him as Josiah filled the doorway with his massive frame.

"Should I take care of this, sir?"

"No! No, no . . ." Benny said, still giddy with the impromptu performance. "What is your name?"

Travis was still breathing hard. "Travis Maddox," he said, wiping Dane's and David's blood off his hands and onto his jeans.

"Travis Maddox, I believe you can help your little girlfriend out."

"How's that?" Travis puffed.

"Dane was supposed to fight tomorrow night. I had a lot of cash riding on him, and it doesn't look like Dane will be fit to win a fight anytime soon. I suggest you take his place, make my bankroll for me, and I'll forgive the remaining fifty-one hundred of Mick's debt."

Travis turned to me. "Pigeon?"

"Are you all right?" I asked, wiping the blood from his face. I bit my lip, feeling my face crumple with a combination of fear and relief.

Travis smiled. "It's not my blood, baby. Don't cry."

Benny stood. "I'm a busy man, son. Pass or play?"

"I'll do it," Travis said. "Give me the when and where and I'll be there."

"You'll be fighting Brock McMann. He's no wallflower. He was barred from the UFC last year."

Travis was unaffected. "Just tell me where I need to be."

Benny's shark's grin spread across his face. "I like you, Travis. I think we'll be good friends."

"I doubt it," Travis said. He opened the door for me and sustained a protective stance until we cleared the front door.

"Jesus Christ!" America cried upon seeing the splattered blood covering Travis's clothing. "Are you guys okay?" She grabbed my shoulders and scanned my face.

"I'm okay. Just another day at the office. For both of us," I said, wiping my eyes.

Travis grabbed my hand and we rushed to the hotel with Shepley and America close behind. Not many paid attention to Travis's appearance. He was covered in blood, and only the occasional out-of-towner seemed to notice.

"What in the hell happened in there?" Shepley finally asked.

Travis stripped down to his Skivvies and disappeared into the bathroom. The shower turned on and America handed me a box of tissues.

"I'm fine, Mare."

She sighed and pushed the box at me once again. "You're not fine."

"This is not my first rodeo with Benny," I said. My muscles were sore from twenty-four hours of stress-induced tension.

"It's your first time to watch Travis go apeshit on someone," Shepley said. "I've seen it once before. It's not pretty."

"What happened?" America insisted.

"Mick called Benny. Passed accountability on to me."

"I'm gonna kill him! I'm going to kill that sorry son of a bitch!" America shouted.

"He's not holding me responsible, but he was going to teach Mick a lesson for sending his daughter to pay off his debt. He called two of his damned dogs on us, and Travis took them out. Both of them. In under five minutes."

"So Benny let you go?" America asked.

Travis appeared from the bathroom with a towel around his waist, the only evidence of his scuffle a small red mark on his cheekbone below his right eye. "One of the guys I knocked out had a fight tomorrow night. I'm taking his place and in return Benny will forgive the last five K Mick owes."

America stood up. "This is ridiculous! Why are we helping Mick, Abby? He threw you to the wolves! I'm going to kill him!"

"Not if I kill him first," Travis seethed.

"Get in line," I said.

"So you're fighting tomorrow?" Shepley asked.

"At a place called Zero's. Six o'clock. It's Brock McMann, Shep."

Shepley shook his head. "No way. No fucking way, Trav. The guy's a maniac!"

"Yeah," Travis said, "but he's not fighting for his girl, is he?" Travis cradled me in his arms, kissing the top of my hair. "You okay, Pigeon?"

"This is wrong. This is wrong on so many levels. I don't know which one to talk you out of first."

"Did you not see me tonight? I'm going to be fine. I've seen Brock fight before. He's tough, but not unbeatable."

"I don't want you to do this, Trav."

"Well, I don't want you to go to dinner with your ex-boyfriend tomorrow night. I guess we both have to do something unpleasant to save your good-for-nothing father."

I had seen it before. Vegas changed people, creating monsters and broken men. It was easy to let the lights and stolen dreams seep into your blood. I had seen the energized, invincible look on Travis's face many times growing up, and the only cure was a plane ride home.

JESSE FROWNED WHEN I LOOKED AT MY WATCH AGAIN.

"You have somewhere to be, Cookie?" Jesse asked.

"Please stop calling me that, Jesse. I hate it."

"I hated it when you left, too. Didn't stop you."

"This is a tired, worn-out conversation. Let's just have dinner, okay?"

"Okay, let's talk about your new man. What's his name? Travis?" I nodded. "What are you doing with that tattooed psychopath? He looks like a reject from the Manson Family."

"Be nice, Jesse, or I'm walking out of here."

"I can't get over how different you look. I can't get over that you're sitting in front of me."

I rolled my eyes. "Get over it."

"There she is," Jesse said. "The girl I remember."

I looked down at my watch. "Travis's fight is in twenty minutes. I better go."

"We still have dessert coming."

"I can't, Jess. I don't want him worrying if I'm going to show up. It's important."

His shoulders fell. "I know. I miss the days when I was important."

I rested my hand on his. "We were just kids. That was a lifetime ago."

"When did we grow up? You being here is a sign, Abby. I thought I'd never see you again and here you sit. Stay with me."

I shook my head slowly, hesitant to hurt my oldest friend. "I love him, Jess."

His disappointment shadowed the small grin on his face. "Then you'd better go."

I kissed his cheek and fled the restaurant, catching a taxi.

"Where you headed?" The cab driver asked.

"Zero's."

The cabby turned to look at me, giving me a once-over. "You sure?"

"I'm sure! Go!" I said, tossing cash over the seat.

Chapter Sixteen
Home

TRAVIS FINALLY BROKE THROUGH THE CROWD WITH Benny's hand on his shoulder, whispering in his ear. Travis nodded and replied. My blood ran cold as I watched him be so friendly to the man who had threatened us less than twenty-four hours before. Travis basked in the applause and congratulations of his triumph as the crowd roared. He walked taller, his smile was wider, and when he reached me, he planted a quick kiss on my mouth.

I could taste the salty sweat mixed with the coppery taste of blood on his lips. He had won the fight, but not without a few battle wounds of his own.

"What was that about?" I asked, watching Benny laugh with his cohorts.

"I'll tell you later. We have a lot to talk about," he said with a broad grin.

A man patted Travis on the back.

"Thanks," Travis said, turning to him and shaking his outstretched hand.

"Looking forward to seeing another match of yours, son," the man said, handing him a bottle of beer. "That was incredible."

"C'mon, Pidge." He took a sip of his beer, swished it around in his mouth, and then spit, the amber liquid on the ground tinged with blood. He weaved through the crowd, taking in a deep breath when we made it to the sidewalk outside. He kissed me once and then led me down the Strip, his steps quick and purposeful.

In the elevator of our hotel, he pushed me against the mirrored wall, grabbed my leg, and pulled it up in a quick motion against his hip. His mouth crashed into mine, and I felt the hand under my knee slide up my thigh and pull up my skirt.

"Travis, there's a camera in here," I said against his lips.

"I don't give a fuck," he chuckled. "I'm celebrating."

I pushed him away. "We can celebrate in the room," I said, wiping my mouth and looking down at my hand, seeing streaks of crimson.

"What's wrong with you, Pigeon? You won, I won, we paid off Mick's debt, and I just got the offer of a lifetime."

The elevator opened and I stood in place as Travis stepped out into the hall. "What kind of offer?" I asked.

Travis reached out his hand, but I ignored it. My eyes narrowed, already knowing what he would say.

He sighed. "I told you, we'll talk about it later."

"Let's talk about it now."

He leaned in and pulled me by the wrist into the hallway and then lifted me off the floor into his arms.

"I am going to make enough money to replace what Mick took from you, to pay for the rest of your tuition, pay off my bike, and buy you a new car," he said, sliding the card key in and out of its slot. He pushed open the door and set me on my feet. "And that's just the beginning!"

"And how exactly are you going to do that?" My chest tightened and my hands began to tremble.

He took my face in his hands, ecstatic. "Benny is going to let me fight here in Vegas. Six figures a fight, Pidge. Six figures a fight!"

I closed my eyes and shook my head, blocking out the excitement in his eyes. "What did you say to Benny?" Travis lifted my chin, and I opened my eyes, afraid he had already signed a contract.

He chuckled. "I told him I'd think about it."

I exhaled the breath I'd been holding. "Oh, thank God. Don't scare me like that, Trav. I thought you were serious."

Travis grimaced and steadied himself before he spoke. "I am serious, Pigeon. I told him I needed to talk to you first, but I thought you'd be happy. He's scheduling one fight a month. Do you have any idea how much money that is? Cash!"

"I can add, Travis. I can also keep my senses when I'm in Vegas, which you obviously can't. I have to get you out of here before you do something stupid." I walked over to the closet and ripped our clothes from the hangers, furiously stuffing them into our suitcases.

Travis gently grabbed my arms and spun me around. "I can do this. I can fight for Benny for a year and then we'll be set for a long, long time."

"What are you going to do? Drop out of school and move here?"

"Benny's going to fly me out, work around my schedule."

I laughed once, incredulous. "You can't be that gullible,

Travis. When you're on Benny's payroll, you aren't just going to fight once a month for him. Did you forget about Dane? You'll end up being one of his thugs!"

He shook his head. "We already discussed that, Pidge. He doesn't want me to do anything but fight."

"And you trust him? You know they call him Slick Benny around here!"

"I wanted to buy you a car, Pigeon. A nice one. Both of our tuitions will be paid in full."

"Oh? The mob is handing out scholarships, now?"

Travis's jaws clenched. He was irritated at having to convince me. "This is good for us. I can sock it away until it's time for us to buy a house. I can't make this kind of money anywhere else."

"What about your Criminal Justice degree? You're going to be seeing your old classmates quite a bit working for Benny, I promise you."

"Baby, I understand your reservations, I do. But I'm being smart about this. I'll do it for a year and then we'll get out and do whatever the hell we want."

"You don't just quit Benny, Trav. He's the only one that can tell you when you're done. You have no idea what you're dealing with! I can't believe you're even considering this! Working for a man that would have beat the hell out of the both of us last night if you hadn't stopped him?"

"Exactly. I stopped him."

"You stopped two of his lightweight goons, Travis. What are you going to do if there are a dozen of them? What are you going to do if they come after me during one of your fights?"

"It wouldn't make sense for him to do that. I'll be making him lots of money."

"The moment you decide you're not going to do that anymore, you're expendable. That's how these people work."

Travis walked away from me and looked out the window, the blinking lights coloring his conflicted features. He had made his decision before he'd ever come to me about it.

"It's going to be all right, Pigeon. I'll make sure it is. And then we'll be set."

I shook my head and turned around, shoving our clothes into our suitcases. When we set down on the tarmac at home, he would be his old self again. Vegas did strange things to people, and I couldn't reason with him while he was intoxicated with the flow of cash and whiskey.

I refused to discuss it further until we were on the plane, afraid Travis would let me leave without him. I buckled my seat belt and clenched my teeth, watching him stare longingly out the window as we climbed into the night sky. He was already missing the wickedness and limitless temptations Vegas had to offer.

"That's a lot of money, Pidge."

"No."

His head jerked in my direction. "This is my decision. I don't think you're looking at the big picture."

"I think you've lost your damn mind."

"You're not even going to consider it?"

"No, and neither are you. You're not going to work for a murderous criminal in Las Vegas, Travis. It's completely ridiculous for you to think I could consider it."

Travis sighed and looked out the window. "My first fight is in three weeks."

My mouth dropped open. "You already agreed to it?"

He winked. "Not yet."

"But you're going to?"

He smiled. "You'll quit being mad when I buy you a Lexus."

"I don't want a Lexus," I seethed.

"You can have anything you want, baby. Imagine how it's going to feel driving into any dealership you want, and all you have to do is pick your favorite color."

"You're not doing this for me. Stop pretending you are."

He leaned over, kissing my hair. "No, I'm doing it for us. You just can't see how great it's going to be."

A cold shiver radiated from my chest, traveling down my spine into my legs. He wouldn't see reason until we were in the apartment, and I was terrified that Benny had made him an offer he couldn't refuse. I shook off my fears; I had to believe Travis loved me enough to forget the dollar signs and false promises Benny had made.

"Pidge? Do you know how to cook a turkey?"

"A turkey?" I said, taken off guard by the sudden change of conversation.

He squeezed my hand. "Well, Thanksgiving break is coming up, and you know my dad loves you. He wants you to come for Thanksgiving, but we always end up ordering pizza and watching the game. I thought maybe me and you could try cooking a bird together. You know, have a real turkey dinner for once in the Maddox house."

I pressed my lips together, trying not to laugh. "You just thaw the turkey and put it in a pan and cook it in the oven all day. There's not much to it."

"So you'll come? You'll help me?"

I shrugged. "Sure."

His attention was diverted from the intoxicating lights below, and I allowed myself to hope that he would see how wrong he was about Benny after all.

TRAVIS SET OUR SUITCASES ON THE BED AND COLLAPSED beside them. He hadn't pushed the Benny issue, and I was hopeful that Vegas had begun to filter out of his system. I bathed Toto, disgusted that he reeked of smoke and dirty socks from being in Brazil's apartment all weekend, and then towel-dried him in the bedroom.

"Oh! You smell so much better!" I giggled as he shook, spraying me with tiny droplets of water. He stood up on his hind legs, covering my face with tiny puppy kisses. "I missed you, too, little man."

"Pigeon?" Travis asked, nervously knotting his fingers together.

"Yeah?" I said, rubbing Toto with the fluffy yellow towel in my hands.

"I wanna do this. I want to fight in Vegas."

"No," I said, smiling at Toto's happy face.

He sighed. "You're not listening. I'm gonna do it. You'll see in a few months that it was the right decision."

I looked up at him. "You're going to work for Benny."

He nodded nervously and then smiled. "I just wanna take care of you, Pidge."

Tears glossed my eyes, knowing he was resolved. "I don't want anything bought with that money, Travis. I don't want anything to do with Benny or Vegas or anything that goes along with it."

"You didn't have a problem with the thought of buying a car with the money from my fights here."

"That's different and you know it."

He frowned. "It's gonna be okay, Pidge. You'll see."

I watched him for a moment, hoping for a glimmer of amusement in his eyes, waiting for him to tell me that he was joking. But all I could see was uncertainty and greed.

"Why did you even ask me, Travis? You were going to work for Benny no matter what I said."

"I want your support on this, but it's too much money to turn down. I would be crazy to say no."

I sat for a moment, stunned. Once it had all sunk in, I nodded. "Okay, then. You've made your decision."

Travis beamed. "You'll see, Pigeon. It's going to be great." He pushed off the bed, walked over to me, and kissed my fingers. "I'm starved. You hungry?"

I shook my head and he kissed my forehead before making his way to the kitchen. Once his footsteps left the hall, I pulled my clothes from their hangers, grateful that I had room in my suitcase for most of my belongings. Angry tears fell down my cheeks. I knew better than to take Travis to that place. I had fought tooth and nail to keep him from the dark edges of my life, and the moment the opportunity presented itself, I dragged him to the core of everything I hated without a second thought.

Travis was going to be a part of that, and if he wouldn't let me save him, I had to save myself.

The suitcase was filled to its limit, and I stretched the zipper over the bulging contents. I yanked it off the bed and down the hall, passing the kitchen without glancing in its direction. I hurried down the steps, relieved that America and Shepley were still kissing and laughing in the parking lot, transferring her things from his Charger to her Honda.

"Pigeon?" Travis called from the doorway of the apartment.

I touched America's wrist. "I need you to take me to Morgan, Mare."

"What's going on?" she said, noting the seriousness of the situation by my expression.

I glanced behind me to see Travis jogging down the stairs and across the grass to where we stood.

"What are you doing?" he said, gesturing to my suitcase.

If I'd told him in that moment, all hope of separating myself from Mick, and Vegas, and Benny, and everything I didn't want would be lost. Travis wouldn't let me leave, and by morning I would have convinced myself to accept his decision.

I scratched my head and smiled, trying to buy some time to think of an excuse.

"Pidge?"

"I'm taking my stuff to Morgan. They have all those washers and dryers and I have a ridiculous amount of laundry to do."

He frowned. "You were going to leave without telling me?"

I glanced to America and then to Travis, struggling for the most believable lie.

"She was coming back in, Trav. You're so freakin' paranoid," America said with the dismissive smile she had used to deceive her parents so many times.

"Oh," he said, still unsure. "You staying here tonight?" he asked me, pinching the fabric of my coat.

"I don't know. I guess it depends on when my laundry gets done."

Travis smiled, pulling me against him. "In three weeks, I'll pay someone to do your laundry. Or you can just throw away your dirty clothes and buy new ones."

"You're fighting for Benny again?" America asked, shocked.

"He made me an offer I couldn't refuse."

"Travis," Shepley began.

"Don't you guys start on me, too. If I'm not changing my mind for Pidge, I'm not changing my mind for you."

America met my eyes with understanding, "Well, we better get you back, Abby. That pile of clothes is gonna take you forever."

I nodded and Travis leaned down to kiss me. I pulled him closer, knowing it would be the last time I felt his lips against mine. "See you later," he said. "Love you."

Shepley lifted my suitcase into the hatchback of the Honda, and America slid into her seat beside me. Travis folded his arms across his chest, chatting with Shepley as America switched on the ignition.

"You can't stay in your room tonight, Abby. He's going to come straight there when he figures it out," America said as she slowly backed away from the parking block.

Tears filled my eyes and spilled over, falling down my cheeks. "I know."

Travis's cheerful expression changed when he saw the look on my face. He wasted no time jogging to my window. "What's wrong, Pidge?" he said, tapping on the glass.

"Go, Mare," I said, wiping my eyes. I focused on the road ahead as Travis jogged alongside the car.

"Pigeon? America! Stop the fucking car!" he yelled, slamming his palm against the glass. "Abby, don't do this!" he said, realization and fear distorting his expression.

America turned onto the main road and pressed on the gas. "I'm never going to hear the end of this—just so you know."

"I'm so, so sorry, Mare."

She glanced into the rearview mirror and pushed her foot to the floor. "Jesus Christ, Travis," she muttered under her breath.

I turned to see him running at full speed behind us, vanishing and reappearing between the lights and shadows of the street lamps. After he reached the end of the block, he turned in the opposite direction, sprinting to the apartment.

"He's going back to get his bike. He's gonna follow us to Morgan and cause a huge scene."

I closed my eyes. "Just . . . hurry. I'll sleep in your room tonight. Think Vanessa will mind?"

"She's never there. He's really going to work for Benny?"

The word was stuck in my throat, so I simply nodded.

America grabbed my hand and squeezed. "You're making the right decision, Abby. You can't go through that again. If he won't listen to you, he's not going to listen to anyone."

My cell phone rang. I looked down to see Travis's silly face and then pressed ignore. Less than five seconds later, it rang again. I turned it off and shoved it into my purse.

"This is going to be a god-awful fucking mess," I said, shaking my head and wiping my eyes.

"I don't envy your life for the next week or so. I can't imagine breaking up with someone that refuses to stay away. You know that's how it's going to be, right?"

We pulled into the parking lot at Morgan, and America held open the door as I lugged my suitcase in. We rushed to her room and I puffed, waiting for her to unlock her door. She held it open and then tossed me the key.

"He's going to end up getting arrested or something," she said.

She ran down the hall and I watched her rush across the parking lot from the window, getting in her car just as Travis pulled up on his bike beside her. He ran around to the passenger side and yanked open the door, looking to Morgan's doors when he realized I wasn't in the car. America backed out while Travis ran into the building, and I turned, watching the door.

Down the hall, Travis pounded on my door, calling my name. I had no idea if Kara was there, but if she was, I felt bad for what she would have to endure for the next few minutes until Travis accepted that I wasn't in my room.

"Pidge? Open the fucking door, dammit! I'm not leaving until you talk to me! Pigeon!" he yelled, banging on the door so loudly the entire building could have heard.

I cringed when I heard Kara's mousy voice.

"What?" she growled.

I pressed my ear against the door, struggling to hear Travis's low murmurs. I didn't have to strain for long.

"I know she's here!" he yelled. "Pigeon?"

"She's not . . . Hey!" Kara squealed.

The door cracked against the cement block wall of our room and I knew that Travis had forced his way in. After a full minute of silence, I heard Travis yell down the hall. "Pigeon! Where is she?"

"I haven't seen her!" Kara shouted, angrier than I'd ever heard her. The door slammed shut, and sudden nausea overwhelmed me as I waited for what Travis would do next.

After several minutes of quiet, I cracked open the door, peering down the wide hallway. Travis sat with his back against the wall with his hands covering his face. I shut the door as quietly as I could, worrying that the campus police had been called.

After an hour, I glanced down the hall again. Travis hadn't moved.

I checked twice more during the night, finally falling asleep around four. I purposefully overslept, knowing I would skip classes that day. I turned on my phone to check my messages, seeing that Travis had flooded my inbox. The endless texts he'd sent me through the night varied from apologies to rants.

I called America in the afternoon, hoping Travis hadn't confiscated her cell phone. When she answered, I sighed.

"Hey."

America kept her voice low. "I haven't told Shepley where you are. I don't want him in the middle of this. Travis is crazy pissed at me right now. I'm probably staying at Morgan tonight."

"If Travis hasn't calmed down . . . good luck getting any sleep here. He made an Oscar-worthy performance in the hall last night. I'm surprised no one called security."

"He was kicked out of History today. When you didn't show, he kicked over both of your desks. Shep heard that he waited for you after all of your classes. He's losin' it, Abby. I told him you were done the second he made the decision to work for Benny. I can't believe he thought for a single second you would be okay with that."

"I guess I'll see you when you get here. I don't think I can go to my room, yet."

America and I were roommates over the next week, and she made sure to keep Shepley away so he wouldn't be tempted to tell Travis of my whereabouts. It was a full-time job avoiding a run-in with him. I avoided the cafeteria at all costs, as well as History class, and I played it safe by leaving my classes early. I knew that I would have to talk to Travis sometime, but

I couldn't until he had calmed down enough to accept my decision.

I sat alone Friday night, lying in bed, holding the phone to my ear. I rolled my eyes when my stomach growled.

"I can come pick you up and take you somewhere for dinner," America said.

I flipped through my History book, skipping over where Travis had doodled and scribbled love notes in the margins. "No, it's your first night with Shep in almost a week, Mare. I'm just going to pop over to the cafeteria."

"You sure?"

"Yeah. Tell Shep I said hi."

I walked slowly to the cafeteria, in no hurry to suffer the stares of those at the tables. The entire school was abuzz with the breakup, and Travis's volatile behavior didn't help. Just when the lights of the cafeteria came into view, I saw a dark figure approach.

"Pigeon?"

Startled, I jerked to a stop. Travis walked into the light, unshaven and pale. "Jesus, Travis! You scared the hell out of me!"

"If you would answer your phone when I call I wouldn't have to sneak around in the dark."

"You look like hell," I said.

"I've been through there once or twice this week."

I tightened my arms around me. "I'm actually on my way to grab something to eat. I'll call you later, okay?"

"No. We have to talk."

"Trav . . ."

"I turned Benny down. I called him Wednesday and told

him no." There was a hopeful glimmer in his eyes, but it disappeared when he registered my expression.

"I don't know what you want me to say, Travis."

"Say you forgive me. Say you'll take me back."

I clenched my teeth together, forbidding myself to cry. "I can't."

Travis's face crumpled. I took the opportunity to walk around him, but he sidestepped to stand in my way. "I haven't slept, or ate . . . I can't concentrate. I know you love me. Everything will be the way it used to be if you'd just take me back."

I closed my eyes. "We are dysfunctional, Travis. I think you're just obsessed with the thought of owning me more than anything else."

"That's not true. I love you more than my life, Pigeon," he said, hurt.

"That's exactly what I mean. That's crazy talk."

"It's not crazy. It's the truth."

"Okay . . . so what exactly is the order for you? Is it money, me, your life . . . or is there something that comes before money?"

"I realize what I've done, okay? I see where you'd think that, but if I'd known that you were gonna leave me, I would have never . . . I just wanted to take care of you."

"You've said that."

"Please don't do this. I can't stand feeling like this . . . it's . . . it's killin' me," he said, exhaling as if the air had been knocked out of him.

"I'm done, Travis."

He winced. "Don't say that."

"It's over. Go home."

His eyebrows pulled in. "You're my home."

His words cut me, and my chest tightened so much that it was hard to breathe. "You made your choice, Trav. I've made mine," I said, inwardly cursing the quivering in my voice.

"I'm going to stay the hell out of Vegas and away from Benny . . . I'm going to finish school. But I need you. I *need* you. You're my best friend." His voice was desperate and broken, matching his expression.

In the dim light I could see a tear fall from his eye, and in the next moment he reached out for me and I was in his arms, his lips on mine. He squeezed me tight against his chest as he kissed me, and then cradled my face in his hands, pressing his lips harder against my mouth, desperate to get a reaction.

"Kiss me," he whispered, sealing his mouth on mine. I kept my eyes and mouth closed, relaxing in his arms. It took everything I had not to move my mouth with his, having longed for his lips all week. "Kiss me!" he begged. "Please, Pigeon! I told him no!"

When I felt hot tears searing down my cold face, I shoved him away. "Leave me alone, Travis!"

I had only made it a few feet when he grabbed my wrist. My arm was straight, outstretched behind me. I didn't turn around.

"I am begging you." My arm lowered and tugged as he fell to his knees. "I'm begging you, Abby. Don't do this."

I turned to see his agonized expression, and then my eyes drifted down my arm to his, seeing my nickname in thick black letters on his flexed wrist. I looked away, toward the cafeteria. He had proven to me what I had been afraid of all along. As much as he loved me, when money was involved, I would be second. Just as I was with Mick.

If I gave in, either he would change his mind about Benny, or he would resent me every time money could have made his life easier. I imagined him in a blue-collar job, coming home with the same look in his eyes that Mick had when he returned after a night of bad luck. It would be my fault that his life wasn't what he wanted it to be, and I couldn't let my future be plagued with the bitterness and regret that I left behind.

"Let me go, Travis."

After several moments he finally released my arm. I ran to the glass door, yanking it open without looking back. Everyone in the room stared at me as I walked toward the buffet, and just as I reached my destination, heads angled to see outside the windows where Travis was on his knees, palms flat on the pavement.

The sight of him on the ground made the tears I'd been holding back rush down my face. I passed the stacks of plates and trays, dashing down the hall to the bathrooms. It was bad enough that everyone had witnessed the scene between me and Travis. I couldn't let them see me cry.

I cowered in the stall for an hour, bawling uncontrollably until I heard a tiny knock on the door.

"Abby?"

I sniffed. "What are you doing in here, Finch? You're in the girls' bathroom."

"Kara saw you come in and came to the dorms to get me. Let me in," he said in a soft voice.

I shook my head. I knew he couldn't see me, but I couldn't

speak another word. I heard him sigh and then his palms slapped on the floor as he crawled under the stall.

"I can't believe you're making me do this," he said, pulling himself under with his hands. "You're going to be sorry you didn't open the door, because I just crawled along that piss-covered floor and now I'm going to hug you."

I laughed once, and then my face compressed around my smile as Finch pulled me into his arms. My knees went out from under me, and Finch carefully lowered me to the floor, pulling me into his lap.

"Ssshh," he said, rocking me in his arms. He sighed and shook his head. "Damn, girl. What am I gonna do with you?"

Chapter Seventeen
No, Thanks

I DOODLED ON THE FRONT OF MY NOTEBOOK, MAKING squares in squares, connecting them to each other to form rudimentary 3-D boxes. Ten minutes before class was to begin, the classroom was still empty. Life was in the beginning stages of normal, but it still took me a few minutes to psych myself up to be around anyone other than Finch and America.

"Just because we're not dating anymore doesn't mean you can't wear the bracelet I bought you," Parker said as he slid into the desk beside me.

"I've been meaning to ask you if you wanted it back."

He smiled, leaning over to add a bow to the top of one of the boxes on the paper. "It was a gift, Abs. I don't give gifts with conditions."

Dr. Ballard flipped on her overhead as she took her seat at the head of the class and then rummaged through papers on her cluttered desk. The room was suddenly abuzz with chatter echoing against the large rain-spattered windows.

"I heard that you and Travis broke up a couple of weeks ago." Parker held up a hand seeing my impatient expression. "It's none of my business. You've just looked so sad, and I wanted to tell you that I'm sorry."

"Thanks," I muttered, turning to a fresh page in my notebook.

"And I also wanted to apologize for my behavior before. What I said was . . . unkind. I was just angry, and I lashed out at you. It wasn't fair, and I'm sorry."

"I'm not interested in dating, Parker," I warned.

He chuckled. "I'm not trying to take advantage. We're still friends, and I want to make sure that you're okay."

"I'm okay."

"Are you going home for Thanksgiving break?"

"I'm going home with America. I usually have Thanksgiving at her house."

Parker began to speak but Dr. Ballard began her lecture. The subject of Thanksgiving made me think of my previous plans to help Travis with a turkey. I thought about what that would have been like, and I found myself worrying that they would be ordering pizza yet again. A sinking feeling came over me. I instantly pushed it from my mind, trying my best to concentrate on Dr. Ballard's every word.

After class, my face flushed when I saw Travis jogging toward me from the parking lot. He was clean-shaven again, wearing a hooded sweatshirt and his favorite red baseball cap, ducking his head away from the rain.

"I'll see you after break, Abs," Parker said, touching my back.

I expected an angry glare from Travis, but he didn't seem to notice Parker as he approached. "Hey, Pidge."

I offered an awkward smile, and he shoved his hands into the front pocket of his sweatshirt. "Shepley said you're going with him and Mare to Wichita tomorrow."

"Yeah?"

"You're spending the whole break at America's?"

I shrugged, trying to seem casual. "I'm really close with her parents."

"What about your mom?"

"She's a drunk, Travis. She won't know it's Thanksgiving."

He was suddenly nervous, and my stomach wrenched with the possibility of a second public breakup. Thunder rolled above us and Travis looked up, squinting as the large drops fell against his face.

"I need to ask you for a favor," he said. "C'mere." He pulled me under the closest awning and I complied, trying to avoid another scene.

"What kind of favor?" I asked, suspicious.

"My uh . . ." He shifted his weight. "Dad and the guys are still expecting you on Thursday."

"Travis!" I whined.

He looked at his feet. "You said you would come."

"I know, but . . . it's a little inappropriate now, don't you think?"

He seemed unaffected. "You said you would come."

"We were still together when I agreed to go home with you. You knew I wasn't going to come."

"I didn't know, and it's too late, anyway. Thomas is flying in, and Tyler took off work. Everyone's looking forward to seeing you."

I cringed, twirling the damp strands of my hair around my finger. "They were going to come anyway, weren't they?"

"Not everyone. We haven't had all of us there for Thanksgiving in years. They all made an effort to be there since I promised them a real meal. We haven't had a woman in the kitchen since Mom died and . . ."

"That's not sexist or anything,"

He tilted his head. "That's not what I meant, Pidge, c'mon. We all want you there. That's all I'm sayin'."

"You haven't told them about us, have you?" I said the words in the most accusatory tone I could manage.

He fidgeted for a moment, and then shook his head. "Dad would ask why, and I'm not ready to talk to him about it. I'd never hear the end of how stupid I am. Please come, Pidge."

"I have to put the turkey in at six in the morning. We'd have to leave here by five . . ."

"Or we could stay there."

My eyebrows shot up. "No way! It's bad enough that I'm going to have to lie to your family and pretend we're still together."

"You act like I'm asking you to light yourself on fire."

"You should have told them!"

"I will. After Thanksgiving . . . I'll tell them."

I sighed, looking away. "If you promise me that this isn't some stunt to try and get back together, I'll do it."

He nodded. "I promise."

Although he was trying to hide it, I could see a spark in his eyes. I pressed my lips together, trying not to smile. "I'll see you at five."

Travis leaned down to kiss my cheek, his lips lingering on my skin. "Thanks, Pigeon."

America and Shepley met me at the door of the cafeteria and we walked in together. I yanked the silverware from its holder and then dropped my plate onto the tray.

"What's with you, Abby?" America asked.

"I'm not coming with you guys tomorrow."

Shepley's mouth fell open. "You're going to the Maddoxes?"

America's eyes darted to mine. "You're what?"

I sighed and shoved my campus ID at the cashier. "I promised Trav I'd go when we were on the plane, and he told them all I'd be there."

"In his defense," Shepley began, "he really didn't think you guys were gonna break up. He thought you'd come around. It was too late by the time he figured out that you were serious."

"That's bullshit, Shep, and you know it," America seethed. "You don't have to go if you don't want to, Abby."

She was right. It wasn't as if I didn't have a choice. But I couldn't do that to Travis. Not even if I hated him. And I didn't.

"If I don't go, he'll have to explain to them why I didn't show, and I don't want to ruin his Thanksgiving. They're all coming home thinking I'm going to be there."

Shepley smiled. "They all really like you, Abby. Jim was just talking to my dad about you the other day."

"Great," I muttered.

"Abby's right," Shepley said. "If she doesn't go, Jim will spend the day bitching at Trav. There's no sense in ruining their day."

America put her arm around my shoulders. "You can still come with us. You're not with him anymore. You don't have to keep saving him."

"I know, Mare. But it's the right thing to do."

THE SUN MELTED INTO THE BUILDINGS OUTSIDE THE window, and I stood in front of my mirror, brushing my hair while trying to decide how I was going to go about pretending with Travis. "It's just one day, Abby. You can handle one day," I said to the mirror.

Pretending had never been a problem for me; it was what was going to happen while we were pretending that I was worried about. When Travis dropped me off after dinner, I was going to have to make a decision. A decision that would be skewed by a false sense of happiness we would portray for his family.

Knock, knock.

I turned, looking at the door. Kara hadn't been back to our room all evening, and I knew that America and Shepley were already on the road. I couldn't imagine who it could be. I set my brush on the table and pulled open the door.

"Travis," I breathed.

"Are you ready?"

I raised an eyebrow. "Ready for what?"

"You said pick you up at five."

I folded my arms across my chest. "I meant five in the morning!"

"Oh. I guess I should call Dad and let him know we won't be staying after all."

"Travis!" I wailed.

"I brought Shep's car so we didn't have to deal with our bags on the bike. There's a spare bedroom you can crash in. We can watch a movie or—"

"I'm not staying at your dad's!"

His face fell. "Okay. I'll uh . . . I'll see you in the morning."

He took a step back and I shut the door, leaning against it. Every emotion I had weaved in and out of my insides, and I heaved an exasperated sigh. With Travis's disappointed expression fresh on my mind, I pulled open the door and stepped out, seeing that he was slowly walking down the hall, dialing his phone.

"Travis, wait." He flipped around and the hopeful look in his eyes made my chest ache. "Give me a minute to pack a few things."

A relieved, appreciative smile spread across his face and he followed me to my room, watching me shove a few things in a bag from the doorway.

"I still love you, Pidge."

I didn't look up. "Don't. I'm not doing this for you."

He sucked in a breath. "I know."

We rode in silence to his dad's house. The car felt charged with nervous energy, and it was hard to sit still against the cold leather seats. Once we arrived, Trenton and Jim walked out onto the porch, all smiles. Travis carried our bags from the car, and Jim patted his back.

"Good to see ya, son." His smiled broadened when he looked at me. "Abby Abernathy. We're looking forward to dinner to-morrow. It's been a long time since . . . Well. It's been a long time."

I nodded and followed Travis into the house. Jim rested his hand on his protruding belly and grinned. "I set you two up in the guest bedroom, Trav. I didn't figure you would wanna fight with the twin beds in your room."

I looked to Travis. It was difficult watching him struggle to speak. "Abby's uh . . . she's going to uh . . . going to take the guest room. I'm going to crash in mine."

Trenton made a face. "Why? She's been staying at your apartment, hasn't she?"

"Not lately," he said, desperately trying to avoid the truth.

Jim and Trenton traded glances. "Thomas's room has been storage for years now, so I was going to let him take your room. I guess he can sleep on the couch," Jim said, looking at the ratty, discolored cushions in the living room.

"Don't worry about it, Jim. We were just trying to be respectful," I said, touching his arm.

His laughter bellowed throughout the house, and he patted my hand. "You've met my sons, Abby. You should know it's damn near impossible to offend me."

Travis nodded toward the stairs, and I followed him. He pushed open the door with his foot and sat our bags on the floor, looking at the bed and then turning to me. The room was lined in brown paneling, the brown carpet beyond normal wear and tear. The walls were a dirty white, the paint peeling in places. I saw only one frame on the wall; enclosed was a picture of Jim and Travis's mother. The background was a generic portrait-studio blue; the couple sported feathered hair and young, smiling faces. It must have been taken before they had the boys; neither of them could have been older than twenty.

"I'm sorry, Pidge. I'll sleep on the floor."

"Damn straight you will," I said, pulling my hair into a ponytail. "I can't believe I let you talk me into this."

He sat on the bed and rubbed his face in frustration. "This is going to be a fucking mess. I don't know what I was thinking."

"I know exactly what you were thinking. I'm not stupid, Travis."

He looked up at me and smiled. "But you still came."

"I have to get everything ready for tomorrow," I said, opening the door.

Travis stood up. "I'll help you."

We peeled a mountain of potatoes, cut up vegetables, set out the turkey to thaw, and started the piecrusts. The first hour was more than uncomfortable, but when the twins arrived, everyone seemed to congregate in the kitchen. Jim told stories about each of his boys, and we laughed about tales of earlier disastrous Thanksgivings when they attempted to do something other than order pizza.

"Diane was a hell of a cook," Jim mused. "Trav doesn't remember, but there was no sense trying after she passed."

"No pressure, Abby," Trenton said. He chuckled, and then grabbed a beer from the fridge. "Let's get out the cards. I want to try to make back some of my money that Abby took."

Jim waved his finger at his son. "No poker this weekend, Trent. I brought down the dominoes; go set those up. No betting, dammit. I mean it."

Trenton shook his head. "All right, old man, all right." Travis's brothers meandered from the kitchen, and Trenton followed, stopping to look back. "C'mon, Trav."

"I'm helping Pidge."

"There's not much more to do, baby," I said. "Go ahead."

His eyes softened at my words, and he touched my hip. "You sure?"

I nodded and he leaned over to kiss my cheek, squeezing my hip with his fingers before following Trenton into the game room.

Jim watched his sons file out of the doorway, shaking his head and smiling. "This is incredible what you're doing, Abby. I don't think you realize how much we all appreciate it."

"It was Trav's idea. I'm glad I could help."

His large frame settled against the counter, taking a swig of his beer while he pondered his next words. "You and Travis haven't talked much. You having problems?"

I squeezed the dish soap into the sink as it filled with hot water, trying to think of something to say that wasn't a bald-faced lie. "Things are a little different, I guess."

"That's what I thought. You have to be patient with him. Travis doesn't remember much about it, but he was close to his mom, and after we lost her he was never the same. I thought he'd grow out of it, you know, with him being so young. It was hard on all of us, but Trav . . . he quit trying to love people after that. I was surprised that he brought you here. The way he acts around you, the way he looks at you . . . I knew you were some-thin' special."

I smiled, but kept my eyes on the dishes I was scrubbing.

"Travis'll have a hard time. He's going to make a lot of mis-takes. He grew up around a bunch of motherless boys and a lonely, grouchy old man for a father. We were all a little lost after Diane died, and I guess I didn't help the boys cope the way I should have.

"I know it's hard not to blame him, but you have to love him, anyway, Abby. You're the only woman he's loved besides his mother. I don't know what it'll do to him if you leave him, too."

I swallowed back the tears and nodded, unable to reply. Jim rested his hand on my shoulder and squeezed. "I've never seen him smile the way he does when he's with you. I hope all my boys have an Abby one day."

His footsteps faded down the hallway and I gripped the edge of the sink, trying to catch my breath. I knew spending the holi-day with Travis and his family would be difficult, but I didn't think my heart would be broken all over again. The men joked and laughed in the next room as I washed and dried the dishes, putting them away. I cleaned the kitchen and then washed my hands, making my way to the stairs for the night.

Travis grabbed my hand. "It's early, Pidge. You're not going to bed, are ya?"

"It's been a long day. I'm tired."

"We were getting ready to watch a movie. Why don't you come back down and hang out?"

I looked up the stairs and then down to his hopeful smile. "Okay."

He led me by the hand to the couch, and we sat together as the opening credits rolled.

"Shut off that light, Taylor," Jim ordered.

Travis reached his arm behind me, resting his arm on the back of the couch. He was trying to keep up pretenses while appeasing me. He had been careful not to take advantage of the situation, and I found myself conflicted, both grateful and disappointed. Sitting so close to him, smelling the mixture of tobacco and his cologne, it was very difficult for me to keep my distance, both physically and emotionally. Just as I had feared, my resolve was wavering. I struggled to block out everything Jim had said in the kitchen.

Halfway through the movie, the front door flew open and Thomas rounded the corner, bags in hand.

"Happy Thanksgiving!" he said, setting his luggage on the floor.

Jim stood up and hugged his oldest son, and everyone but Travis stood to greet him.

"You're not going to say hi to Thomas?" I whispered.

He didn't look at me when he spoke, watching his family hug and laugh. "I got one night with you. I'm not going to waste a second of it."

"Hi there, Abby. It's good to see you again," Thomas smiled.

Travis touched my knee with his hand and I looked down and then to Travis. Noticing my expression, Travis took his hand off my leg and interlocked his fingers in his lap.

"Uh-oh. Trouble in paradise?" Thomas asked.

"Shut up, Tommy," Travis grumbled.

The mood in the room shifted, and I felt all eyes on me, waiting for an explanation. I smiled nervously and took Travis's hand into both of mine.

"We're just tired. We've been working all evening on the food," I said, leaning my head against Travis's shoulder.

He looked down at our hands and then squeezed, his eyebrows pulling in a bit.

"Speaking of tired, I'm exhausted," I breathed. "I'm gonna head to bed, baby." I looked to everyone else. "Good night, guys."

"Night, sis," Jim said.

Travis's brothers all bade me good night, and I headed up the stairs.

"I'm gonna turn in, too," I heard Travis say.

"I bet you are," Trenton teased.

"Lucky bastard," Tyler grumbled.

"Hey. We're not going to talk about your sister like that," Jim warned.

My stomach sank. The only real family I'd had in years was America's parents, and although Mark and Pam had always looked out for me with true kindness, they were borrowed. The six unruly, foul-mouthed, loveable men downstairs had welcomed me with open arms, and tomorrow I would tell them goodbye for the last time.

Travis caught the bedroom door before it closed and then froze. "Did you want me to wait in the hall while you dressed for bed?"

"I'm going to hop in the shower. I'll just get dressed in the bathroom."

He rubbed the back of his neck. "All right. I'll make a pallet, then."

I nodded, making my way to the bathroom. I scrubbed myself raw in the dilapidated shower, focusing on the water stains and soap scum to fight the overwhelming dread I felt for both the night and the morning. When I returned to the bedroom, Travis dropped a pillow on the floor on his makeshift bed. He offered a weak smile before leaving me to take a turn in the shower.

I crawled into bed, pulling the covers to my chest, trying to ignore the blankets on the floor. When Travis returned, he stared at the pallet with the same sadness that I did, and then turned off the light, situating himself on his pillow.

It was quiet for a few minutes, and then I heard Travis heave a miserable sigh. "This is our last night together, isn't it?"

I waited a moment, trying to think of the right thing to say. "I don't wanna fight, Trav. Just go to sleep."

Hearing him shift, I turned onto my side to look down at him, pressing my cheek into the pillow. He supported his head with his hand and stared into my eyes.

"I love you."

I watched him for a moment. "You promised."

"I promised this wasn't a stunt to get back together. It

wasn't." He reached up his hand to touch mine. "But if it meant being with you again, I can't say I wouldn't consider it."

"I care about you. I don't want you to hurt, but I should have followed my gut in the first place. It would've never worked."

"You did love me, though, right?"

I pressed my lips together. "I still do."

His eyes glossed over, and he squeezed my hand. "Can I ask you for a favor?"

"I'm sort of in the middle of the last thing you asked me to do," I said with a smirk.

His features were taut, unaffected by my expression. "If this is really it . . . if you're really done with me . . . will you let me hold you tonight?"

"I don't think it's a good idea, Trav."

His hand gripped tight over mine. "Please? I can't sleep knowing you're just a foot away, and I'm never gonna get the chance again."

I stared into his desperate eyes for a moment and then frowned. "I'm not having sex with you."

He shook his head. "That's not what I'm asking."

I searched the dimly lit room with my eyes, thinking about the consequences, wondering if I could tell Travis no if he changed his mind. I shut my eyes tight and then pushed away from the edge of the bed, turning down the blanket. He crawled into bed beside me, hastily pulling me tight into his arms. His bare chest rose and fell with uneven breaths, and I cursed myself for feeling so peaceful against his skin.

"I'm going to miss this," I said.

He kissed my hair and pulled me to him. He seemed unable to get close enough to me. He buried his face in my neck and

I rested my hand on his back in comfort, although I was just as heartbroken as he was. He sucked in a breath and pressed his forehead against my neck, pressing his fingers into the skin of my back. As miserable as we were the last night of the bet, this was much, much worse.

"I . . . I don't think I can do this, Travis."

He pulled me tighter and I felt the first tear fall from my eye down my temple. "I can't do this," I said, clenching my eyes shut.

"Then don't," he said against my skin. "Give me another chance."

I tried to push myself out from under him, but his grip was too solid for any possibility of escape. I covered my face with both hands as my quiet sobs shook us both. Travis looked up at me, his eyes heavy and wet.

With his large, gentle fingers, he pulled my hand away from my eyes and kissed my palm. I took a faltering breath as he looked at my lips and then back to my eyes. "I'll never love anyone the way I love you, Pigeon."

I sniffed and touched his face. "I can't."

"I know," he said, his voice broken. "I never once convinced myself that I was good enough for you."

My face crumpled and I shook my head. "It's not just you, Trav. We're not good for each other."

He shook his head, wanting to say something but thinking better of it. After a long, deep breath, he rested his head against my chest. When the green numbers on the clock across the room read eleven o'clock, Travis's breaths finally slowed and evened out. My eyes grew heavy, and I blinked a few times before slipping out of consciousness.

*   *   *

"OW!" I YELPED, PULLING MY HAND FROM THE STOVE AND automatically nursing the burn with my mouth.

"You okay, Pidge?" Travis asked, shuffling across the floor and slipping a T-shirt over his head. "Shit! The floor's fucking freezing!" I stifled a giggle as I watched him hop on one foot and then the other until the soles of his feet acclimated to the frigid tile.

The sun had barely peeked through the blinds, and all but one of the Maddoxes were sleeping soundly in their beds. I pushed the antique tin pan further into the oven and then closed the door, turning to cool my fingers under the sink.

"You can go back to bed. I just had to put the turkey in."

"Are you coming?" he asked, wrapping his arms around his chest to ward off the chill in the air.

"Yeah."

"Lead the way," he said, sweeping his hand toward the stairs.

Travis yanked his shirt off as we both shoved our legs under the covers, pulling the blanket up to our necks. He tightened his arms around me as we shivered, waiting for our body heat to warm the small space between our skin and the covers.

I felt his lips against my hair, and then his throat moved when he spoke. "Look, Pidge. It's snowing."

I turned to face the window. The white flakes were only visible in the glow of the street lamp. "It kind of feels like Christmas," I said, my skin finally warming up against his. He sighed and I turned to see his expression. "What?"

"You won't be here for Christmas."

"I'm here, now." He pulled his mouth up on one side and leaned down to kiss my lips. I leaned back and shook my head. "Trav . . ."

His grip tightened and he lowered his chin, his chestnut eyes determined. "I've got less than twenty-four hours with you, Pidge. I'm gonna kiss you. I'm gonna kiss you a lot today. All day. Every chance I get. If you want me to stop, just say the word, but until you do, I'm going to make every second of my last day with you count."

"Travis—" I thought about it for a moment, and I reasoned that he was under no illusions about what would happen when he took me home. I had come there to pretend, and as hard as it would be for us both later, I didn't want to tell him no.

When he noticed me staring at his lips, the corner of his mouth turned up again, and he leaned down to press his soft mouth against mine. It began sweet and innocent, but the moment his lips parted, I caressed his tongue with mine. His body instantly tensed, and he took a deep breath in through his nose, pressing his body against me. I let my knee fall to the side and he moved above me, never taking his mouth from mine.

He wasted no time undressing me, and when there was no more fabric between us, he gripped the iron vines of the headboard with both hands, and in one quick movement, he was inside me. I bit my lip hard, stifling the cry that was clawing its way up my throat. Travis moaned against my mouth, and I pressed my feet against the mattress, anchoring myself so I could raise my hips to meet his.

One hand on the iron and the other on the nape of my neck, he rocked against me over and over, and my legs quivered with his firm, determined movements. His tongue searched my mouth, and I could feel the vibration of his deep groans against my chest as he kept to his promise to make our last day together memorable. I could spend a thousand years trying to block that moment from my memory, and it would still be burned into my mind.

An hour had passed when I clenched my eyes shut, my every nerve focused on the shuddering of my insides. Travis held his breath as he thrust inside me one last time. I collapsed against the mattress, completely spent. Travis heaved with deep breaths, speechless and dripping with sweat.

I could hear voices downstairs and I covered my mouth, giggling at our misbehavior. Travis turned on his side, scanning my face with his soft, brown eyes.

"You said you were just going to kiss me." I grinned.

As I lay next to his bare skin, seeing the unconditional love in his eyes, I let go of my disappointment and my anger and my stubborn resolve. I loved him, and no matter what my reasons were to live without him, I knew it wasn't what I wanted. Even if I hadn't changed my mind, it was impossible for us to stay away from each other.

"Why don't we just stay in bed all day?" he smiled.

"I came here to cook, remember?"

"No, you came here to help me cook, and I don't report for duty for another eight hours."

I touched his face; the urge to end our suffering had become unbearable. When I told him I had changed my mind and that things were back to normal, we wouldn't have to spend the day pretending. We could spend it celebrating instead.

"Travis, I think we . . ."

"Don't say it, okay? I don't want to think about it until I have to." He stood up and pulled on his boxers, walking over to my bag. He tossed my clothes on the bed and then yanked his shirt over his head. "I want to remember this as a good day."

I made eggs for breakfast and sandwiches for lunch, and when the game began, I started dinner. Travis stood behind me at every opportunity, his arms wrapped around my waist, his lips on my neck. I caught myself glancing at the clock, eager to find a moment alone with him to tell him my decision. I was anxious to see the look on his face and to get back to where we were.

The day was filled with laughter, conversation, and a steady stream of complaints from Tyler about Travis's constant display of affection.

"Get a room, Travis! Jesus!" Tyler groaned.

"You are turning a hideous shade of green," Thomas teased.

"It's because they're making me sick. I'm not jealous, douche-bag," Tyler sneered.

"Leave 'em alone, Ty," Jim warned.

When we sat down for dinner, Jim insisted on Travis carving the turkey, and I smiled as he proudly stood up to comply. I was a bit nervous until the compliments washed in. By the time I served the pie, there wasn't a morsel of food left on the table.

"Did I make enough?" I laughed.

Jim smiled, pulling his fork through his lips to get ready for dessert. "You made plenty, Abby. We just wanted to tide ourselves over until next year . . . unless you'd like to do this all over again at Christmas. You're a Maddox, now. I expect you at every holiday, and not to cook."

I glanced over at Travis, whose smiled had faded, and my heart sank. I had to tell him soon. "Thanks, Jim."

"Don't tell her that, Dad," Trenton said. "She's gotta cook. I haven't had a meal like this since I was five!" He shoveled half a slice of pecan pie into his mouth, humming with satisfaction.

I felt at home, sitting at a table full of men who were leaning back in their chairs, rubbing their full bellies. Emotion overwhelmed me when I fantasized about Christmas and Easter and every other holiday I would spend at that table. I wanted nothing more than to be a part of this broken, loud family that I adored.

When the pies were gone, Travis's brothers began to clear the table and the twins manned the sink.

"I'll do that," I said, standing.

Jim shook his head. "No, you don't. The boys can take care of it. You just take Travis to the couch and relax. You've worked hard, sis."

The twins splashed each other with dishwater and Trenton cussed when he slipped on a puddle and dropped a plate. Thomas chastised his brothers, getting the broom and dustpan to sweep up the glass. Jim patted his sons on the shoulders and then hugged me before retreating to his room for the night.

Travis pulled my legs onto his lap and slipped off my shoes, massaging the soles of my feet with his thumbs. I leaned my head back and sighed.

"This was the best Thanksgiving we've had since Mom died."

I pulled my head up to see his expression. He was smiling, but it was tinged with sadness.

"I'm glad I was here to see it."

Travis's expression changed and I braced myself for what he was about to say. My heart pounded against my chest, hoping he would ask me back so I could say yes. Las Vegas seemed like a lifetime ago, sitting in the home of my new family.

"I'm different. I don't know what happened to me in Vegas. That wasn't me. I was thinking about everything we could buy with that money, and that was all I was thinking about. I didn't see how much it hurt you for me to want to take you back there, but deep down, I think I knew. I deserved for you to leave me. I deserved all the sleep I lost and the pain I've felt. I needed all that to realize how much I need you and what I'm willing to do to keep you in my life."

I chewed on my lip, impatient to get to the part where I said yes. I wanted him to take me back to the apartment and spend the rest of the night celebrating. I couldn't wait to relax on the new couch with Toto, watching movies and laughing like we used to.

"You said you're done with me, and I accept that. I'm a different person since I met you. I've changed . . . for the better. But no matter how hard I try, I can't seem to do right by you. We were friends first, and I can't lose you, Pigeon. I will always love you, but if I can't make you happy, it doesn't make much sense for me to try to get you back. I can't imagine being with anyone else, but I'll be happy as long as we're friends."

"You want to be friends?" I asked, the words burning in my mouth.

"I want you to be happy. Whatever that takes."

My insides wrenched at his words, and I was surprised at the overpowering pain I felt. He was giving me an out, and it was exactly when I didn't want it. I could have told him that I had changed my mind, and he would take back everything he'd just said, but I knew that it wasn't fair to either of us to hold on just when he had let go.

I smiled to fight the tears. "Fifty bucks says you'll be thanking me for this when you meet your future wife."

Travis's eyebrows pulled together as his face fell. "That's an easy bet. The only woman I'd ever wanna marry just broke my heart."

I couldn't fake a smile after that. I wiped my eyes and then stood up. "I think it's time you took me home."

"C'mon, Pigeon. I'm sorry, that wasn't funny."

"It's not that, Trav. I'm just tired, and I'm ready to go home."

He sucked in a breath and nodded, standing up. I hugged his brothers goodbye, and asked Trenton to say goodbye to Jim for me. Travis stood at the door with our bags as they all agreed to come home for Christmas, and I held my smile long enough to get out the door.

WHEN TRAVIS WALKED ME TO MORGAN, HIS FACE WAS still sad, but the torment was gone. The weekend wasn't a stunt to get me back after all. It was closure.

He leaned over to kiss my cheek and held the door open for me, watching as I walked inside. "Thanks for today. You don't know how happy you made my family."

I stopped at the bottom of the stairs. "You're going to tell them tomorrow, aren't you?"

He looked out to the parking lot and then at me. "I'm pretty sure they already know. You're not the only one with a poker face, Pidge."

I stared at him, stunned, and for the first time since I'd met him, he walked away from me without looking back.

Chapter Eighteen
The Box

FINALS WERE A CURSE FOR EVERYONE BUT ME. I KEPT busy, studying with Kara and America in my room and at the library. I only saw Travis in passing when the schedules changed for tests. I went home with America for winter break, thankful that Shepley had stayed with Travis so I wouldn't suffer their constant displays of affection.

The last four days of break I caught a cold, giving me a good reason to stay in bed. Travis said he wanted to be friends, but he hadn't called. It was a relief to have a few days to wallow in self-pity. I wanted to get it out of my system before returning to school.

The return trip to Eastern seemed to take years. I was eager to start the spring semester, but I was far more eager to see Travis again.

The first day of classes, a fresh energy had swept over the campus along with a blanket of snow. New courses meant new friends and a new beginning. I didn't have a single class with Travis, Parker, Shepley, or America, but Finch was in all but one of mine.

I anxiously waited for Travis at lunch, but when he came in he simply winked at me and then sat at the end of the table with the rest of his frat brothers. I tried to concentrate on America and Finch's conversation about the last football game of the season, but Travis's voice kept catching my attention. He was regaling tales of his adventures and brushes with the law he'd had over break, and news of Trenton's new girlfriend they'd met one night while they were at the Red Door. I braced myself for mention of any girl he'd brought home or met, but if he had, he wasn't sharing it with his friends.

Red and gold metallic balls still hung from the ceiling of the cafeteria, blowing with the current of the heaters. I pulled my cardigan around me, and Finch noticed, hugging me to him and rubbing my arm. I knew that I was paying far too much attention to Travis's general direction, waiting for him to look up at me, but he seemed to have forgotten that I was sitting at the table.

He seemed impervious to the hordes of girls that approached him after news of our breakup, but he was also content with our relationship returning to its platonic state, however strained. We had spent almost a month apart, leaving me nervous and unsure about how to act around him.

Once he finished his lunch, my heart fluttered when he walked up behind me and rested his hands on my shoulders.

"How's your classes, Shep?" he asked.

Shepley's face pinched. "First day sucks. Hours of syllabi and class rules. I don't even know why I show up the first week. How about you?"

"Eh . . . it's all part of the game. How 'bout you, Pidge?" he asked.

"The same," I said, trying to keep my voice casual.

"Did you have a good break?" he asked, playfully swaying me from side to side.

"Pretty good," I said. I tried my best to sound convincing.

"Sweet. I've got another class. Later."

I watched him make a beeline for the doors, shoving them both open and then lighting a cigarette as he walked.

"Huh," America said in a high-pitched tone. She watched Travis cut across the greens through the snow and then shook her head.

"What?" Shepley asked.

America rested her chin on the heel of her hand, seeming vexed. "That was kind of weird, wasn't it?"

"How so?" Shepley asked, flicking America's blond braid back to brush his lips across her neck.

America smiled and leaned into his kiss. "He's almost normal . . . as normal as Trav can be. What's up with him?"

Shepley shook his head and shrugged. "I don't know. He's been that way for a while."

"How backward is that, Abby? He's fine and you're miserable," America said, unconcerned with listening ears.

"You're miserable?" Shepley asked with a surprised expression.

My mouth fell open and my face flamed with instant embarrassment. "I am not!"

She pushed her salad around in the bowl. "Well, he's damn near ecstatic."

"Drop it, Mare," I warned.

She shrugged and took another bite. "I think he's faking it."

Shepley nudged her. "America? You goin' to the Valentine's Day date party with me or what?"

"Can't you ask me like a normal boyfriend? Nicely?"

"I have asked you . . . repeatedly. You keep telling me to ask you later."

She slumped in her chair, pouting. "I don't wanna go without Abby."

Shepley's face screwed with frustration. "She was with Trav the whole time last time. You barely saw her."

"Quit being a baby, Mare," I said, throwing a stick of celery at her.

Finch elbowed me. "I'd take you, Cupcake, but I'm not into the frat-boy thing, sorry."

"That's actually a damn good idea," Shepley said, his eyes bright.

Finch grimaced at the thought. "I'm not Sig Tau, Shep. I'm not anything. Fraternities are against my religion."

"Please, Finch?" America asked.

"Déjà vu," I grumbled.

Finch looked at me from the corner of his eye and then sighed. "It's nothing personal, Abby. I can't say I've ever been on a date . . . with a girl."

"I know." I shook my head dismissively, waving away my deep embarrassment. "It's fine. Really."

"I need you there," America said. "We made a pact, remember? No parties alone."

"You'll hardly be alone, Mare. Quit being so dramatic," I said, already annoyed with the conversation.

"You want dramatic? I pulled a trash can beside your bed, held a box of Kleenex for you all night, and got up to get you cough medicine twice when you were sick over break! You owe me!"

I wrinkled my nose. "I have kept your hair vomit free so many times, America Mason!"

"You sneezed in my face!" she said, pointing to her nose.

I blew my bangs from my eyes. I could never argue with America when she was determined to get her way. "Fine," I said through my teeth.

"Finch?" I asked him with my best fake smile. "Will you go to the stupid Sig Tau Valentine's date party with me?"

Finch hugged me to his side. "Yes. But only because you called it stupid."

I walked with Finch to class after lunch, discussing the date party and how much we were both dreading it. We picked out a pair of desks in our Physiology class, and I shook my head when the professor began my fourth syllabus of the day. The snow began to fall again, drifting against the windows, politely begging entrance and then falling with disappointment to the ground.

After class was dismissed, a boy I'd met only once at the Sig Tau house knocked on my desk as he walked by, winking. I offered a polite smile and then glanced over to Finch. He shot me a wry grin, and I gathered my book and laptop, shoving them into my backpack with little effort.

I lugged my bag over my shoulders and trudged to Morgan along the salted sidewalk. A small group of students had started a snowball fight on the greens, and Finch shuddered at the sight of them, covered in white powder.

I wobbled my knee, keeping Finch company as he finished his cigarette. America scurried beside us, rubbing her bright green mittens together.

"Where's Shep?" I asked.

"He went home. Travis needed help with something, I guess."

"You didn't go with him?"

"I don't live there, Abby."

"Only in theory," Finch winked at her.

America rolled her eyes. "I enjoy spending time with my boyfriend, so sue me."

Finch flicked his cigarette into the snow. "I'm heading out, ladies. I'll see you at dinner?"

America and I nodded, smiling when Finch first kissed my cheek and then America's. He stayed on the wet sidewalk, careful to stay in the middle so that he wouldn't miss and step into the snow.

America shook her head at his efforts. "He is ridiculous."

"He's a Floridian, Mare. He's not used to the snow."

She giggled and pulled me toward the door.

"Abby!"

I turned to see Parker jogging past Finch. He stopped, catching his breath a moment before he spoke. His puffy gray coat heaved with each breath, and I chuckled at America's curious stare as she watched him.

"I was . . . whew! I was going to ask you if you wanted to grab a bite to eat tonight."

"Oh. I uh . . . I already told Finch I'd eat with him."

"All right, it's no big deal. I was just going to try that new burger place downtown. Everyone's saying it's really good."

"Maybe next time," I said, realizing my mistake. I hoped that he wouldn't take my flippant reply as a postponement. He nodded and shoved his hands into his pockets, quickly walking back the way he came.

Kara was reading ahead in her brand-new books, grimacing at America and me when we walked in. Her demeanor hadn't improved since we'd returned from break.

Before, I had spent so much time at Travis's that Kara's insufferable comments and attitude were tolerable. Spending every evening and night with her during the two weeks before the semester ended made my decision not to room with America more than just regrettable.

"Oh, Kara. How I've missed you," America said.

"The feeling is mutual," Kara grumbled, keeping her eyes on her book.

America chatted about her day and plans with Shepley for the weekend. We scoured the Internet for funny videos, laughing so hard we were wiping away tears. Kara huffed a few times at our disruption, but we ignored her.

I was grateful for America's visit. The hours passed so quickly that I didn't spend a moment wondering if Travis had called until she decided to call it a night.

America yawned and looked at her watch. "I'm going to bed, Ab . . . aw, shit!" she said, snapping her fingers. "I left my makeup bag at Shep's."

"That's not a tragedy, Mare," I said, still giggling from the latest video we'd watched.

"It wouldn't be if I didn't have my birth control in there. C'mon. I have to go get it."

"Can't you just get Shepley to bring them?"

"Travis has his car. He's at the Red with Trent."

I felt sick. "Again? Why is he hanging out with Trent so much, anyway?"

America shrugged. "Does it matter? C'mon!"

"I don't want to run into Travis. It'll be weird."

"Do you ever listen to me? He's not there, he's at the Red. Come on!" she whined, tugging on my arm.

I stood up with mild resistance as she pulled me from the room.

"Finally," Kara said.

We pulled up to Travis's apartment, and I noted that the Harley was parked under the stairs and that Shepley's Charger was missing. I breathed a sigh of relief and followed America up the icy steps.

"Careful," she warned.

If I'd known how unsettling it would be to set foot in the apartment again, I wouldn't have let America talk me into going there. Toto scampered around the corner at full speed, crashing into my legs when his tiny paws failed to get traction on the entryway tile. I picked him up, letting him greet me with his baby kisses. At least he hadn't forgotten me.

I carried him around the apartment, waiting while America searched for her bag.

"I know I left it here!" she said from the bathroom, stomping down the hall to Shepley's room.

"Did you look in the cabinet under the sink?" Shepley asked.

I looked at my watch. "Hurry, Mare. We need to get going."

America sighed in frustration from the bedroom.

I looked down at my watch again, and then jumped when the front door burst open behind me. Travis stumbled in, his arms wrapped around Megan, who was giggling against his mouth. A box in her hand caught my eye, and I felt sick when I realized what it was: condoms. Her other hand was on the back of his neck, and I couldn't tell whose arms were tangled around who.

Travis did a double take when he saw me standing alone in the middle of the living room, and when he froze, Megan looked up with a residual smile still on her face.

"Pigeon," Travis said, stunned.

"Found it!" America said, jogging out of Shepley's room.

"What are you doing here?" he asked. The stench of whiskey blew in with the flurry of snowflakes, and my uncontrollable anger overcame any need to feign indifference.

"It's good to see you're feeling like your old self, Trav," I said. The heat that radiated from my face burned my eyes and blurred my vision.

"We were just leaving," America snarled. She grabbed my hand as we slid past Travis.

We flew down the steps toward her car, and I was thankful that it was just a few steps further, feeling the tears well up in my eyes. I almost fell backward when my coat snagged on something midstep. America's hand slipped from mine and she flipped around the same time I did.

Travis had a fistful of my coat, and my ears caught fire, stinging in the cold night air. His lips and collar were a ridiculous shade of deep red.

"Where are you going?" he said, a half-drunk, half-confused look in his eyes.

"Home," I snapped, straightening my coat when he released me.

"What are you doing here?"

I could hear the packed snow crunch under America's feet as

she walked up behind me, and Shepley flew down the stairs to stand behind Travis, his wary eyes fixed on his girlfriend.

"I'm sorry. If I'd known you were going to be here, I wouldn't have come."

He shoved his hands in his coat pockets. "You can come here anytime you want, Pidge. I never wanted you to stay away."

I couldn't manage the acidity in my voice. "I don't want to interrupt." I looked to the top of the stairs, where Megan stood with a smug expression. "Enjoy your evening," I said, turning away.

He grabbed my arm. "Wait. You're mad?"

I yanked my coat from his grip. "You know . . . I don't even know why I'm surprised."

His eyebrows pulled in. "I can't win with you. I can't win with you! You say you're done . . . I'm fucking miserable over here! I had to break my phone into a million pieces to keep from calling you every minute of the damn day—I've had to play it off like everything is just fine at school so you can be happy . . . and you're fucking mad at me? You broke my fuckin' heart!" His last words echoed into the night.

"Travis, you're drunk. Let Abby go home," Shepley said.

Travis grabbed my shoulders and pulled me to him. "Do you want me or not? You can't keep doing this to me, Pidge!"

"I didn't come here to see you." I said, glaring up at him.

"I don't want her," he said, staring at my lips. "I'm just so fucking unhappy, Pigeon." His eyes glossed over and he leaned in, tilting his head to kiss me.

I grabbed him by the chin, holding him back. "You've got her lipstick on your mouth, Travis," I said, disgusted.

He took a step back and lifted his shirt, wiping his mouth. He stared at the red streaks on the white fabric and shook his head. "I just wanted to forget. Just for one fuckin' night."

I wiped an escaped tear. "Then don't let me stop you."

I tried to retreat to the Honda, but Travis grabbed my arm again. In the next moment, America was wildly hitting his arm with her fists. He looked at her, blinking for a moment in stunned disbelief. She balled up her fists and pounded them against his chest until he released me.

"Leave her alone, you bastard!"

Shepley grabbed her and she pushed him away, turning to slap Travis's face. The sound of her hand against his cheek was quick and loud, and I flinched with the noise. Everyone froze for a moment, shocked at America's sudden rage.

Travis frowned, but he didn't defend himself. Shepley grabbed her again, holding her wrists and pulling her to the Honda while she thrashed about.

She fought him violently, her blond hair whipping around with her attempts to get away. I was amazed at her determination to get at Travis. Pure hate glowed in her usually sweet, carefree eyes.

"How could you? She deserved better from you, Travis!"

"America, STOP!" Shepley yelled, louder than I'd ever heard him.

Her arms fell to her side as she glared at Shepley with incredulity. "You're defending him?"

Although he seemed nervous, he stood his ground. "Abby broke up with him. He's just trying to move on."

Her eyes narrowed and she pulled her arm from his grip.

"Well then, why don't you go find a random WHORE—" she looked at Megan—"from the Red and bring her home to fuck and then let me know if it helps you get over me."

"Mare," Shepley grabbed for her but she evaded him, slamming the door as she sat behind the wheel. I sat beside her, trying not to look at Travis.

"Baby, don't leave," Shepley begged, leaning down into the window.

She started the car. "There is a right side and a wrong side here, Shep. And you are on the wrong side."

"I'm on your side," he said, his eyes desperate.

"Not anymore you're not," she said, backing out.

"America? America!" Shepley called after her as she raced to the road, leaving him behind.

I sighed. "Mare, you can't break up with him over this. He's right."

America put her hand on mine and squeezed. "No he's not. Nothing about what just happened was right."

When we pulled into the parking lot beside Morgan, America's phone rang. She rolled her eyes as she answered. "I don't want you calling me anymore. I mean it, Shep," she said. "No, you're not . . . because I don't want you to, that's why. You can't defend what he's done; you can't condone him hurting Abby like that and be with me . . . that's exactly what I mean, Shepley! It doesn't matter! You don't see Abby screwing the first guy she sees! It's not Travis that's the problem, Shepley. He didn't ask you to defend him! Ugh . . . I'm done talking about this. Don't call me again. Goodbye."

She shoved her way out of the car and stomped across the

road and up the steps. I tried to keep in step with her, waiting to hear his side of their conversation.

When her phone rang again, she turned it off. "Travis made Shep take Megan home. He wanted to come by on his way back."

"You should let him, Mare."

"No. You're my best friend. I can't stomach what I saw tonight, and I can't be with someone that will defend it. End of conversation, Abby, I mean it."

I nodded and she hugged my shoulders, pulling me against her side as we walked up the stairs to our rooms. Kara was already asleep, and I skipped the shower, crawling into bed fully dressed, coat and all. I couldn't stop thinking about Travis stumbling in the door with Megan or the red lipstick smeared across his face. I tried to block out the sickening images of what would have happened had I not been there, and I crossed over several emotions, settling on despair.

Shepley was right. I had no right to be angry, but it didn't help me to ignore the pain.

FINCH SHOOK HIS HEAD WHEN I SAT IN THE DESK BESIDE him. I knew that I looked awful; I barely had the energy to change clothes and brush my teeth. I had only slept an hour the night before, unable to shake the sight of the red lipstick on Travis's mouth or the guilt over Shepley and America's breakup.

America chose to stay in bed, knowing once the anger subsided, depression would set in. She loved Shepley, and although she was determined to end things because he had picked the wrong side, she was prepared to suffer the backlash of her decision.

After class, Finch walked with me to the cafeteria. As I had feared, Shepley was waiting at the door for America. When he saw me, he didn't hesitate.

"Where's Mare?"

"She didn't go to class this morning."

"She's in her room?" he said, turning for Morgan.

"I'm sorry, Shepley," I called after him.

He froze and wheeled around with the face of a man who had reached his limit. "I wish you and Travis would just get your shit together! You're a goddamn tornado! When you're happy, it's love and peace and butterflies. When you're pissed, you take the whole fucking world down with you!"

He stomped away, and I exhaled the breath I was holding. "That went well."

Finch pulled me into the cafeteria. "The whole world. Wow. Think you could work your voodoo before the test on Friday?"

"I'll see what I can do."

Finch chose a different table, and I was more than happy to follow him there. Travis sat with his frat brothers, but he didn't get a tray and he didn't stay long. He noticed me just as he was leaving, but he didn't stop.

"So America and Shepley broke up, too, huh?" Finch asked while he chewed.

"We were at Shep's last night and Travis came home with Megan and . . . it was a mess. They took sides."

"Ouch."

"Exactly. I feel terrible."

Finch patted my back. "You can't control the decisions they make, Abby. So I guess this means we get to skip the Valentine's thing at Sig Tau?"

"Looks that way."

Finch smiled. "I'll still take you out. I'll take you and Mare both out. It'll be fun."

I leaned on his shoulder. "You're the best, Finch."

I hadn't thought about Valentine's, but I was glad I had plans. I couldn't imagine how miserable I would feel spending it with America alone, hearing her rant about Shepley and Travis all night. She would still do that—she wouldn't be America if she didn't—but at least it would be a limited tirade if we were in public.

THE WEEKS OF JANUARY PASSED, AND AFTER A COM-mendable but failed attempt by Shepley to get America back, I saw less and less of both him and Travis. By February, they stopped coming to the cafeteria altogether, and I only saw Travis a handful of times on my way to class.

The weekend before Valentine's Day, America and Finch talked me into going to the Red, and on the entire drive to the club, I dreaded seeing Travis there. We walked in, and I sighed with relief to see no sign of him.

"First round's on me," Finch said, pointing out a table and sliding through the crowd to the bar.

We sat down and watched as the dance floor went from being empty to overflowing with drunken college students. After our fifth round, Finch pulled us to the dance floor, and I finally felt relaxed enough to have a good time. We giggled and bumped against each other, laughing hysterically when a man swung his dance partner around and she missed his hand, sliding across the floor on her side.

America raised her hands above her head, shaking her curls

to the music. I laughed at her signature dance face and then stopped abruptly when I saw Shepley walk up behind her. He whispered something in her ear and she flipped around. They traded words and then America grabbed my hand, leading me to our table.

"Of course. The one night we go out, and he shows up," she grumbled.

Finch brought each one of us two more drinks, including a shot each. "I thought you might need them."

"You thought right." America tilted her head back before we could toast, and I shook my head, clinking my glass to Finch's. I tried to keep my eyes on my friends' faces, worried that with Shepley being there, Travis wouldn't be far behind.

Another song came over the speakers and America stood up. "Fuck it. I'm not sitting at this table the rest of the night."

"Atta girl!" Finch smiled, following her to the dance floor.

I followed them, glancing around for Shepley. He had disappeared. I relaxed again, trying to shake off the feeling that Travis would show up on the dance floor with Megan. A boy I'd seen around campus danced behind America, and she smiled, welcoming the distraction. I had a suspicion that she was making a show of enjoying herself in hopes that Shepley would see. I looked away for a second, and when I looked back to America, her dance partner was gone. She shrugged, continuing to shake her hips to the beat.

The next song began to play and a different boy appeared behind America, his friend dancing next to me. After a few moments, my new dance partner maneuvered behind me, and I felt a bit unsure when I felt his hands on my hips. As if he'd read my mind, his hands left my waist. I looked behind me, and he was gone. I looked up at America, and the man behind her was gone as well.

Finch seemed a bit nervous, but when America raised an eyebrow at his expression, he shook his head and continued dancing.

By the third song, I was sweaty and tired. I retreated to our table, resting my heavy head on my hand, and laughed as I watched yet another hopeful ask America to dance. She winked at me from the dance floor, and then I stiffened when I saw him yanked backward, disappearing through the crowd.

I stood up and walked around the dance floor, keeping my eye on the hole he was pulled through, and felt the adrenaline burn through the alcohol in my veins when I saw Shepley holding the surprised man by his collar. Travis was beside him, laughing hysterically until he looked up and saw me watching them. He hit Shepley's arm, and when Shepley looked in my direction, he shoved his victim backward onto the floor.

It didn't take me long to figure out what was going on: they had been yanking the guys who were dancing with us off the dance floor and threatening them to get them to stay away from us.

I narrowed my eyes at them both and then made my way to America. The crowd was thick, and I had to shove a few people out of my way. Shepley grabbed my hand before I made it to the dance floor.

"Don't tell her!" he said, trying to subdue his smile.

"What the hell do you think you're doing, Shep?"

He shrugged, still proud of himself. "I love her. I can't let other guys dance with her."

"Then what's your excuse for yanking the guy that was dancing with me?" I said, crossing my arms.

"That wasn't me," Shepley said, quickly glancing at Travis. "Sorry, Abby. We were just having fun."

"Not funny."

"What's not funny?" America said, glaring at Shepley.

He swallowed, shooting a pleading look in my direction. I owed him a favor, so I kept my mouth shut.

He sighed in relief when he realized I wouldn't rat him out, and then he looked at America with sweet adoration. "Wanna dance?"

"No, I don't wanna dance," she said, walking back to the table. He followed her, leaving Travis and me standing together.

Travis shrugged. "Wanna dance?"

"What? Megan's not here?"

He shook his head. "You used to be a sweet drunk."

"Happy to disappoint you," I said, turning toward the bar.

He followed, pulling two guys from their seats. I glared at him for a moment, but he ignored me, sitting down and then watching me with an expectant expression.

"Are you gonna sit? I'll buy you a beer."

"I thought you didn't buy drinks for girls at the bar."

He tilted his head in my direction with an impatient frown. "You're different."

"That's what you keep telling me."

"C'mon, Pidge. What happened to us being friends?"

"We can't be friends, Travis. Obviously."

"Why not?"

"Because I don't want to watch you maul a different girl every night, and you won't let anyone dance with me."

He smiled. "I love you. I can't let other guys dance with you."

"Oh yeah? How much did you love me when you were buying that box of condoms?"

Travis winced and I stood up, making my way to the table. Shepley and America were in a tight embrace and making a scene while they kissed passionately.

"I think we're going to the Sig Tau Valentine's date party again," Finch said with a frown.

I sighed. "Shit."

Chapter Nineteen
Hellerton

AMERICA HADN'T BEEN BACK TO MORGAN HALL SINCE her reunion with Shepley. She was consistently absent at lunch, and her phone calls were few and far between. I didn't begrudge them the time to make up for the time they'd spent apart. Truthfully, I was happy that America was too busy to call me from Shepley and Travis's apartment. It was awkward hearing Travis in the background, and I felt a little jealous that she was spending time with him and I wasn't.

Finch and I were seeing more of each other, and I was selfishly thankful that he was just as alone as I was. We went to class, ate together, and studied together, and even Kara grew accustomed to having him around.

My fingers were beginning to get numb from the frigid air as I stood outside Morgan while he smoked.

"Would you consider quitting before I get hypothermia from standing here for moral support?" I asked.

Finch laughed. "I love you, Abby. I really do, but no. Not quitting."

"Abby?"

I turned to see Parker walking down the sidewalk with his hands shoved into his pockets. His full lips were dry under his red nose, and I laughed when he put an imaginary cigarette to his mouth and blew out a puff of misty air.

"You could save a lot of money this way, Finch," he smiled.

"Why is everyone trashing on my smoking habit today?" he asked, annoyed.

"What's up, Parker?" I asked.

He fished two tickets from his pocket. "That new Vietnam movie is out. You said you wanted to see it the other day, so I thought I would grab us some tickets for tonight."

"No pressure," Finch said.

"I can go with Brad if you have plans," he said with a shrug.

"So it's not a date?" I asked.

"Nope, just friends."

"And we've seen how that works out for you," Finch teased.

"Shut up!" I giggled. "That sounds fun, Parker, thanks."

His eyes brightened. "Would you like to get some pizza or something before? I'm not a big fan of theater food, myself."

"Pizza's great," I nodded.

"The movie's at nine, so I'll pick you up at six thirty or so?"

I nodded again and Parker waved goodbye.

"Oh, Jesus," Finch said. "You're a glutton, Abby. You know that's not going to fly with Travis when he gets wind of it."

"You heard him. It's not a date. And I can't make plans based on what is okay with Travis. He didn't clear it with me before he brought Megan home."

"You're never going to let that go, are you?"

"Probably not, no."

+ + +

WE SAT IN A CORNER BOOTH, AND I RUBBED MY MITTENS together, trying to get warm. I couldn't help but notice we were in the same booth Travis and I sat in when we first met, and I smiled at the memory of that day.

"What's funny?" Parker asked.

"I just like this place. Good times."

"I noticed the bracelet," he said.

I looked down at the sparkling diamonds on my wrist. "I told you I liked it."

The waitress handed us menus and took our drink orders. Parker updated me on his spring schedule, and talked about the progress in his studies for the MCAT. By the time the waitress served our beers, Parker had barely taken a breath. He seemed nervous, and I wondered if he wasn't under the impression that we were on a date, regardless of what he'd said.

He cleared his throat. "I'm sorry. I think I've monopolized the conversation long enough." He tipped his beer bottle and shook his head. "I just haven't talked to you for any length of time in so long that I suppose I had a lot to say."

"It's fine. It has been a long time."

Just then, the door chimed. I turned to see Travis and Shepley walk in. It took Travis less than a second to meet my stare, but he didn't look surprised.

"Jesus," I muttered under my breath.

"What?" Parker asked, turning to see them sit in a booth across the room.

"There's a burger place down the street we can go to," Parker said in a hushed voice. As nervous as he was before, it had been taken to a whole new level now.

"I think it would be more awkward to leave at this point," I grumbled.

His face fell, defeated. "You're probably right."

We tried to continue our conversation, but it was noticeably forced and uncomfortable. The waitress spent an extended period of time at Travis's table, raking her fingers through her hair and shifting her weight from one foot to the other. She finally remembered to take our order when Travis answered his cell phone.

"I'll have the tortellini," Parker said, looking to me.

"And I'll have . . ." I trailed off. I was distracted when Travis and Shepley stood up.

Travis followed Shepley to the door, but he hesitated, stopped, and turned around. When he saw me watching him, he walked straight across the room. The waitress had an expectant smile, as if she thought he had come to say goodbye. She was quickly disappointed when he stood beside me without so much as blinking in her direction.

"I've got a fight in forty-five minutes, Pidge. I want you there."

"Trav . . ."

His face was stoic, but I could see the tension around his eyes. I wasn't sure if he didn't want to leave my dinner with Parker to fate or if he truly wanted me there with him, but I had made my decision the second he'd asked.

"I need you there. It's a rematch with Brady Hoffman, the guy from State. It's a big crowd, lots of money floating around . . . and Adam says Brady's been training."

"You've fought him before, Travis, you know it's an easy win."

"Abby," Parker said quietly.

"I need you there," Travis said.

I looked at Parker with an apologetic smile. "I'm sorry."

"Are you serious?" he said, his eyebrows shooting up. "You're just going to leave in the middle of dinner?"

"You can still call Brad, right?" I asked, standing up.

The corners of Travis's mouth turned up infinitesimally as he tossed a twenty on the table. "That should cover it."

"I don't care about the money . . . Abby . . ."

I shrugged. "He's my best friend, Parker. If he needs me there, I have to go."

I felt Travis's hand encapsulate mine as he led me away. Parker watched with a stunned look on his face. Shepley was already on the phone in his Charger, spreading the word. Travis sat in the back with me, keeping my hand firmly in his.

"I just got off the phone with Adam, Trav. He said the State guys all showed up drunk and padded with cash. They're already riled up, so you might wanna keep Abby out of the way."

Travis nodded. "You can keep an eye on her."

"Where's America?" I asked.

"Studying for her Physics test."

"That's a nice lab," Travis said. I laughed once and then looked to Travis, who had a small grin on his face.

"When did you see the lab? You haven't had Physics," Shepley said.

Travis chuckled and I elbowed him. He pressed his lips together until the urge to laugh subsided, and then he winked at me, squeezing my hand once again. His fingers intertwined in mine, and I heard a small sigh escape his lips. I knew what he was thinking because I felt the same. In that sliver of time, it was as if nothing had changed.

We pulled into a dark patch of the parking lot, and Travis refused to let go of my hand until we crawled into the window of the basement of the Hellerton Science Building. It had been built just the year before, so it didn't suffer from stagnant air and dust like the other basements we'd snuck into.

Just as we entered the hallway, the roar of the crowd reached our ears. I poked my head out to see an ocean of faces, many of them unfamiliar. Everyone had a bottle of beer in their hand, but the State students were easy to pick out of the crowd. They were the ones that swayed with their eyes half closed.

"Stay close to Shepley, Pigeon. It's going to get crazy in here," he said from behind me. He scanned the crowd, shaking his head at the sheer numbers.

Hellerton's basement was the most spacious on campus, so Adam liked to schedule fights there when he expected a larger crowd. Even with the addition of space, people were being rubbed against the walls and shoving one another to get a good spot.

Adam rounded the corner and didn't try to hide his dissatisfaction with my presence. "I thought I told you that you couldn't bring your girl to the fights anymore, Travis."

Travis shrugged. "She's not my girl anymore."

I kept my features smooth, but he had said the words so matter-of-factly that I felt a stabbing sensation in my chest.

Adam looked down at our intertwined fingers and then up at Travis. "I'm never gonna figure you two out." He shook his head and then glanced to the mob. People were still streaming in from the stairs, and those on the floor were already packed together. "We've got an insane pot tonight, Travis, so no fuckin' off, okay?"

"I'll make sure it's entertaining, Adam."

"That's not what I'm worried about. Brady's been training."

"So have I."

"Bullshit," Shepley laughed.

Travis shrugged. "I got in a fight with Trent last weekend. That little shit is fast."

I chuckled and Adam glared at me. "You better take this seriously, Travis," he said, staring into his eyes. "I have a lot of money riding on this fight."

"And I don't?" Travis said, irritated with Adam's lecture.

Adam turned, holding the bullhorn to his lips as he stood upon a chair above the multitude of drunken spectators. Travis pulled me against his side as Adam greeted the crowd and then went over the rules.

"Good luck," I said, touching his chest. I hadn't felt nervous watching his fights other than the one he'd had with Brock McMann in Vegas, but I couldn't shake the ominous feeling I'd had since we stepped foot in Hellerton. Something was off, and Travis felt it, too.

Travis grabbed my shoulders and planted a kiss on my lips. He pulled away quickly, nodding once. "That's all the luck I need."

I was still stunned from the warmth of Travis's lips when Shepley pulled me to the wall beside Adam. I was bumped and elbowed, reminding me of the first night I watched Travis fight, but the crowd was less focused, and some of the State students were getting hostile. Easterners cheered and whistled for Travis when he broke into the Circle, and State's crowd alternated between booing Travis and cheering for Brady.

I was in prime position to see Brady tower over Travis, twitching impatiently for the bullhorn to sound. As usual, Travis had a slight grin on his face, unaffected by the madness around him. When Adam began the fight, Travis intentionally let Brady get in the first punch. I was surprised when his face jerked hard to the side with the blow. Brady had been training.

Travis smiled, his teeth a bright red, and then he focused on matching every punch Brady dealt.

"Why is he letting him hit him so much?" I asked Shepley.

"I don't think he's letting him anymore," Shepley said, shaking his head. "Don't worry, Abby. He's getting ready to take it up a notch."

After ten minutes Brady was winded, but he still landed solid blows into Travis's sides and jaw. Travis caught Brady's shoe when he tried to kick him, and held his leg high with one hand, punching him in the nose with incredible force and then lifting Brady's leg higher, causing him to lose his balance. The crowd exploded when Brady fell, but he wasn't on the floor for long. He stood, but with the addition of two lines of dark red streaming from his nose. In the next moment, he landed two more punches to Travis's face. Blood rose from a cut on Travis's eyebrow and dripped down his cheek.

I closed my eyes and turned away, hoping Travis would end the fight soon. The small shift of my body caught me in the current of onlookers, and before I could right myself, I was several feet from a preoccupied Shepley. Efforts to fight against the crowd were ineffective, and before long I was being rubbed against the back wall.

The nearest exit was on the other side of the room, an equal distance to the door we'd come in. My back slammed against the concrete wall, knocking the wind out of me.

"Shep!" I yelled, waving my hand above me to get his attention. The fight was at its peak. No one could hear me.

A man lost his footing and used my shirt to right himself, spilling his beer down my front. I was soaked from neck to waist, reeking with the bitter stench of cheap beer. The man still had my shirt bunched in his fist as he tried to pull himself from the floor, and I ripped his fingers open two at time until he released me. He didn't look twice at me, pushing his way forward through the crowd.

"Hey! I know you!" Another man yelled into my ear.

I leaned away, recognizing him right away. It was Ethan, the man Travis threatened at the bar—the man that had somehow escaped sexual assault charges.

"Yeah," I said, looking for a hole in the crowd as I straightened my shirt.

"That's a nice bracelet," he said, running his hand down my arm and grabbing my wrist.

"Hey," I warned, pulling my hand away.

He rubbed my arm, swaying and grinning. "We were rudely interrupted last time I tried to talk to you."

I stood on my tiptoes, seeing Travis land two blows into Brady's face. He scanned the crowd between each one. He was looking for me instead of focusing on the fight. I had to get back to my spot before he was too distracted.

I had barely made headway into the crowd when Ethan's fingers dug into the back of my jeans. My back slammed into the wall once more.

"I wasn't finished talking to you," Ethan said, scanning my wet shirt.

I pulled his hand from the back of my jeans, digging in my nails. "Let go!" I yelled when he resisted.

Ethan laughed and pulled me against him. "I don't wanna let go."

I scanned the crowd for a familiar face, trying to push Ethan away at the same time. His arms were heavy, and his grip was tight. In a panic, I couldn't distinguish State students from Easterners. No one seemed to notice my scuffle with Ethan, and it was so loud no one could hear me protest, either. He leaned in, reaching his hand around to my backside.

"I always thought you'd be a nice piece of ass," he said, breathing stale beer in my face.

"Get OFF!" I screamed, pushing him.

I looked for Shepley, and saw that Travis had finally picked me out of the crowd. He instantly pushed against the packed bodies surrounding him.

"Travis!" I screamed, but it was muffled against the cheering. I pushed Ethan with one hand and reached for Travis with the other.

Travis made little progress before being shoved back into the Circle. Brady took advantage of Travis's distraction and rammed an elbow in the side of his head.

The crowd quieted down a bit when Travis punched someone in the crowd, trying once again to get to me.

"Get the fuck off her!" Travis yelled.

In a line between where I stood and Travis's desperate attempt to reach me, heads turned in my direction. Ethan was oblivious, trying to keep me still long enough to kiss me.

He ran his nose across my cheekbone and then down my neck.

"You smell really good," he slurred.

I pushed his face away, but he grabbed my wrist, unfazed.

Wide-eyed, I searched for Travis again. He desperately pointed me out to Shepley. "Get her! Shep! Get Abby!" he said, still trying to push through the crowd. Brady pulled him back into the circle and punched him again.

"You're fucking hot, you know that?" Ethan said.

I closed my eyes when I felt his mouth on my neck. Anger welled up within me and I pushed him again. "I said get OFF!" I yelled, ramming my knee into his groin.

He doubled over, one hand automatically flying to the source of the pain, the other still gripping my shirt, refusing to let go.

"You bitch!" he cried.

In the next moment, I was free. Shepley's eyes were wild, staring into Ethan's as he gripped him by the collar of his shirt. He held Ethan against the wall while he nailed him with his fist repeatedly in the face, stopping only when the blood poured from Ethan's mouth and nose.

Shepley pulled me to the stairs, shoving anyone who stood in his path. He helped me through an open window, and then down a fire escape, catching me when I leapt the few feet to the ground.

"You okay, Abby? Did he hurt you?" Shepley asked.

One sleeve of my white sweater hung only by a few threads; otherwise I had escaped unscathed. I shook my head, still stunned.

Shepley gently took my cheeks in his hands, looking into my eyes. "Abby, answer me. Are you all right?"

I nodded. As the adrenaline absorbed into my blood stream, the tears began to flow. "I'm okay."

He hugged me, pressing his cheek against my forehead, and then stiffened. "Over here, Trav!"

Travis ran at us full speed, slowing only when had me in his arms. He was covered in blood, his eye dripping and his mouth spattered with red.

"Jesus Christ . . . is she hurt?" he asked.

Shepley's hand was still on my back. "She said she's okay."

Travis held me at arm's length by my shoulders and frowned. "Are you hurt, Pidge?"

Just as I shook my head, I saw the first of the mob from the basement trickling down from the fire escape. Travis kept me tight in his arms, silently scanning the faces. A short, squat man hopped down from the ladder and froze when he noticed us standing on the sidewalk.

"You," Travis snarled.

He let me go, running across the grass, tackling the man to the ground.

I looked to Shepley, confused and horrified.

"That's the guy that kept shoving Travis back in the Circle," Shepley said.

A small crowd gathered around them as they scuffled on the ground. Travis pounded his fist into the man's face over and over. Shepley pulled me into his chest, still panting. The man stopped fighting back, and Travis left him on the ground in a bloody heap. Those gathered around him fanned out, giving Travis a wide berth, seeing the rage in his eyes.

"Travis!" Shepley yelled, pointing to the other side of the building.

Ethan hobbled in the shadows, using the brick wall of Hellerton to hold himself up. When he heard Shepley yell for Travis, he turned just in time to see his assailant charge. Ethan limped across the lawn, throwing down the beer bottle in his hands and moving as fast as his legs could carry him to the street. Just as he reached his car, Travis grabbed him and slammed him against it.

Ethan pleaded with Travis, even as Travis gripped his shirt and rammed his head into the car door. The begging was cut off with the loud thud of his skull against the windshield, and then Travis pulled him to the front of the car and shattered the headlight with Ethan's face. Travis launched him onto the hood, pressing his face into the metal while shouting obscenities.

"Shit," Shepley said. I turned to see Hellerton glow blue and red from the lights of a quickly approaching police cruiser. Droves of people jumped from the landing, forming a human waterfall down the fire escape, and a flurry of running students burst into every direction.

"Travis!" I screamed.

Travis left Ethan's limp body on the hood of the car to sprint toward us. Shepley pulled me to the parking lot, ripping open his door. I jumped into the backseat, anxiously waiting for them both to get in. Cars flew from their spots and out of the driveway, screeching to a halt when a second police car blocked the drive.

Travis and Shepley jumped into their seats, and Shepley cursed when he saw the trapped cars backing from the only exit. He slammed the car into drive, and the Charger bounced as it jumped the curb. He spun out over the grass, and we flew between two buildings, bouncing again when he hit the road behind the school.

The tires squealed and the engine snarled when Shepley slammed his foot on the accelerator. I slid across the seat into the wall of the cab when we took a turn, bumping my already sore elbow. The streetlights streaked across the window as we raced to the apartment, but it seemed like an hour had passed by the time we pulled into the parking lot.

Shepley threw the Charger into park, and turned off the ignition. The boys opened their doors in silence, and Travis reached into the backseat, lifting me into his arms.

"What happened? Holy shit, Trav, what happened to your face?" America said, running down the stairs.

"I'll tell you inside," Shepley said, guiding her to the door.

Travis carried me up the stairs, through the living room and down the hall without a word, setting me on his bed. Toto pawed at my legs, jumping onto the bed to lick my face.

"Not now, buddy," Travis said in a hushed voice, taking the puppy to the hall and shutting the door.

He knelt in front of me, touching the frayed edges of my sleeve. His eye was in the beginning stages of a bruise, red and swollen. The angry skin above it was cut and wet with blood. His lips were smeared with scarlet, and the hide had been ripped away from some of his knuckles. His once-white T-shirt was now soiled with a combination of blood, grass, and dirt.

I touched his eye and he winced, pulling away from my hand. "I'm so sorry, Pigeon. I tried to get to you. I tried..." He cleared his throat of the anger and worry that choked him. "I couldn't get to you."

"Will you ask America to take me back to Morgan?" I said.

"You can't go back there tonight. The place is crawling with cops. Just stay here. I'll sleep on the couch."

I sucked in a faltering breath, trying to ward off any more tears. He felt bad enough.

Travis stood up and opened the door.

"Where are you going?" I asked.

"I've gotta get a shower. I'll be right back."

America shoved past him, sitting beside me on the bed, pulling me into her chest. "I'm so sorry I wasn't there!" she cried.

"I'm fine," I said, wiping my tearstained face.

Shepley knocked on the door as he entered, bringing me a short glass half full of whiskey.

"Here," he said, handing it to America. She cupped my hands around it and nudged me.

I tipped back my head, letting the liquid flow down my throat. My face compressed as the whiskey burned its way to my stomach. "Thanks," I said, handing the glass back to Shepley.

"I should have gotten to her sooner. I didn't even realize she was gone. I'm sorry, Abby. I should've . . ."

"It's not your fault, Shep. It's not anyone's fault."

"It's Ethan's fault," he seethed. "That sick bastard was dry-fucking her against the wall."

"Baby!" America said, appalled. She pulled me to her side.

"I need another drink," I said, shoving my empty glass at Shepley.

"Me, too," Shepley said, returning to the kitchen.

Travis walked in with a towel around his waist, holding a cold can of beer against his eye. America turned her back to us as Travis slipped on his boxers, and then he grabbed his pillow.

Shepley brought four glasses this time, all full to the brim with amber liquor. We all knocked back the whiskey without hesitation.

"I'll see you in the morning," America said, kissing my cheek.

Travis took my glass, setting it on the nightstand. He watched me for a moment and then walked over to his closet, pulling a T-shirt off the hanger and tossing it to the bed.

"I'm sorry I'm such a fuckup," he said, holding the beer to his eye.

"You look awful. You're going to feel like shit tomorrow."

He shook his head, disgusted. "Abby, you were attacked tonight. Don't worry about me."

"It's hard not to when your eye is swelling shut," I said, situating his shirt on my lap.

His jaw tensed. "It wouldn't've happened if I'd just let you stay with Parker. But I knew if I asked you, you'd come. I wanted to show him that you were still mine, and then you get hurt."

The words took me off guard, as if I hadn't heard him right. "That's why you ask me to come tonight? To prove a point to Parker?"

"It was part of it," he said, ashamed.

The blood drained from my face. For the first time since we'd met, Travis had fooled me. I had gone to Hellerton with him thinking he needed me, thinking that despite everything, we were back to where we were before. I was nothing more than a water hydrant; he had marked his territory, and I had allowed him to do it.

My eyes filled with tears. "Get out."

"Pigeon," he said, taking a step toward me.

"Get OUT!" I said, grabbing the glass from the nightstand and throwing it at him. He ducked, and it shattered against the wall in hundreds of tiny, glistening shards. "I hate you!"

Travis heaved as if the air had been knocked out of him, and with a pained expression, he left me alone.

I yanked off my clothes and pulled the T-shirt on. The noise that burst from my throat surprised me. It had been a long time since I had sobbed uncontrollably. Within moments, America rushed into the room.

She crawled into the bed and wrapped her arms around me. She didn't ask questions or try to console me; she only held me as I let the tears drench the pillowcase.

Chapter Twenty
Last Dance

JUST BEFORE THE SUN BREACHED THE HORIZON, AMERica and I quietly left the apartment behind. We didn't speak on the way to Morgan. I was glad for the silence. I didn't want to talk, I didn't want to think, I just wanted to block out the last twelve hours. My body felt heavy and sore, as if I'd been in a car accident. When we walked into my room, I saw that Kara's bed was made.

"Can I stick around a while? I need to borrow your flatiron," America asked.

"Mare, I'm fine. Go to class."

"You're not fine. I don't want to leave you alone right now."

"That's all I want to be at the moment."

She opened her mouth to argue but sighed. There would be no changing my mind. "I'm coming back to check on you after class. Get some rest."

I nodded, locking the door behind her. The bed squeaked beneath me as I fell onto it with a huff. All along I believed that I was important to Travis, that he needed me. But in that moment, I felt like the shiny new toy Parker said I was. He wanted to prove to Parker that I was still his. His.

"I'm nobody's," I said to the empty room.

As the words sunk in, I was overwhelmed with the grief I'd felt from the night before. I belonged to no one.

I'd never felt so alone in my life.

FINCH SET A BROWN BOTTLE IN FRONT OF ME. NEITHER of us felt like celebrating, but I was at least comforted by the fact that, according to America, Travis would avoid the date party at all costs. Red-and-pink craft paper covered empty beer cans hanging from the ceiling, and red dresses in every style walked past. The tables were covered with tiny foil hearts, and Finch rolled his eyes at the ridiculous decorations.

"Valentine's Day at a frat house. Romantic," he said, watching the couples walk by.

Shepley and America had been downstairs dancing from the moment we arrived, and Finch and I protested our presence by pouting in the kitchen. I drank the contents of the bottle quickly, determined to blur the memories of the last date party I'd attended.

Finch popped open another cap and handed me another, aware of my desperation to forget. "I'll get more," he said, returning to the fridge.

"The keg is for guests, the bottles are for Sig Tau," a girl sneered beside me.

I looked down at the red cup in her hand. "Or maybe your boyfriend just told you that because he was counting on a cheap date."

She narrowed her eyes and pushed away from the counter, taking her cup elsewhere.

"Who was that?" Finch asked, setting down four more bottles.

"Random sorority bitch," I said, watching her walk away.

By the time Shepley and America rejoined us, six empty bottles sat on the table beside me. My teeth were numb, and it felt a bit easier to smile. I was more comfortable, leaning against my spot on the counter. Travis had proven to be a no-show, and I could survive the remainder of the party in peace.

"Are you guys going to dance or what?" America asked.

I looked to Finch. "Are you going to dance with me, Finch?"

"Are you going to be able to dance?" he asked, raising an eyebrow.

"There's only one way to find out," I said, pulling him downstairs.

We bounced and shook until a thin sheen of sweat began to form under my dress. Just when I thought my lungs would burst, a slow song came over the speakers. Finch peered uncomfortably around us, glancing at the people pairing off and getting close.

"You're going to make me dance to this, aren't you?" he asked.

"It's Valentine's Day, Finch. Pretend I'm a boy."

He laughed, pulling me into his arms. "It's hard to do that when you're wearing a short pink dress."

"Whatever. Like you've never seen a boy in a dress."

Finch shrugged. "True."

I giggled, resting my head against his shoulder. The alcohol made my body feel heavy and sluggish as I tried to move to the slow tempo.

"Mind if I cut in, Finch?"

Travis stood beside us, half amused, half prepared for my reaction. The blood under my cheeks immediately burst into flames.

Finch looked at me, and then at Travis. "Sure."

"Finch," I hissed as he walked away. Travis pulled me against him, and I tried to keep as much space between us as possible. "I thought you weren't coming."

"I wasn't, but I knew you were here. I had to come."

I looked around the room, avoiding his eyes. Every movement he made I was acutely aware of. The pressure changes of his fingers at the points where he touched me, his feet shuffling beside mine, his arms shifting, brushing against my dress. I felt ridiculous pretending not to notice. His eye was healing, the bruise had almost vanished, and the red blotches on his face were absent as if I had imagined them. All evidence of that horrible night had disappeared, leaving only the stinging memories.

He watched my every breath, and when the song was half over, he sighed. "You look beautiful, Pidge."

"Don't."

"Don't what? Tell you you're beautiful?"

"Just . . . don't."

"I didn't mean it."

I huffed in frustration. "Thanks."

"No . . . you look beautiful. I meant that. I was talking about what I said in my room. I'm not going to lie. I enjoyed pulling you from your date with Parker . . ."

"It wasn't a date, Travis. We were just eating. He won't speak to me now, thanks to you."

"I heard. I'm sorry."

"No you're not."

"Y-you're right," he said, stuttering when he saw my impatient expression. "But I . . . that wasn't the only reason I took you to the fight. I wanted you there with me, Pidge. You're my good-luck charm."

"I'm not your anything," I snapped, glaring up at him.

His eyebrows pulled in and he stopped dancing. "You're my everything."

I pressed my lips together, trying to keep the anger at the surface, but it was impossible to stay mad at him when he looked at me that way.

"You don't really hate me . . . do you?" he asked.

I turned away from him, putting more distance between us. "Sometimes I wish that I did. It would make everything a whole hell of a lot easier."

A cautious smile spread across his lips in a thin, subtle line. "So what pisses you off more? What I did to make you wanna hate me? Or knowing that you can't?"

The anger returned. I shoved past him, running up the stairs to the kitchen. My eyes were beginning to gloss over but I refused to be a sobbing mess at the date party. Finch stood beside the table and I sighed with relief when he handed me another beer.

For the next hour, I watched Travis fend off girls and suck down shots of whiskey in the living room. Each time he caught my eye, I looked away from him, determined to get through the night without a scene.

"You two look miserable," Shepley said.

"They couldn't look more bored if they were doing it on purpose," America grumbled.

"Don't forget . . . we didn't want to come," Finch reminded them.

America made her famous face that I was just as famous for giving in to. "You could pretend, Abby. For me."

Just when I opened my mouth for a sharp retort, Finch touched my arm. "I think we've done our duty. You ready to go, Abby?"

I drank the remainder of my beer in a quick swig and then took Finch's hand. As anxious as I was to leave, my legs froze when the same song that Travis and I danced to at my birthday party floated up the stairs. I grabbed Finch's bottle and took another swig, trying to block out the memories that came with the music.

Brad leaned against the counter beside me. "Wanna dance?"

I smiled at him, shaking my head. He began to say something else, but he was interrupted.

"Dance with me." Travis stood a few feet from me, his hand outstretched to mine.

America, Shepley, and Finch were all staring at me, waiting for my answer as anxiously as Travis.

"Leave me alone, Travis," I said, crossing my arms.

"This is our song, Pidge."

"We don't have a song."

"Pigeon . . ."

"No."

I looked to Brad and forced a smile. "I would love to dance, Brad."

Brad's freckles stretched across his cheeks as he smiled, gesturing for me to lead the way to the stairs.

Travis staggered backward, the hurt plainly displayed in his eyes. "A toast!" he yelled.

I flinched, turning just in time to see him climbing onto a chair, stealing a beer from the shocked Sig Tau brother closest to him. I glanced to America, who watched Travis with a pained expression.

"To douchebags!" he said, gesturing to Brad. "And to girls that break your heart," he bowed his head to me. His eyes lost focus. "And to the absolute fucking horror of losing your best friend because you were stupid enough to fall in love with her."

He tilted back the beer, finishing what was left, and then tossed it to the floor. The room was silent except for the music playing in the lower level, and everyone stared at Travis in mass confusion.

Mortified, I grabbed Brad's hand and led him downstairs to the dance floor. A few couples followed behind us, watching me closely for tears or some other response to Travis's tirade. I smoothed my features, refusing to give them what they wanted.

We danced a few stiff steps and Brad sighed. "That was kind of . . . weird."

"Welcome to my life."

Travis pushed his way through the couples on the dance floor, stopping beside me. It took him a moment to steady his feet. "I'm cutting in."

"No, you're not. Jesus!" I said, refusing to look at him.

After a few tense moments I glanced up, seeing Travis's eyes boring into Brad's. "If you don't back away from my girl, I'll rip out your fucking throat. Right here on the dance floor."

Brad seemed conflicted, his eyes nervously darting from me to Travis. "Sorry, Abby," he said, slowly pulling his arms away. He retreated to the stairs and I stood alone, humiliated.

"How I feel about you right now, Travis . . . it very closely resembles hate."

"Dance with me," he pleaded, swaying to keep his balance.

The song ended and I sighed with relief. "Go drink another bottle of whiskey, Trav." I turned to dance with the only single guy on the dance floor.

The tempo was faster, and I smiled at my new, surprised dance partner, trying to ignore the fact that Travis was just a few feet behind me. Another Sig Tau brother danced behind me, grabbing my hips. I reached back, pulling him closer. It reminded me of the way Travis and Megan danced that night at the Red, and I did my best to recreate the scene I had wished on many occasions that I could forget. Two pairs of hands were on nearly every part of my body, and it was easy to ignore my more reserved side with the amount of alcohol in my system.

Suddenly, I was airborne. Travis threw me over his shoulder, at the same time shoving one of his frat brothers hard, knocking him to the floor.

"Put me down!" I said, pounding my fists into his back.

"I'm not going to let you embarrass yourself over me," he growled, taking the stairs two at a time.

Every pair of eyes we passed watched me kick and scream as Travis carried me across the room. "You don't think," I said as I struggled, "this is embarrassing? Travis!"

"Shepley! Is Donnie outside?" Travis said, ducking from my flailing limbs.

"Uh . . . yeah?" he said.

"Put her down!" America said, taking a step toward us.

"America," I said, squirming, "don't just stand there! Help me!"

Her mouth turned up and she laughed once. "You two look ridiculous."

My eyebrows turned in at her words, both shocked and angry that she found any part of the situation funny.

Travis headed for the door and I glared at her. "Thanks a lot, friend!"

The cold air struck the bare parts of my skin, and I protested louder. "Put me down, dammit!"

Travis opened a car door and tossed me into the backseat, sliding in beside me. "Donnie, you're the DD tonight?"

"Yeah," he said, nervously watching me struggle to escape.

"I need you take us to my apartment."

"Travis . . . I don't think . . ."

Travis's voice was controlled, but frightening. "Do it, Donnie, or I'll shove my fist through the back of your head, I swear to God."

Donnie pulled away from the curb and I lunged for the door handle. "I'm not going to your apartment!"

Travis grabbed one of my wrists and then the other. I leaned down to bite his arm. He closed his eyes, and then a low grunt escaped through his clenched jaw as my teeth sunk into his flesh.

"Do your worst, Pidge. I'm tired of your shit."

I released his skin and jerked my arms, struggling against his grip. "My shit? Let me out of this fucking car!"

He pulled my wrists close to his face. "I love you, dammit! You're not going anywhere until you sober up and we figure this out!"

"You're the only one that hasn't figured it out, Travis!" I said. He released my wrists and I crossed my arms, pouting the rest of the way to the apartment.

When the car slowed to a stop, I leaned forward. "Can you take me home, Donnie?"

Travis pulled me out of the car by the arm and then he swung me over his shoulder again, carrying me up the stairs. "Night, Donnie."

"I'm calling your dad!" I cried.

Travis laughed out loud. "And he'd probably pat me on the shoulder and tell me that it's about damn time!"

He struggled to unlock the door as I kicked and waved my arms, trying to get away. "Knock it off, Pidge, or we're going to fall down the stairs!" Once he opened the door, he stomped into Shepley's room.

"Put. Me. Down!" I screamed.

"Fine," he said, dropping me onto Shepley's bed. "Sleep it off. We'll talk in the morning."

The room was dark; the only light a rectangular beam shooting into the doorway from the hall. I fought to focus through the darkness, beer, and anger, and when he turned into the light, it illuminated his smug smile.

I pounded the mattress with my fists. "You can't tell me what to do anymore, Travis! I don't belong to you!"

In the second it took him to turn and face me, his expression had contorted into anger. He stomped toward me, planting his hands on the bed and leaning into my face.

"WELL, I BELONG TO YOU!" The veins in his neck bulged as he shouted, and I met his glare, refusing to even flinch.

He looked at my lips, panting. "I belong to you," he whispered, his anger melting as he realized how close we were.

Before I could think of a reason not to, I grabbed his face, slamming my lips against his. Without hesitation, Travis lifted me into his arms. In a few long strides, he carried me into his bedroom, both of us crashing to the bed.

I yanked his shirt over his head, fumbling in the dark with his belt buckle. He jerked it open, ripped it off, and threw it to the floor. He lifted me from the mattress with one hand and unzipped my dress with the other. I pulled it over my head, tossing it somewhere in the dark, and then Travis kissed me, moaning against my mouth.

With just a few quick movements, his boxers were off and he pressed his chest against mine. I grabbed his backside, but he resisted when I tried to pull him into me.

"We're both drunk," he said, breathing hard.

"Please." I pressed my legs against his hips, desperate to relieve the burning between my thighs. Travis was set on us getting back together, and I had no intentions of fighting the inevitable, so I was more than ready to spend the night tangled up in his sheets.

"This isn't right," he said.

He was just above me, pressing his forehead against mine. I hoped that it was just halfhearted protesting, and that I could persuade him somehow that he was wrong. The way we couldn't seem to stay away from each other was unexplainable, but I didn't need an explanation anymore. I didn't even need an excuse. In that moment, I only needed him.

"I want you."

"I need you to say it," he said.

My insides were screaming for him, and I couldn't stand it a second longer. "I'll say whatever you want."

"Then say that you belong to me. Say that you'll take me back. I won't do this unless we're together."

"We've never really been apart, have we?" I asked, hoping it was enough.

He shook his head, his lips sweeping across mine. "I need to hear you say it. I need to know you're mine."

"I've been yours since the second we met."

My voice took the tone of begging. Any other time I would have been embarrassed, but I was beyond regret. I had fought my feelings, guarded them, and bottled them up. I had experienced the happiest moments of my life while at Eastern, all of them with Travis. Fighting, laughing, loving, or crying, if it was with him, I was where I wanted to be.

One side of his mouth turned up as he touched my face, and then his lips touched mine in a tender kiss. When I pulled him against me, he didn't resist. His muscles tensed, and he held his breath as he slid inside me.

"Say it again," he said.

"I'm yours," I breathed. Every nerve, inside and out, ached for more. "I don't ever want to be apart from you again."

"Promise me," he said, groaning with another thrust.

"I love you. I'll love you forever." The words were more of a sigh, but I met his eyes when I said them. I could see the uncertainty in his eyes vanish, and even in the dim light, his face brightened.

Finally satisfied, he sealed his mouth over mine.

+ + +

TRAVIS WOKE ME WITH KISSES. MY HEAD FELT HEAVY and fogged from the multiple drinks I'd had the night before, but the hour before I fell asleep replayed in my mind in vivid detail. Soft lips showered every inch of my hand, arm, and neck, and when he reached my lips, I smiled.

"Good morning," I said against his mouth.

He didn't speak; his lips continued working against mine. His solid arms enveloped me, and then he buried his face in my neck.

"You're quiet this morning," I said, running my hands over the bare skin of his back. I let them continue down his backside, and then I hooked my leg over his hip, kissing his cheek.

He shook his head. "I just want to be like this," he whispered.

I frowned. "Did I miss something?"

"I didn't mean to wake you up. Why don't you just go back to sleep?"

I leaned back against the pillow, pulling up his chin. His eyes were bloodshot, the skin around them blotchy and red.

"What in the hell is wrong with you?" I asked, alarmed.

He put one of my hands in his and kissed it, pressing his forehead against my neck. "Just go back to sleep, Pigeon. Please?"

"Did something happen? Is it America?" With the last question, I sat up. Even seeing the fear in my eyes, his expression didn't change. He simply sighed and sat up with me, looking at my hand in his.

"No . . . America's fine. They got home around four this morning. They're still in bed. It's early, let's just go back to sleep."

Feeling my heart pounding against my chest, I knew there

was no chance of falling back asleep. Travis put both hands on each side of my face and kissed me. His mouth moved differently, as if he were kissing me for the last time. He lowered me to the pillow, kissed me once more, and then rested his head on my chest, wrapping both arms tightly around me.

Every possible reason for Travis's behavior flipped through my mind like television channels. I hugged him to me, afraid to ask. "Have you slept?"

"I . . . couldn't. I didn't wanna . . ." his voice trailed off.

I kissed his forehead. "Whatever it is, we'll get through it, okay? Why don't you get some sleep? We'll figure it out when you wake up."

His head popped up and he scanned my face. I saw both mistrust and hope in his eyes. "What do you mean? That we'll get through it?"

My eyebrows pulled in, confused. I couldn't imagine what had happened while I was sleeping that would cause him so much anguish. "I don't know what's going on, but I'm here."

"You're here? As in you're staying? With me?"

I knew that my expression must have been ridiculous, but my head was spinning from both the alcohol and Travis's bizarre questions. "Yes. I thought we discussed this last night?"

"We did." He nodded, encouraged.

I searched the room with my eyes, thinking. His walls were no longer bare as they were when we had first met. They were now peppered with trinkets from places that we'd spent time together, and the white paint was interrupted by black frames holding pictures of me, us, Toto, and our group of friends. A larger frame of the two of us at my birthday party replaced the sombrero that once hung by a nail above his headboard.

I narrowed my eyes at him. "You thought I was going to wake up pissed at you, didn't you? You thought I was going to leave?"

He shrugged, making a poor attempt at the indifference that used to come so easily to him. "That is what you're famous for."

"Is that what you're so upset about? You stayed up all night worrying about what would happen when I woke up?"

He shifted as if his next words would be difficult. "I didn't mean for last night to happen like that. I was a little drunk, and I followed you around the party like some fucking stalker, and then I dragged you out of there, against your will . . . and then we . . ." He shook his head, clearly disgusted with the memories playing in his mind.

"Had the best sex of my life?" I smiled, squeezing his hand.

Travis laughed once, the tension around his eyes slowly melting away. "So we're okay?"

I kissed him, touching the sides of his face with tenderness. "Yes, dummy. I promised, didn't I? I told you everything you wanted to hear, we're back together, and you're still not happy?"

His face compressed around his smile.

"Travis, stop. I love you," I said, smoothing the worried lines around his eyes. "This absurd standoff could have been over at Thanksgiving, but . . ."

"Wait . . . what?" he interrupted, leaning back.

"I was fully prepared to give in on Thanksgiving, but you said you were done trying to make me happy, and I was too proud to tell you that I wanted you back."

"Are you fucking kidding me? I was just trying to make it easier on you! Do you know how miserable I've been?"

I frowned. "You looked just fine after break."

"That was for you! I was afraid I'd lose you if I didn't pretend to be okay with just being friends. I could have been with you this whole time? What the fuck, Pigeon?"

"I . . ." I couldn't argue; he was right. I had made us both suffer, and I had no excuse. "I'm sorry."

"You're sorry? I damn near drank myself to death, I could barely get out of bed, I shattered my phone into a million pieces on New Year's Eve to keep from calling you . . . and you're sorry?"

I bit my lip and nodded, ashamed. I had no idea what he'd been through, and hearing him say the words made a sharp pain twist inside my chest. "I'm so . . . so sorry."

"You're forgiven," he said with a grin. "Don't ever do it again."

"I won't. I promise."

He flashed his dimple and shook his head. "I fucking love you."

Chapter Twenty-One
Smoke

THE WEEKS PASSED, AND IT WAS A SURPRISE TO ME how quickly spring break was upon us. The expected stream of gossip and stares had vanished, and life had returned to normal. The basements of Eastern U hadn't held a fight in weeks. Adam made a point of keeping a low profile after the arrests had led to questions about what exactly had gone on that night, and Travis grew irritable waiting for a phone call to summon him to his last fight of the year, the fight that would pay most of his bills for the summer and well into the fall.

The snow was still thick on the ground, and on the Friday before break, one last snowball fight broke out on the crystalline lawn. Travis and I weaved through the flying ice to the cafeteria, and I held tight to his arm, trying to avoid both the snowballs and falling to the ground.

"They're not going to hit you, Pidge. They know better," Travis said, holding his red, cold nose to my cheek.

"Their aim isn't synonymous with their fear of your temper, Trav."

He held me against his side, rubbing my coat sleeve with his hand as he guided me through the chaos. We came to an abrupt halt when a handful of girls screamed past as they were pelted by the merciless aim of the baseball team. Once they cleared the path, Travis led me safely to the door.

"See? I told you we'd make it," he said with a smile.

His amusement faded when a tightly packed snowball exploded against the door, just between our faces. Travis's glare scanned the lawn, but the sheer numbers of students darting in every direction doused his urge to retaliate.

He pulled open the door, watching the melting snow slide down the painted metal to the ground. "Let's get inside."

"Good idea," I nodded.

He led me by the hand down the buffet line, piling different steaming dishes on one tray. The cashier, used to our routine, had given up her predictable baffled expression weeks before.

"Abby," Brazil nodded to me and then winked at Travis. "You guys have plans next week?"

"We're staying here. My brothers are coming in," Travis said, distracted as he organized our lunches, dividing the small Styrofoam plates in front of us on the table.

"I'm going to kill David Lapinski!" America announced, shaking snow out of her hair as she approached.

"Direct hit!" Shepley laughed. America shot him a warning glare and his laugh turned into a nervous chuckle. "I mean . . . what an asshole."

We laughed at his regretful expression as he watched her stomp to the buffet line, following quickly after.

"He's so whipped," Brazil said with a disgusted look on his face.

"America's a little uptight," Travis explained. "She's meeting his parents this week."

Brazil nodded, his eyebrows shooting up. "So they're . . ."

"There," I said, nodding with him. "It's permanent."

"Whoa," Brazil said. The shock didn't leave his face as he picked at his food, and I could see the confusion swirl around him. We were all young, and Brazil couldn't wrap his head around Shepley's commitment.

"When you have it, Brazil . . . you'll get it," Travis said, smiling at me.

The room was abuzz with excitement from both the spectacle outside and the quickly approaching last hours before break. As the seats filled, the steady stream of chatter grew to a loud echo, the volume rising as everyone began talking over the noise.

By the time Shepley and America returned with their trays, they had made up. She happily sat in the empty seat next to me, prattling on about her impending meet-the-parents moment. They would leave that evening for his parents' house. It was the perfect excuse for one of America's infamous meltdowns.

I watched her pick at her bread as she fretted about what to pack and how much luggage she could take without appearing pretentious, but she seemed to be holding it together.

"I told you, baby. They're gonna love you. Love you like I love you, love you," Shepley said, tucking her hair behind her ear. America took a breath and the corners of her mouth turned up in the way they always did when he made her feel more at ease.

Travis's phone shivered, causing it to glide a few inches across the table. He ignored it, regaling Brazil with the story of our first game of poker with his brothers. I glanced at the display, tapping Travis on the shoulder when I read the name.

"Trav?"

Without apology, he turned away from Brazil and gave me his undivided attention. "Yeah, Pigeon?"

"You might want to get that."

He looked down at his cell phone and sighed. "Or not."

"It could be important."

He pursed his lips before holding the receiver to his ear. "What's up, Adam?" His eyes searched the room as he listened, nodding occasionally. "This is my last fight, Adam. I'm not sure yet. I won't go without her and Shep's leaving town. I know . . . I heard you. Hmmm . . . that's not a bad idea, actually."

My eyebrows pulled in, seeing his eyes brighten with whatever idea Adam had enlightened him with. When Travis hung up the phone, I stared at him expectantly.

"It's enough to pay rent for the next eight months. Adam got John Savage. He's trying to go pro."

"I haven't seen him fight, have you?" Shepley asked, leaning forward.

Travis nodded. "Just once in Springfield. He's good."

"Not good enough," I said. Travis leaned in and kissed my forehead with soft appreciation. "I can stay home, Trav."

"No," he said, shaking his head.

"I don't want you to get hit like you did last time because you're worried about me."

"No, Pidge."

"I'll wait up for you," I said, trying to seem happier with the idea than I felt.

"I'm going to ask Trent to come. He's the only one I'd trust so I can concentrate on the fight."

"Thanks a lot, asshole," Shepley grumbled.

"Hey, you had your chance," Travis said, only half teasing.

Shepley's mouth pulled to the side with chagrin. He still felt at fault for the night at Hellerton. He apologized to me daily for weeks, but his guilt finally became manageable enough for him to suffer in silence. America and I tried to convince him that he wasn't to blame, but Travis would always hold him accountable.

"Shepley, it wasn't your fault. You pulled him off of me, remember?" I said, reaching around America to pat his arm. I turned to Travis, "When is the fight?"

"Next week sometime," he shrugged. "I want you there. I need you there."

I smiled, resting my chin on his shoulder. "Then I'll be there."

Travis walked me to class, his grip tensing a few times when my feet slipped on the ice. "You should be more careful," he teased.

"I'm doing it on purpose. You're such a sucker."

"If you want my arms around you, all you have to do is ask," he said, pulling me into his chest.

We were oblivious to the students passing and the snowballs flying overhead as he pressed his lips against mine. My feet left the ground and he continued to kiss me, carrying me with ease across campus. When he finally set me on my feet in front of the door of my classroom, he shook his head.

"When we make our schedules for next semester, it would be more convenient if we had more classes together."

"I'll work on that," I said, giving him one last kiss before making my way to my seat.

I looked up, and Travis gave me one last smile before making his way to his class in the next building. The students around me were as used to our shameless displays of affection as his class was used to him being a few minutes late.

I was surprised that the time ticked by so quickly. I turned in my last test of the day and made my way to Morgan Hall. Kara sat in her usual spot on her bed as I rifled through my drawers for a few needed items.

"You going out of town?" Kara asked.

"No, I just needed a few things. I'm headed over to the Science building to pick up Trav, and then I'll be at the apartment all week."

"I figured," she said, keeping her eyes on the pages of her book.

"Have a good break, Kara."

"Mmmhmm."

The campus was nearly empty, with only a few stragglers left. When I turned the corner, I saw Travis standing outside, finishing a cigarette. He wore a knit cap over his shaved head and one hand was shoved in the pocket of his worn dark-brown leather jacket. Smoke drifted from his nostrils as he looked down to the ground, deep in thought. It wasn't until I was just a few feet from him that I noticed how distracted he was.

"What's on your mind, baby?" I asked. He didn't look up. "Travis?"

His lashes fluttered when my voice registered and the troubled expression was replaced with a contrived smile. "Hey, Pigeon."

"Everything okay?"

"It is now," he said, pulling me against him.

"Okay. What's up?" I said. With a raised eyebrow and a frown, I made a show of my skepticism.

"Just have a lot on my mind," he sighed. When I waited expectantly, he continued. "This week, the fight, you being there . . ."

"I told you I would stay home."

"I need you there, Pidge," he said, flicking his cigarette to the ground. He watched it disappear into a deep footprint in the snow and then cupped his hand around mine, pulling me toward the parking lot.

"Have you talked to Trent?" I asked.

He shook his head. "I'm waiting for him to call me back."

America rolled down the window and poked her head out of Shepley's Charger. "Hurry up! It's freaking freezing!"

Travis smiled and picked up the pace, opening the door for me to slide in. Shepley and America repeated the same conversation they'd had since she learned she would be meeting his parents while I watched Travis stare out of the window. Just as we pulled into the parking lot of the apartment, Travis's phone rang.

"What the fuck, Trent?" he answered. "I called you four hours ago. It's not like you're productive at work or anything. Whatever. Listen, I need a favor. I've got a fight next week. I need you to go. I don't know when it is, but when I call you, I need you there within an hour. Can you do that for me? Can you do it or not, douchebag? Because I need you to keep an eye on Pigeon. Some asshole put his hands on her last time and . . . yeah." His voice lowered to a frightening tone. "I took care of it. So if I call . . . ? Thanks, Trent."

Travis clicked his phone shut and leaned his head against the back of the seat.

"Relieved?" Shepley asked, watching Travis in the rearview mirror.

"Yeah. I wasn't sure how I was going to do it without him there."

"I told you," I began.

"Pidge, how many times do I have to say it?" he frowned.

I shook my head at his impatient tone. "I don't understand it, though. You didn't need me there before."

His fingers lightly grazed my cheek. "I didn't know you before. When you're not there, I can't concentrate. I'm wondering where you are, what you're doing . . . if you're there and I can see you, I can focus. I know it's crazy, but that's how it is."

"And crazy is exactly the way I like it," I said, leaning up to kiss his lips.

"Obviously," America muttered under her breath.

IN THE SHADOWS OF KEATON HALL, TRAVIS HELD ME tight against his side. The steam from my breath entangled with his in the cold night air, and I could hear the low conversations of those filtering in a side door a few feet away, oblivious to our presence.

Keaton was the oldest building at Eastern, and although the Circle had been held there before, I was uneasy about the venue. Adam expected a full house, and Keaton wasn't the most spacious of basements on campus. Beams formed a grid along the aging brick walls, just one sign of the renovations taking place inside.

"This is one of the worst ideas Adam has had yet," Travis grumbled.

"It's too late to change it, now," I said, looking up at the scaffolds.

Travis's cell phone lit up and he popped it open. His face was tinged with blue against the display, and I could finally see the two worry lines between his eyebrows I already knew were there. He clicked buttons and then snapped the phone shut, gripping me tighter.

"You seem nervous tonight," I whispered.

"I'll feel better when Trent gets his punk ass here."

"I'm here, you whiny little girl," Trenton said in a hushed voice. I could barely see his outline in the darkness, but his smile gleamed in the moonlight.

"How ya been, sis?" he said. He hugged me with one arm, and then playfully shoved Travis with the other.

"I'm good, Trent."

Travis immediately relaxed, and then he led me by the hand to the back of the building.

"If the cops show and we get separated, meet me at Morgan Hall, okay?" Travis said to his brother. We stopped at an open window low to the ground, the signal that Adam was inside and waiting.

"You're fuckin' with me," Trenton said, staring down at the window. "Abby's barely gonna fit through there."

"You'll fit," Travis assured him, crawling down into the blackness inside. Like so many times before, I leaned down and pushed myself backward, knowing Travis would catch me.

We waited for a few moments, and then Trenton grunted as

he pushed off the ledge and landed on the floor, nearly losing his balance as his feet hit the concrete.

"You're lucky I love Abby. I wouldn't do this shit for just anyone," Trenton grumbled, brushing off his shirt.

Travis jumped up, pulling the window closed with one quick movement. "This way," he said, leading us through the dark.

Hallway after hallway, I gripped Travis's hand in mine, feeling Trenton pinching the fabric of my shirt. I could hear small pieces of gravel scrape the concrete as I shuffled along the floor. I felt my eyes widen, trying to adjust to the blackness of the basement, but there was no light to help them focus.

Trenton sighed after the third turn. "We're never gonna find our way out of here."

"Just follow me out. It'll be fine," Travis said, irritated with Trenton's complaining.

When the hallway grew lighter, I knew we were close. When the low roar of the crowd came to a feverish pitch of numbers and names, I knew we had arrived. The room where Travis waited to be called usually had only one lantern and one chair, but with the renovations, it was full of desks and chairs and random equipment covered in white sheets.

Travis and Trenton discussed strategy for the fight as I peeked outside. It was as packed and chaotic as the last fight, but with less room. Furniture covered in dusty sheets lined the edges of the walls, pushed aside to make room for the spectators.

The room was darker than usual, and I guessed that Adam wanted to be careful not to draw attention to our whereabouts. Lanterns hung from the ceilings, creating a dingy glow on the cash being held high as bets were still being called.

"Pigeon, did you hear me?" Travis said, touching my arm.

"What?" I said, blinking.

"I want you to stand by this doorway, okay? Keep hold of Trent's arm at all times."

"I won't move. I promise."

Travis smiled, his perfect dimple sinking into his cheek. "Now you look nervous."

I glanced to the doorway and then back to him. "I don't have a good feeling about this, Trav. Not about the fight, but... something. This place gives me the creeps."

"We won't be here long," Travis assured me. Adam's voice came over the horn, and then a pair of warm, familiar hands were on each side of my face. "I love you," he said. He wrapped his arms around me and lifted me off the floor, squeezing me to him as he kissed me. He lowered me to the ground and then hooked my arm around Trenton's. "Don't take your eyes off of her," he said to his brother, "Even for a second. This place'll get crazy once the fight starts."

"...so let's welcome tonight's contender—JOHN SAVAGE!"

"I'll guard her with my life, little brother," Trenton said, tugging on my arm. "Now go kick this guy's ass and let's get out of here."

"...TRAVIS 'MAD DOG' MADDOX!" Adam yelled through the horn.

The volume was deafening as Travis made his way through the crowd. I looked up to Trenton, who had the tiniest crook of a smile on his face. Anyone else might not have noticed, but I could see the pride in his eyes.

When Travis reached the center of the Circle, I swallowed. John wasn't much bigger, but he looked different from anyone Travis had fought before, including the man he fought in Vegas.

He wasn't trying to intimidate Travis with a severe stare like the others; he was studying him, preparing the fight in his mind. As analytical as his eyes were, they were also absent of reason. I knew before the fight began that Travis had more than a fight on his hands; he was standing in front of a demon.

Travis seemed to notice the difference as well. His usual smirk was gone, an intense stare in its place. When the horn sounded, John attacked.

"Jesus," I said, gripping Trenton's arm.

Trenton moved as Travis did, as if they were one. I tensed with each swing John threw, fighting the urge to shut my eyes. There were no wasted movements; John was cunning and precise. All of Travis's other fights seemed sloppy in comparison. The raw strength behind the punches alone was awe-inspiring, as if the whole thing had been choreographed and practiced to perfection.

The air in the room was heavy and stagnant; the dust from the sheets had been disturbed and caught in my throat each time I gasped. The longer the fight lasted, the worse the ominous feeling became. I couldn't shake it, and yet I forced myself to stay in place so Travis could concentrate.

In one moment, I was hypnotized by the spectacle in the middle of the basement; in the next, I was shoved from behind. My head jerked back with the blow, but I tightened my grip, refusing to budge from my promised spot. Trenton turned and grabbed the shirts of two men behind us and tossed them to the ground as though they were rag dolls.

"Back the fuck up, or I'll kill you!" he yelled to those staring at the fallen men. I gripped his arm tighter and he patted my hand. "I got ya, Abby. Just watch the fight."

Travis was doing well, and I sighed when he drew first blood. The crowd grew louder, but Trenton's warning kept those around us at a safe distance. Travis landed a solid punch and then glanced at me, quickly returning his attention to John. His movements were lithe, almost calculating, seeming to predict John's attacks before he made them.

Noticeably impatient, John wrapped his arms around Travis, pulling him to the ground. As one unit, the crowd surrounding the makeshift ring tightened around them, leaning in as the action fell to the floor.

"I can't see him, Trent!" I cried as I bounced on my tiptoes.

Trenton looked around, finding Adam's wooden chair. In a dancelike motion, he passed me from one arm to the other, helping me as I climbed above the mob. "Can you see him?"

"Yeah!" I said, holding Trenton's arm for balance. "He's on top, but John's legs are around his neck!"

Trenton leaned forward on his toes, cupping his free hand around his mouth, "SLAM HIS ASS, TRAVIS!"

I glanced down to Trenton and then leaned forward to get a better look at the men on the floor. Suddenly Travis was on his feet, John holding tight around Travis's neck with his legs. Travis fell on his knees, slamming John's back and head against the concrete in a devastating blow. John's legs went limp, releasing Travis's neck, and then Travis reared back his elbow, pummeling John over and over with his clenched fist until Adam pulled him away, throwing the red square on John's flaccid body.

The room erupted, cheering as Adam lifted Travis's hand into the air. Trenton hugged my legs, calling out victory to his brother. Travis looked up at me with a broad, bloody smile; his right eye had already begun to swell.

As the money passed hands and the crowd began to meander about, preparing to leave, my eyes drifted to a wildly flickering lantern swaying back and forth in the corner of the room behind Travis. Liquid was dripping from its base, soaking the sheet below it. My stomach sank.

"Trent?"

Catching his attention, I pointed to the corner. In that moment, the lantern fell from its clip, crashing into the sheet below, immediately bursting into flames.

"Holy shit!" Trenton said, gripping my legs.

A few men around the fire jumped back, watching in awe as the flames crawled to the adjacent sheet. Black smoke bellowed from the corner, and in unison, every person in the room flew into a panic, pushing their way to the exits.

My eyes met Travis's. A look of absolute terror distorted his face.

"Abby!" he screamed, pushing at the sea of people between us.

"C'mon!" Trenton yelled, pulling me from the chair to his side.

The room darkened, and a loud popping noise sounded from another side of the room. The other lanterns were igniting and adding to the fire in small explosions. Trenton grabbed my arm, pulling me behind him as he tried to force his way through the crowd.

"We can't get out that way! We'll have to go back the way we came!" I cried, resisting.

Trenton looked around, forming a plan of escape in the center of the confusion. I looked to Travis again, watching as he tried to make his way across the room. As the crowd surged, Travis was pushed farther away. The excited cheering from be-

fore was now horrified shrieks of fear and desperation as everyone fought to reach the exits.

Trenton pulled me to the doorway, and I looked back. "Travis!" I yelled, reaching out for him.

He was coughing, waving the smoke away.

"This way, Trav!" Trenton called to him.

"Just get her out of here, Trent! Get Pigeon out!" he said,
coughing.

Conflicted, Trenton looked down to me. I could see the fear
in his eyes. "I don't know the way out."

I looked to Travis once more, his form flickering behind the
flames that had spread between us. "Travis!"

"Just go! I'll catch up to you outside!" His voice was drowned
out by the chaos around us, and I gripped Trenton's sleeve.

"This way, Trent!" I said, feeling the tears and smoke burn
my eyes. Dozens of panicked people were between Travis and
his only escape.

I tugged on Trenton's hand, shoving anyone in my path. We
reached the doorway, and then I looked back and forth. Two
dark hallways were dimly lit by the fire behind us.

"This way!" I said, pulling on his hand again.

"You sure?" Trenton asked, his voice thick with doubt and fear.

"C'mon!" I said, tugging on him again.

The farther we ran, the darker the rooms became. After
a few moments, my breaths were easier as we left the smoke
behind, but the screams didn't subside. They were louder and
more frantic than before. The horrific sounds behind us fueled
my determination, keeping my steps quick and purposeful. By
the second turn, we were walking blindly through the darkness.

I held my hand in front of me, feeling along the wall with my free hand, gripping Trenton's hand with the other.

"Do you think he got out?" Trenton asked.

His question undermined my focus, and I tried to push the answer from my mind. "Keep moving," I choked out.

Trenton resisted for a moment, but when I tugged on him again, a light flickered. He held up a lighter, squinting into the small space for the way out. I followed the light as he waved it around the room, and gasped when a doorway came into view.

"This way!" I said, tugging on him again.

As I rushed through to the next room, a wall of people crashed into me, throwing me to the ground. Three women and two men, all with dirty faces and wide, frightened eyes looked down at me.

One of the boys reached down to help me up. "There's some windows down here we can get out of!" he said.

"We just came from that way. There's nothing down there," I said, shaking my head.

"You must have missed it. I know they're this way!"

Trenton tugged on my hand. "C'mon, Abby, they know the way out!"

I shook my head. "We came in this way with Travis. I know it."

He tightened his grip. "I told Travis I wouldn't let you out of my sight. We're going with them."

"Trent, we've been down that way . . . there were no windows!"

"Let's go, Jason!" a girl cried.

"We're going," Jason said, looking to Trenton.

Trenton tugged on my hand again and I pulled away. "Trent, please! It's this way, I promise!"

"I'm going with them," he said, "Please come with me."

I shook my head, tears flowing down my cheeks. "I've been here before. That's not the way out!"

"You're coming with me!" he yelled, pulling on my arm.

"Trent, stop! We're going the wrong way!" I cried.

My feet slid across the concrete as he pulled me along, and when the smell of smoke grew stronger, I yanked away, running in the opposite direction.

"ABBY! ABBY!" Trenton called.

I kept running, holding my hands out in front of me, anticipating a wall.

"Come on! She's gonna get you killed!" a girl said.

My shoulder crashed into a corner and I spun around, falling to the ground. I crawled along the floor, holding my trembling hand in front of me. When my fingers touched Sheetrock, I followed it up, rising to my feet. The corner of a doorway materialized under my touch and I followed it into the next room.

The darkness was endless, but I willed away the panic, carefully keeping my footsteps straight, reaching out for the next wall. Several minutes passed by, and I felt the fear well up inside me as the wails from behind rung in my ears.

"Please," I whispered in the blackness, "let this be the way out."

I felt another corner of a doorway, and when I made my way through, a silver stream of light glowed before me. Moonlight filtered through the glass of the window, and a sob forced its way from my throat.

"T-trent! It's here!" I called behind me. "Trent!"

I squinted, seeing a tiny bit of movement in the distance. "Trent?" I called out, my heart beat fluttering wildly in my chest. Within moments, shadows danced against the walls, and my eyes widened with horror when I realized what I thought were people, was actually the flickering light of approaching flames.

"Oh my God," I said, looking up at the window. Travis had closed it behind us, and it was too high for me to reach.

I looked around for something to stand on. The room was lined with wooden furniture covered in white sheets. The same sheets that would feed the fire until the room turned into an inferno.

I grabbed a piece of white cloth, yanking it from a desk. Dust clouded around me as threw the sheet to the ground and lugged the bulky wood across the room to the space beneath the window. I shoved it next to the wall and climbed up, coughing from the smoke that slowly seeped into the room. The window was still a few feet above me.

I grunted as I tried to shove it open, clumsily twisting the lock back and forth between each push. It wouldn't budge.

"Come on, dammit!" I yelled, leaning into my arms.

I leaned back, using my body weight with the little momentum I could manage to force it open. When that didn't work, I slid my nails under the edges, pulling until I thought my nails had pulled away from the skin. Light flashed from the corner of my eye, and I cried out when I saw the fire barreling down the white sheets lining the hallway I had traveled just moments before.

I looked up at the window, once again digging my nails into

the edges. Blood dripped from my fingertips, the metal edges sinking into my flesh. Instinct overcame all other senses, and my hands balled into fists, ramming into the glass. A small crack splintered across the pane, along with my blood smearing and spattering with each blow.

I hammered the glass once more with my fist, and then pulled off my shoe, slamming it with full force. Sirens wailed in the distance and I sobbed, beating my palms against the window. The rest of my life was just a few inches away, on the other side of the glass. I clawed at the edges once more and then began slapping the glass with both palms.

"HELP ME!" I screamed, seeing the flames draw nearer. "SOMEBODY HELP ME!"

A faint cough sputtered behind me. "Pigeon?"

I flipped around to the familiar voice. Travis appeared in a doorway behind me, his face and clothes covered in soot.

"TRAVIS!" I cried. I scrambled off the desk and ran across the floor to where he stood, exhausted and filthy.

I slammed into him, and he wrapped his arms around me, coughing as he gasped for air. His hands grabbed my cheeks.

"Where's Trent?" he said, his voice raspy and weak.

"He followed them!" I bawled, tears streaming down my face. "I tried to get him to come with me, but he wouldn't come!"

Travis looked down at the approaching fire and his eyebrows pulled in. I sucked in a breath, coughing when smoke filled my lungs. He looked down at me, his eyes filling with tears. "I'm gonna get us outta here, Pidge." His lips pressed against mine in one quick, firm movement, and then he climbed on top of my makeshift ladder.

He pushed at the window and then twisted the lock, the

muscles of his arms quivering as he used all of his strength against the glass.

"Get back, Abby! I'm gonna break the glass!"

Afraid to move, I could only take one step away from our only way out. Travis's elbow bent as he reared back his fist, yelling as he rammed it into the window. I turned away, shielding my face with my bloody hands as the glass shattered above me.

"Come on!" he yelled, holding his hand out to me. The heat from the fire took over the room, and I soared into the air as he lifted me from the ground and pushed me outside.

I waited on my knees as Travis climbed out, and then helped him to his feet. The sirens were blaring from the other side of the building, and red and blue lights from fire engines and police cruisers danced across the brick on the adjacent buildings.

We ran to the crowd of people standing in front of the building, scanning the dirty faces for Trenton. Travis yelled his brother's name, his voice becoming more and more hopeless with each call. He pulled out his cell phone to check for a missed call and then slammed it shut, covering his mouth with his blackened hand.

"TRENT!" Travis screamed, stretching his neck as he searched the crowd.

Those that had escaped were hugging and whimpering behind the emergency vehicles, watching in horror as the pumper truck shot water through the windows and firefighters ran inside, pulling hoses behind them.

Travis ran his hand over the stubble on his scalp, shaking his head. "He didn't get out," he whispered. "He didn't get out, Pidge."

My breath caught as I watched the soot on his cheeks streak with tears. He fell to his knees, and I fell with him.

"Trent's smart, Trav. He got out. He had to have found a different way," I said, trying to convince myself as well.

Travis collapsed into my lap, gripping my shirt with both fists. I held him. I didn't know what else to do.

An hour passed. The cries and wailing from the survivors and spectators outside the building had grown to an eerie quiet. We watched with waning hope as the firefighters brought out two people, and then continuously came out empty-handed. As the paramedics tended to the injured and ambulances tore into night with burn victims, we waited. Half an hour later, the bodies they returned with were those who were beyond saving. The ground was lined with casualties, far outnumbering those of us that had escaped. Travis's eyes didn't leave the door, waiting for them to pull his brother from the ashes.

"Travis?"

We turned at the same time to see Adam standing beside us. Travis stood up, pulling me along with him.

"I'm glad to see you guys made it out," Adam said, looking stunned and bewildered. "Where's Trent?"

Travis didn't answer.

Our eyes returned to the charred remains of Keaton Hall, the thick black smoke still billowing from the windows. I buried my face into Travis's chest, shutting my eyes tight, hoping at any moment I would wake up.

"I have to uh ... I have to call my dad," Travis said, his eyebrows pulling together as he opened his cell phone.

I took a breath, hoping my voice would sound stronger than

I felt. "Maybe you should wait, Travis. We don't know anything, yet."

His eyes didn't leave the number pad, and his lip quivered. "This ain't fucking right. He shoulda never been there."

"It was an accident, Travis. You couldn't have known something like this was going to happen," I said, touching his cheek.

His face compressed, his eyes shutting tight. He took in a deep breath and began to dial his father's number.

Chapter Twenty-Two
Jet Plane

THE NUMBERS ON THE SCREEN WERE REPLACED WITH A name as the phone began to ring, and Travis's eyes widened when he read the display.

"Trent?" A surprised laugh escaped his lips, and a smile broke out on his face as he looked at me. "It's Trent!" I gasped and squeezed his arm as he spoke. "Where are you? What do you mean you're at Morgan? I'll be there in a second, don't you fucking move!"

I surged forward, my feet struggling to keep up with Travis as he sprinted across the campus, dragging me behind him. When we reached Morgan, my lungs were screaming for air. Trenton ran down the steps, crashing into both of us.

"Jesus H. Christ, brother! I thought you were toast!" Trenton said, squeezing us so tightly I couldn't breathe.

"You asshole!" Travis screamed, shoving his brother away. "I thought you were fucking dead! I've been waiting for the fire-fighters to carry your charred body from Keaton!"

Travis frowned at Trenton for a moment, and then pulled him into a hug. His arm shot out, fumbling around until he felt my shirt, and then pulled me into a hug as well. After several moments, Travis released Trenton, keeping me close beside him.

Trenton looked at me with an apologetic frown. "I'm sorry, Abby. I panicked."

I shook my head. "I'm just glad you're okay."

"Me? I would have been better off dead if Travis had seen me come out of that building without you. I tried to find you after you ran off, but then I got lost and had to find another way. I walked along the building looking for that window, but I ran into some cops and they made me leave. I've been flippin' the fuck out over here!" he said, running his hand over his short hair.

Travis wiped my cheeks with his thumbs, and then pulled up his shirt, using it to wipe the soot from his face. "Let's get out of here. The cops are going to be crawling all over the place soon."

After hugging his brother once more, we walked to America's Honda. Travis watched me buckle my seat belt and then frowned when I coughed.

"Maybe I should take you to the hospital. Get you checked out."

"I'm fine," I said, interlacing my fingers in his. I looked down, seeing a deep cut across his knuckles. "Is that from the fight or the window?"

"The window," he answered, frowning at my bloodied nails.

"You saved my life, you know."

His eyebrows pulled together. "I wasn't leaving without you."

"I knew you'd come," I said, squeezing his fingers between mine.

We held hands until we arrived at the apartment. I couldn't

tell whose blood was whose as I washed the crimson and ash from my skin in the shower. Falling into Travis's bed, I could still smell the stench of smoke and smoldering skin.

"Here," he said, handing me a short glass filled with amber liquid. "It'll help you relax."

"I'm not tired."

He held out the glass again. His eyes were exhausted, blood-shot and heavy. "Just try to get some rest, Pidge."

"I'm almost afraid to close my eyes," I said, taking the glass and gulping the liquid down.

He took the glass and set it on the nightstand, sitting beside me. We sat in silence, letting the last hours sink in. I shut my eyes tight when the memories of the terrified cries of those trapped in the basement filled my mind. I wasn't sure how long it would take me to forget, or if I ever would.

Travis's warm hand on my knee pulled me from my conscious nightmare. "A lot of people died tonight."

"I know."

"We won't find out until tomorrow just how many."

"Trent and I passed a group of kids on the way out. I wonder if they made it. They looked so scared . . ."

I felt the tears fill my eyes, but before they touched my cheeks, Travis's solid arms were surrounding me. Immediately I felt protected, flush against his skin. Feeling so at home in his arms had once terrified me, but in that moment, I was grateful that I could feel so safe after experiencing something so horrific. There was only one reason I could ever feel that way with anyone.

I belonged to him.

It was then that I knew. Without a doubt in my mind, without worry of what others would think, and having no fear of mistakes or consequences, I smiled at the words I would say.

"Travis?" I said against his chest.

"What, baby?" he whispered into my hair.

Our phones rang in unison, and I handed his to him as I answered mine. "Hello?"

"Abby?" America shrieked.

"I'm okay, Mare. We're all okay."

"We just heard! It's all over the news!"

I could hear Travis explaining to Shepley next to me, and I tried my best to reassure America. Fielding dozens of her questions, trying to keep my voice steady while recounting the scariest moments of my life, I relaxed the second Travis covered my hand with his.

It seemed I was telling someone else's story, sitting in the comfort of Travis's apartment, a million miles away from the nightmare that could have killed us. America wept when I finished, realizing how close we came to losing our lives.

"I'm going to start packing now. We'll be home first thing in the morning," America sniffed.

"Mare, don't leave early. We're fine."

"I have to see you. I have to hug you so I'll know you're all right," she cried.

"We're fine. You can hug me on Friday."

She sniffed again. "I love you."

"I love you, too. Have a good time."

Travis looked at me and then pressed the phone tight against his ear. "Better hug your girl, Shep. She sounds upset. I know, man . . . me, too. See you soon."

I hung up seconds before Travis did, and we sat in silence for a moment, still processing what had happened. After several moments, Travis leaned back against his pillow, and then pulled me against his chest.

"America all right?" he asked, staring up at the ceiling.

"She's upset. She'll be okay."

"I'm glad they weren't there."

I clenched my teeth. I hadn't even thought about what might have happened had they not stayed with Shepley's parents. My mind flashed to the terrified expressions of the girls in the basement, fighting against the men to escape. America's frightened eyes replaced the nameless girls in that room. I felt nauseated thinking about her beautiful blond hair soiled and singed along with the rest of the bodies laid out on the lawn.

"Me, too," I said with a shiver.

"I'm sorry. You've been through a lot tonight. I don't need to add anything else to your plate."

"You were there, too, Trav."

He was quiet for several moments, and just when I opened my mouth to speak again, he took a deep breath.

"I don't get scared very often," he said finally. "I was scared the first morning I woke up and you weren't here. I was scared when you left me after Vegas. I was scared when I thought I was going to have to tell my dad that Trent had died in that building. But when I saw you across the flames in that basement . . . I was terrified. I made it to the door, was a few feet from the exit, and I couldn't leave."

"What do you mean? Are you crazy?" I said, my head jerking up to look into his eyes.

"I've never been so clear about anything in my life. I turned around, made my way to that room you were in, and there you were. Nothing else mattered. I didn't even know if we would make it out or not, I just wanted to be where you were, whatever that meant. The only thing I'm afraid of is a life without you, Pigeon."

I leaned up, kissing his lips tenderly. When our mouths parted, I smiled. "Then you have nothing to be afraid of. We're forever."

He sighed. "I'd do it all over again, you know. I wouldn't trade one second if it meant we were right here, in this moment."

My eyes felt heavy, and I took in a deep breath. My lungs protested, still burning from the smoke. I coughed a bit and then relaxed, feeling Travis's warm lips against my forehead. His hand glided over my damp hair, and I could hear his heart beating steady in his chest.

"This is it," he said with a sigh.

"What?"

"The moment. When I watch you sleeping . . . that peace on your face? This is it. I haven't had it since before my mom died, but I can feel it again." He took another deep breath and pulled me closer. "I knew the second I met you that there was something about you I needed. Turns out it wasn't something about you at all. It was just you."

The corner of my mouth turned up as I buried my face into his chest. "It's us, Trav. Nothing makes sense unless we're together. Have you noticed that?"

"Noticed? I've been telling you that all year!" he teased. "It's official. Bimbos, fights, leaving, Parker, Vegas . . . even fires . . . our relationship can withstand anything."

I lifted my head up once more, noticing the contentment

in his eyes as he looked at me. It was similar to the peace I had seen on his face after I lost the bet to stay with him in the apartment, after I told him I loved him for the first time, and the morning after the Valentine's dance. It was similar, but different. This was absolute—permanent. The cautious hope had vanished from his eyes, unqualified trust taking its place.

I recognized it only because his eyes mirrored what I was feeling.

"Vegas?" I asked.

His brow furrowed, unsure of where I was headed. "Yeah?"

"Have you thought about going back?"

His eyebrows shot up. "I don't think that's a good idea for me."

"What if we just went for a night?"

He looked around the dark room, confused. "A night?"

"Marry me," I said without hesitation. I was surprised at how quickly and easily the words came.

His mouth spread into a broad smile. "When?"

I shrugged. "We can book a flight tomorrow. It's spring break. I don't have anything going on tomorrow, do you?"

"I'm callin' your bluff," he said, reaching for his phone. "American Airlines," He said, watching my reaction closely as he was connected. "I need two tickets to Vegas, please. Tomorrow. Hmmmm . . ." He looked at me, waiting for me to change my mind. "Two days, round trip. Whatever you have."

I rested my chin on his chest, waiting for him to book the tickets. The longer I let him stay on the phone, the wider his smile became.

"Yeah . . . uh, hold on a minute," he said, pointing to his wallet. "Grab my card, would ya, Pidge?" He waited again for my reaction. I happily leaned over, pulled his credit card from his wallet, and handed it to him.

Travis called out the numbers to the agent, glancing up at me after each set. When he gave the expiration date and saw my lack of protesting, he pressed his lips together. "Er, yes, ma'am. We'll just pick them up at the desk. Thank you."

He handed me his phone and I set it on the night table, waiting for him to speak.

"You just asked me to marry you," he said, still waiting for me to admit some kind of trickery.

"I know."

"That was the real deal, you know. I just booked two tickets to Vegas for noon tomorrow. So that means we're getting married tomorrow night."

"Thank you."

His eyes narrowed. "You're going to be Mrs. Maddox when you start classes on Monday."

"Oh," I said, looking around.

Travis raised an eyebrow. "Second thoughts?"

"I'm going to have some serious paperwork to change next week."

He nodded slowly, cautiously hopeful. "You're going to marry me tomorrow?"

I smiled. "Uh-huh."

"You're serious?"

"Yep."

"I fucking love you!" He grabbed each side of my face, slamming his lips against mine. "I love you so much, Pigeon," he said, kissing me over and over.

"Just remember that in fifty years when I'm still kicking your ass in poker," I giggled.

He smiled, triumphant. "If it means sixty or seventy years with you, baby . . . you have my full permission to do your worst."

I raised one eyebrow. "You're gonna regret that."

"I bet I won't."

I smiled with as much deviance as I could muster. "Are you confident enough to bet that shiny bike outside?"

He shook his head, a serious expression replacing the teasing smile he had just seconds before. "I'll put in everything I have. I don't regret a single second with you, Pidge, and I never will."

I held out my hand and he took it without hesitation, shaking it once and then bringing it to his mouth, pressing his lips tenderly against my knuckles. The room was quiet, his lips leaving my skin and the air escaping his lungs the only sound.

"Abby Maddox . . ." he said, his smile beaming in the moonlight.

I pressed my cheek against his bare chest. "Travis and Abby Maddox. Has a nice ring to it."

"Ring?" he said, frowning.

"We'll worry about rings later. I sort of sprung this on you."

"Uh . . ." he trailed off, watching me for the reaction he expected.

"What?" I asked, feeling myself tense.

"Don't freak out," he said as he shifted nervously. His grip around me tightened. "I kind of . . . already took care of that part."

"What part?" I said, my head craning to see his face.

He stared up at the ceiling and sighed. "You're going to freak out."

"Travis . . ."

I frowned as he pulled one arm away from me, reaching for the drawer of his nightstand. He felt around for a moment.

I blew my damp bangs from my eyes. "What? You bought condoms?"

He laughed once. "No, Pidge." His eyebrows pulled together as he made more of an effort, reaching farther into the drawer. Once he found what he was looking for, his focus changed, and he watched me as he pulled a small box from its hiding place.

I looked down as he placed the small velvet square on his chest, reaching behind him to rest his head on his arm.

"What's that?" I asked.

"What does it look like?"

"Okay. Let me rephrase the question: When did you get that?"

Travis inhaled, and as he did, the box rose with his chest and fell when he pushed the air from his lungs. "A while ago."

"Trav . . ."

"I just happened to see it one day, and I knew there was only one place it could belong . . . on your perfect little finger."

"One day when?"

"Does it matter?" he rebutted. He squirmed a bit, and I couldn't help but laugh.

"Can I see it?" I smiled, suddenly feeling a bit giddy.

His smile matched mine, and he looked to the box. "Open it."

I touched it with one finger, feeling the lush velvet under my fingertip. I grasped the golden seal with both hands, slowly pulling the lid open. A glimmer caught my eye and I slammed the lid shut.

"Travis!" I wailed.

"I knew you'd freak out!" he said, sitting up and cupping his hands over mine.

I could feel the box pressing against both of my palms, feeling like a prickly grenade that could detonate at any moment. I closed my eyes and shook my head. "Are you insane?"

"I know. I know what you're thinking, but I had to. It was the One. And I was right! I haven't seen one since that was as perfect as this one!"

My eyes popped open and instead of the anxious pair of brown eyes I expected, he was beaming with pride. He gently peeled my hands from the case and pulled the lid open, pulling the ring from the tiny slit that held it in place. The large, round diamond glittered even in the dim light, catching the moonlight in every facet.

"It's . . . my God, it's amazing," I whispered as he took my left hand in his.

"Can I put it on your finger?" he asked, peering up at me. When I nodded, he pressed his lips together, sliding the silver band over my knuckle, holding it in place for a moment before letting go. "Now it's amazing."

We both stared at my hand for a moment, equally shocked at the contrast of the large diamond sitting atop my small, slender finger. The band spanned the bottom of my finger, splitting in two on each side as it reached the solitaire, smaller diamonds lining each sliver of white gold.

"You could have put a down payment on a car for this," I said under my breath, unable to put any strength behind my voice.

My eyes followed my hand as Travis brought it up to his lips. "I've imagined what this would look like on your hand a million times. Now that it's there . . ."

"What?" I smiled, watching him stare at my hand with an emotional grin.

He looked up at me. "I thought I was going to have to sweat five years before I'd feel like this."

"I wanted it as much as you did. I've just got a hell of a poker face," I said, pressing my lips against his.

Epilogue

Travis squeezed my hand as i held my breath. I tried to keep my face smooth, but when I cringed, his grip became tighter. The white ceiling was tarnished in some places by leak stains. Other than that, the room was immaculate. No clutter, no utensils strewn about. Everything had its place, which made me feel moderately at ease about the situation. I had made the decision. I would go through with it.

"Baby . . ." Travis said, frowning.

"I can do this," I said, staring at spots in the ceiling. I jumped when fingertips touched my skin, but I tried not to tense. I could see the worry in Travis's eyes when the buzzing began.

"Pigeon," Travis began again, but I shook my head dismissively.

"All right. I'm ready." I held the phone away from my ear, wincing from both the pain and the inevitable lecture.

"I'm going to kill you, Abby Abernathy!" America cried. "Kill you!"

"Technically, it's Abby Maddox, now," I said, smiling at my new husband.

"It's not fair!" she whined, the anger subsiding from her tone. "I was supposed to be your maid of honor! I was supposed to go dress shopping with you and throw a bachelorette party and hold your bouquet!"

"I know," I said, watching Travis's smile fade as I winced again.

"You don't have to do this, you know," he said, his eyebrows pulling together.

I squeezed his fingers together with my free hand. "I know."

"You said that already!" America snapped.

"I wasn't talking to you."

"Oh, you're talking to me," she fumed. "You are sooo talking to me. You are never going to hear the end of this, do you hear me? I will never, ever forgive you!"

"Yes you will."

"You! You're a . . . ! You're just plain mean, Abby! You're a horrible best friend!"

I laughed, causing the man seated beside me to jerk. "Hold still, Mrs. Maddox."

"I'm sorry," I said.

"Who was that?" America snapped.

"That was Griffin."

"Who the hell is Griffin? Let me guess, you invited a total stranger to your wedding and not your best friend?" Her voice became shriller with each question.

"No. He didn't go to the wedding," I said, sucking in a breath of air.

Travis sighed and shifted nervously in his chair, squeezing my hand.

"I'm supposed to do that to you, remember?" I said, smiling up at him through the pain.

"Sorry. I don't think I can take this," he said, his voice thick with distress. He relaxed his hand, looking to Griffin.

"Hurry up, would ya?"

Griffin shook his head. "Covered in tats and can't take your girlfriend getting a simple script. I'll be finished in a minute, mate."

Travis's frown deepened. "Wife. She's my wife."

America gasped once the conversation processed in her mind. "You're getting a tattoo? What is going on with you, Abby? Did you breathe toxic fumes in that fire?"

I looked down at my stomach, to the smeared black mess just to the inside of my hipbone, and smiled. "Trav has my name on his wrist." I sucked in another breath when the buzzing continued. Griffin wiped ink from my skin and began again. I spoke through my teeth, "We're married. I wanted something, too."

Travis shook his head. "You didn't have to."

I narrowed my eyes. "Don't start with me. We discussed this."

America laughed once. "You've gone crazy. I'm committing you to the asylum when you get home." Her voice was still piercing and exasperated.

"It's not that crazy. We love each other. We have been practically living together on and off all year. Why not?"

"Because you're nineteen, you idiot! Because you ran off and didn't tell anyone, and because I'm not there!" she cried.

"I'm sorry, Mare, I have to go. I'll see you tomorrow, okay?"

"I don't know if I want to see you tomorrow! I don't think I want to see Travis ever again!" she sneered.

"I'll see you tomorrow, Mare. You know you want to see my ring."

"And your tat," she said, a smile in her voice.

I clicked the phone shut, handing it to Travis. The buzzing resumed again, and my attention focused on the burning sensation followed by the sweet second of relief as he wiped the excess ink away. Travis shoved my phone in his pocket, gripping my hand with both of his, leaning down to touch his forehead to mine.

"Did you freak out this much when you got your tattoos?" I asked him, smiling at the apprehensive expression on his face.

He shifted, seeming to feel my pain a thousand times more than I. "Uh . . . no. This is different. This is much, much worse."

"Done!" Griffin said with as much relief in his voice as was on Travis's face.

I let my head fall back against the chair. "Thank God!"

"Thank God!" Travis sighed, patting my hand.

I looked down at the beautiful black lines on my red and angry skin:

MRS. MADDOX

"Wow," I said, rising up on my elbows to get a better look.

Travis's frown instantly turned into a triumphant smile. "It's beautiful."

Griffin shook his head. "If I had a dollar for every inked-up new husband that brought his wife in here and took it worse than she did . . . well. I wouldn't have to tat anyone ever again."

"Just tell me how much I owe, smart-ass," Travis mumbled.

"I'll have your bill at the counter," Griffin said, amused with Travis's retort.

I looked around the room at the shiny chrome and posters of sample tattoos on the wall and then back down to my stomach. My new last name shined in thick, elegant black letters. Travis watched me with pride, and then peered down at his titanium wedding band.

"We did it, baby," he said in a hushed voice. "I still can't believe you're my wife."

"Believe it," I said, smiling.

He helped me from the chair and I favored my right side, conscious of every movement I made that caused my jeans to rub against my raw skin. Travis pulled out his wallet, signing the receipt quickly before leading me by the hand to the cab waiting outside. My cell phone rang again, and when I saw that it was America, I let it ring.

"She's going to lay the guilt trip on thick, isn't she?" Travis said with a frown.

"She'll pout for twenty-four hours after she sees the pictures—then she'll get over it."

Travis shot me a mischievous grin. "Are you sure about that, Mrs. Maddox?"

"Are you ever going to stop calling me that? You've said it a hundred times since we left the chapel."

He shook his head as he held the cab door open for me. "I'll quit calling you that when it sinks in that this is real."

"Oh, it's real all right," I said, sliding to the middle of the seat to make room. "I have wedding night memories to prove it."

He leaned against me, running his nose up the sensitive skin of my neck until he reached my ear. "We sure do."

"Ow . . ." I said when he pressed against my bandage.

"Oh, dammit, I'm sorry, Pidge."

"You're forgiven," I said with a smile.

We rode to the airport hand in hand, and I giggled as I watched Travis stare at his wedding band without apology. His eyes held the peaceful expression I was becoming accustomed to.

"When we get back to the apartment, I think it will finally hit me, and I'll quit acting like such a jackass."

"Promise?" I smiled.

He kissed my hand and then cradled it in his lap between his palms. "No."

I laughed, resting my head on his shoulder until the cab slowed to a stop in front of the airport. My cell phone rang again, displaying America's name once again.

"She's relentless. Let me talk to her," Travis said, reaching for my phone.

"Hello?" he said, waiting out the shrill stream on the other end of the line. He smiled. "Because I'm her husband. I can answer her phone now." He glanced at me and then shoved open the cab door, offering his hand. "We're at the airport, America. Why don't you and Shep pick us up and you can yell at us both on the way home? Yes, the whole way home. We should arrive around three. All right, Mare. See you then." He winced with her sharp words and then handed me the phone. "You weren't kidding. She's pissed."

He tipped the cabby and then threw his bag over his shoulder, pulling up the handle to my rolling luggage. His tattooed arms tensed as he pulled my bag, his free hand reaching out to take mine.

"I can't believe you gave her the green light to let us have it for an entire hour," I said, following him through the revolving door.

"You don't really think I'm going to let her yell at my wife, do you?"

"You're getting pretty comfortable with that term."

"I guess it's time I admit it. I knew you were going to be my wife pretty much from the second I met you. I'm not going to lie and say I haven't been waiting for the day I could say it . . . so I'm going to abuse the title. You should get used to it, now." He said this all matter-of-factly, as if he were giving a practiced speech.

I laughed, squeezing his hand. "I don't mind."

He peered at me from the corner of his eye. "You don't?" I shook my head and he pulled me to his side, kissing my cheek. "Good. You're going to get sick of it over the next few months, but just cut me some slack, okay?"

I followed him through the hallways, up escalators, and past lines of security. When Travis walked through the metal detector, a loud buzzer went off. When the airport guard asked Travis to remove his ring, his face turned severe.

"I'll hold onto it, sir," the officer said. "It will only be for a moment."

"I promised her I'd never take it off," Travis said through his teeth.

The officer held out his palm; patience and amused understanding wrinkled the thin skin around his eyes.

Travis begrudgingly removed his ring, slammed it into the guard's hand, and then sighed when he walked through the doorway. He didn't set off the alarm, but he was still annoyed. I walked through without event, handing over my ring as well.

Travis's expression was still tense, but when we were allowed to pass, his shoulders relaxed.

"It's okay, baby. It's back on your finger," I said, giggling at his overreaction.

He kissed my forehead, pulling me to his side as we made our way to the terminal. When I caught the eyes of those we passed, I wondered if it was obvious that we were newlyweds, or if they simply noticed the ridiculous grin on Travis's face, a stark contrast to his shaved head, inked arms, and bulging muscles.

The airport was abuzz with excited tourists, the beeping and ringing of slot machines, and people meandering in every direction. I smiled at a young couple holding hands, looking as excited and nervous as Travis and I did when we arrived. I didn't doubt that they would leave feeling the same mixture of relief and bewilderment that we felt.

In the terminal, I thumbed through a magazine, and gently touched Travis's wildly bouncing knee. His leg froze and I smiled, keeping my eyes on the pictures of celebrities. He was nervous about something, but I waited for him to tell me, knowing he was working it out internally. After a few minutes, his knee bobbed again, but this time he stopped it on his own and then slowly slumped down into his chair.

"Pigeon?"

"Yeah?"

A few moments passed, and then he sighed. "Nothing."

The time passed too quickly, and it seemed we had just sat down when our flight number was called to board. A line quickly formed, and we stood up, waiting our turn to show our tickets and walk down the long hall to the airplane that would take us home.

Travis hesitated. "I can't shake this feeling," he said under his breath.

"What do you mean? Like a bad feeling?" I said, suddenly nervous.

He turned to me with concern in his eyes. "I have this crazy feeling that once we get home, I'm going to wake up. Like none of this was real."

I slid my arms around his waist, running my hands up the lean muscles of his back. "Is that what you're worried about?"

He looked down to his wrist and then glanced to the thick silver band on his left finger. "I just can't shake the feeling that the bubble's going to burst, and I'm going to be lying in my bed alone, wishing you were there with me."

"I don't know what I'm going to do with you, Trav! I've dumped someone for you—twice—I've picked up and gone to Vegas with you—twice—I've literally gone through hell and back, married you, and branded myself with your name. I'm running out of ideas to prove to you that I'm yours."

A small smile graced his lips. "I love it when you say that."

"That I'm yours?" I asked. I leaned up on the balls of my feet, pressing my lips against his. "I. Am. Yours. Mrs. Travis Maddox. Forever and always."

His small smile faded as he looked at the boarding gate and then down to me. "I'm gonna fuck it up, Pigeon. You're gonna get sick of my shit."

I laughed. "I'm sick of your shit now. I still married you."

"I thought once we got married, that I'd feel a little more reassured about not losing you. But I feel like if I get on that plane . . ."

"Travis? I love you. Let's go home."

His eyebrows pulled in. "You won't leave me, right? Even when I'm a pain in the ass?"

"I vowed in front of God—and Elvis—that I wouldn't, didn't I?"

His frown lightened a bit. "This is forever, right?"

One corner of my mouth turned up. "Would it make you feel better if we made a wager?"

Other passengers began to walk around us, however slowly, watching and listening to our ridiculous conversation. As before, I was glaringly aware of prying eyes, but this time was different. The only thing I could think about was the peace returning to Travis's eyes.

"What kind of husband would I be if I bet against my own marriage?"

I smiled. "The stupid kind. Didn't you listen to your dad when he told you not to bet against me?"

He raised an eyebrow. "So you're that sure, huh? You'd bet on it?"

I wrapped my arms around his neck and smiled against his lips. "I'd bet my firstborn. That's how sure I am."

And then the peace returned.

"You can't be that sure," he said, the anxiousness absent from his voice.

I raised an eyebrow, my mouth pulling up on the same side. "Wanna bet?"

Acknowledgments

I AM SO INCREDIBLY THANKFUL FOR MY BEST FRIEND and sister, Beth. Without her encouragement, I would never have embarked on this journey. It's because of her enthusiastic cheerleading that I am living my dream. I cannot say thank you enough. Thank you to my children for their endless patience, hugs, and understanding.

To my mother, Brenda, for her assistance in any way she could, whenever I asked. Many thanks to fellow authors and dear friends Jessica Park, Tammara Webber, Tina Reber, Stephanie Campbell, Abbi Glines, Liz Reinhardt, Elizabeth Reyes, Nichole Chase, Laura Bradley Rede, Elizabeth Hunter, Killian McRae, Colleen Hoover, Eyvonna Rains, Lani Wendt Young, Karly Blakemore-Mowle, Michele Scott, Tracey Garvis-Graves, Angie Stanton, and E L James for their overwhelming support, love, and advice. You are the best thing to come from my writing career. Truly.

Thank you to my agent Rebecca Watson, who is as brilliant as she is funny, and my agents at the Intercontinental Literary Agency for their diligence and hard work.

Enormous gratitude to Judith Curr at Atria Books for your unwavering support, and to my editor, Amy Tannenbaum, who has been passionate about this project from the very beginning. Thank you for believing in this story. And thanks to everyone else at Atria who made this happen so quickly, including Peter Borland, Chris Lloreda, Kimberly Goldstein, Samantha Cohen, Paul Olsewski, Isolde Sauer, Dana Sloan, Jessica Chin, Benjamin Holmes, Michael Kwan, James Pervin, Susan Rella, and James Walsh.

Thank you to Dr. Ross Vanhooser for your invaluable advice, and for believing in my talent before even I knew I had any.

Thank you so much to Maryse and Lily of Maryse.net and to reader Nikki Estep for loving Travis and Abby's story so much that they made it their mission to share it!

Last, but never least, endless love and appreciation to my darling husband who's infinitely supportive and patient, and loves me even when I'm ignoring him for fictional people. He is my everything, and I wouldn't think of doing any of this without him . . . I wouldn't want to. It's because of him that I know how to write about intense love. Jeff, thank you so much for being everything that you are.

About the Author

JAMIE MCGUIRE IS THE *NEW YORK TIMES* BESTSELLING author of three other novels: *Providence, Requiem,* and *Eden.* She and her husband, Jeff, live with their children just outside Enid, Oklahoma, with four dogs, four horses, and a cat named Rooster.

To learn more about Jamie McGuire, visit her at:

Facebook
https://www.facebook.com/Jamie.McGuire.Author

Twitter
@JamieMcGuire_

Simon & Schuster Author Page
http://authors.simonandschuster.co.uk/Jamie
-McGuire/408106960

Author website
www.jamiemcguire.com